LAND OF DREAMS

Books by Lauraine Snelling

LAND
OF
DREAMS

LAURAINE SNELLING

with Kiersti Giron

BETHANYHOUSE

a division of Baker Publishing Group
Minneapolis, Minnesota

© 2025 by Lauraine Snelling

Published by Bethany House Publishers
Minneapolis, Minnesota
BethanyHouse.com

Bethany House Publishers is a division of
Baker Publishing Group, Grand Rapids, Michigan

Printed in the United States of America

Library of Congress Cataloging-in-Publication Data
Names: Snelling, Lauraine, author. | Giron, Kiersti, author.
Title: Land of dreams / Lauraine Snelling with Kiersti Giron.
Description: Minneapolis, Minnesota : Bethany House Publishers, a division of Baker
    Publishing Group, 2025. | Series: Home to Green Creek ; 1
Identifiers: LCCN 2024039013 | ISBN 9780764243523 (paperback) | ISBN
    9780764244476 (cloth) | ISBN 9780764244483 (large print) | ISBN 9781493449002
    (ebook)
Subjects: LCGFT: Christian fiction. | Romance fiction. | Novels.
Classification: LCC PS3569.N39 L35 2025 | DDC 813/.54—dc23/eng/20240830
LC record available at https://lccn.loc.gov/2024039013

Scripture quotations are from the King James Version of the Bible.

This is a work of historical reconstruction; the appearances of certain historical figures are therefore inevitable. All other characters, however, are products of the author's imagination, and any resemblance to actual persons, living or dead, is coincidental.

Cover design by Dan Thornberg, Design Source Creative Services

Published in association with Books & Such Literary Management, www.booksandsuch .com.

Baker Publishing Group publications use paper produced from sustainable forestry practices and postconsumer waste whenever possible.

25 26 27 28 29 30 31   7 6 5 4 3 2 1

*The HOME TO GREEN CREEK series
is dedicated to both sides of my family,
those who emigrated to America
and those who remained in Norway.
God bless.*

ONE

The sound of the splash ripped her heart in two.

Amalia Gunderson stared straight ahead, one hand gripping the ship's rail. Today the horizon held no sense of promise. Mor and Far were gone, their bodies now sunk beneath the ocean's churning waves, along with their dream to find their son, her older brother, in the new land. What was she to do now?

Slowly she became aware of a small hand shaking her own.

"Bitte, Mor needs you. Please come now."

Glancing down, Amalia saw tears streaming down the little girl's pale cheeks.

"What is it, Ruthie?"

The five-year-old girl shook her head, setting her long braids to swinging. "Mor said it is very important. Her voice is so faint I could barely hear her." Ruth wiped her runny nose on the back of her mitten.

Amalia fought back the tears that insisted on dripping down her cheeks. She sniffed again and obeyed the tugging hand.

The captain of the ship stepped in to take her other arm. "I am so sorry, Miss Gunderson. Be careful going down the stairs now."

He closed the door against the wind, and the silence was broken only by their breathing and the tapping of their shoes.

Amalia wanted to stop at her room that now only she occupied, climb into the curtained bed, and forget the world existed. She had been taking care of several people recovering from the cholera, along with her own fading mother, who had now left her with no family of her own.

But like Amalia, little Ruth had already suffered the loss of her father in this dreadful epidemic, and if her mother made it through another night, it would be a miracle.

"Here." Captain Alberg stopped at another door, tapped, and turned the knob, pushing the door open. Ruth threw herself into her seated mother's arms.

Holding her daughter close, Hilda Forsberg looked into Amalia's tear-reddened eyes. "Thank you for coming." She paused to breathe. "I have the greatest favor to ask." Another pause for breath. "As you know, we are on our way . . . to inherit a farm with a large house . . . in the state of Iowa . . . near a town called Decorah."

Amalia nodded. "Of course, both of our families have talked about our lives ahead." *And there are only three of us remaining. Lord God, hold us close.*

Ruth sniffed again, and her mother pulled a handkerchief from her sleeve to mop her daughter's nose and eyes. Her hand trembled to nearly missing contact. Pleading, she looked to Amalia.

Her own eyes nearly blinded by tears, she took the bit of cloth, dried the child's cheeks, and tucked the square into the coat pocket. The two women exchanged a look that made Amalia want to run from the room.

The captain cleared his throat. "I need to tend to more matters on deck."

Hilda nodded. She held a packet of papers out to him. "Could you please explain why we are meeting?"

"Are you sure you . . . ?" He cleared his throat again.

"Ja, I am sure."

The captain turned to Amalia. "Miss Gunderson, these are legal documents that say if Mrs. Forsberg passes on to her heavenly home before this ship docks, you will become the legal guardian of Ruth Forsberg, and as such, will manage the estate until Ruth reaches a legal age of twenty-one when she will assume the inheritance."

"But . . ." Amalia stared from the extended packet to the shivering woman in front of her.

"Please, there is no one else that I can trust." Her words were punctuated with panting breaths, as if she'd been running rather than sitting huddled in a shawl-covered blanket.

When Amalia looked to Captain Alberg, his shrug did nothing to reassure her.

Lord God above, what do I do? Her plea brought no answers.

"Mor, I will stay with you," Ruth insisted.

"Ja, that you will." She rested her cheek on Ruth's near-to-white braids, braided the last few mornings by Amalia.

Amalia accepted the packet. "What do I need to do?"

"Sign where I tell you." The captain set an inkstand on the small table and pulled a quill pen from another pocket. "You can read and sign your name?"

"Ja, if it be in Norwegian."

"It is," Ruth's mor whispered.

The captain untied and rolled out the papers, smoothing them to lie flat. "You will sign here and here, under Mrs. Forsberg's signature, and fill your name in here."

Holding the page in the light of the porthole, Amalia read the document. "This will stand up in court if anyone ever contests it?"

"Yes." Captain Alberg glanced up at a thud from overhead.

Lord, I trust you. Please help Mrs. Forsberg become well enough that we will not have to use this. She sucked in a breath, signed on all the lines, and handed the document back to the captain.

He checked to make sure all the lines were filled and tied the tasseled cord around the roll. Handing it to the shivering woman in the chair, he snugged his hat down on his head, bowed, and with a "please, excuse me," exited the room.

"Takk, my dear friend. And now could you please help me back to bed?"

"Of course." Amalia slid her arm around the woman's back and lifted her to her feet, so thin the lifting was easy. She half carried Ruth's mor to the curtained bunk bed, sat her down, and leaving her shoes on, lifted her feet into the bed and tucked the quilt around her. Lying on her side, Hilda held up her arm so her little daughter could snuggle in spoon fashion.

"Takk." Her eyes drifted shut.

"I need to go check on the others, so Ruthie, you stay here." The little girl nodded. "I will bring you some soup for supper after a while." A nod was the only answer.

Amalia closed the door behind her and strode down the hall, past her door and two more. She tapped on the door. "It's me, Mrs. Haugen, just coming to see if I can do anything for you."

"Ja, bitte. Come in."

While her patient lay covered in the lower bunk, her voice sounded stronger than at breakfast. Amalia pulled back the curtain and earned a smile from the older woman inside. "You look and sound better."

A nod. "Ja, I am. Can I please have a drink of water?"

Amalia poured water from the pitcher and, after sitting on the edge of the bunk, held it for Mrs. Haugen to sip. "Perhaps tomorrow I can help you to the chair."

"As small as this cabin is, how can the chair look so far away?" The ghost of a smile made Amalia want to dance across the room. Finally, one of her patients was getting better. *Takk, Lord God.*

"How is Ruthie's mor?"

Amalia blew out a breath. "Please keep praying for her." The three women had all agreed to pray for the sick on the ship. Mrs. Haugen's husband had been one of the first to succumb.

"And yours?"

"She splashed into the waves earlier today." How could that already seem like it happened days ago, when only an hour or so had passed? Time that she would have spent huddled under her quilts, soaking them with her tears.

"Oh, my dear friend." Mrs. Haugen reached out a shaky hand to squeeze Amalia's.

Amalia fought a losing battle against the tears, then mopped the drips away with her own square of cloth, made by her mor with a forget-me-not embroidered in one corner. Something to treasure of her mor's love.

"I must go check on the others." Back in Norway, she and her mor had often gone on rounds through their village, caring for the sick—it had felt only natural to do so here once the cholera began. She refused to ponder the question of whether her mor would have caught the disease if she'd stayed away. To ignore the suffering went contrary to her mother's nature. As for Amalia herself, she seemed immune—why, no one could say.

Now two other surviving patients shared one cabin, and the rest slept in steerage. She hated going down the ladder nailed against the wall. Invariably she'd hear and see rats scurrying around, and the stench burned her nose. If only she could convince the captain to allow those still living to be moved up into an empty cabin. Cholera was no respecter of wealth.

Amalia drew a breath and tucked away her damp handkerchief. "I will bring you soup when it is ready. Lars will check on you?"

"He always does. My good son."

Squeezing the woman's hand, Amalia tucked the quilt in around her and shut the door behind her. After blowing her nose again, she made her way out onto the deck and over to the closed opening to steerage and waved one of the deckhands over. "Could you please open this for me?"

He shook his head as he came. "Not good for you to go down there."

Surely by now they knew that would not stop her. "Will you please light the lantern for me?"

Grumbling all the way, he descended the ladder, struck the match to light the lantern, and returned to the deck.

"Takk." She closed her eyes going down the ladder and breathed through her mouth. As far as she knew, there were no dead bodies down there, but the stench was still beyond belief. Once she was on the floor, she took down the lantern and made her way to the occupied bunk beds, throwing shadows against the walls and the row of bed frames. As others had died, she had the living move closer to the ladder.

An older man who said he'd lived through cholera before had the children gathered around him for school. On sunny days, he brought the children up to the deck for school and a chance to run around. The huge steam stacks provided protection from the wind, so the remaining passengers often clustered there. Amalia had attended the classes on speaking English rather than Norwegian. She often wondered if her brother had learned any English on his way to America. If Erik was still alive, where was he and what was he doing? Why had he never written letters home?

"Good afternoon," the man said in greeting.

"Ja, good—" She stumbled over the word. "Afternoon."

"I believe your patients are improving." He spoke slowly.

"Takk, er, thank you." She turned to the right a couple of bunk rows later to find another patient sitting on the edge of the bunk, a quilt wrapped around his shoulders. "God dag. Good to see you sitting up."

"Ja, finally." He coughed into the corner of the quilt. "For a change, I am looking forward to feeding myself soup and bread. Takk for your care for those of us who are getting stronger."

"Thank our Lord God, He is the one who does the healing."

"Ja, that is so." He lay back down with the quilt wrapped around him. "I run out of energy quickly."

Amalia checked on several others, finding some improving, others unchanged. She carried water and changed one bed of soiled linens, then returned to deck and insisted a deckhand help her carry down a kettle of the soup the cook had simmering. At last she climbed the ladder back to the upper deck and made her way back to her own empty cabin. As soon as she closed the door behind her, weeping for her mother attacked like a ferocious beast. She wrapped herself in the quilts that no longer comforted her mor and cried herself to sleep.

Sometime later, the clanging of the supper bell jerked her up from the deep well. She threw back the covers and, crossing to the mirror, smoothed her hair back into the bun at the nape of her neck. She still had passengers too weak to feed themselves. Ruth's mother especially.

Amalia carried the bowls of soup into the Forsberg cabin where Ruth was still in bed with her mor. "I brought you supper."

"Takk." Ruth slipped out of her mor's embrace. "I don't think Mor wants any supper. She won't wake up."

Amalia felt her heart clench. She set Ruth in the chair and pulled the little table up in front of her. Setting the soup and bread on the table, she tried to smile. "Let's say grace. I Jesu navn . . ." The little girl helped her complete the prayer.

"Should we save some for Mor?" Ruth dipped her bread in the soup.

"Nei, you go ahead and finish." *Oh Lord God, how do I tell her?* While Ruth ate her meal, Amalia slipped over to the bunk and felt Hilda's still face and hands to be sure. Cold—cold as her own

13

mor's that morning. She swallowed back the tears and returned to the little girl.

"Finished?" At the child's nod, Amalia took Ruth on her lap. "You know how much your mor loved you?"

Ruth nodded and turned to look in Amalia's eyes. She heaved a sigh that came clear from her toes. "She's gone to heaven to be with Far and Jesus, hasn't she?"

Amalia nodded and hugged the little girl close, not even attempting to fight the tears. *Oh, Lord, I am so tired of cholera and burying people at sea. Will we never reach land?* She sniffed and blew her nose. "I must go tell the captain."

"You will be my mor now?"

"Um, perhaps your Tante Amalia? We will move your things into my cabin but leave the trunks and boxes in here." *After all, your family paid for their tickets.*

Ruth wiped her nose and eyes on her sleeve and stood up. Blinking, she took the hanky offered and wiped again. "Tante Amalia."

"Ja, little one." Amalia stood, settled her skirts, and secured her hat on her head. "All will be well. God said so, and He never makes mistakes."

They found Captain Alberg in his cabin.

"She's gone?" he asked.

Amalia nodded.

"We will commit her after dawn. Good thing she took care of her daughter's future when she did." He looked at Ruth with a sad shake of his head. "I am so sorry. Your far and mor were good people, you can remember them with pride." He stood. "Dear God, I pray this is our last burial."

Amalia tucked Ruth into her bunk and when she was asleep returned to the other cabin. She left Hilda in her shift and wrapped her shawl around her, folding all the daytime wear of woolen skirt, vest, woolen petticoats, blouse, long stockings, coat, hat, and gloves and storing them in a trunk. She tucked the boots in along the edge, closed and locked the trunk. The roll of papers, she stored in her own trunk. Holding the lantern high, she saw the Forsberg family Bible at the foot of the bunk. "Takk, Lord. Someday Ruth will appreciate that." She locked the cabin and returned to her own.

Amalia cuddled Ruth close when she climbed into her own bunk. She could see the stars out the porthole with the ship running smooth after the last storm.

She woke to a knock on the door. "Ja?"

"Captain said to tell you the ceremony will be in half an hour, just before breakfast served in the dining room."

"Takk, we will be ready." Leaving Ruth sleeping, she got herself ready for the day, braiding her hair and wrapping the long golden rope around her head, then woke Ruth. "Dress quickly and I will braid your hair." She'd contemplated leaving Ruth asleep until the morning meal but decided the little girl would want to say good-bye.

They stood in the cold wind, watching the sun rising. Captain Alberg read the service, the people gathered sang the Norwegian hymn Amalia had requested, "I Know of a Sleep in Jesus' Name," and the wrapped body was lowered into the sea. Ruth hid her face in Amalia's coat, clinging so tightly to her hand, it started to cramp.

The captain raised his voice. "Thank you all for gathering. Breakfast is now being served in the dining room. Thank God for smooth sailing today."

"Any idea when we will see land?" one of the men asked.

"Today or tomorrow, I should think."

The next morning, they woke to the sound of a tugboat meeting the ship. Within minutes, it pulled away, returning to the harbor.

The passengers clustered around the captain.

"I am sorry to announce that due to the cholera that took so many lives, we will not be allowed to dock in New York Harbor. Food will be brought out to us, but no one from the ship may disembark. I will try to find some other port that will take us in, or we may have to remain in the harbor in quarantine for some time."

"So what will we do?"

"Pray God intervenes." The captain turned and strode to his cabin.

Amalia took Ruth's hand. "Come, we will go eat and then I need to take care of those below." *Lord God, I know you have a plan. You must.*

Two

S he had to get their clothes clean.

Amalia knelt at a washtub on the ship's deck, scrubbing little Ruth's extra woolen skirt till her hands burned red from the scrap of lye soap she'd begged from another immigrant woman. The work gave her something to do, something to occupy her mind other than this endless waiting, sitting aboard ship in New York Harbor.

Certainly not how she'd imagined their welcome to Amerika.

"Can I help you, Tante Malia?" A little hand tapped her shoulder.

Amalia twisted her head to see Ruthie standing close. "I thought you were playing with Brigit, den lille."

"I was." The little girl worried her bottom lip between her teeth. "But I want to be with you."

Amalia smothered a sigh. Poor little one, she seemed barely able to let her "new tante" out of her sight these days. Small wonder, with all she'd been through, yet sometimes Amalia felt nearly stifled. She shook her head at herself for the thought. Yes, she'd lost her parents too, but Ruthie was so little and lost.

"Come, help me squeeze out the dirty water."

A smile peeked through, and Ruthie knelt on the deck beside her and reached for the tub.

"Ah-ah." Amalia reached to block her from plunging her blouse sleeves deep in the dirty water. "Push up your sleeves first."

Ruth obeyed, the wind over the harbor blowing wisps of fair hair across her pale little face. "After we get our clothes clean, will they let us off the ship?"

"I hope they will soon."

"How soon?"

"I don't know. It's been almost three weeks already." Three weeks of sitting in harbor on this "death ship," as the quarantine inspector had called them. Ships carrying cholera must isolate in the harbor, he'd declared, unless passengers could be taken to one of the two quarantine islands out in the bay. But right now, those were all full.

April inched forward, the sun baking them on the deck on the warmest days, rain and wind rocking the ship on others. Nearly three weeks of carrying water to the sufferers and sponging fevered foreheads, though finally new cases had stopped breaking out now. Of holding little Ruthie close in the night when she cried for her mor, the little one's gasping sobs springing Amalia's own tears to leak down the neck of her shift, raw grief squeezing out in the darkness. Of wondering why she herself stayed healthy when so many others sickened and perished. *Mor and Far . . . however will I manage in this new land without you? And how will I find Erik?* Her mor's last words, "Find your brother," simmered at the back of her mind, though with Ruth now in her charge and the child's inheritance to claim, she didn't know how to begin that quest even once they were allowed on shore.

"Tante Amalia?"

Amalia swiped her sleeve across her eyes and tried to smile at the little girl, staring up at her so soberly. How long before smiles would come easy again? "Ja, what is it, den lille?"

Ruth stood, hands dripping, and pointed behind her. "What's everybody looking at?"

Amalia glanced about them. A surge of immigrants hurried to the rail, murmurs rising to a swell. *The inspector*, she heard the words tossed from one side of the ship to another.

The quarantine inspector? He was back? Amalia dropped the sodden skirt in the dirty water and pushed to her feet. She let Ruthie tug her toward the railing, not that they could see anything with others pushing ahead.

"Back, back." Sailors and the captain made a pathway through the crowd. "Out of the way, make room."

Amalia snatched Ruthie back and held the little girl against her, hands over the child's shoulders.

The quarantine inspector, a short man with piercing blue eyes and an official-looking badge, marched across the gangplank and onto the deck, his shoes clipping on the boards. He scanned the lines of immigrants with thinned lips beneath his mustache.

"You claim the epidemic has ceased, Captain?"

Captain Alberg, with his sea-creased face and sideburns flecked with gray, nodded. "No new cases for over two weeks now."

The inspector hmphed and drew a handkerchief from his coat pocket to hold over his nose and mouth. "Take me to steerage and I'll see for myself."

The two men disappeared below deck.

Murmurs rose in the milling crowd. One woman started to weep, hushed by her husband.

"Come." Amalia squeezed Ruth's shoulders. "I should get our clothes from the washtub before someone else does."

The little girl helped Amalia dip their few garments in the shared rinse tub, then wring the water from them as best they could.

"Do you think the man will let us get off the ship now?" Ruth handed over a still-dripping blouse.

"I don't know." Amalia gave the garment another wring, then piled the sodden clothes in the basket lent to her by kind Mrs. Haugen, now recovering from her illness. Amalia would have to hang the laundry items between their bunks and hope they'd dry.

"What is he doing down below the deck?"

"Checking to see how sick people still are, I guess."

"What if he thinks they're too sick? Will he send us back to Norway?"

"I don't know. I hope not." Or did she? Amalia's chest squeezed. What was there for her in this new land, without her parents? Erik, of course—but was he even still alive, somewhere? She looked down into the little face upturned to hers. Still, she had Ruth, tied to her legally on paper as well as, now, by heart. She couldn't go back home—to Norway—even if she wanted to.

The murmurs around them rose again, then silenced, and Amalia looked up to see the quarantine inspector emerging from the hold.

"Well." The inspector removed the handkerchief from his nose and brushed at his sleeve. "It seems the epidemic has run its course." He glared around the crowd of immigrants as if holding each of them personally responsible for the plague, then up at the captain. "*If* the situation continues to improve over the next three days with no new cases, you may be permitted to dock at that point. And *if* you scour this ship top to bottom." He flicked his gaze over them all again and shook his head, then made his way back toward the gangplank. The crowd parted for him this time without being told.

Ruth twisted to look up at Amalia. "Does that mean we finally get to step onto Amerika?"

Amalia ran her hand over the little girl's braids wound around her head. Ruthie had asked Amalia to pin her braids over her head this morning, like Amalia's own plaited crown of dark gold. The color of aged honey, Mor always said. Her throat tightened again, but she made herself smile at Ruth, even if her lips trembled with the effort.

"I think it does, den lille." *Far i himmelen, guide us in this new land. I don't know what I'm doing.*

Did everything in Amerika screech and smell of smoke?

Amalia flinched at the screaming of the locomotive's brakes as it jerked to a halt in front of them, billowing choking black puffs. She'd cover her ears but for clinging to Ruth's hand. With the crowd of strangers pressing around them from every direction, she would not let go of the little girl for a moment, even if deafened.

"Come. This way." Behind her, Mrs. Haugen took Amalia's other arm and guided her through the rising sea of people toward the belching train. The woman had taken her and Ruth under her wing once she heard they were all heading west, insisting they travel with her and her grown son, Lars, at least as far as Iowa. The Haugens were traveling farther, to Dakota Territory. Lars even spoke decent English.

Amid the crush of people, Amalia boosted Ruthie up on the train carriage steps after Mrs. Haugen, then nearly tripped trying to clamber aboard herself, caught by Lars's outstretched hand. Finally steady, she grasped her satchel firmly with one hand and Ruthie with the other, following Mrs. Haugen's shoulders, thinner now since her sickness, down the narrow aisle of the railway car. They found their way to an open corner in the third-class car and collapsed onto the wooden benches.

"Finally." Mrs. Haugen settled back, panting slightly. "I sometimes thought we'd never make it this far."

Amalia's throat tightened. Despite her lingering weakness, Mrs. Haugen always seemed so strong, yet tears sheened the older woman's gray eyes as she gazed at the ashy smoke billowing beyond the carriage window. She had been one of the first to lose someone to the cholera aboard ship, her husband, not to mention weathering the sickness herself. And now she must start this new life without him.

Amalia reached across the gap between their benches and squeezed her hand. "We've survived the voyage, the epidemic, and three weeks sitting in the harbor. I think we're going to make it."

"Not to mention surviving Castle Garden." Lars quirked a brow.

They all chuckled, though Amalia held back a shudder at the memory of all of them shuttled through the enormous fortress-like building from one official department to another like a herd of human cattle, even if most of the officials had proven helpful and kind.

"Ja." Mrs. Haugen's smile creased the corners of her eyes again. "I am thankful for the agents there who helped us get railroad tickets. I wouldn't have had the first idea how to get from New York to Dakota Territory." She spoke the unfamiliar words with care, enunciating each strange syllable.

"And without being cheated, as I hear so many immigrants have been." Lars shook his head and pushed back his cap. "Now as long as we don't run into any train robbers, we should be fine."

"Hush." His mother patted his leg. "Don't even speak of such things."

Amalia leaned against the hard back of the seat and put her arm around Ruthie. The little girl cuddled against her and laid her head in Amalia's lap, where she stroked back the wisps of hair always springing loose against the child's ear and cheek. With a jolt and a hiss, the train rumbled forward, chugging slowly at first, then swaying and clacking, faster and faster. Ruthie sprang up again to stare out the window, pressing her face against the glass.

Amalia's own middle trembled at the speed. Surely they would reach Iowa by nightfall, hurtling over the rails like this.

By the next morning, after nearly twenty-four hours of the hard seats and jolting train, their hair and eyes full of soot and Ruthie whimpering with hunger, she realized Amerika stretched much larger than she'd thought.

"Hush, den lille." Amalia scrounged in her satchel for remnants of the food she'd bought with precious new American coins at Castle Garden. She held up their last roll, now going hard and stale. "Here. Nibble on this."

The little girl subsided, leaning against the hard back of the seat and gnawing on the crust.

Mrs. Haugen pressed a brown paper package into Amalia's hand. "Share this between you."

Amalia peeked under the wrapper to see soft bread and cheese, then pushed it back. "This is yours. We can't."

"Of course you can." The woman firmed her chin. "You are responsible for that little one, aren't you?"

The weight of that settled on Amalia's chest again, and she nodded. "Mange takk." She held out the package to Ruthie.

"Nei, I said for the two of you. You need your strength too."

Her throat tightening, Amalia broke off part of the sandwich, then handed the larger portion to Ruthie. "What do you say to Mrs. Haugen?"

"Mange takk," the little girl mumbled around her mouthful.

The older woman smiled, then leaned her head back and closed her eyes.

Amalia nibbled her own portion, the fragrant bread and cheese tasting of sheer heaven. The pinch in her middle eased, she leaned her head against the train car window and nodded off to sleep.

She woke sometime later, head stuffy and eyes blurry, to find the wooden bench beside her empty. Ruthie was gone.

"Ruth. Ruthie!" Amalia lurched to her feet, legs stiff, chest clamping with panic. She jerked her gaze to the seat across. Mrs. Haugen snored against the window. Lars's seat sat empty too.

Maybe Ruthie was with Lars. Amalia staggered down the swaying aisleway. That had to be it—Lars had taken the little girl for a drink of water or something, hadn't wanted to waken the women. *Please, God, please—*

Stumbling through the packed aisles, a multitude of languages peppering the air and unwashed bodies souring it, she scanned each crowded seat.

"Miss Gunderson?" A familiar voice turned her round.

"Lars? Do you know where Ruthie is?"

The young man frowned. "No. I heard there was coffee in second class and went to get us some." He held out a steaming cup.

Amalia shook her head hard. "Nei. I have to find Ruthie. I fell asleep, and now she is gone—" She clutched a nearby seat back, fighting to breathe. *Far i himmelen, how could I let this happen?*

Surely a little girl couldn't get lost on a train. She wouldn't have gotten off by herself. But what if someone got hold of her, someone with evil intent? Amalia's knees threatened to buckle.

"Come." Lars caught her elbow. "Maybe she's back at our seats by now. She could have just gone to use the necessary."

The necessary—yes, that could be. Amalia sucked air into her lungs again and followed Lars back to their seats, scanning each bench once more on the way back.

But no Ruthie sat perched on their bench, gazing out the train window.

Amalia braced herself in the aisleway while Lars woke his mother. She shook her buzzing head to clear it, scouring up and down the crowded car. Which way to look next? She wanted to run down the aisleway screaming.

The train-car door hissed open, and a conductor stepped through, wearing a gilt-edged cap and badge. And holding a child's hand—

"Ruthie!" Amalia careened down the aisle and caught the little girl into her arms. "Where were you? You gave me such a fright." She looked up at the conductor. "Mange takk, tusen takk. Where did you find her?"

24

The conductor's bushy brows drew together, and he shook his head, spilling out words she couldn't understand and pointing behind him.

Amalia straightened and held Ruthie out from her. "Where did you go?"

The little girl shrank from Amalia's tone. "I just went to the necessary, but then I forgot how to get back. I smelled something good to eat, so I followed the smell and found a car that was so beautiful, full of pretty ladies and soft chairs and they had hot chicken on fancy plates and—"

"You went into the first-class car?" Amalia's fingers tightened on the child's shoulders.

Ruthie hung her head.

Amalia inhaled deep through her nose and looked up to meet the conductor's gaze. Stern, yet she thought a touch of humor glinted deep in his eyes.

"Jeg beklager så mye." His deepened frown said he'd no understanding of her apology. How she wished she'd taken time to learn more English before leaving the ship. "Mange takk." She laid her hand on her chest. Surely he could at least understand gratitude.

The conductor shook his head again, but then patted Ruthie's. He said something to both of them, the words a jumble but the tone communicating clearly that such must not happen again. Then he smiled at Ruthie, gave Amalia another headshake, and headed back toward the other car.

Amalia blew out a long breath, then gripped Ruthie by the hand. "Back to the seats, young lady. We must have a talk."

Later that afternoon, a chagrined Ruthie huddled in the bench corner by the window, and Amalia fought to stay awake, determined not to close her eyes on her small charge again. When the train stopped at a town around suppertime, Amalia used some of her precious coins to buy them each a hunk of bread and cheese, splurging on a sausage and an apple for Ruthie. Hilda had left the rest of their family's funds for the trip with Amalia, and she had some from her parents too. But who knew what really awaited them at their journey's end? She wanted to be careful. Lars said some men he'd spoken to assured him they'd reach Iowa by tomorrow evening. Then they would see.

"Come, den lille. Let me tell you a story." Amalia tucked away the remnants of their simple supper, then reached to draw Ruthie toward her as the sun slanted low over the prairie beyond the sooty window. Prairie—another new word. So strange to see expanses of grass and sprouting cornfields with no mountains and hardly any trees. Though spring wildflowers dotted the fields, her chest ached for the whispering evergreens, steep slopes, and icy blue fjords of Norway.

"You are not angry anymore?" Ruthie cuddled against her side, the pitiful whisper melting Amalia's heart.

"Nei." She pressed a kiss to the little girl's head. "I was just so frightened, you understand? And I know you will never do such again."

"I was just hungry."

"I know. But now you've had food, and by tomorrow, we will be at the boardinghouse, where you have a cousin, ja? She will have hot food, maybe some potato leek soup. Now let me tell you the story of the princess on the glass mountain."

"My mor used to tell me that one."

Amalia swallowed. "Mine too."

Ruthie snuggled closer, and Amalia let the familiar tale carry them back to their birth land, to Mor's gentle voice telling the story by the hearth at home, her spinning wheel and loom in the corner, firelight dancing on the rosemaled trunk and beloved family faces about—Mor's, Far's. Erik's. Where was he? If only she knew so she could send him a letter, tell him what had happened, where she was, ask him to come for her . . .

Ruthie's shifting made her realize she'd trailed off mid-story, so

Amalia picked up again. "So there sat the princess atop the glass hill, with three golden apples in her lap. And her father the king decreed, whoever could manage to climb the hill and fetch the golden apples, that man could have not only half the kingdom, but the princess as his wife . . ."

Ruthie nodded off soon after the story finished, and Amalia, her head resting on the little girl's atop her shoulder, let her own eyes close as well, the train's rolling rumble lulling her too.

One more day, and then—they would be in Decorah, Iowa. Whatever that strange-sounding place would hold.

Please, Lord, guide us and show us the way.

THREE

That woman better not be headed in here."

Bent over a volume of case law, Absalom Karlsson barely registered his father's grumble by the front window of their Decorah law office, or rather the front rooms of their home that they used as an office. Absalom pushed his spectacles up his nose and ran his finger down the page, peering close to better see the words. Yes—this looked promising. All week he'd been searching for a key precedent to help them win the Jorstad family's case. Recent immigrants from Norway, the Jorstads had been cheated out of nearly all their money by an unscrupulous landlord. And now, almost first thing this morning, he'd found—

"Absalom!"

"Father?" He lifted his head, blinking.

"She's coming. That woman means nothing but trouble." His father limped away from the window, hobbling toward his private office off to the side. He moved faster than Absalom would have thought possible, since his father had lost the lower half of his leg back in the war.

"Who?" Shaking his head to clear it, Absalom stood from behind the mahogany counter where he'd been working.

"Zelda Berg." His father jerked his thumb over his shoulder. "Whatever happens, don't let her in my office." With a final glance toward the front window, he slammed the door shut.

What on earth? Absalom ran his hands through his mop of curly dark hair. And just when he'd been so close to a break-through. That one paragraph he'd just started reading could set a tenable precedent . . . he reached for the book again, interrupted by the jingle of the bell hung on their front door.

With a sigh, Absalom marked the page and looked up. The opening door admitted a fresh April breeze—and Miss Zelda Berg. The middle-aged woman sniffed as if testing the air in the room.

He put on a polite smile. "Miss Berg. How might I assist you this afternoon?"

"I have a legal question. An important legal question." Her voice seemed set in a perpetual whine, while her sharp eyes darted from one corner of the room to another. "I've been trying to speak to your father about it all week. Is he in?"

"He's busy at present. How may I help you?"

"It's a delicate matter, involving family inheritance and such." She fingered the strings of her pocketbook with fingers that couldn't seem to still. "I'd much prefer to speak with the magistrate."

"I have experience in handling such matters." Keeping his tone even, Absalom reached for his volume on inheritance laws. "I just helped another family settle a difficult inheritance dispute last week. What is the nature of your concern?"

"It's really rather delicate for a legal clerk." With another sniff, she took a step to the right, toward his father's private office. "Where is your father?"

"I don't believe my father has any room in his appointment schedule today. And I will be an attorney myself soon." Absalom firmed his voice. Honey over vinegar only went so far—and attracted wasps as well as flies. "If I cannot help you, perhaps you'd like to try another of the law offices in Decorah."

Zelda Berg sighed and pursed her lips. "When will the *magistrate* be available, then?"

Biting the inside of his cheek, Absalom checked the appointment book. "Two o'clock Thursday?"

"Nothing sooner? It's a terribly long walk all the way from Green Creek. I've no conveyance of my own, you know." With a last glance about the waiting room, as if she might discover his father hiding in a corner like a mouse, Miss Berg turned to go. Then, with a sudden flail, she stumbled back and clutched the edge of the counter behind her.

"Are you quite well, ma'am?" Absalom stepped around the corner and hurried to her side.

"Certainly not," she snapped. "I've a sudden dizzy spell. Haven't you anywhere I can sit down?"

Absalom smothered a sigh. "Of course." He took her elbow—even her joints poked sharp—and guided her to one of the straight-backed chairs in their waiting area.

She waved her hand at him. "Water."

He headed for the water pitcher they kept on the counter to quench clients' thirst, filled a cup, and brought it to her.

She sipped without a word of thanks, then loosened her coat and pulled a handkerchief from her handbag to dab at her forehead and neck. "Uff da. It's dreadfully warm in here."

He thought the heat from the fire crackling in the potbellied stove felt nice, since this morning's heavy blanket of clouds brought to mind more December than April. But Miss Berg would complain to God himself, as he'd heard someone say once. *Stay put,* he mentally ordered his father in the other room. "More water, Miss Berg?"

"I need to put my feet up. Perhaps your father's office?"

He'd known she was brazen, but this? "I'm afraid not, ma'am."

"Hmmph." Her face twisted.

Absalom cast a longing glance at the counter, imagining the work behind it as the morning ticked away.

"I suppose you'll just send me on my way." By Miss Berg's tone, Absalom rivaled Genghis Khan for heartlessness.

"Not till you're quite well, of course, ma'am." He gentled his tone. After all, Christ commanded to love the unlovable. "Another glass of water?"

"I wouldn't dream of troubling you." She shoved the empty cup back into his hand. "Just help me up."

Gripping his arm, Zelda Berg attempted to stand—or gave the appearance of trying, at least.

Absalom veritably dragged her to her feet, suppressing the urge to shove her out the door.

"Thank you," she said, though her tone communicated anything but. She jerked her elbow away and headed for the door, tottering slightly. "Tell your father I'll see him—oh." She swayed on her feet, arms outstretched.

Absalom rushed forward to catch her as Miss Berg rolled her eyes back and collapsed to the floor, knocking over their brass umbrella stand with a crash along the way. *Splendid.* He shifted her weight in his arms, having just kept her head from hitting the floorboards. Just terrific, in both the old and new meanings of the word.

"Miss Berg?" Absalom shook the woman. Her head flopped to the side. He tried to haul her up to set her in the chair again, but she proved heavier than she looked.

His father's office door banged open. "What on earth?"

"Sorry. I tried." Absalom pointed his chin at the limp woman in his arms.

His father sighed and rubbed his hand over his face. "Bring her in."

Together, his father's prosthetic leg notwithstanding, they

managed to haul Miss Berg into his father's office, hoisting her into one of the green velvet armchairs kept there for client comfort.

After trying to ensure she wouldn't slide off, Absalom headed for another glass of water, tamping down the urge to throw the contents straight into the blasted woman's face. He'd bet good money she'd never fainted in her life, however slack her face hung just now. But appearances could be deceiving, as he knew well— especially where women were concerned.

He winced and stamped down the uncharitable thought. *Lord, forgive me.* But when he had to push aside actually urgent cases, all because of a self-centered . . . well, it got his dander up.

He returned with the water just as Miss Berg's eyelids fluttered. "Where—what happened?"

"You collapsed in the front room." Absalom kept his words careful. He held out the water without further comment.

"Oh my." She sipped with a trembling hand. "What can be the matter with me?" She glanced about the small room as if noticing where she was for the first time, then landed her gaze on his father. "Magistrate Karlsson. Dear me, I didn't mean to intrude on your private office."

Her sharp tones sure could turn molasses-sweet in a hurry. Absalom turned his head away to roll his eyes.

"Miss Berg." His father inclined his head. "Are you feeling better?"

"A bit, thank you, Magistrate." She sat up straight with a coy smile. "You are always so solicitous."

His father's face nearly snorted a laugh from Absalom's chest. Behind the chaise beyond Miss Berg's view, Absalom lifted his hands in a shrug. The woman was incorrigible.

"Would you like some more water, Miss Berg? Before I help you out?" He emphasized the last word just enough, he hoped.

"This is adequate, thank you." She took a minuscule sip. "And now, Magistrate, since I'm here, perhaps we might discuss that legal question I mentioned to you the other day."

"I, well—" His father's mouth twisted.

Absalom cleared his throat. "Miss Berg, might I remind you of our appointment Thursday?"

"And as I'm sure your father knows, some legal matters cannot wait," she snapped. "I merely want to know the details of my cousin, Else Forsberg's, will. Concerning her property and suchlike."

His father rubbed a hand down one gray sideburn. "And as I told you in the mercantile the other day, Miss Berg, I'm not permitted to divulge that information. Not unless you're a client, and—"

"Then I'll become one. Why do you suppose I'm here, after all?"

"—and even then, only if you're a beneficiary in the will."

"You mean I'm not?" Her sallow cheeks reddened.

His father sighed. "As I said, I'm not permitted to—"

"Ja, ja." She tightened a fist in her lap. "I understand well enough you're not going to help me."

"You are welcome to still come to the office Thursday, Miss Berg," Absalom put in.

"And for what? To be condescended to again? Consider my appointment cancelled. As you suggested earlier, I can seek out legal help elsewhere in Decorah. And on your own heads be it." She jutted out her chin. "I suppose I must walk myself home now." When neither gentleman responded, she sniffed and pushed to her feet, clipping toward the door with startling energy for a woman who'd just fainted.

Absalom exchanged a look with his father and followed Miss Berg to the front door.

She pushed it open, then clucked her tongue. "Would you believe, it's begun to snow. My, these unpredictable Iowa springs." She flashed a triumphant glance.

Could she be serious? Absalom reached his arm above her head to press the door open farther and nearly groaned. Sure enough, fitful flakes spurted down from the sky.

"Absalom." His father's eyes apologized. "Would you be so kind as to drive Miss Berg home in the buggy?"

Absalom clamped the inside of his cheek so hard he flinched. "Of course. One moment, Miss Berg, while I get my umbrella." He glanced around for one, found it still knocked on the floor from the upended umbrella stand. Expelling a silent breath, he set the stand to rights and grasped the umbrella's handle to shield them from the heavying snowfall on the way to the buggy. *Lord, you sure must think I need to cultivate the virtue of patience.*

Miss Berg stayed mercifully silent on their drive the couple of snowy miles to Green Creek. The old boardinghouse where she lived sat back a bit from the rest of the small town, surrounded by farmland. Not that she appeared to use it as a boardinghouse. In fact, Absalom had very little idea what she did with the dilapidated building, now that her cousin had passed away. Perhaps that was why she'd been in such a tizzy to speak with his father?

"Thank you, that will do." She released his arm after he helped her out of the buggy. Absalom followed her toward the porch, intending to see her to the door with his umbrella, but she turned, holding out her palm to halt him on the steps.

"You needn't come in. I'll be quite all right now."

He paused, one foot up on a step. All this, now she shooed him off like a stray dog? He glanced up at the three-story building, scanning the aging gingerbread trim, now frosted with snow. Stunning in architecture, though showing want of care. Not only peeling paint but shutters coming loose. What did the woman do, rattling around in it by herself?

"Good day to you, then, Miss Berg."

She stood watching him, eyes boring as if she expected him to—what, steal the rickety rocking chair on the porch? He saw barely a curtain in the window.

Tipping his hat, he turned away and climbed back into the buggy, letting their black mare, Maybelle, have her head along the white-scattered road back toward Decorah. The snow lightened already, a few sunrays peeking out through parting dark clouds and gleaming on the snowy fields around him, the farmland that had just been starting to show hints of green. Absalom shook his head. Iowa springs indeed. He blinked against the brightness and gently slapped the reins, thinking of the book on his desk. He'd see if his father thought the precedent solid for the Jorstads, then perhaps could still get a letter in the afternoon mail. If he hurried.

"So what do you make of Miss Berg?" he asked his father that evening as they tidied up the front office rooms before supper. He sorted through the mail, setting aside a bill and the latest issue of the *American Law Register* to peruse later.

His father puffed out his cheeks with a breath. "She's been tailing me all week about her cousin's will. After that message about the Forsbergs, I figure I better not give her an inch till we know more."

Absalom raised a brow. "You mean the letter from Else Forsberg's nephew? Coming from Norway?"

"No, that was weeks ago. Didn't I show you the telegram last week—I was sure I did. You must have been out on a case." His father patted his pockets, then dug through his desk drawer. He held out the yellow slip of paper. "Here."

Absalom read the stilted lines, a knot settling in his gut. "How awful."

"Indeed. Epidemics surely can humble our modern sense of how far we've come in a trice." He took the paper back from Absalom. "Both parents gone, just like that. The poor child."

Absalom thought of his mother, taken in an influenza epidemic when he was only a small boy. "You know anything about this Miss Gunderson?"

"No more than is in the telegram. We won't know much till they arrive. But till then, with Miss Berg . . ."

Absalom nodded. "I understand. Best to steer clear." A relative nosing about a family will always raise questions, but now with a vulnerable child and unknown young woman in the mix . . . the back of Absalom's neck prickled. They'd have to keep a sharp eye out so no one got taken advantage of. He stacked the last papers on his desk, placing the Jorstads' file on top for continued attention tomorrow. His father agreed on the precedent; now he just needed to type up the necessary documents for the upcoming hearing.

"Ready to go eat?"

Absalom hesitated, then grabbed the volume on inheritance law to review this evening by the parlor stove. "I am now." A whiff of beef stew wafted through the double doors that led to their private rooms in the back of the large house, rumbling his stomach. Their housekeeper, Mrs. Skivens, was working her culinary magic, as usual. For only coming in a few times a week, she certainly kept them well fed.

His father stepped toward the door, then hesitated. "By the way, I've been meaning to tell you. I saw Rebecca in town last week."

The name stilled Absalom from the inside out. "And?"

"Nothing much, I didn't speak to her—that is, to them. Just passed and nodded on the street. They must have moved here recently."

"She was with—her new husband?"

"Yes. And, well . . ." His father cleared his throat. "She was, ah, in a family way, son."

A lump stuck in his throat. "I see."

His father laid a hand on his shoulder, heavy and warm. "Just thought you should know. I'm sorry if I—"

"No. Thank you for telling me." Absalom pushed toward the door and opened it, ignoring the tremble of his fingers on the knob. "Ready to go?" His voice came almost steady.

His father followed him into the darkened hallway, light gleaming at the end of it with the clink of dishes. Absalom breathed

36

deep of the scent of fresh bread along with the stew. He stopped off in his own room to drop off the book, then headed to join his father and Mrs. Skivens in the kitchen, the warmth and lamplight easing the tightness in his chest. Helping him not think too much of what his father had shared.

Rebecca . . . that child could have been his, if things had been different. If *she* had been different.

They bid the housekeeper good-night and sent her home to her own family, then Absalom served the bowls of stew while his father cut the bread, the rhythm familiar, consoling, as the wind after the snowstorm whistled around the eaves of their home.

"Thanks, for your help with Miss Berg today." His father set his cane in the corner and sat down in the dining room. "Not sure what I would've done without you, with all her shenanigans."

"Good thing you don't need to." Absalom quirked a brow at him and unfolded his napkin. They'd been there for each other, as long as he could remember. He didn't plan on changing that anytime soon.

He wasn't about to let anyone take advantage of his father. Nor of anyone else.

FOUR

A surprise spring snowstorm blew through as the train crossed into Iowa, late on the first of May.

That evening, the sun peeked through storm clouds above the horizon before disappearing in a burst of crimson and orange as the train pulled into Decorah. The new station building boasted yellow siding and a peaked roof, but Amalia's weary legs ached too much to care. Snow lay patchy on the fields, the clouds still lowering heavy. The conductor hoisted to the platform the two trunks and a crate that now held all their worldly possessions, Amalia's and Ruth's combined, except for the carpetbags they clutched.

"God be with you." Mrs. Haugen hugged Amalia on the train steps. "I'm so glad He made our paths cross."

"Me too." Amalia clung to the older woman with one arm, the other holding Ruthie fast. Panic suddenly clamped her chest. What on earth was she doing, alighting in this unknown place with a child in tow, completely alone and friendless? Would it not be better to go on with the Haugens to Dakota Territory? But she'd sent that telegram to the magistrate in Decorah. He'd be expecting them—she hoped.

"All aboard!" bellowed the conductor, nearly straight into Amalia's ear.

"We will write to you." Mrs. Haugen squeezed her hand, then released her to climb down the steps, helped by the conductor's insistent hand. "Then you write back, let us know how things went. If worse comes to worst, we'll only be a few days away by train."

"Ja, I suppose so. Tusen takk, for everything." Amalia gripped Ruthie's hand, pulling her back farther on the platform as the train let out a screech and billowed smoke. Lars flapped his cap, grinning.

Amalia waved hard, ignoring the tears leaking down her cheeks.

Ruthie tugged at her hand. "Where do we go, Tante Malia? I'm hungry."

"Let's see." Amalia sucked a breath and reached for the precious letter tucked into her vest. "I have the address here from your mor. Forsberg House, Green Creek." Her tongue stumbled over the words. Green Creek—did that mean another town, or an actual creek? She scanned the dusking streets, cold falling fast. If only they'd arrived here earlier in the day. *Lord, help.*

A porter stopped beside her. "Pardon, miss. You need these trunks taken somewhere?"

She shook her head. "Jeg vet ikke."

At his quirked brow, she tried switching to the halting words of English she'd learned on the ship. "I—don't—know."

"Aha. Well, how about if I just move these into the station for now? You can try talkin' to the stationmaster in there."

"Mange takk." She cleared her throat. "Th-thank you."

The man grinned and hoisted one trunk, hefting it into the station as if it weighed no more than a sack of flour. Amalia and Ruthie followed.

Father, perhaps you send angels as railroad porters sometimes. Thank you.

"Got a couple young ladies here might could use some help, Mr. Gruber." The porter jerked his thumb back at them, speaking to a man behind the ticket counter. "Think they might be some of your Norwegians."

The stationmaster lifted a brow and came out from behind the counter. "God dag. How may I help you?"

At hearing the familiar language, Amalia's eyes pricked. "Mange takk. We have just arrived on the train." *After a horrible voyage, and losing our parents, and part of me wants to flee back to Norway right now . . .* "I need to find this address."

The man scanned the paper as the porter headed back outside for their other trunk. "Ah. The old Forsberg place, out in Green Creek." He glanced at Amalia, then Ruth. "Miss Zelda know you folks are comin'?"

"I, uh." Amalia swallowed. Who was Zelda? The cousin? "I believe she knew this little girl and her parents were. They died aboard ship, and her mor gave Ruth into my care. I know they'd written, so I trust she's expecting them."

"Well." The stationmaster handed the letter back. "Green Creek's a coupla miles from here. Bit of a far piece for you ladies to walk on your own at this time of night."

"We haven't anywhere else to go." Amalia forced down the bubble of panic in her throat and firmed her voice. "If you can just point us in the right direction . . ." She glanced at the window. Deepening gray showed darkness falling fast. "Might we leave our trunks here till we find a way to take them to the boardinghouse, perhaps tomorrow?" The other man thumped their crate on the floor by the trunks as she spoke.

He nodded. "Sure thing. I'll lock 'em in the back storeroom. But I ain't lettin' you ladies go off by yourselves. I live in Green Creek myself. Don't have room to haul the trunks just now, but I can give you a lift in my buggy."

Air rushed into Amalia's lungs. "Oh, thank you. Mange takk."

"Not to worry. Was about to head home for supper. Just give me a few minutes to close up."

Gratitude balming her heart, Amalia and Ruthie waited on one of the benches in the train station until the stationmaster reappeared, shrugging on his coat. He lit a lantern and held the door for his two guests, then locked it behind them. The porter had already left, doubtless for his own hearth and supper.

Amalia wrapped both the little girl's woolen shawl and her own more closely once they stepped out into the chilling dusk.

"That wind blows right sharp across the prairie, as you'll learn. Shouldn't get any more snow after this, but never can tell." Mr. Gruber hoisted Ruthie up into the buggy and then gave Amalia a hand before climbing in himself. He hupped the horse, and they started off at a gentle trot.

In the back seat, Amalia hugged Ruthie against her side. The gentle rock of the buggy came as soothing to their weary muscles as the fresh, cold air of the prairie to their lungs after the soot and smoke of the train.

"So how's the little one related to Zelda Berg?"

"I'm not sure." Amalia shifted in her seat. "Sorry, but that doesn't sound like the name I read on the papers I signed. But Ruth's far was nephew to Else Forsberg."

"Ah." The man nodded. "How'd he and her mor pass?"

"We had a cholera outbreak on the ship." Amalia's throat tightened.

He shook his head and blew out a breath. "Lord have mercy."

Amalia pushed back the crowding memories of her own parents. "Else Forsberg used to own and run the boardinghouse, is that right?"

Mr. Gruber nodded. "Right you are. 'Long with her husband, Amund, till he passed some years ago. Right fine lady Else was too, whole town loved her. Always doing good, would take in strays who couldn't afford to pay much, yet her boardinghouse still held a fine reputation. Pity she took ill and died, just last year it was. Matter of fact, she used to talk about her family in

Norway, some folks she hoped might come over. Must have been this little one's parents."

"Ja." Amalia's voice lifted. "So Zelda has been living here awhile?"

"Mrs. Forsberg invited her out to live with her a few years ago, she's a cousin, I believe. Most folks in town didn't think she—but never mind, I should mind my own business." He thumbed toward a cluster of flickering lights on the prairie horizon. "That's Green Creek, up ahead."

Ruthie leaned over the edge of the buggy to see better, Amalia keeping firm hold of her. "That's it, Tante Amalia? Our new home?"

"I guess so, den lille." Amalia swallowed. *Home.* When would she know the real meaning of that word again?

"You're her tante?" Mr. Gruber clucked to the horses, turning them onto a rutted track leading toward the cluster of lights.

"Not really." Amalia drew Ruth back to sit against her again. "But when Hilda passed, and Ruthie's father and my parents were gone too—she asked me to, well . . ."

"I see." Mr. Gruber's voice came gentle as a father's. "And it would seem she made a right fine choice in that sorrowful time."

Amalia's eyes stung. "Takk."

They said little else as the buggy rumbled down the main street of the little town. Small, but not too rustic, at least from what Amalia could tell in the dimness—wooden sidewalks, and a respectable little line of shops. Mr. Gruber turned down off a lane that led between muddy fields and along a tree-lined creek, then finally stopped in front of a three-story house and a few other outbuildings, barely visible in the falling darkness.

"Well, ladies, here you are." He wrapped the reins around the buggy frame and jumped down to help them out.

"Mange takk, Mr. Gruber." Amalia gripped his hand. "You've been God's angel to us."

"I don't know about that. But my missus and I aren't far away, just over on Butterworth Street, other side of Main. You let us know if you need anything, now." He glanced up at the boardinghouse, a frown creasing his face in the lantern light.

"Won't you come up with us? I'm sure Miss Berg would like to thank you also."

"No, no, I'd best be gettin' home to my wife. Miss Berg won't want to see me anyhow. She doesn't—well. You'll see soon enough." He set their bags at the foot of the steps, then patted Ruth's head. "You be good for your tante, now."

"I will." Ruth squeezed Amalia's hand.

"I'll bring your trunks and the crate out in the morning, if I can manage it."

"You are so kind. Tusen takk."

With the buggy slushing away, Amalia turned toward the boardinghouse, hard to see in the darkness. The building stretched tall, with a wraparound porch. One light glowed in a lower window.

At least someone is home. Amalia clutched that thought as tightly as Ruthie clung to her hand. The wind bit through her coat and into her bones. She felt for the step with the toe of her boot and shifted her weight. They had to get out of the weather. Sucking in a deep breath, she squeezed the little hand and together they mounted three steps.

"Our bags?"

"I'll get them after. . . ." She raised her hand and rapped on the door. And waited. No answer. She rapped again, harder. Nothing. *Please Lord . . .* This time she pounded. Surely whoever was in that room could hear her. Unless she was sleeping. But one did not sleep with a lit candle or lantern. Dredging up her faltering courage, she fumbled for the knob and pushed the door open. The two of them stepped inside. She could barely see a stairway to the left, thanks to a dim glow from a room near the door.

"Hallo?" she called. "Is anyone here?"

"I have a gun, go away." A woman's voice preceded a growing light from the room.

"I am Amalia Gunderson, and this is Ruth Forsberg with me. We came from Norway. The stationmaster said this is the Forsberg House. Are we in the right place?"

The woman raised her candleholder. "Ja, but you cannot stay here. This is my house now." She too spoke in Norwegian, which was a small comfort.

Ruthie sneezed and shifted closer to Amalia.

"Surely you have a place we can sleep. On the floor by the stove will be fine. Our trunks are still at the station but . . ."

"Nei! I do not know you. I cannot have strangers sleeping in my house."

Dear God, surely . . .

Amalia straightened her shoulders. "This is Ruth Forsberg, daughter of Hilda and Carl. Carl, nephew to Else Forsberg?" She looked the woman in the eye, hoping she remembered the relations right.

Something flickered in the woman's gaze, and she glanced down at Ruthie. "Carl's daughter?"

"Ja." Amalia put her arms around Ruth's shivering form. "This child is your family."

"Well, but—"

"I am going out to get our bags and we will sleep by the stove in the kitchen. We are not going any farther tonight." She bent down and said, "Ruth, you stay right here by the door, and I will be right back."

"Nei, I stay with you." Her voice broke as she threw her arms around Amalia.

"Please . . ."

"I never gave you permission to be here. I should throw you both out."

"I do not know who you are, but we will talk in the morning."

Fierce, biting anger made her shake all over as she stalked back out to the porch, Ruthie hanging on her hand. All the strain of the trip, and now—how could anyone be so cruel as to turn out even strangers in the dark and cold like this? *Dear God, help us.* "Let go of me and stay right here so I can get our bags," Amalia ordered her charge.

"Ja." Ruth's teeth chattered in the cold, and she was shaking so hard she could barely stand.

Amalia snatched up the two bags and swung them to the porch. "Now, we go back inside. You go open the door."

"C-c-c an't." Sobs smothered Amalia's heart.

She threw the bags close to the door and scooped the child up in her arms. "Now, all will be well." When she stepped back in the house, the woman with the candle stood in the doorway of the room. Amalia set Ruth down, reached out to grab the bags, and stood upright feeling like she might collapse at any moment.

"Shut the door!"

"Sorry." Amalia carefully clicked the door shut, much preferring to slam it. How could anyone . . . ?

The woman led the way to the kitchen, still faintly warm from the heat of the cooking stove. "You'll have to sleep under the table." She left the room with her candle.

Was that permission to stay, then? However grudging? Amalia jerked the two quilts out of the bags and after wrapping one around Ruth stood her next to the stove. "You can lean against the stove, help warm you up." Why was she whispering? "Ruthie, did you hear me?" Instead she spoke softly.

"Ja."

The brief candlelight had at least shown her the layout of the kitchen. The stove stood against the inner wall, the table and chairs near the window. She patted the stove to find the lid lifter and set the lid to the side. Sure enough, several coals winked at her from the ashes. But were they enough to fire up new wood? She fumbled around to find a box of kindling, then lifted the back lid and the divider. She couldn't find any starter so laid several sticks of kindling on the coals and opened all the vents.

Turning, she located a chair with the toe of her boot, the screech setting her teeth on edge, and lifted the chair over to set by the stove. Settling Ruth on the chair, she whispered, "You can lean against the stove, it's not hot." The smell of smoke made her want to dance for joy. After blowing on the kindling till it burst into flame, she added three sticks of wood and settled the lids back in place.

Ruthie whimpered. "I have to use the pot."

Amalia closed her eyes, the better to think. She unwrapped Ruth, took her over to the sink, and after stripping down her leggings, set and held her on the edge of the sink until she finished. *I will scrub the sink in the morning*, she promised herself and settled Ruth's clothing back in place.

Laying bundled Ruth down by the stove, Amalia fetched the other blanket off a chair at the table and, wrapping it around them both, pulled Ruth as close as she could.

"Takk."

She squeezed the little one gently. *Amen, Lord, amen.*

A snap from the fire made her smile. She'd get up in a bit to turn down the vents.

The fire was nearly out when she woke, so she added more wood and left the vents open in the hope it would start again. Who was the woman who met them—Zelda Berg? What made her treat them as she did? What would they do in the morning? Where might she find a chamber pot? Cautiously, she slipped from their sleeping place to turn down the vents as the fire now crackled and the warmth penetrated her coat. How long would it be until daylight? Would the woman chase them out again? They had to take the papers and go see the magistrate in Decorah first thing. Mr. Gruber had said he would bring their trunks out in the morning. Thoughts and fears jumbled together like a twisted hank of yarn. She yawned and blew out a breath before sleep claimed her again.

Pounding jerked her upright. A dream? No, there it came again. Someone was at the door, and daylight showed frost-painted windows.

"I am coming!" the woman called. "Who's there?"

"Mr. Gruber from the train station. I have the trunks for your guests, I'll leave them here on the porch."

"No!" The door banged open. "They are not my guests, and they will not be staying here."

Amalia stood and debated. Should she go see what she could do? After all, this was legally Ruth's house. Her stomach rumbled. She had the paperwork. Should she show it to the woman? But she'd clearly recognized Carl Forsberg's name. She knew Ruth was family.

She had to get to that magistrate in town, the one mentioned in the papers. Had he received her message?

The door slammed.

"I'm hungry." The little voice came from the pile on the floor.

"I know. You stay wrapped up, and I will get the fire going again. We'll see what there might be to eat." She could hear noises from the other room, making her think the woman was probably getting dressed. She started the stove again and put water to heat to sterilize the sink, then stared around the kitchen. Two doors. The first opened into a pantry without a lot in it. The second opened onto the back porch with a barn and what might be a chicken house out back.

The teakettle whistled. Amalia quickly scrubbed out the sink with lye soap, then poured boiling water over it. There—that should take care of last night. She washed her hands and headed back to the pantry. Out the window hung a side of bacon, but it was plenty cold enough in the room to keep food. Cupboards lined both sides of the narrow room with counters separating top and bottom. Eggs in a bowl, bread in a wooden box along with butter, and a pitcher of milk closer to the window.

The door slammed against the wall. "What are you doing in my pantry?"

Amalia kept herself from flinching. "Looking for something to make for breakfast. We have not eaten since. . . ." She could hear Ruthie whimpering. "I will make breakfast, and then we will go to the magistrate's office to introduce ourselves and show him the papers I have. I am Amalia Gunderson, the legal guardian for Ruth Forsberg. And you are?" She couldn't believe what she was doing, as she gathered the bowl of eggs and the bread to take into the kitchen.

The woman followed her. "You . . . you . . . have no right."

"So you say. But as I said, I have legal papers." She set the food on the counter and returned to the pantry for the pitcher and the butter, ignoring the slight tremble in her hands at her own temerity. "Ruthie, pick up the quilts and stuff them back into our bags."

Ruth did as she was told, sneaking glances at the other woman. She didn't look quite as scary as she'd sounded last night—not as tall as Amalia, but bigger-boned. She seemed all angles, with sharp chin and elbows, shapeless dress hanging on her frame, mouse-brown hair pulled into a messy bun. Amalia drew a breath and nodded at her. "Please tell me your name, that will be much easier."

"Zelda Berg. And I have lived and worked here for the last five years since I was invited to help my cousin, who was ailing." At least Zelda wasn't screaming anymore. "She left this place to me."

"Oh." Was that possible? But what about . . . ? Amalia brought down a frying pan from the shelf above the warming oven. "Would you like to eat with us?" This had to be the strangest day ever.

Zelda lifted an apron from the hook on the pantry door and pulled it over her head. She turned to Ruth. "The outhouse is out back."

"Takk." Amalia beckoned Ruth to come with her. When they

came back in after stomping their boots on the steps, the fragrance of warming bread met them at the door. Ruthie squeezed her hand. A coffeepot steamed on the stove while Zelda turned the scrambled eggs.

"The dishes are in that cupboard." Zelda pointed to one by the window. "But right after breakfast, you either show me those papers or leave."

"Ruthie, put your coat on the bags." Amalia set the plates and utensils on the table, along with a cup for milk. She wasn't showing Zelda anything till she met with the magistrate.

Ruth did as she was told and stood behind a chair, as if hiding.

They took places at the table, and after a slight pause, Amalia bowed her head. "I Jesu navn . . ." Ruth joined her in the traditional table grace.

As soon as they had eaten, Amalia pumped water into a pan in the sink and Ruth handed her the dishes. Zelda poured herself another cup of coffee and took it back to her room.

When they finished the dishes, Amalia got the hairbrush out of a bag and, after brushing Ruth's hair, rebraided it and then did her own. "We can't go looking like waifs," she whispered to Ruth, who smiled up at her.

"That felt so good."

"I know." She patted Ruthie's shoulder. "Now get your coat and hat, mittens too, and we will go find the magistrate. I'm certain Miss Zelda does not want to come with us."

"What about our trunks?"

Uff da, she'd forgotten. Had the stationmaster managed to leave them, or had Zelda made him cart them back to the station?

Opening the front door revealed both trunks huddled on the porch along with their crate, near where a spindle or two gapped missing in the railing.

Amalia smiled and released a breath. "They'll wait on the porch just fine."

Sun glinting off the snow nearly blinded them as they returned the way they had come the night before. A train whistle echoed over the prairie as they walked, drawing their attention to a church steeple ahead. Ice-clad trees raised their arms to the sun, perhaps in supplication for spring to come. Someone on the train said that this was an unusually late snowstorm, not expected but welcomed for the extra moisture to seep into the ground.

"Do you think there is still more snow coming at home?" Ruth asked.

"Probably."

"I miss home."

"I know, me too." Perhaps, had they never tried immigrating, her parents would still be alive and Ruthie's too. All those people who were buried at sea on their voyage. Uff da. Amalia sniffed and inhaled a breath of clean air, so welcome after the putrid stench of the ship. Would she ever forget the horrors they had lived through? And now how was she to find Erik with Ruth and a boardinghouse to care for?

She turned at the song of harness bells.

The wagon driver, a young father with a small boy peeking out of the wagon bed, pulled up and smiled at them. "Can I give you a ride?" He spoke Norwegian.

"We're almost there, but takk."

He set the brake and jumped down. "Come along and I'll take you right to your destination." As he handed them up onto the seat, he smiled. "You're new in town."

"Ja, we arrived on the train last evening."

"Welcome to Decorah. Tell me, where do you need to go?"

"To see the magistrate."

"Ah, Magistrate Karlsson."

She could feel him studying her, so she kept her gaze straight ahead, between the horses' twitching ears. Should she have accepted a ride from a stranger? So many unknowns in this new land.

"Well, if he isn't in the office, his son will be. Hate for your walk to be in vain." He pointed out the Lutheran church and the mercantile before stopping in front of a two-story house, set back under spreading trees and enclosed by a wraparound porch. A sign on the picket fence announced Magistrate.

"Is he expecting you?"

"He knew we were coming." *I think.* Amalia shook out her skirts as she waited for him to help Ruthie down. "Tusen takk." She laid her hands on Ruth's shoulders. "You have been most kind."

"I'm sure I'll be seeing you again. Green Creek isn't that far from Decorah."

"Again, takk." Automatically, she checked her bag to make sure the papers were still there. Their driver pushed open the gate and motioned them through.

He tipped his hat and smiled at the little girl. "God bless."

Taking Ruthie's hand, Amalia and her charge followed the shoveled path to the steps and climbed to the porch. *Thank you for that man's kindness, and please, Lord, make this go well.* She could feel Ruth shaking. Surely it wasn't that cold, but she knew she was shaking too, only inside. Sucking in a deep breath, she rapped on the carved wooden door.

"Come on in, it's open," a man's voice invited.

She thumbed down the brass handle, and with a small push, the door swung open. Warm air welcomed them to enter. Placing Ruth gently before her, Amalia managed to make herself smile.

The curly-headed, bespectacled young man behind the walnut desk looked up. "Good morning. And who do I have the privilege of welcoming this glorious morning?"

Amalia knew her smile trembled, but she nodded, though she only caught the "good morning" part of his words. "I am Amalia Gunderson, and this is Ruth Forsberg. From Norway?"

He stood and immediately switched to Norwegian. "We were

beginning to worry about you. My father is the magistrate, and I am Absalom Karlsson, his clerk."

"We sent you a message as soon as we were finally able to leave the ship."

He nodded. "Ja, my father received that. Sounds like that was a horrendous crossing." He paused. "Let me make sure the magistrate is in his office." He stepped over to another carved wooden door, apparently leading to a private office. "Sir?"

"Yes, I heard, bring them in."

The voice even sounded important.

The lump in her throat had grown. Amalia glanced down to see Ruth staring up at her, her eyes wide, her lips trembling. "It's all right, little one. All will be well." She nodded as she spoke and gently squeezed the small hand in hers.

"Please, come this way." The younger man motioned them to go ahead of him.

Within the smaller room, the older man levered himself to his feet behind his desk. "Miss Gunderson. I am so glad to finally meet you." He looked to Ruth. "And you too, Miss Ruth." He bowed slightly. "Please be seated, and may we offer you coffee or tea?"

"Coffee please, and possibly milk for Ruth?" She helped with Ruthie's coat and then felt hands lifting her coat off.

"Of course. Absalom will take care of your coats and bring in a tray while you tell me what has happened since your message." He motioned them to be seated and sat down again himself, a barely noticeable wince as he did so.

Amalia filed her observation away for future thought and, clearing her throat, gave him an abbreviated version of their westbound trip. "The stationmaster gave us a ride out to the boardinghouse and said he would bring out our trunks this morning, which he did." She paused.

"And?" He leaned back in his chair and steepled his fingers, never taking his gaze off her.

While his voice was gentle, Amalia knew with absolute certainty that she never wanted to do anything to make him angry. "And she, Miss Berg, did not want to answer the door last night. I knew someone was there because of light in a room by the door."

"And what did you do?"

"I finally pushed open the door, and we stepped inside."

He nodded for her to continue.

"She stood in her doorway, holding a candle, and told us to get out. We could not stay there."

He sighed with a slight shake of his head and a glance at his son. "And?"

"I said we were too tired and had nowhere to go and we weren't leaving. She took us to the kitchen, said we could sleep under the table, and went back to her room."

"And did not even give you a light?"

"At least I had seen the kitchen, so I rebuilt a fire in the stove. . . ."

"All in the dark . . ."

She nodded. "Anyway, we slept there, and this morning she did let me make breakfast before telling us we had to leave."

He tipped his head back and blew out a breath. "So at least you have slept, eaten, and now you are here."

"A very kind man insisted we ride with him in his wagon and brought us here." She leaned over and pulled the rolled documents out of her bag to lay on the desk. "With these."

ᏟIVE

He couldn't abide folks being ill-treated. Much less a vulnerable young woman and little girl.

Absalom Karlsson adjusted his spectacles to better focus as he read the legal papers, leaning over his father's shoulder behind the desk. The document clearly stated that, following the death of her husband, if Mrs. Forsberg died before their ship docked, legal guardianship of her daughter would pass to Amalia Gunderson, who would manage the boardinghouse till Ruth came of age, at which time she would assume her inheritance.

"You signed this on board the ship?" Absalom glanced up to meet Miss Gunderson's blue-gray gaze.

"Ja. The captain oversaw and witnessed it."

"Well, he'd have the authority to do that." Absalom examined the signatures—Mrs. Forsberg's, Miss Gunderson's, the captain's, and turned the page over to be sure he hadn't missed anything on the back. He looked to his father, who sat leaning back in his chair, watching him.

"What do you think?" asked his quirked gray brows.

Absalom tipped his head. All seemed in order. No wonder Zelda Berg had seemed worried about her prospects, though how much of this she'd suspected, he'd no idea. But that she had nearly turned these two out the door in the dark of night, only relenting to let them sleep on the kitchen floor—something burned in his chest. He straightened, watching the pair as they watched his father, Miss Gunderson seeming to hold her breath for his verdict. Despite all she'd been through, she sat erect, her crown of honey-blonde braids tidy, shoulders straight beneath her shawl, blouse, and the embroidered vest so many immigrants from Norway wore. The little girl, Ruth, swung her feet from her velvet chair, picking at the gilded braid curved around the arm. She glanced up to catch his gaze and snatched her hand back to her lap, head ducking, then peeked out at him from beneath white-blonde wisps escaping from her braids.

Absalom smiled at her. An answering smile flickered on Ruth's face, like a shy sunbeam peeking from behind clouds to see if it were safe to come out. What heartache this little one had already known in her short life, all in a few weeks' time.

"Well, Miss Gunderson." His father stacked the papers neatly on his desk. "All looks to be legal and aboveboard. These papers are impeccable. Mrs. Forsberg seems to have been a woman of foresight."

Miss Gunderson's slim shoulders relaxed a touch. "That's good. But what do we do now?"

"You say Miss Berg is refusing to honor the papers?"

"I haven't actually shown them to her yet." She twisted her fingers in the lap of her woolen skirt. "I wanted to be sure, first, that—"

"That they were valid." The magistrate nodded. "You were wise, but they are. If you don't mind my asking, Miss Gunderson, how old are you?"

"Twenty." She swallowed. "I'll be twenty-one in the fall. Is that all right?"

He nodded. "Legal guardians only have to be eighteen. You have much put on your young shoulders—yet I see already you are bearing it well."

"Takk." She ran her hand over Ruthie's head. "May I ask where this boardinghouse came from, and why it is Ruthie's?"

"The owners of the house, Amund and Else Forsberg, inherited the place from his parents, who settled here in 1850 when he was a young man. They built there because of the creek, you know, that runs right through the property. Miss Else married into the family and was a fine woman; everyone in town thought highly of her. Amund's parents died soon after, leaving the property to him. He and Else had no children but I believe Carl visited them once as a boy, and they decided to leave it to him as their nephew, especially as he kept in touch and planned to bring his family over. Else ran it as a boardinghouse for some time after Amund's early death, but as she grew older and needed more help about the place, she invited Miss Zelda Berg—a cousin of her husband's—to come live with her." His father grimaced. "Not that Miss Berg proved much help. The place just went to sixes and sevens, along with Else's health. She died last year, but it's been oh, at least four years since they took in boarders. Would you agree, Absalom?"

He nodded. "Three or four, I'd say." And longer since the place had any success.

"I know Hilda and Carl hoped to get it up and running again—they'd laid all their hopes for a future in America on it. And now, it belongs to their daughter." Miss Gunderson squeezed the little girl's hand. "But what are we to do about Miss Berg?"

"Absalom will go with you to speak with her." His father nodded at him.

Absalom pushed up his spectacles and smiled at Miss Gunderson. "Of course."

"I'd go myself, but this bum leg keeps me close to my desk." His father gave his knee a tap where it joined with his prosthetic leg, a relic of the Civil War over two decades ago. "Absalom is a legal clerk, soon to be an attorney. He can assure Miss Berg of the legal authenticity of your claim—and the consequences should she dispute it."

"Mange takk." Miss Gunderson blinked hard. "I am—we are— very grateful, to both of you."

Little Ruth wriggled on her chair, tugging on her guardian's arm.

"Ssh, den lille. Just a moment more."

"And you, young lady." His father opened his desk drawer. "You've been mighty patient sitting here while we grown-ups droned on. I do believe I've got a peppermint stick in here for little girls who wait so quietly. If it's all right with Miss Gunderson, that is."

The young woman nodded, and Ruth took her treat, eyes shining.

"What do you say?" came the gentle whisper from her guardian.

Ruth pulled the candy from her mouth. "Mange takk."

"You're most welcome."

Cool yet fresh with spring, the prairie wind caressed their faces a short while later as Absalom drove their buggy toward the smaller town of Green Creek, a couple of miles outside Decorah. Under the bright sunshine, snow melted on the fields. Little Ruth perched beside him on the seat, still sucking her peppermint stick and squeezed between him and Miss Gunderson.

Keeping his hands steady on the mare's reins, Absalom stole another glance at the slender young immigrant woman. Only twenty, nearly six years younger than he, yet what strength she had. Losing her parents, arriving in a new land, now both guardian and champion of a young child . . . he could see the strain in her lovely gray-blue eyes, yet she kept her arm firm around Ruthie between them, as if all her being now focused on protecting this little one entrusted to her care.

She glanced his way and caught him staring. Absalom shifted his gaze back to the reins, his neck heating.

Miss Gunderson cleared her throat. "I'm very grateful to you, Mr. Karlsson, and your father, for your kindness. I'm sorry to impose on you like this."

"No imposition at all. All part of my job." He sent her a smile, hoping to set her at ease.

"Really?" She cocked her head.

"Much of my work involves helping immigrants recently arrived in this area. We have such a large Norwegian community here, you know. Sad to say, immigrants from the old country can be vulnerable to those who might take advantage. Greedy landlords, dishonest money changers. Many have been robbed long before they make it to Iowa." Like the Jorstad family. Had the judge in Decorah received his legal briefing yet? The court date should be next week.

She nodded slowly. "I've heard about that. So you help them. You have a good heart."

His chest warmed at her words. So different from Rebecca's scorn for his "charity cases." He shook his head to squash that thought, jouncing his tousle of dark curls. Maybelle, the mare, chose that moment to shake hers as well, jingling the harness and bringing a giggle from Ruth. Absalom met Miss Gunderson's gaze over the child's head, and they both chuckled.

"Here we are." He turned onto the main road through Green Creek.

"It's down that way." Miss Gunderson lifted her hand to point, then tucked it back into her lap. "I'm sorry, you probably know."

"A reminder never hurts." He turned down the lane, passing the trees bordering the creek, then stopped Maybelle in front of the boardinghouse land and set the brake. He jumped down, rounding the buggy to help Miss Gunderson. Ruthie next jumped into his arms, beaming when he caught her.

Chuckling at her delight in such a small thing, Absalom set her on the ground. "Now. Let's go sort this out with Miss Berg."

Though he kept his tone light, his gut tightened as before entering a courtroom. Groundless as the woman's opposition might be, Zelda Berg wasn't a force to take lightly. If the way she'd finagled past his father hadn't told him that, the shadow that fell over little Ruth's face now would have. Her smile gone, she clung to Miss Gunderson's hand and hung behind her skirts as they approached the gingerbread-trimmed building. Its dilapidation struck him afresh in the sunshine—dull white paint faded and flaking off, blue trim peeling. An upper window broken. Why couldn't Zelda see she needed help?

Lord, let me get through to this woman. Protect these innocent ones from further fracas. They'd been through enough already.

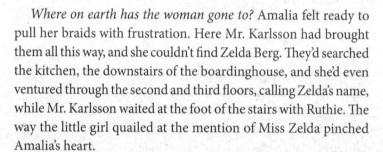

Where on earth has the woman gone to? Amalia felt ready to pull her braids with frustration. Here Mr. Karlsson had brought them all this way, and she couldn't find Zelda Berg. They'd searched the kitchen, the downstairs of the boardinghouse, and she'd even ventured through the second and third floors, calling Zelda's name, while Mr. Karlsson waited at the foot of the stairs with Ruthie. The way the little girl quailed at the mention of Miss Zelda pinched Amalia's heart.

The upper floors stunned her, too, with their empty, cobwebbed rooms, a cracked window in one letting in cold air. The third floor wasn't finished into rooms at all, just one long, open space. This had once been a thriving, bustling boardinghouse—what on earth had happened to all the furniture?

"I'm so sorry." Amalia hurried back downstairs, blowing out a long breath. "I don't know where she is."

"Maybe outside?" Ruth piped up, courage regained now that she had Amalia by the hand again.

"Good idea." They hadn't explored the grounds yet. Amalia headed through the kitchen, Mr. Karlsson holding the door for her and Ruthie as they stepped into the sunshine onto the back porch, where dried weeds poked through broken floorboards. Amalia shielded her eyes with her hand and scanned the backyard. A chicken coop as she'd thought, a barn that looked mostly empty, a couple of outbuildings. What looked like farm fields stretched beyond the barn, though still streaked with melting snow. Who farmed those fields? She couldn't imagine Zelda behind a plow.

At the edge of the property, a slender line of just-leafing trees must mark the creek she'd heard cut through the land—Green Creek, which lent the town its name. How Ruthie would love to splash there this summer. On the other side of the boarding-house lay a garden patch, brave sprouts of green poking between the snow patches, and from the edge stretched a clothesline to the corner of the boardinghouse. Unpinning a few items from the line stood Zelda with her back to them, shawl flapping in the fresh breeze.

"Miss Berg!" Relief and frustration warred in Amalia's voice, chasing out her trepidation for the moment. Ruthie's hand firm in hers, she marched off the back porch and across to the garden. "I've been looking all over for you."

The woman turned and glared at them. "Hoped I'd seen the last of you."

Amalia stared at her, then shook her head. "Well, you haven't. This is Mr. Karlsson. His father is the—"

"Magistrate. I know." Zelda flicked her gaze over Absalom as if he were something a cat dragged in. "Guess it's no surprise whose side you're on."

The legal clerk cleared his throat and stepped up by Amalia's shoulder. Though only a few inches taller than she, his presence radiated confidence. And assurance of the legal papers he held out in his hand.

"Perhaps you're unaware, Miss Berg, that Carl and Hilda Fors-berg were to inherit this boardinghouse from Carl's aunt, Else

Forsberg. After Carl passed, Hilda left the inheritance, upon her death, to her daughter, Ruth. She appointed Miss Gunderson, here, as her legal guardian and in charge of the estate till Ruth comes of age."

Zelda yanked a nightdress from the clothesline and rolled it into a ball. "My cousin Else left this boardinghouse to me."

"She said that?" At Amalia's words, Mr. Karlsson shot her a glance as if warning her to watch her words. She pressed her lips together.

"I'm her cousin. I helped her run this boardinghouse till she died. Laws of all common decency say it should go to me." Zelda tilted her chin and glared at the curly-haired young man.

"And laws of common decency say you don't turn a young woman and child out into the streets late at night. Especially family."

"*She* isn't family." Zelda jutted her chin at Amalia. "And I didn't turn them out of the house. They slept perfectly warm inside."

"Little thanks to you, as I understand it." Mr. Karlsson's tone sharpened, and he drew a breath as if to calm himself. "Regardless, these papers are perfectly legal, Miss Berg. Are you saying you have other papers from your cousin that prove she left the building to you?"

Zelda's gaze flickered from the legal clerk to Amalia, landing on Ruth. She said nothing.

"I said, do you have papers that—"

"Last I knew a woman didn't need papers to show she lives in a place," Zelda snapped. "And I've lived here for five years. Everyone in town knows that. I've got plans for it."

"And living in a place where you've no legal right is called squatting." Mr. Karlsson's voice could cut steel. "Miss Gunderson would have the right to turn you out."

Zelda's face slackened. The nightgown dropped from her hands to the muddy ground, unheeded. "She has no—"

"She *has* the right. Whether she chooses to exercise it is up to her." He glanced at Amalia and adjusted his spectacles. "But I would strongly suggest moderating your tone, Miss Berg."

Zelda Berg opened her mouth, then shut it. She raised her gaze to meet Amalia's, jutting her chin. "So. Shall I pack my bags?"

"I . . ." Amalia moistened her lips and squeezed Ruthie's hand. "I can't do that." Even if Zelda had nearly done the same to them, she couldn't turn the woman out into the streets. Not that she relished the thought of her company, but her parents had raised her with "Love your enemies" since her mother's knee. "You are welcome to stay with us for the time being, Miss Berg. But I hope we can try to live harmoniously together."

Zelda sniffed, but at a hard look from the legal clerk, she mumbled a "takk."

"Now." Mr. Karlsson rubbed his hands together and glanced at Amalia. "I saw a couple of trunks on the porch, Miss Gunderson. Might I carry them in for you?"

"Ja." Amalia drew a breath. "We would appreciate that. I saw an empty room with two pallets on the second floor when I was looking for you, Miss Berg." Among many other empty rooms. "Is it all right if Mr. Karlsson puts our trunks there for now?" Not that she should need the woman's permission, but Zelda *had* lived in this place as her home for some time. Amalia would do her best to live in peace "as far as it depended on her."

The older woman sighed. "I suppose. And call me Zelda, I'm sick to death of this infernal 'Miss Berg.'" She turned back to her laundry.

A nearly civil reply. Amalia smiled down at Ruthie and squeezed her hand. "Shall we go see our new room?"

The little girl's smile melted her heart anew.

They led the way upstairs, Mr. Karlsson lugging the first of their trunks behind. The weight made him puff by the time he reached the top.

Amalia turned down the hallway to the right and stepped into the room she'd seen on her search earlier. With Miss Berg using the room downstairs, they had the entire second floor to themselves until boarders moved in. Assuming they could actually get boarders.

The legal clerk thumped the trunk near the foot of one of the pallets. "I'll get the other one." He glanced about the room, empty save for the two straw ticks on the floor, each covered with a dusty quilt. "Whatever happened to all the boardinghouse furniture?"

"I've been wondering the same thing. Most of the other rooms don't even have pallets."

"Unbelievable." Mr. Karlsson headed back down the stairs. By the time he thudded the second trunk by the other pallet, he was breathing hard. "There you are. Do you want the crate up here too?" He stood a moment to catch his breath.

"Mange takk. You shouldn't have had to do that all by yourself." She shook her head. "The crate can remain below since it contains garden seeds and starts along with a few tools."

He waved his hand and pushed his spectacles up his nose, dark curly hair flying askew all over his head. "No trouble at all. Good for this lazy legal clerk to get a bit of exercise." He winked at Ruthie.

"What do we say to Mr. Karlsson?" Amalia nudged her.

"Tusen takk." Ruthie plunked onto one of the pallets and gave a little bounce, bringing puffs of dust from the faded blue and brown quilt thrown across it. "Can this be my bed? I want to be by the window."

"I don't see why not. But get up for now, we need to wash those quilts." And all the bedding and scrub this entire place down. Amalia shook her head. How long since this building knew a proper cleaning?

"I'll let you get settled, then." Absalom Karlsson stepped to the door, then turned back, one hand on the doorframe. "Well done, out there. Zelda Berg is a force to be reckoned with. But clearly, so are you." His brown eyes crinkled.

"Takk." Amalia sighed. "Life surely takes turns we don't expect, doesn't it?" She shut down any further pondering for the moment, suddenly so tired she wanted to fall on a pallet, dust and all, and cry. "But I'm grateful you came with us, Mr. Karlsson. I don't think things would have gone the same without you."

"Happy to help." He gave the doorframe a pat. "Oh. Do you mind if I take those papers back to my father's office for a few days? I'd like to type up official copies so we can have them on record and make an English translation also."

Amalia hesitated. She'd rather not let the papers out of her hands. But wouldn't it be better to have typed copies, as Mr. Karlsson said? What if she lost them, or, worse, Zelda took them? "Ja. I suppose that would be good." She held the papers out.

"I'll bring them back as soon as I can." He tucked the papers into his jacket with a care that reassured her. "Hopefully no later than the day after tomorrow."

She nodded. "Mange takk again."

After he headed downstairs, she turned to see the little girl gazing out the window, both hands pressed against the dusty pane.

"Can we go outside, Tante Amalia? I want to see the creek."

"Ja, den lille. Let's explore our new home."

It surely didn't feel like home, yet. But now they had a roof over their heads. And though she'd only met them this morning, she sensed Magistrate Karlsson and his son would not let any harm come to them, if they could help it.

Clinging to that thought, Amalia followed the tug of Ruthie's hand down the stairs and out into the sunshine.

Six

"I s this really our house?"

Back in the sun-striped kitchen after taking a peek at the creek, Amalia smiled down at the little girl's upturned face and nodded. "Ja, this is our new home."

"But Miss Zelda does not want us here. I don't think she likes me."

I don't think she likes anybody. Amalia squatted down so she could be eye to eye with her charge. "I know. So it is our job to love her anyway."

"I know that is what Jesus said, but He lived a long time ago, and He never knew her."

It took all Amalia's strength to not burst out laughing. Instead she slid her arms around Ruth and drew her in close. "Ah, my little one. Good thing we have our God helping us then, is it not?"

Ruthie heaved a sigh right from her toes and stared deep into Amalia's eyes. She twisted her mouth around, sniffed, sniffed again, and nodded. "I'm hungry."

Small wonder. Noon had come and gone by the time Mr. Karlsson left. After they ate, she would carry a bucket of soapy water up to their room, and as soon as she threw the pallets out the window, they would begin scrubbing. Surely there was a broom out on the back porch.

Before fixing anything, Amalia filled a large kettle with water and set it on the stove. She added more wood to the firebox and opened the drafts. There was plenty of hot water in the reservoir, but the job upstairs would take a lot.

After a glass of milk with a slice of buttered bread, Ruthie followed her in her search out to the porch for a bucket and rags for cleaning. "Where is Miss Zelda?"

"I suppose she is in her room."

"Will she help us?"

Doubtful. Amalia shrugged and paused. A bird was singing from the tree near the porch. She swapped grins with Ruth, but as soon as they moved to the railing, the bird flew off. The song of the windmill out beyond the lilac bushes reminded her how fortunate they were to not have to haul water from the creek. Treetops above the small rise bordered the creek they could see from their upstairs window. The family that homesteaded this land and passed it down, now to the third generation, had foresight indeed.

And to think that little Ruth was now legally the owner. No wonder Miss Berg, Zelda, was fighting so hard to keep it. Despite the broken window and railing, the weeds choking the bushes around the porch, this place was a treasure. It just needed some care.

"Let's go get this done." She snagged rags off a nail on the wall, handed the pile to Ruthie, and with broom in one hand and bucket in the other, they returned to the kitchen. Zelda had been in there—the coffeepot was pulled over to the hotter part of the stove. She poured the hot water from the kettle into the bucket, shaved lye soap into it, and she and Ruth headed for the stairs. Zelda's door was closed. Should she rap on it and request help? Best not today.

Intimidating was a good word for their room. How many years had the dust and cobwebs been moving in? A little breeze from the open window stirred the dust and set the cobwebs to swinging. "You throw those pallets out the window, and I'll attack the cobwebs."

Ruthie giggled. "Really?"

"We're not dragging all that dirt down the stairs."

Dust rose in a cloud when Ruth picked up a corner of one pallet and dragged it over to the window. "Ishta," she muttered, and tilting her head way back, she lifted the straw-stuffed pallet to the windowsill and sent it careening to the ground. The second followed quickly whereupon she dusted her hands together. "Ja!"

Grinning, Amalia wrapped one of the rags around the broom and swept down cobwebs all around the room before moving to the ceiling. She sneezed. *I should have wrapped both of our heads before we started.* Mor always did that, but she never had filth like this to contend with. In Norway farmers even dusted cobwebs out of their barns, since most cattle spent the winter underneath the houses.

Once the entire room was swept, she used the rag-covered broom to wash the ceiling and the upper walls. She glanced over to see Ruth, elbows on the windowsill, watching the outside world go by.

"What do you see out there?" Amalia set the broom in a corner. "I'm going down to get another bucket of water."

"There's a cat out there, hunting."

"Hope she catches a mouse."

"Not a bird."

"Ja." Another bird singing made them both smile.

After the next bucket of water Amalia dipped from the reservoir, she fed the fire and returned up the stairs. The water running down the walls from washing the upper portion left streaks on the whitewash. The difference between the washed and to-be-washed made her shudder.

Finally she and Ruth stood in the doorway, looking over the clean room. Hooks for their clothing lined one wall, their trunks another. Spring air flowing in the window made inhaling a delight.

"Once we get the pallets clean and dry . . ." She paused. "What will we stuff them with?"

"There is a haystack over by the barn next door, maybe they will give us some hay."

Amalia picked up the cleaning supplies. "Good observation, den lille."

Together they made their way downstairs, Ruth dragging the broom behind her. In the kitchen Amalia leaned over the woodbox and frowned. Nearly out of wood. One more thing to do. And they needed more water. What needed to be done first? The coffeepot sat on top of the reservoir. Zelda managed to have coffee when she wanted. Surely she would come do something. Meals did not fix themselves.

"Come on, Ruthie, we need to go scrub the pallets." Amalia grabbed the bucket of dirty rags and the broom and led the way to the back porch where she wrung out the dirty rags and emptied the bucket over a bush off to the right of the steps. "But we better get water first." So many things in her head clamoring for right now!

The handle on the pump at the windmill made her hands burn it was so cold. A pipe ran water to a watering trough for stock someday when they would have some. After filling the bucket she dumped it into a tub she'd found on the porch wall, repeated that twice, and carried the next bucket into the house, pouring part of it into the reservoir and the remainder into the tall pot by the sink. She leaned on the sink to catch her breath and looked down to see Ruth watching her, worry wrinkling her forehead.

Amalia smiled. "I'm all right." She sucked in a deep breath. "Ruthie, please bring some wood from that stack on the porch for the woodbox."

The little girl nodded and returned to the porch. Amalia followed her. "After we finish this, we will drag these pallets over and shake them out over the garden." Together they did that, the younger wrinkling her nose.

"They even stink out here."

"Ja, you have a good smeller."

Ruth giggled. "Oh look." She pointed ahead of them to where a tiger cat was dragging something brown and furry away. "At least it is not a bird." She looked up at Amalia. "You think she has kittens?"

Amalia shook her head. "I think it is early for kittens. Fold open the end on the pallet and shake hard." She did hers and helped Ruth. Dirty old straw scattered across the garden, the dust blowing back in their faces.

Ruth scrubbed her wrist under her nose. "Ishta." She held up one pallet. "Good thing we did not sleep on these last night. They probably have bugs too." The little girl shook her hands. "Mor said there were fleas and lice on people in the hold of the ship."

"True." And cholera. Fleas and lice were a nuisance, but people did not die from the pests. Amalia brushed off the front of her skirt. She should have put on an apron; what was she thinking, or not thinking? "We will bring in more wood so we can boil these on the stove. Might be the only way we can kill any bugs left in the material."

So to scrub the filthy things now or wait till morning? She dumped her armload of wood into the woodbox. The coffeepot sat back on the hot portion of the stove. The thought of a cup of hot coffee . . . she returned to the back porch and carried in another armload of wood. She would have coffee with supper. Perhaps Zelda would fix the meal, though by all appearances the woman seemed intending to stay in her room all day, aside from taking down her laundry this morning. What on earth could she be doing?

"Tante Malia?" Ruth dumped more wood in the box.

"Ja?"

"There is a big pot out on the porch. Mor had one like that for washing clothes."

"Really?"

Ruth took her hand. "Come on, I will show you."

Sure enough. It was turned over so water would not rust it. Amalia tipped the pot on its side and together they rolled it to the steps and down. So that was what that bare spot with a few blackened coals was for. She should have realized that. If they were going to set up, there must be other wash to do. Perhaps Zelda had already washed all her winter things. Amalia shook her head. No, this had not been used for who knew how long, at least since last fall. Doing wash for one person need not entail this big old pot, but she was sure that back in the days when this was a boarding-house, it had seen plenty.

Amalia looked around. Where had Ruth gone? She heaved a sigh of relief when her charge came out of the outhouse, shaking her skirt down as she strolled back. "We do not have any more kindling," she announced.

One more thing. At least Zelda could have shown them around. Should she go and ask?

"Malia, look." Ruth had squatted down to see better. Amalia joined her.

A crocus, no, a whole bed of purple and gold with a few white, the narrow green leaves framing buds in various stages of growth.

"They are so pretty." She beamed up at Amalia. "Do they smell good?"

"Not that I remember. These are blooming late, I think. I remember them poking through the snow at home. First flower to bloom every year."

"Mor loved flowers." The wistful tone made Amalia's eyes burn.

"My mor did too. She brought some seeds with her, in the crate." She sniffed. If only they had stayed in Norway, she would still have a family. If only she could find her brother, if he was still alive. Her mor always said that looking back was a waste of time and energy. Look forward. Look to Jesus. Live now. Amalia could hear that dear voice. *"Jesus is right here with us, now."* She sniffed again and blinked away the threatening tears.

"Come, den lille." She held out her hand. "Let's explore some more."

"What about the pallets?"

"I will set them to boiling on the stove." While she did that, Ruth brought in more wood till the box was nearly full. Together they went back outside and circled the house, looking carefully at plants poking up through the dirt. They opened the door to the chicken house, which had a row of nest boxes on one wall and a small door for the chickens to use. There was also a small building, which held shovels, hoes, rakes, and various other garden things on the shelves, and the barn, with stanchions for six cows, box stalls, and wider stalls for the horses. Cobwebs curtained the windows and all the corners. Outside the barn stood a roofed, round building with walls of wooden slats. A three-sided building housed a plow, scythes on the wall, and what looked to be a forge.

This farm must have been a big success in the past. Amalia looked over the fields toward the creek. Someone had been farming this land but who? Surely not Zelda.

Questions stacked in her mind like split wood.

She looked down to smile at Ruth who had slipped her hand into Amalia's. "Some place, is it not?"

"I want to go see the creek again."

"We will do that another day. I want to get the pallets out on the clothesline. Let the sun help clean them tomorrow."

Hands swinging between them, they returned to the house. "I hope we get chickens. I like chickens. And eggs. And baby chicks." Ruthie grinned up at her. "We had a rooster at home. He was mean, and sometimes he chased me. Mor said if he did not behave, she was going to put him in the stewpot." Together they mounted the steps, loaded their arms with wood, and entered the kitchen. The big pot with the pallets bubbling in it was now steaming above the oven, near to the reservoir. Zelda again.

Amalia almost shook her head. Instead she blew out a breath

and pulled the pot to the reservoir where she could reach it more easily. She found a wooden spoon in one drawer, along with other cooking utensils. Somewhere there was most likely a thick stick and a scrubbing board. Probably out on the porch with the other wash things.

"Ruth, would you please go out on the back porch and see if you can find a scrubboard?"

"There is one in that cupboard."

"Why did you not tell me?"

She shrugged. "You didn't ask."

"Would you please get it for me?" Amalia could feel her grin and shook her head as the little girl headed for the back porch.

After scrubbing and rinsing and scrubbing again, Amalia tried twisting the pallets to get some water out. When that did not work, she dumped the drippy mess into a bucket and hauled that outside. By the time they were dripping on the clothesline, the thought of sitting down with a cup of coffee was more appealing than ever. She headed back inside and stepped into the pantry. What was she going to make for supper?

"Malia," Ruth whispered, tugging on her guardian's skirt.

"What is it?"

Ruth pointed. "She is digging in the garden."

"Who?"

"Miss Berg."

What could she be doing? Amalia looked out the pantry window. Sure enough. Was it time to start getting the garden ready for planting? Perhaps that was something the woman planned to do.

She scanned the shelves for what she could make into supper. Some milk left in the pitcher, butter, one egg. Flour in the cupboard. She sniffed a jar—sourdough starter. Brown sugar, less than half a loaf of bread, dried beans, coffee beans and a grinder, rice, and spices. Salt and pepper sat on the stove shelf. She could use the starter for breakfast. They would not starve. But three ate a lot more than one. And it was too late to soak the beans to eat tonight. She glanced out the window again. Zelda was still there with a basket by her side.

Amalia set the jar of sourdough starter and the flour on the counter. Using a bowl from the cupboard, she poured in about a cup of starter, added warm water, and beat it with a wooden spoon. After sprinkling in flour, she continued beating the batter in order to add as much air to it as she could, watching to see air bubbles. She set the bowl on the warming shelf and covered it with a clean dish towel to rise till morning. How long since they had had pancakes? On the ship? She thought back to helping the cook in the galley, while they were moored in New York Harbor. All the time they spent scrubbing the ship, the people and the cargo, not that there was much of anything left.

She closed her eyes against the memories. *And still, what do I do for supper, Lord?*

"Malia, what is wrong?"

"Nothing is wrong, den lille." She inhaled. "Now doesn't that smell good?"

"Smells like bread baking."

"That it does and . . ."

The back door opened, and Zelda carried in a basket. She put it in the sink.

Amalia could not resist. "What do you have there?"

"Rutabagas. Wintered over in the garden."

Rutabagas? Amalia hurried to peer into the sink. The large, round tubers half filled the basket, purple tops and yellow-orange flesh glinting through the dirt, ready to be chopped and simmered into sweet and nourishing stew.

Her exhale came followed by a smile. And now they had supper for today. *Thank you, Lord.*

Seven

"We can't thank you enough, Mr. Karlsson. Mange takk." Absalom gripped Mr. Jorstad's hand and patted the man's shoulder. "Absalom, please. And you're welcome. It was a privilege to help." He couldn't stop the grin on his own face.

"That's what I call a case closed soundly." Beside him, his father put his hat on his head with a smile. As magistrate, he'd come along to add his legal clout to the case. "Must say I enjoyed the look on that man's face when you brought up that case precedent, son."

Absalom chuckled. That unscrupulous landlord had been soundly beaten in court, thanks to the case he'd built. The judge had ordered that scoundrel to pay the Jorstads back not only what he'd cheated from them but legal expenses as well. Not that Absalom wouldn't have done this job for free—and often did, for this type of case.

It was one of the reasons Rebecca had declared him unfit for a husband. The thought undercut his smile, but he pushed it away. Someday, he might have to be more careful about bringing in enough income, but for now, his father still put a roof over his head. And as a legal clerk still finishing his law degree by correspondence, he could afford to charge little—or sometimes nothing—to families who needed it.

After all, doing good sparked his joy in the job.

With a light step, Absalom bid farewell to the Jorstads and headed down the Decorah courthouse steps, his father following more slowly with his cane. Their buggy waited in the shade of a new-leafed tree, Maybelle lifting her head with a nicker as they approached.

"Now that's what I call a good day's work, girl. And it's only midmorning." Absalom rubbed her velvety black nose while his father climbed in, then led the mare to the nearby water trough before mounting the driver's seat and clucking her toward home. He relaxed against the seat, the spring sunshine warming his shoulders and easing his muscles. The recent snowfall had nearly disappeared, only a few patches of slush left on the gutters.

"So, what do you plan to turn your attention to now, son? Got plenty of hours left in the day."

"I've got some studying to catch up on. A paper on immigrant law I've been meaning to finish for a week."

His father chuckled. "Been too busy actually applying it to write it, eh?"

True. Between the Jorstads and helping Amalia Gunderson and little Ruth. "That's another thing. I finished typing up the Forsberg papers, need to deliver those to Miss Gunderson." The thought of seeing her again brought the sun's warmth clear through his middle. What did that mean? He'd hardly noticed another woman since Rebecca jilted him, nearly two years ago now. And he couldn't go having improper feelings about a client. Protective, that's all he could allow.

Back at their office, they found two angry farmers waiting for them, needing arbitration over a boundary line dispute. It took both him and his father till the dinner hour to get them to agree on a compromise, then Absalom devoured a sandwich at his desk while working on his paper. A set appointment with another client came next, so that the afternoon had half passed before he finally set off for Green Creek, the typed copies and English translation secured in his files in the office drawer, another copy with the original folded safe in his inner jacket pocket.

At the boardinghouse, he mounted the steps two at a time and rapped on the door. He looked forward to seeing little Ruth again, should have brought another peppermint stick to coax out one of her sunshine smiles.

But no one appeared in answer to his knock. He rapped again, harder. Perhaps they were in the kitchen, or upstairs. He scanned the peeling doorframe for a bell. Hadn't Mrs. Forsberg used to have a large one, for announcing boarders? He jogged down the rickety porch steps to check around back.

"Hello there, young feller."

At the call, Absalom veered away from rounding the corner of the building and scanned for the source of the gravelly voice. A middle-aged man with a gray beard and farmer's hat leaned over the fence marking the property line.

Absalom approached and tipped his hat. "Absalom Karlsson."

"The magistrate's son." The farmer nodded. "I know who you are. Abram Miller here. I own this farm over here, plus been share-cropping Mrs. Forsberg's fields, rest her soul, for nigh on six years now." He jutted his chin at the building. "Been seein' a passel more activity over there than in a long spell. Couple of young ladies too. Heard somethin' about them bein' kin to Mrs. Forsberg?"

"The little girl is." Absalom eyed the man, debating how much to say. "They've recently arrived from Norway."

"Ah." The man rubbed his beard, a spark of recognition in his eyes. "I heard talk some of Else and Amund's family might be comin' from the old country to take over the boardinghouse. Thought it'd be a married couple, though. Where's the husband?"

"Actually, both parents died on the voyage. Young Ruth now has a legal guardian."

"You don't say." Miller's eyes widened, then he shook his head. "Bet Zelda Berg had two kinds of fits about that."

The man had more insight than he'd at first given him credit for. But then, Miss Berg doubtless made few friends in this town. "You say you've farmed the boardinghouse fields for some time?"

Miller nodded and spat. "I plant 'em in wheat and corn, then always gave Mrs. Forsberg her portion of the harvest proceeds." He squinted at the building. "Never did give anything to Miss Berg last year, didn't quite feel right about it, if you get my meaning. But the money's safe in the bank, was saving it up for when the rightful folks came. Might be you could advise me what to do with it?"

Money in the bank. Now that would be welcome news to Miss Gunderson. But he'd need to speak to his father to confirm the legal proceedings. "I'll speak to the magistrate. Thank you for letting me know."

Just then, the topics of their conversation rounded the corner of the boardinghouse, Miss Gunderson carrying a large, empty basket, her young charge tagging along behind. Ruth stopped short when she saw Absalom, then dashed toward him, beaming and braids flying, setting red ribbons to fluttering.

"Mr. Karlsson!" She threw her arms around his legs.

"Well." He patted her head, grinning. "What did I do to deserve that sort of welcome?"

"We found some more bedding for our beds. Now it's all hanging on the line back there." She pointed behind the boardinghouse.

"Just let me set this basket down." Miss Gunderson glanced from Abram Miller to Absalom, a question in her eyes, then headed to the porch with her basket.

When she returned, Absalom nodded toward the farmer. "Miss Gunderson, this is Abram Miller, from the next farm over. He's been farming the Forsberg fields for some years now."

"So those are our fields. I'd wondered." She lifted her hand to brush back loose tendrils of hair that had escaped from her braids. "God dag." She smiled at Miller.

The farmer doffed his hat. "Sorry. I ain't so good with Norwegian."

"Oh." She twisted her hands in her apron, face flushing. "I'm— sorry." Her tongue still stumbled over the English words.

"Not your fault, just my own laziness. Sometimes feel outnumbered in this town full of Norskies." He chuckled, taking any insult out of the words.

Absalom's tongue itched to tell her of the money in the bank, but he held himself back till he checked with his father. He didn't want to misspeak in case he missed some legal detail, nor risk giving her false hope.

Miller cleared his throat. "I wanted to ask, Would you like your animals back?"

"Animals?" She looked from the man to Absalom as if unsure she understood the meaning.

"Animals—livestock." Absalom switched to Norwegian for her. "Husdyr."

"Ja, but—I didn't know we had any." She pushed back those strands of hair again, blowing over her face in the breeze. "What animals?"

Miller let out a low whistle. "Miss Berg sure keeps things close to the chest, don't she? You've got a cow and a heifer, a team of horses, and a passel of chickens over at my place, young lady. Been keepin' them in my barn, since Miss Zelda don't want to be troubled. But if you could use some milk and eggs for the little one, you're more'n welcome to come get 'em once you're ready here."

"Oh, ja." She clasped her hands, face lighting. "That would be such a gift. Mange takk."

Absalom peered at her, questions pinching. Had they been struggling to find enough to eat? Ruth seemed hale enough, but did Miss Gunderson's cheeks look thinner? He kicked himself for not checking on them sooner, though it had only been a couple of days.

"Did you hear that, Ruthie?" She smoothed her hand over the little girl's hair. "We will have chickens to go in the henhouse."

"Milk and eggs, hurra!" Ruth danced in a circle, her muddy boots capering.

Mr. Miller cast Absalom a glance as if wondering the same as he. "Why don't you young ladies come over with me right now? 'Less you've got somethin' else to do at the moment."

"Ja, mange takk. Let me just tell Miss Berg."

"Oh, before I forget." Absalom reached into his pocket for the papers. "As promised. I typed an extra copy for you too."

"Tusen takk. I appreciate it." She took the papers, and untying her apron as she went, Miss Gunderson hurried up the steps and into the boardinghouse.

So Miss Berg was in the building and had either not heard or ignored Absalom's knock. He chewed the inside of his cheek. And not helping with the laundry out back at all? What did the woman do with herself?

Miss Gunderson came down the steps a few moments later. A bit of color in her cheeks and a spark in her eyes made him wonder what the older woman had said this time, but she only held out a little shawl for Ruthie and said, "We are ready."

Wishing he could think of an excuse to tag along, Absalom bid them all good-bye and headed back to Maybelle and the buggy. He'd ask his father about that money in the bank first thing.

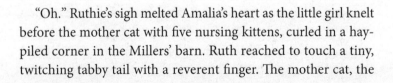

"Oh." Ruthie's sigh melted Amalia's heart as the little girl knelt before the mother cat with five nursing kittens, curled in a hay-piled corner in the Millers' barn. Ruth reached to touch a tiny, twitching tabby tail with a reverent finger. The mother cat, the same orange tabby they had seen crossing their field, purred and curled closer around her kittens.

So it hadn't been too early for kittens after all.

"You should take one of them for her, once they're weaned." Mr. Miller gave Amalia a nod, speaking slowly enough that she could gather what he meant.

"Maybe." She couldn't think about that just yet—but cats always proved helpful around the house and barn, after all, for keeping away rodents. And the rapt look on Ruthie's face . . .

For now, though, she had other animals to think of.

"Where are the chickens?"

"Out foraging in the yard just now. We can bring 'em over once you have a chance to clean out your henhouse. Got yourself a round dozen of Rhode Island Reds, half that of Barred Rocks. And one of the Reds is a rooster."

What richness, though Amalia didn't recognize the English names for the breeds.

The barn door opened, admitting a tall, broad-shouldered younger man, perhaps in his late twenties, carrying an empty milk pail in each hand.

"Ah. This here's my son, Eben—come over here, Eben. He's going to do the milking, can show you your cow. Son, this is Miss Amalia Gunderson. She's taken on the Forsberg place next door, adjoining farms, as it were. We'll be neighbors." Miller gave his towering son's shoulder a slap. "I'm sure Eben will be glad to help you out any way he can, Miss Gunderson. He's not married." He said the last words very loudly, as if wanting to make sure Amalia understood. "Ain't that right, son?"

"Sure." Eben grinned down at her, reminding her of an awkward calf, all lanky arms and legs. "Glad to help."

"I, uh, mange takk. I mean, thank you." Amalia's cheeks warmed. "So where is—our cow?"

Eben swung one long arm ahead to point the way, clanging the milk pail. "Right up ahead yonder. I'll show you."

Amalia followed, eagerness to see their milk cow winning over the momentary discomfort.

Eben led the way past a line of cows waiting at stanchions for their grain, then stopped by a smallish, golden-brown cow who lowed insistently at their approach.

"Hey there, girl." Eben scratched between her horns. "Well, here she be."

"She is beautiful." Amalia stepped closer. "What is her name?"

"Mrs. Forsberg called her Honey." He shrugged. "She's a good milker. Dry now, though, she's due to calve again in a month or so. That fawn-colored heifer is hers from last year. Can take her too, if you like."

Honey—it suited her well, with her golden coat and soft big brown eyes. Plus another heifer to breed next year and a calf coming too! Amalia reached to stroke the smooth neck, then scratched Honey's broad cheek. The cow turned her head toward her, blinking, stretching her chin up for Amalia to scratch under her jaw. Amalia grinned and followed the silent request. This reminded her of the cows at home. She'd always enjoyed brushing them.

"Go ahead and milk the others, Eben, then we'll send some milk back with the ladies." Mr. Miller approached from behind.

"Sure thing, Pa." Eben poured a portion of grain for Honey, then a larger helping for a cow in the next stanchion, a large black-and-white milker. He swung a stool next to her and collapsed his frame onto it. Within seconds milk hissed into the bucket, steamy and frothing.

Amalia swallowed, mouth watering. Despite how she'd tried to stretch it, Zelda's milk pitcher had been empty since yesterday morning, and she'd only snapped when Amalia asked where to get more. And now, abundant milk—for porridge and for Ruthie, for cream in coffee, for butter and cheese and sour cream cookies. And soon, a milking cow of their own. *Thank you, Father.*

"Want to see your horses?" Mr. Miller asked at her shoulder.

She'd forgotten about the team. Amalia followed him to the other side of the large barn, where he showed her a fine pair, one chestnut and one bay.

"Been usin' them as a spare to trade out with my team for plowing. But they belonged to Mrs. Forsberg, so you can take 'em if you want."

Amalia nibbled her lip. "I don't know." Could she handle feeding and caring for a team just now? Managing the cow and chickens seemed enough to start, and even that would take work to prepare for. "The barn has hay?"

He shrugged and spat. "Probably all old and stale by now. You'll want to wait to bring the cow over till the pasture grows enough for grazing. We'll share milk with you till she freshens."

"I'll need to clean the barn out too." And how was she to do that, with only a five-year-old's help? If only Zelda . . .

"Me an' Eben can help with that. And if you ain't sure about the horses, leave them here for the time being. I don't mind boardin' 'em, if'n you don't mind me usin' them in the fields. I treat 'em well, no overwork, so don't fret your mind about that."

Amalia nodded. Having one decision made for her, at least, eased the tension in her middle. "Mange takk. That will be good." They could bring the horses later, once they got the boardinghouse up and running. *And how to do that?* The thought still took her breath away. Never would she have dreamed she'd be charged with running a boardinghouse on coming to America. *"One step at a time,"* she heard her mother's voice in her head. That's all she could do.

After coaxing Ruthie away from the kittens by promising to visit them again soon, Amalia led her after Mr. Miller into the white farmhouse with its spreading front porch. Mrs. Miller, a short, round lady with a broad smile, welcomed them in a familiar language into a kitchen that smelled of cinnamon and ginger.

"I just took these out of the oven. I don't suppose you'd be willing to sample them for me?"

Wide-eyed, Ruthie took a ginger cookie and bit in. The grin on her face brought one to Amalia's. "Mange takk."

"Velbekommen." Mrs. Miller popped half a dozen more hot cookies onto a plate and set it before Ruthie, then gestured to Amalia. "For you too."

Amalia hesitated, then reached for a cookie, inhaling the fragrance before biting in. Crisp on the outside, warm and soft and spicy on the inside. Had they stepped into heaven? "Mange takk, indeed. You speak Norwegian?"

"My mother was Norwegian." Mrs. Miller wrapped a dozen more cookies in a cloth and bustled over to a large basket on the table, already filled with several bundles and jars. She tucked the cookies in. "Can't get Mr. Miller to learn three words, but I speak it well enough to get by, ja?" She glanced at Amalia, a twinkle in her eye.

She did, and the music of her mother tongue came as balm to her ears. Of course, Zelda spoke Norwegian, but her harsh tones grated whatever the language. *"I won't have you filling this place with dirty livestock again."* The memory of the woman's words flung before they left to come over here made Amalia flinch. She'd had to remind Zelda the choice wasn't hers to make, and that Ruthie needed decent food to eat—which hadn't gone over well, but she'd abated into muted grumbles. So Miss Berg couldn't abide good healthy livestock, but happily let the rest of the place dissolve into dust and shambles? Amalia shook her head. It made no sense.

"Got a lot on your mind, haven't you?" Mrs. Miller's voice came gently.

Amalia's ears heated. She gave a slight shrug and smile. "Does it show?"

"What shows is that you've been carrying far too heavy a load on your young shoulders." She clucked her tongue. "Mercy, whenever I walk by that place, I want to scrub the porch and wash the windows."

Amalia sighed. "And I haven't even gotten to those yet. I've been focused on washing our bedding and scrubbing the inside rooms. Which reminds me, we saw a haystack outside your barn—would you mind if we took a bit to stuff our pallets? We had to dump what was inside, all musty and filled with vermin."

"Oh, goodness, we have plenty of straw. I'll have Abram and Eben drive some over tonight, give you enough for the straw ticks and a start for bedding your animals once they come." Mrs. Miller hefted the basket over to Amalia, plunking it down on the table before her. "And there. That oughta hold you over for a few days at least. You both need some color in your cheeks."

Ruthie knelt up on her chair to peer into the basket, pressing against Amalia's shoulder. Two loaves of bread, a smoked ham. Cheeses and pickles, a jar of lard and one of preserves. The cookies and a dozen eggs. And if she weren't mistaken, that small, cold crock must be butter.

Tears stung Amalia's eyes. "Mange takk. May God bless you."

"Oh, He does." Mrs. Miller patted their shoulders. "And now, let's go see about those chickens."

With the sun lowering over the western horizon, the chickens flapped toward their coop, eager for their evening feed and ready to roost. Ruthie danced on her toes watching them, then Mr. Miller and Eben filled the wagon with straw to drive over to the boardinghouse. Eben drove the wagon the short distance from one farm to the other. Ruthie giggled in the back, nestled amid the straw, while Amalia sat by the driver, the basket in her lap and a jug of milk at her feet.

Halting the wagon by the barn, Eben forked the straw into a stack just inside the barn door.

"Mange takk—thank you." Amalia laid her hands on Ruth's shoulders and met the young man's eyes. "We are so grateful."

"Anytime, Miss Gunderson. Hope we'll be seein' a lot of you." With another grin, he doffed his work-stained hat and hopped back up in the wagon seat, driving home under the last rays of the setting sun.

They peeked inside the barn at the straw stack. A slight breeze stirred the air, stinking of musty hay and old manure, and made Ruthie sneeze.

"Tomorrow we will start cleaning the barn." And she needed to write a letter to her relatives back home. So much to tell—the sad, and the good. She hadn't even told them yet that her parents had died, so much had been happening. Setting the thought aside for now, she held out her hand for Ruthie's small one. "Come, let's go inside."

Amalia caught sight of Zelda standing on the back porch, watching them. The woman shook her head, then walked inside and slammed the door.

Amalia fought a sinking in her middle. Would nothing please that woman?

EIGHT

Who filled the woodbox before we came here? Or does Zelda just see us as servants now?

She felt heat creep up her neck. *Amalia Marie Gunderson, whatever has come over you? Whatever happened to be thankful in all things? Start counting your blessings—now.* She wasn't sure if the voice in her mind was her mor's or her own.

"Malia, can I go see the kittens?" Ruth dumped her armload in the box and smiled up at her guardian.

"Nei, we will have breakfast soon, so bring in more wood."

The little girl heaved a sigh big enough to make Amalia need to hide a smile. "We're having pancakes for breakfast."

"Really?" Now even Ruthie's blue eyes danced. She darted toward the back door. "I'm getting more wood—" She skidded to a stop, before tiptoeing to the porch.

What in the world? Amalia followed, a slight breeze kissing her cheeks when she stopped in the doorway. Such a glorious day—what a shame to miss any of the sunshine. The mama cat from their neighbor's sat on the top step, using one white paw to clean her whiskers. How long had it been since she last saw a cat preening? It felt like another lifetime. And they would soon have a kitten for Ruthie to play with.

Ruth beamed up a smile and loaded her arms with wood. Amalia followed suit and together they returned to the kitchen. Several more trips took care of that job.

Amalia set a frying pan on the stove and stirred the batter she had prepared earlier. Sourdough perfumed the room. After adding more wood to the firebox, she slid the frying pan to heat, poured grease into the pan, and gave the batter another stir. "Go ahead and set the table, then bring the butter and jam from the pantry."

"Milk?"

Amalia nodded to the pitcher on the counter.

Ruthie hummed as she did what she was told. "Should I go knock on her door?" She nodded over her shoulder, her eyebrows raised in question.

Amalia started to say no, do not bother her, but instead nodded. Something along the line of heaping coals on an adversary's head made her swallow. She moved the coffeepot to sit beside the skillet.

"Can I have coffee too?" Ruth set three cups in place and paused.

Amalia nodded again. The amount of coffee in Ruth's cup would barely warm the drink, but it would smell like coffee and taste like it a bit. She poured the batter into the smoking fry pan, making three circles, much easier to flip than a full pan-sized one. Even so the puddles ran together, creating new shapes.

Ruthie skipped back into the room. "She said she already ate."

Amalia shrugged. Oh well, they tried. She flipped the pancakes to a plate warming on the stove shelf and set the plate in the warming oven. She fixed about half the batter, saving the remainder to thicken and make into biscuits for supper.

The first bite made her close her eyes in delight before she opened them abruptly. "Oh! We forgot to say grace." Together they bowed their heads. "I Jesu navn . . . amen." *Thank you, Lord, we have so much to be grateful for.*

Ruthie buttered her last pancake, spread jam on it, and rolled it carefully. She picked up the roll and looked to Amalia. "This all right?"

"Ja." Accompanied by a nod. "I will do the same when we have pancakes again. My brother always sprinkled sugar on his when we had some." Thoughts of Erik and her family made her eyes burn. How could she try to find him, especially when so much else demanded to be done? She sniffed and pushed back her chair. "I'll fix our coffee."

They carried their cups outside and sat down on the top step to sip while looking to see which bird was singing at the moment. A green haze clothed each tree as the leaves were emerging, and a slight mist rose out in the fields. Amalia studied the horizon. No snow-crowned mountains like at home, the creek meandering rather than tumbling down steep hills. She tossed the dregs of her coffee on what looked like a rosebush rising through the weeds off to her right. Her mor wanted to bring starts of her roses, but Far talked her out of it. Said they'd never make it. Amalia rubbed her forehead. Oh, how she missed them.

Ruth leaned against her shoulder. "You are sad?"

"Homesick."

"Me too. Far said we would have a dog here."

"We'll see. And start with a kitten." Amalia stood and stretched. "We need a stool for you so you can learn to knead dough and wash dishes." Amalia looked down at her charge. "There are beans in the pantry. We'll wash and soak them. I saw cornmeal, too, so . . ."

"Corn bread." Ruth leaped to her feet. "And soon I can go see the kittens."

They loaded their arms at the dwindling stack of wood and dumped it in the woodbox. Sometime later, with the dough rising on the warming shelf, the kitchen set back to rights, and beans soaking in a kettle, Amalia filled the bucket with hot water and shaved in soap.

Ruth ran to the porch to grab the rags and broom. "You said to cover our hair next time."

"Takk." She tied cloth around their heads and headed upstairs to the middle floor. "Now we even have straw to stuff our pallets."

"Good, floor's hard."

They were just going down for a bucket of clean water when they heard a "halloo" from outside. Ruth ran the rest of the way downstairs and tugged open the front door. "Mr. Eben is here!"

Zelda stuck her head out of her bedroom door. "I told you, no hollering in the house." She slammed the door shut.

Ruth stumbled back up the stairs to meet Amalia coming down. "I—I forgot."

That . . . Amalia couldn't think of the right word. She took the little hand, and together they met the farmer's son at the front gate.

"God dag." Amalia shaded her eyes with one hand.

"I brought your chickens."

"Oh, but we don't have the chicken house cleaned out yet."

He shrugged. "Then I'll help you clean it."

"You are so kind. Takk."

He backed up his team and followed the lane toward the barn. After parking the team in the shadow of the barn, he stepped down and tied them to a post.

Amalia grabbed a flat shovel and a pitchfork and sent Ruth to the house for the broom.

She returned empty-handed and with a frown. "Miss Zelda said we can't use the house broom in the filthy chicken house."

Another thing they would be discussing. Amalia clamped her jaw. Tight. As if she did not know how to wash a broom.

Eben swung the door open. "Shovel works better anyway." He stopped in the doorway to look around. "Lots of spiders, good chicken food."

"We don't have anything else to feed them."

"I brought a bag of oats for now. They'll find plenty when they start scratching around. Keep 'em in the house for a day or two to settle in, give 'em a pan for water." While he talked, he started shoveling. "You got a wheelbarrow?"

"No idea, I'll go see what's in the shed. Ruth, you start cleaning out the nest boxes."

Once they reached the dirt floor of the henhouse, Eben drove the team over and forked straw in to cover the floor. Ruth and Amalia stuffed straw in the nest boxes and stood back for Eben to bring in the two crates. He opened the tops and stepped back.

Ruth giggled when two hens stuck their heads up to look around.

"Where do you want the oats?"

"Ah, in the barn, I guess. Might there be a grain bin out there?" She should have been more prepared.

Eben set the sack of oats in the grain bin and stepped back up on the wagon. "Anything else I can do for you?"

"Not right now. Takk, tusen takk. I mean, thank you."

He tipped his hat and grinned. "Velbekommen. My ma taught me some words." He clucked the team, took a couple of paces, and stopped. "Almost forgot, Ma wants you all to come for supper Saturday night. Miz Berg too."

"Takk."

"Can I play with the kittens?"

He grinned down at Ruth. "Sure thing." He looked to Amalia. "Just set the crates outside when they are empty. And make sure you put water in there."

"Takk." *What can I put water in?* "Ruthie, can you think of something to put water in?"

"A bucket?"

"Good thought, but we need something more shallow." She motioned with her fingers spread wide. "I wonder what they used to use?" She heaved a sigh. "I better go cut the biscuits, they need time to rise again."

Back in the kitchen, she dumped the risen dough out on a

floured cloth on the table and patted it into a big circle, flipping it over once to form it more. Using a biscuit cutter, she cut them as close as she could. After greasing the cookie sheet, she spaced the dough far enough apart to give them space to rise and formed the leftovers to finish the rows.

"Some of the chickens are still in the crates." Ruth popped back in from outside and dumped more wood in the woodbox.

"Takk, den lille. You knew we were getting low. And don't worry, the chickens will come out once they feel comfortable enough. I'll be right back out."

"How long do the beans need to soak?" Ruthie peeked into the kettle.

"Till supper." She spread a cloth over the pan. "Then they can simmer all night."

"But the fire goes almost out."

"I'll just have to stoke it better." Too many things to keep track of. If only she could figure out a waterer for the chickens. If only she didn't have to confront Zelda. Amalia sighed. At least they could take care of the pallets. "Come on, Ruthie, let's go stuff our pallets with straw so we sleep better tonight."

They used much of the remaining straw in the barn for the pallets. "Stuff as much as you can into the tick, it'll pack down when you sleep on it. Here." Amalia swapped ticks and shook the new one, then stuffed in more straw and folded the end into place. Shame there wasn't a wheelbarrow or wagon they could use. Instead she half carried, half dragged one up to the back door and then the other. The porch steps were bad enough but the stairs . . .

"Maybe we should sleep in the parlor."

Amalia swallowed a chuckle at the way Ruth was studying the pallets. "Takk, little one, we'll get them . . ." Oh, oh, she'd not put wood in the stove for too long.

She hurried into the kitchen and found the coffeepot steaming. Zelda had taken care of the stove. At least she was doing something.

The thought of a cup of coffee made Amalia stomp back out to the porch, grab one of the pallets, carry it to the stairs, and drag it up. "Uff da," she muttered to herself as she almost sat down on one of the steps. *Lord, help me.* By the time both pallets were on the floor in their room, all she wanted to do was lie down on one and take a nap.

"Can we have a pancake with our coffee?"

Our coffee. Her inside chuckle sent her downstairs to pour her coffee and fix one for Ruth. Together they sat down at the table, spread preserves from the Miller basket on their leftover pancakes from breakfast, and rolled them up. For some reason, the first bite made her smile. "What a good idea."

Ruth grinned back at her and lifted her cup. "Takk."

"There's straw on the stairway!"

Zelda. Her door slammed again.

Amalia inhaled a deep breath. "Have you finished your coffee?" Talking gently was difficult with a tight jaw.

Ruth nodded, her eyes wide.

"Good, then you go out and see how the chickens are doing. See if you can find something to put their water in."

Ruth nodded and, setting her cup on the counter, escaped out the door.

Amalia heaved a big sigh and pushed herself upright. She checked to make sure the biscuits were about ready for the oven and rapped on the downstairs bedroom door.

"Go away."

"Do you want to talk in there or out here?"

"We have nothing to talk about."

"We, or at least I, will talk now." Amalia turned the knob and pushed open the door. She glanced around the fully furnished room that once must have been a small parlor at the front of the house. "First, takk for keeping the stove going while we worked outside. Now, I don't care if you talk with me or not, but you will not yell at Ruth. Not ever again. Life has been terribly hard on her, leaving home, losing her parents, and then to have someone be cruel to her." Her words stumbled over each other. "You do know this house and farm is now hers, and her mor appointed me to be her guardian. That means you will answer to me, not an innocent child!" She paused, gripping her hands together. "So to put this bluntly, you have two choices."

"But I . . ."

Amalia waved Zelda's words aside. "You can remain here if you do your share of the work and are not unkind to Ruth. Or you can pack your things and move somewhere else." Hopefully far away.

Zelda sat on the edge of her unmade bed and, arms clamped around her middle, stared arrows at Amalia. "You have no right . . ."

"I have every right. I am Ruth's legal guardian and as such it is my job to protect her. You have no right to scream at her, or me either, for that matter. You have until Saturday to decide."

Amalia shut the door with a snap and leaned her forehead against the doorframe to help stop her shaking. Her heart pounded, drumming in her ears. All she wanted to do was get out of the house before the tears drowned her.

But she needed to add more wood to the fire and slide the biscuits into the oven. Mopping the moisture from her cheeks, she returned to the kitchen. Good thing the table was there to hold her up. Never in her life had she talked to someone like that. *Dear God, did I yell at her, or did it just feel like it?* A bubble of hysteria almost made her laugh. She opened the oven door to be greeted with a burst of hot air. The oven was plenty hot. She carefully placed the tray of biscuits inside.

Ruth met her at the steps. "I can't make the pump work."

"You found a waterer?"

The little girl shrugged. "If it will hold water."

Amalia pumped a bucket full of water and carried it to the chicken house.

"See the little trough, I think they used it before."

Amalia poured it full of water. They stepped back. One of the chickens came over, cocked her head to see them better, dipped her beak in the water and tipped her head back.

"I can see her swallow." Ruth grinned up at Amalia.

"I know." She wanted to grab Ruthie up and whirl her around. Oh, such joy in a small package.

Another hen and then two more came to drink, watching carefully to make sure no one was going to grab at them.

"The biscuits!" Amalia spun around, the chickens at the water trough flew up squawking, and she ran for the house. She burst into the kitchen. The golden-brown biscuits cooled in the middle of the table.

Did this mean Zelda wanted to stay?

NINE

W e are all invited to the Millers' for supper."
    At the breakfast table Saturday morning, Zelda
    buttered her biscuit, her head wagging slowly.

"I get to see the kittens." Ruthie wriggled on her chair, earning herself a glare from Zelda.

Having Zelda at the table took all the strength Amalia owned to not make some comment. She had been starting the fire in the stove when Amalia and Ruth came down the stairs. The shock had been almost too much. Ruthie squeezed her hand and looked up at her, eyes wide, mouth in an O. She'd returned the squeeze with a slight nod. *Thank you, Lord. And please give me wisdom and strength.* She'd almost been wishing for, or at least contemplating, Zelda moving out. But maybe Amalia standing up to her the other day had actually made a difference.

Amalia set the bowl of scrambled eggs on the table.

"Say grace?" Ruth asked.

"Ja. Takk." Amalia sat down at the table and bowed her head. "I Jesu navn . . ." At the *amen*, she breathed a sigh of relief.

"Eggs, we have eggs." Ruthie grinned. "Do you think our chickens laid any eggs?"

"You can go see after breakfast. Zelda, could you please pass the biscuits? And thank you for making the coffee." Right now Amalia was grateful they could all speak Norwegian, but they did need to work on their new language. *I wonder if Zelda would teach us how to speak English.* She chewed a bite of her biscuit along with golden egg. Better not expect too much.

When they were finished and Zelda said she would do the dishes—another miracle—Amalia followed Ruth out to the chicken house. The little girl paused at the door.

"Hear that?"

Amalia nodded. "Hens like to announce when they've laid an egg. You need to pay attention to that rooster, though. Sometimes they can be mean."

"Can we let them out in their yard?"

"Ja, but not let them loose, until they know this is where they live now."

"How will we get them in at night?"

"They'll mostly go in. We might have to remind some of them, but chickens are smart." She opened the door and motioned for Ruth to go first. One of the hens in the nest boxes jumped to the floor. Another hen stayed in her box.

"The water is empty." Ruth looked up at Amalia. "The straw is wet, I think it leaked out."

"Not surprising. Wood shrinks when it gets really dry but then swells when wet. We'll soak it in the bucket at the pump." She looked down to see the big red rooster pecking and scratching closer than he had been. "Ruth, pay attention to the rooster."

"Shoo." She fluttered her hands at him. He shook himself and flapped his wings but kept staring at her, even while pecking at something.

Amalia stepped between the rooster and the child. "Come on, we'll go get the oats for them. That should make him more friendly."

"Why can't I stay here?"

"Just because." They shut the door behind them and strolled over to the barn.

"I hope we can have baby chicks soon." Ruth tipped her head back to better feel the sunshine. "The ladies will like being outside better."

"Ladies?"

"Ja, they are ladies, and he is a gentleman."

Amalia scooped oats from the sack and poured the grain in the bucket. Together they swung the pail between them. Birds serenaded the new day, with the rooster crowing counterpoint. Morning songs to make her heart sing. It had been so very long since she'd lived with chickens, horses, and the cows living in the barn beneath their house built into the hillside. Homesickness flooded through her. She sucked in deep breaths.

Delight shone in Ruth's face. She glanced up at Amalia. "Oh, please don't be sad."

"Sorry, I thought of home . . . in Norway."

"But this is our home now." She swung her arm around to encompass her new world.

"Ja, it is. Takk."

Back in the chicken house, Amalia showed her how to scatter the grain with her hand so all the flock came running. Surrounded by pecking chickens, Ruth trickled oats closer to her feet. A couple of hens cocked their heads, staring at her before moving closer.

"You can come close, I won't hurt you." She looked. "Malia, how come the rooster isn't eating?"

"He's a good rooster, making sure his flock feeds first."

"He needs a name." Ruth threw a handful toward the rooster. "He's red, lotsa colors of red. I have to think about this." She tipped the last grains out of the bucket and watched them disappear into the straw. "Do chickens see better than people?"

"Perhaps." Where did she come up with another one of those questions? She could hear her mother's answer when she had asked a plethora of questions. *"God made it so and so it is."* She stooped down to pick up the water trough. "You bring the bucket and we'll set this to soaking."

"We have to open their door."

"Right." She grabbed the wood handle and lifted, but when it moved only an inch, she wiggled the thin rectangle of wood back and forth to loosen it. A few more jerks and wiggles raised the door. *Thank you, Lord.*

One of the hens wandered over then darted outside. Others followed.

Ruthie giggled and clapped. "We'll bring you water too."

At the windmill, Amalia pumped the bucket full, and Ruth set the trough in to soak. Together they returned to the house, loaded their arms with wood, and dumped the chunks into the nearly full woodbox.

A cloth-draped bowl of bread dough sat rising in the sun from the window. But where was Zelda?

Amalia lifted the cloth and saw the dough needed more rising time, so she added wood to the stove and started dipping hot water from the reservoir into a pail. "Ruthie, please bring in those rags and the broom from the porch." While she did that, Amalia shaved soap into the pail, and together they climbed the stairs to the third floor. A cool breeze blew in from the open windows on the second floor as they passed. At the end of the open, stuffy third story, Amalia grunted as she tried to lift the window sash. If only she knew whether or not they had a crowbar, but rather than wasting time looking for one, she sent Ruth down to the kitchen for a knife. Blowing out a breath, she tied a cloth around her head, a rag around the broom, and set to the cobwebs on walls and ceiling.

Ruth returned and handed her a table knife. "Miss Berg said knives belong in the kitchen."

"She did, did she?"

"She was kneading the sourdough. It sure smells good."

After running the knife blade between window and sill, and

along the top, Amalia got it to move. "You lift on the bottom."
With the heels of her hands pushing the upper frame and Ruth
pulling up on the bottom, they forced the window to rise. "Good."
She shook Ruthie's hand. "Takk, tusen takk."

Ruth propped her elbows on the windowsill and leaned out.
"Smells much better out here." She grinned over her shoulder. "I
can almost touch the leaves on the tree."

"Be careful!"

The little girl pulled herself back in and rolled her eyes. "I wasn't
going to fall."

Amalia finished sweeping the ceiling and the walls and handed
the broom to Ruth. "You sweep the floor, while I wash the window."

They stopped for a quick dinner, then went back to work. When
they finished scrubbing half the floor of the huge space late afternoon, Amalia's shoulders burned, her lower back aching. And they
still had another half to go. *I wonder what they used this open story
for? How will we find boarders to fill this place?* The thought was
nothing new. *And what about beds or at least more pallets?* She
jerked her thoughts back. She'd read in her Bible, "In every thing
give thanks." She'd heard sermons on the same thing. Her mor kept
a list of things she gave thanks for. But her mor was gone, and her
far, and she didn't know where Erik was, and . . . she looked down
to see Ruthie staring at her.

"You look sad," she whispered and sniffed.

"Forgive me." She bent over and wrapped the little girl in her
arms. "I'm sorry."

Ruth stole her arms around Amalia's neck and kissed her cheek.
"Don't like it when you are sad."

Amalia kissed her back and stood straight. "Neither do I. We
better get going, supper with the Millers." A nod accompanied
her smile. "We should probably freshen up a bit."

Ruth looked up at her. "You have a cobweb on your head."

Two loaves of baked bread sat on the table, covered by a dish towel. The thought of cutting off a heel and spreading butter on it made her mouth water. Where was Zelda now?

"Ruth, see if you can find Zelda."

The little girl nodded and darted out the door only to be back immediately. "She is digging rutabagas."

"Takk." Amalia knew the woman had said no to the invitation for tonight, but perhaps she had changed her mind.

She hadn't.

Well, nothing ever changed all at once. Amalia brought in an armload of wood to dump into the woodbox. "Get the hairbrush." While Ruthie did that, she dipped a cloth in the reservoir and wiped her own face. "Here wipe your face, arms and hands too, and I'll braid your hair." She'd not done that this morning, so now was necessary. By the time they finished and stepped out the front door, the sun was sliding toward the horizon.

"I get to see the kittens," Ruthie sang, skipping beside her.

Mrs. Miller met them at the door and stepped back. "Come in, come in. I was about to send Eben for you." She glanced out the door. "Zelda refused to come?"

"I'm sorry."

"Don't you be sorry. She is a hard woman to deal with." She led the way to the kitchen where the table was already set, and both Mr. Miller and Eben smiled their greetings.

"Welcome and how about you sit here, Miss Ruth." Mr. Miller patted the chair next to him and motioned for Amalia to sit on the next chair. "One of these days we'll make sure you meet our Lisa. She must be about your age, and she loves to come to the farm."

"Our oldest son's daughter. They live on the other side of Deco-rah." Mrs. Miller pulled a pan out of the oven and set it on the stove. "Baked chicken."

Ruth looked up to Amalia, her eyes wide.

"May I help you?" Amalia asked, patting Ruth's knee.

"If you would like to put the bowls on the table while I cut this up. Didn't want it to get cold." She motioned to the bowls on the stove warming shelf. "I made noodles since we ran out of potatoes. Always look forward to new potatoes. And dried pole beans with bacon. You ever dried pole beans?"

Amalia shook her head. "I've not even heard of such a thing. Gardening is different in Norway."

Mrs. Miller set the platter of cut up chicken on the table and sat down. "Now did I miss anything?" She popped up again. "The rolls are in the warming oven."

When she sat back down, Mr. Miller bowed his head. "Thank thee, Lord, for this food thou hast given us. Let us use it for thy service. I thank thee too for our new neighbors. In the name of the Father, the Son, and the Holy Spirit, Amen. And now everyone, pass your plate here for chicken, and Eben, please start the bowl in front of you."

Amalia served both Ruth and herself and passed the bowls on. So much food. When had she last seen a meal like this? Even to the pickled beets, butter, and jam in the center of the table. The pitcher must be cream for the coffee.

"Ruth, would you like more milk?"

She shook her head. "Takk." And looked up to Amalia who nodded her approval.

Eben leaned forward. "How are your chickens?"

Ruth's grin dimpled her cheeks. "Two eggs this morning." Her English was coming along.

"When we finish eating, want to see the kittens?"

Her face lit up.

He smiled back. "Thought so."

When they had finished the gingerbread covered in applesauce, Eben and Ruth went out to find the kittens while the dishes soaked in a pan on the stove. Mrs. Miller refilled coffee cups and sat back down.

"Now, tell me how you are getting along. I know it can't be easy with Zelda."

Amalia stirred cream into her coffee and heaved a sigh. Might as well be honest; they knew the woman far better than she did. "I can ignore her rudeness, staying in her room, but she screamed at Ruth a couple of times and made her cry. So finally on Thursday, I knocked on her door. She told me to go away, but I barged in and . . ." Amalia studied her hands clasped around the coffee cup, then glanced up with a tiny shrug. "Well, I told her she had two options. Stay and do her share of the work, without yelling at Ruth, or leave."

"Good for you." Mrs. Miller reached over and covered one of Amalia's hands with her own. "And don't worry, you're not telling us anything new. Ever since Else passed on to her reward and left Zelda alone, she has become more difficult to deal with." Since they'd been speaking in Norwegian, she gave a quick translation for her husband.

"We helped her as much as we could." Mr. Miller shrugged. "But she's got to be more of a recluse."

"Zelda asked us to go on farming the land, which we've done since before Amund, Else's husband, passed away. She asked Zelda to come help her with the boardinghouse, but when Else's health started to fail—it was more than the two of them could handle. The boarders just slowly stopped coming."

More questions than she could sort through and ask kept Amalia quiet. Finally she asked, "What about all the furniture?"

The two exchanged a look.

"I think Zelda sold or traded it for food. She did tend the garden though, even brought us some vegetables at times." Mr. Miller wagged his head slowly, as if it were heavy.

"Ja, her rutabagas have been helping keep us fed."

"We have done as much as we could, but now we can go days without seeing her out of the house. When she doesn't answer the door, we leave milk and eggs in a box with a cover on her front porch. Eben goes over and splits wood. Last year one of the oak trees on the farm blew over so we cut it into stove lengths and split the wood between the two places."

"Mr. Miller, Mrs. Miller, I think you have been wonderful neighbors to her. Such a shame . . ." Amalia exhaled slowly. Then shook her head. "Takk, tusen takk doesn't begin to cover our debt to you. I had no idea what I was getting into when I agreed to be Ruth's guardian." She shook her head again. "I don't think her parents did either, they were both so excited about inheriting this place. They had dreamed of coming here . . . someday, of working on Carl's aunt's big farm and fancy boardinghouse. Talked about it on the ship. A new life for their children, they still hoped to have more."

"As my mor used to say, life changes in an instant, and we have no control over it whatsoever." Mrs. Miller pushed back her chair. "I want to send these leftovers home with you. I know there is not a lot to eat there, because I don't think Zelda's been to the store in a long time."

"Takk." Amalia turned as Ruth danced back into the room.

"I got to hold one of the kittens, the mama cat let me."

"She'll start weaning them pretty soon, so in a few weeks you can take one or two if you would like. Now that there will be feed in your barn, there will be more mice. You'll need barn cats too."

With every word, the little girl's eyes grew rounder.

Eben grinned at them both. "You know chickens like to catch mice too."

"Chickens eat mice?"

"Chickens eat most anything."

Mrs. Miller set a basket on the table. "I tucked more of the gingerbread in here too. I thought a certain little girl might like that."

Ruthie looked up at Amalia and whispered, "Does she mean me?"

"What do you think?" Amalia gave her a squeeze and hefted the basket. "You are so good to us. Takk for maten."

"Velbekommen, and come back soon."

Amalia and Ruth strolled down the short road to home, Ruthie more spinning than walking.

"Oh, Malia." Ruth stopped. "Look, the moon!" As they watched, the silvery disk broke free of the earth and started the climb into the deepening sky.

She turned back to face west, seeing a thin band of brilliant sunset had yet to fade.

A perfect end to today. What will tomorrow bring?

TEN

Why hadn't he foreseen this?

Absalom stared at the hymnal in his hands, trying to focus on the words amid the usual Sunday morning chorus around him at First Lutheran Church of Decorah. His father stood beside him, belting out "A Mighty Fortress Is Our God" in his usual off-key bass, apparently unaware of the young woman's dark head two rows in front of them.

Of course Rebecca would come to church here, if she'd moved back to town. Her family had always attended First Lutheran, and they'd attended together, those months they'd been engaged. He hadn't seen her last Sunday, but they must have been still getting settled.

If only the Einersen family had left with the others who had split off to form Faith Lutheran Church this January—then Rebecca and her husband would have followed. Absalom winced at the uncharitable thought. He'd never rejoice over a schism in the family of God—and over predestination, of all things.

He forced his mouth to start shaping the familiar words.

> "And though this world with devils filled,
> Should threaten to undo us,
> We will not fear, for God hath willed
> His truth to triumph through us. . . ."

Not that theology wasn't important, but weren't such issues as whether or not God chose the elect before the foundations of the world up to Him, after all? It wasn't like people could do anything about it, either way. His father had stuck with First Lutheran, having deep roots there, and so had Absalom, but the emptier pews and invisible tension between their congregation and their former church members a few blocks down the street weighed on his heart.

His father nudged him, a general rustle reminding him the congregation was seating. Absalom snapped the book shut and sat in the pew, ears warming. His father quirked a brow at him, but Absalom just shook his head and reached for his Bible. He turned the fragile pages, forcing himself not to look up, not to glance over to see what Rebecca was doing now, seated up there by her new husband. He tried to shut out the memories of when she used to sit beside him, in this very church, gloved hands proper in her lap, full skirt brushing over his boots. What was the matter with him? He thought he'd moved past this.

It wasn't that he still pined over Rebecca. He knew now they weren't right together—after all, if she only loved him for the station she thought he'd bring her, not who he really was, then she hadn't loved him at all. His throat tightened. Even if he'd loved her. But seeing her here unexpectedly, real and alive, only a few pews ahead—well, it stirred up all sorts of feelings he'd thought long gone.

The slight press of his father's trousered knee against his gave him pause, and he drew a long breath. Was it intentional? Did his father know? Regardless, the touch steadied him. He let the breath out and focused on the pages he'd unseeingly turned, since paying attention to the sermon, begun from the carved wooden pulpit ahead, didn't seem quite realistic at the moment.

He ran his finger down the black printed column before him.

"I had fainted, unless I had believed to see the goodness of the LORD in the land of the living. Wait on the LORD: be of good courage, and he shall strengthen thine heart: wait, I say, on the LORD."

He blinked away a blur behind his spectacles. The end of Psalm 27 . . . one of his mother's favorites, his father had always said. He lifted his head and drew another long breath, finding it possible now to listen to the sermon, even when the dark-haired man next to Rebecca bent toward her solicitously, whispering something. Absalom stood for the creed, went forward and knelt for communion, thankful for the familiar rhythms of Lutheran liturgy, that he could worship in body and spirit even if his mind struggled at times.

After the service, he and his father turned to greet the Jorstad family, who had filled the pew behind them. Carl and his wife, Anja, surrounded by their six children, expressed their gratitude once again.

"We have found our land, not far outside of town." Carl shook his head and gripped Absalom's hand, his voice husky. "Thanks to you, we have enough to start building our house and barn. We can never say mange takk enough."

Absalom found it easy to smile now. "To God be the glory, my friend."

His father shifted his feet and leaned on his cane. "Well, I'm afraid this leg of mine insists I get a move on." He tapped his thigh. "God's blessings on you, Mr. and Mrs. Jorstad."

"One more question." Carl leaned toward Absalom.

"Go ahead, Father, I'll be there in a moment." Absalom turned back. "Of course, how can I help?"

"Is there anywhere you could suggest my daughter Inga might find work?" He tipped his head at a tall girl with a long blonde braid, the eldest of the Jorstad daughters.

"Don't you need her help at home?"

"We need all help, of course." Carl spread his hands. "But despite all your assistance, our funds are tight. I need her brothers' help more, to build on our land. She is handy about a house, if you know anyone who could use a good hired girl."

Absalom thought of Miss Gunderson and the boardinghouse. Much assistance was needed there, but even if she knew of the money in the bank, he highly doubted she could afford to hire anyone yet, not without boarders. "I'm not sure, but I'll let you know."

"Mange takk."

He headed down the pew the way his father had gone, pausing at the aisle to let an elderly couple precede him, then glanced back to see if the way was clear. And looked straight into Rebecca's brown eyes.

Her presence so close still socked him in the gut. He thought surely she'd left already, while he'd been talking with the Jorstads.

She clasped her hands over her swelling middle. "Hello, Absalom."

"Hello." The word rasped only slightly. With her figure blooming with motherhood, she'd never looked lovelier.

Her eyes darted from him to the tall man coming up behind her. "This is my husband, Dr. David Armitage. David, Absalom Karlsson."

A doctor? So she'd found a man who could do more than "keep her in bread and butter." Absalom pushed back the memory. He would not give into bitterness, he'd already determined that. He stuck out his hand.

The man shook it. "A pleasure." He glanced between them. "Did you go to school together, here in Decorah?"

"We did." Absalom eyed Rebecca. Had she told her husband nothing of him, then?

The flush deepened in her cheeks.

"When did you move back to town?" The words sounded almost natural.

"Just last month. We want to be closer to family, with, well . . ." She shrugged and glanced down, her cheeks scarlet.

"Ah, yes. Congratulations." He'd once imagined a home with her, their hearthside, her rocking a cradle with their child . . . but it wasn't to be.

"And I'm taking over Dr. Esselstrom's practice in town." Armitage smiled down at his wife.

"I see." Absalom nodded. Clearly he'd been so embedded in immigrant cases he'd missed all the latest town news.

"Absalom's father is the magistrate here. He himself is going to be an attorney. Or already is?" She quirked a brow, but hesitantly, without the scorn he'd known from her last they met.

"Soon." He cleared his throat. "I take my exams in August."

"Ah, excellent." The doctor laid his hand on Rebecca's shoulder. "Well, perhaps we should . . ."

"Yes." She shifted, placing a hand to her lower back as if it ached. "It was good to see you, Absalom."

He nodded. "You too." Was that true? He couldn't untangle his thoughts enough to know. They turned down the aisle, disappeared in the dwindling crowd at the door. He closed his eyes and leaned on the corner of the empty pew, blowing out a long breath. At least that was over. Surely the first encounter would be the most awkward.

"Ah, there you are, son." The tap of his father's cane on the aisle neared him. "I was beginning to wonder where you'd got to."

"Carl Jorstad had a question." Absalom straightened. "And I talked to Rebecca and her husband."

"Ah." His father stilled. "I'm sorry, son. I didn't realize—I should have stayed."

"It's all right. I'm glad it happened, actually." He rounded the pew and patted his father's shoulder. "Let's go home."

That afternoon, after Sunday dinner, Absalom spent some time in the front garden, pulling away last year's dead grass and weeds from around his mother's rosebushes, now putting forth leaves of a fresh, deep green. He could already see tiny buds that would swell over the coming weeks and explode in blooms of white, pale pink, and deep rose by June. Spring sunshine warmed his back, last week's snowfall only a memory.

Peace seeped into his muscles with the pull of manual labor. As a man of the desk and pen, he knew he lacked the strength of the farmers, blacksmiths, and builders around him. But that didn't mean he didn't like to use his hands at times. Clipping away the crumbling vines, pulling out the dead grass to make room for the new sprouting through, piling it all in a heap beside their simple stable round back to break down for compost—it cleared his head and lungs. Perhaps a parable for what was happening in his own soul?

He slowed, digging his fingers into the earth to loosen a stubborn clump of old rooted grass. Old words and wounds couldn't be tugged out as easily as dry weeds, but out here, with the breeze tangling his hair and the smell of dirt in his nose, he sensed a new freeing and opening of his spirit. He didn't want to live tangled in the dead roots of the past, but make room for new growth, whatever the Lord might want that to be.

He grinned and tugged out a recalcitrant root. He was healing, thanks be to God.

The next morning, he headed down the street with a spring in his step, the world washed bright and gleaming by an overnight shower.

"Morning." He smiled and tipped his hat at two older ladies coming out of the mercantile. They nodded and smiled back. Everyone seemed in a bright mood today.

A burst of hollers farther down the street halted his steps, then sped them. A boy burst out of an office front a few doors down, followed by a man shouting after him.

"Thief! Stop that boy!"

The lad careened straight toward Absalom, then veered into the street. Absalom leapt after the child, snatching him out of the way of an oncoming wagon and thudding them both to the ground. They rolled into the gutter, lay there stunned an instant, then the boy scratched and kicked to get away.

"Hang on there, son." Absalom wrestled to a sitting position, holding tight to the boy's skinny arm.

"Lemme go!" The boy reared back with balled fist, twisting toward him, then froze when he saw Absalom's face. "Oh, it's you."

"Hank?" Absalom grabbed the boy by both shoulders. "What in land sakes—"

"Ah, you got him, thank you. He got away from me, the slippery little devil." A suit-coated arm reached into the gutter and snatched the boy up by his collar onto the board sidewalk.

Absalom felt for his spectacles, finding them in the gutter beside him. He winced but put them back on, scratches notwithstanding. Standing, he looked up several inches into the approving gaze of Dr. David Armitage.

He grimaced. Of all people for the boy to rob. He stepped back up on the sidewalk, bringing himself at least closer to level with Rebecca's husband.

"We meet again, if under less pleasant circumstances." Armitage gave the boy a shake, flapping Hank's tattered shirtsleeves. "Found this young rascal absconding with a bottle of expensive medicine."

"Ain't that expensive." The boy spat into the street, still clutching the small brown bottle.

"Then why not pay for it, you young reprobate?" The doctor wrested the bottle from dirty, clenching fingers. "Where's the sheriff in this town?"

Absalom shot a glance at Hank. Though the boy flinched at the word *sheriff*, he kept his face expressionless. *Lord, give me wisdom.* "Doctor, I know this boy."

Trimmed brows shot up. "You *know* him?"

"Yes." He ignored the look. "Let me take charge of him. I'll see he gives you no further trouble."

Armitage huffed a laugh. "Surely he's too poor to pay for a lawyer."

"I'm not a lawyer." Not yet. "But I don't think we need involve the sheriff. This time." He met Rebecca's husband's eyes. "I give you my word."

The man held his gaze a moment, then shrugged and shoved Hank toward Absalom. "If you say so, your father being magistrate and all. But I'll hold you responsible for any further monetary losses, Karlsson."

"Wait." Absalom dug in his pocket. "I'll pay for that medicine he took."

"Why would you do that?"

"He wouldn't take it without reason."

The man stared at him a moment. "Thirty cents, then. On your own head be it." He accepted Absalom's coins, tossed over the bottle, then headed back into his office, shaking his head.

Absalom gripped the boy's arm, half expecting Hank to bolt at any moment. "What were you thinking?"

He tried to wrest his shoulder away. "That doc ain't near as nice as Doc Esselstrom. He useta give me medicine when I needed it."

"Did you try asking this 'doc,' as you say?"

Hank rolled his eyes. "I can tell he wouldn't give nobody nothin'."

Absalom squelched a laugh. He'd always known Hank to be a solid judge of character. If that was the type of man Rebecca wanted, he should be glad she'd done Absalom the courtesy of jilting him. *Focus, Absalom.* "That doesn't make it right, and you know that.

Why did you need medicine anyway?" He examined the bottle. A simple laudanum cough syrup. "Are you sick?"

"Ain't for me. For a friend."

Absalom eyed him. "Another of your 'friends,' huh?"

"It's true, Mr. Karlsson! He's coughin' real bad."

"And where does this friend live?"

Hank hung his head, swiped his raggedy sleeve across his nose. "He don't like folks comin' around."

"Hank." Absalom waited till the boy dragged his gaze up to meet his eyes. He waggled the little glass bottle in his hands. "If you want this, you'll tell me."

The boy sighed as if he could win a medal for long-suffering. "Fine. But you tell ol' JJ you didn't give me no choice."

He quoted the doctor's words. "On my own head be it."

At Absalom's insistence, they stopped by the magistrate's office to tell his father of their errand. He wouldn't have his father worrying if he was absent long.

"Another mysterious errand of mercy, eh?" His father looked up from his desk and shook his head. "That boy has his finger on the pulse of this town far better than any child of ten should."

Absalom tipped his head and turned for the door. He couldn't deny it.

"Wait." His father stood with a grunt, then stepped near to slip a folded bill into Absalom's pocket. "If it seems needed. You know."

He squeezed his father's shoulder. Never wanting to be noticed, that was him. "Thanks."

He found Hank nearly dancing with impatience on the porch, where he'd insisted on waiting. "Took you long enough. C'mon, he's waiting."

"So who is this 'he'?" Absalom fell into step beside the boy.

"My friend, James Johann. Goes by JJ."

"And where does he live?"

"You'll see."

The way this young one had him and his father wrapped around his finger . . . Absalom shook his head and half laughed at himself but kept following. He expected Hank to lead him toward the outskirts of Decorah, perhaps the other side of the railroad tracks, but after some time he realized they were heading across the prairie toward Green Creek, eventually winding their way down toward the creek itself.

"You might have told me to get the buggy. Hold up a minute." Absalom leaned on a new-leafed sapling, puffing a moment, the sweat beginning to trickle beneath his three-piece suit. Water burbled unseen, the smell of mud and creek water filtering through the canopy of trees and vines.

"Like a buggy could get down here. Ain't too much further."

Sure enough, they wended through a parting of trees to a small shack set back a bit from the creek bank. Hank whistled, and a giant black hound lumbered up from the ramshackle porch, loping his way toward Hank with tongue hanging out.

"I told Dog to keep watch here. Good boy." Hank knelt to rub the dog's ears and jowls, the hound slopping the boy's face with his tongue.

Absalom watched the pair. He'd seen Dog with Hank before; in fact, he had rarely seen him without the animal. He wondered where the dog came from. There was so much of Hank's story he didn't know—though not for want of trying. How many times had he and his father tried to get Hank to . . .

"Whatcha standin' there for? Come on." Lifting his chin, Hank strode toward the hut and up the rickety steps, Dog stuck to his side like a burr.

Absalom followed, the bottle of cough syrup tight in his hand, wary where he stepped on the porch. Several boards had already rotted through or fallen out, and he nearly put his foot through another.

Inside he blinked in the dimness, the only light gleaming faintly through one paper-covered window. Two chickens clucked and pecked on the floor, the place neat enough but sparsely furnished. An old man lay on a pallet in the corner.

"Hey there, Mr. JJ." Hank's voice came soft as the spring breeze. He knelt by the pallet. "I brought you some medicine. And a friend."

Friend? Absalom's chest warmed at the word. He lowered one knee to crouch beside Hank at the beside. "Good day to you, sir. I'm Absalom Karlsson."

"James Johann. Folks call me JJ." The man coughed, his spindly frame jerking on the pallet. "Hank here shouldnta brought you. No use troublin' a fancy man over the likes of me."

"I insisted. We really should take you to a doctor." Absalom scanned the room for provisions. He couldn't see much, but a closed cupboard by the simple table might hold something.

"Don't need no doctor. Hank shoulda left well enough alone, but you know what it's like to try and talk sense into him."

Absalom grinned. "I do."

"Here." Hank took the bottle from Absalom and shoved it at JJ. "This syrup should help your cough."

"Didn't steal it, did ya, boy?" JJ's wrinkled face pulled between his balding head and gray beard.

Hank flushed. "Nope. He didn't let me."

"Then you *have* got yourself a friend." With sudden energy, JJ propped himself up on his elbow and took a swig from the bottle. "There. Feel better already." A harsh cough belied his words.

"Can I get you some provisions from town, sir?" Absalom adjusted his crouch, the dirt floor grinding into his knee. "Just tell me what you need."

"I've got enough to get by for now." The man lay back down, his voice raspy. "Got my chickens for eggs, and a mite of bread left in the cupboard. Wild plum jam too, made it myself from the trees by the creek last summer." He cracked a grin. "Live like a king, most times. 'Course, usually I do handiwork for folks as'll hire me. Haven't been able to do that here lately. But I'll be up and around." He thumbed in Hank's direction. "This young feller won't give me no peace till then."

"'Cause otherwise you won't take care of yourself." Hank looped his arm around Dog's neck.

Before they left, Absalom slipped the bill from his father—twenty dollars, the figure made him blink—under a pitcher on the table. Surely JJ could make good use of that. So much good his father did in this town, and few folks ever knew. But that was how he wanted it.

"So." Absalom slung his arm over Hank's shoulders as they trudged back toward town. "Are you ready for me to reach out to that new Lutheran orphanage up in Stanton? I've heard good things."

Hank shrugged his arm off and glared. "I told you. I'm fine how I am."

"So you say, but Hank . . ." Absalom blew out a breath. "A boy your age shouldn't be on his own. You need a home. A family."

"I got a family." Hank rested his hand on his hound's head, trotting at his side with tongue still lolling. "Dog is all I need."

Absalom sighed. "At least have something to eat with the magistrate and me when we get back. Must be nearly noontime by now."

Hank waited so long Absalom thought he'd offended him yet again. At last he snuck a grin over his shoulder. "I guess I could do that."

Absalom shook his head and chuckled, but still something rankled deep in his middle. He couldn't keep letting a ten-year-old child live on the streets. But with a boy slippery and streetwise as Hank—what were they to do?

ᴄELEVEN

S he'd never seen such a pile of straw.
Ruth stared at the golden stack, striped with sunshine from the half-open barn door. Mr. Miller and Mr. Eben had hauled more straw in their wagon, to be ready when they brought over the animals.

Specks of straw caught the sunrays as they floated in the air, like stars or fairy dust from one of Tante Amalia's stories.

But when she tried to climb the stack, the straw slid away. Ruth took a few steps at the scattered bottom, her feet slipping in the straw. So, instead of trying to climb, she flopped down on her back like making snow angels. Snow didn't prickle, but straw did.

She could see the barn swallows, tucked in their nests in the eaves like little baskets. See the cobwebs too that Tante Amalia couldn't reach with her broom. Maybe Ruth could, if she had brought a ladder in. She could do that next time before the straw-stack was all gone. She was a good helper, Tante Malia said. And Tante Malia sure needed help.

She could see her now, if she craned her neck to peek through the slice of open barn door. Tante Amalia stood over at the chicken coop letting the chickens out to scratch. Ruth helped sometimes, but she didn't like that mean rooster. That's why she had slipped into the barn this morning.

When she tried to stand up, the straw shifted beneath her feet, almost making her lose her balance. Ruth plopped onto her bottom. This was comfier anyway. She gave a little bounce, the flying straw making her giggle, then sneeze.

Instead of standing, she tumbled head over heels in the loose straw at the bottom, landing toward the back of the stack by the empty stalls in a heap of petticoat and giggles.

A dog barked. Almost in her ear.

Ruth sat up, face-to-face with a big black dog. It stared at her, pink tongue lolling out, then barked again. A rustle came from the stall she sat against. A boy staggered out of the stall, brushing straw out of his hair and yawning.

With a shriek, Ruth scrambled to her feet and dashed out of the barn.

Was that Ruthie? Amalia whirled around from latching the chicken coop. She scanned the empty yard. Had she imagined the shriek? Did she hear a bark—a dog? Lifting her skirts, she ran toward the barn. "Ruthie!" *Lord, please protect her.*

The child burst from the barn, running pell-mell.

"Tante Malia." She skidded to a stop and threw her arms around Amalia's knees. "There was a boy sleeping in our barn. With a big black dog."

"What?" Amalia loosened the child's arms and hurried for the barn, grabbing a shovel on the way. "Stay back, Ruthie."

She pushed the heavy door farther open, then peeked inside. Nothing save the empty stalls and freshly-piled strawstack. "Where?"

"Over here," Ruthie whispered loudly. She tiptoed toward the stall.

"Ruthie," Amalia hissed. "Be careful, let me—"

But Ruth stood staring into the stall as if bereft of a cherished friend.

"What is it, den lille?"

"He—he's gone."

Amalia followed to see rumpled fresh straw in the stall. No other sign of anyone having been there, but Ruthie wouldn't have made something like this up. And they hadn't put straw in the stalls yet—someone must have tried to make a bed.

The child bent and held up a small black object. "A button." She pressed it into Amalia's hand. "See?"

Amalia fingered the worn button, walking around the straw-stack to the other side, then peeking inside each empty stall. "Hallo? Hello?" She tried both languages, but nothing, just plenty of dust and old straw to make her sneeze. "We need to get the rest of these stalls cleared out." Once the pasture had grown enough, they would bring over Honey, the heifer, and the horses.

"I think he's gone. The dog would have barked otherwise." Ruthie tipped up her chin to scan the rafters.

"Good point." Amalia pulled straw stems from Ruthie's hair. "Were you playing in the strawstack?"

She wrinkled her small nose. "Maybe?"

Amalia chuckled. "Well, no one's here now. I'll ask Zelda if she knows who it could have been." Not that it sounded like Zelda much cared to know her neighbors, from what the Millers had said. But worth a try, anyway. She set the shovel back against the side of the barn and headed for the boardinghouse. She'd gotten chores finished, at least. "Perhaps we can check the garden later, see what else needs to be planted."

"I don't think Miss Zelda likes other people working in her garden."

"Well, it's not just her garden now. We live here too."

"She talks to the vegetables sometimes. I think she likes them better than people."

Amalia halted and stared down at Ruthie. "How did you learn that?"

Ruthie shrugged. "I listen."

Better than she did, apparently. Amalia gave the little girl's shoulders a squeeze, then brushed more straw from the back of her pinafore and her stockings. "Uff da. Let's get you cleaned up."

"Musta been one of them tramps from the railroad." Zelda's lips thinned and turned down even more than usual. She thwacked her knife through a sturdy rutabaga on the kitchen worktable, preparing to add it to the soup Amalia had simmering for dinner. "Lazy good-for-nothings."

"Ruthie said it was a boy." Amalia scraped chopped onion into the pot. "How big a boy was he?"

Ruth shrugged. "I don't know. Bigger'n me."

"Still coulda been a tramp. Or some runaway from one of them orphan trains."

"Orphan trains?"

"They load up youngsters from off the streets in big cities back east, ship 'em out here. Some folks adopt them, but they often come to no good, from what I've heard." Zelda sniffed in rhythm with her knife.

"What's an orphan?" Ruthie leaned on the counter, looking up at Zelda.

"A child whose parents have died."

Ruthie slipped her hands off the counter and stepped back. "Oh."

Amalia's chest pinched. She set the wooden spoon down and squeezed Ruth's shoulder as she headed to the pantry for the sourdough she'd baked yesterday. They were both orphans, now. "Well, at any rate, he was gone by the time I got there."

"You should tell the sheriff. Downright dangerous, having some stranger sleeping in our barn, none of us the wiser."

A shiver tightened Amalia's spine. She didn't want to give credence to Zelda's fearmongering. But could they be in danger? They had no man on the property, after all. If someone came after Ruthie . . . Amalia slammed down the loaf of bread on the counter, cutting off that thought.

"We'll go see the magistrate after dinner, Ruthie. I have some other questions for him anyway."

"Hurra!" Ruthie spun in a circle, her pinafore twirling, bits of leftover straw falling from her skirt. "I like Magistrate Karlsson."

Zelda shook her finger at the child. "No spinning in the kitchen. It's not safe."

Ruthie stopped short and hung her head. She sidled over to Amalia.

Amalia bit back a sharp retort. Maybe Zelda was right about safety, but . . . She smoothed her hand over the drooping part between Ruthie's braids. "We just want you to be safe, den lille." She shot Zelda a look, which the woman either didn't see or ignored. Amalia stifled a sigh. How long would they have to put up with this oppressive atmosphere in their own home? But it was Zelda's home first.

They ate a silent meal of soup and bread, then Zelda headed back to her own room. Not feeling up to following her to ask for help with the dishes today, Amalia washed them herself, Ruthie wiping the bowls and spoons. At least Zelda had helped with dinner. Small mercies.

She hung the dishrag over the side of the basin to dry, then turned to smile at Ruthie. "Ready?"

"Will we walk the whole way?" Ruth dashed for the door without waiting for an answer.

No running in the house. Amalia bit back the rebuke. She would *not* be like Zelda. "That's the only way we've got right now. But we have good strong legs, ja?"

Ruthie grinned. "Ja."

A few minutes later, they trod the rutted dirt road toward Decorah, new grass sprouting between the wagon tracks.

"Can we see Mr. Absalom again?" Ruthie skipped beside Amalia, swinging their joined hands.

"Maybe. If he's there." They'd a long walk ahead of them, with
no wagon in sight to give a lift along the way. Not that she'd have
thought two or three miles a long walk back home. But here the
May sun beat down on their shoulders, through their woolen vests
and skirts. Already a trickle of sweat dampened her collar. Soon
she and Ruth would need new summer clothes, that she could
tell—with how warm the Iowa sun already shone, their Norwegian
clothes would swelter them come July.

She ran her questions for the magistrate through her mind.
How could she bring in money? The cow and chickens helped,
as did Zelda's rutabagas, but to truly get this place up and running again as a boardinghouse—they had to have more. She still
had some from her parents' savings for the trip, along with that
of Ruthie's family, but she'd rather save that for emergencies and
for Ruthie's future. They needed more groceries soon and a few
other necessities. With Mr. Miller farming the land, they'd have
more to work with come harvest, but that still stretched months
away. They needed to get the boardinghouse up and running—
boarders remained the only way she could think of to actually
bring in regular funds. But how to do that? How to advertise, and
how to get the building in proper shape to begin with, with only
herself, Ruthie, and Zelda's occasional and reluctant hands? Her
head swam with it all.

Even Ruthie dragged her feet by the time they reached the
magistrate's home office. They pushed open the gate and walked
under the soothing shade of the trees, then up the front porch.
Half out of breath, Amalia knocked, then pressed the door open,
welcoming the jingle of the bell and the coolness inside.

Absalom Karlsson bent over the counter, talking with a stooped, older woman with graying blonde hair twisted in a fragile bun. The legal clerk glanced up at Amalia and Ruthie, a smile lighting his brown eyes behind his spectacles. "I'll be right with you."

She nodded and led Ruthie over to the waiting area.

"I'm thirsty." Ruthie plopped on a chair and fidgeted.

"We'll have to wait. Just rest here a minute." Amalia smoothed back the little girl's hair, damp with sweat. Perhaps she shouldn't have made her walk such a long way—but what else could she do? She didn't want to leave her with Zelda. The very thought heated the back of her scalp. Perhaps they did need to ask Mr. Miller to bring over their team of horses—he could still borrow them for field work easy enough, being right next door. But the pasture didn't look high enough for grazing yet. Amalia chewed her lip. So many questions, so few answers.

"Mange takk, Mr. Karlsson. You are a gift from God." The quavery voice of the old woman neared them as she hobbled to the door with Mr. Karlsson supporting her arm.

"Of course, Mrs. Nordberg. Anytime. We'll have those papers ready for you by the end of the week."

Amalia watched through the front window as the young man helped Mrs. Nordberg out the door and into her buggy. With his attention elsewhere, she had a chance to study him better. Not overly tall, nor burly-built like Eben Miller. Yet Absalom Karlsson had a quickness about him, a purpose to his step, a kindness that shone from his eyes beneath that shock of rather tumbled dark curls, in the ready smile above his cleft chin. And that kindness seemed extended to anyone around him, young or old, especially anyone who had need. Though he certainly could turn lawyerly sharp at times, as she'd seen with Zelda.

"Well, Miss Gunderson and Miss Ruthie. What a pleasant surprise." Absalom Karlsson stepped back into the building, that familiar smile lighting his face as he rubbed his hands. "How are you ladies today?"

"I'm hot." Ruth sat forward on her chair, legs dangling. "And thirsty."

"Ruthie," Amalia whispered.

"Well, let's see what we can do about that." He winked at Ruthie and crossed to the counter. Amalia hadn't noticed the pitcher there before. He filled two tin cups and carried them over, handing one to Ruth and one to Amalia. "You two walked all the way from Green Creek?"

Ruthie's face disappeared behind her cup, chugging with hands on both sides.

"Mange takk." The cup cooled Amalia's palm as the water slid down her throat like cold heaven. She drained it halfway at once, hardly realizing she'd been so parched. "I mean, thank you."

His brown eyes twinkled. "Your English is improving."

"I need to figure out how to learn faster. If only Zelda would teach me."

"Miss Zelda doesn't like us." Ruthie emerged from her cup with a long breath.

"Well, that's her loss. But I could teach you." He hesitated, hands behind his back. "Both of you. That is, if you'd like me to."

Was his neck reddening? "That's very kind." Amalia found her ears warming for some reason, or perhaps still just the heat from the walk. "But we wouldn't want to impose on you, Mr. Karlsson. I know you're very busy with your work."

"I could make time." He drew a breath. "And by the way, perhaps we're good enough friends now you could call me Absalom? Mr. Karlsson's liable to get me confused with my father." He cracked a half grin.

"If you're sure that's not disrespectful." Amalia couldn't help but smile back. "Then I suppose you must call me Amalia."

"If you insist." He clasped his hands. "But you must have had reason for walking all this way. Is anything wrong?"

"I found a boy in our barn!" Ruthie blurted the news just as

Magistrate Karlsson opened the door of his private office and stepped out.

"A boy? What's this?" The magistrate cocked bushy gray brows.

"Ruth says she found him sleeping in our barn this morning. By the time I got there, he was gone."

The magistrate frowned. "How old a boy?"

"I don't *know*." Ruthie spread her hands as if she wished grown-ups would stop asking her that. "But he had a big black dog."

The magistrate and Absalom's faces cleared as suddenly as a summer storm, in such unison Amalia nearly laughed.

"Oh, that's all right, then. Must have been Hank."

"Who's Hank?" Ruthie enunciated the strange name.

Magistrate Karlsson shook his head. "He ran away from an orphan train that came through Decorah, oh, a year or so ago now."

"Closer to two," Absalom put in.

"You could be right. Left the train with his older brother, who died of a fever when they were camped out down by the creek. We've tried to no end to get him into a proper home or orphanage somewhere, but he always refuses. He's a slippery young one."

"But a heart of gold," Absalom added. "You've nothing to fear from Hank. He has his finger on the pulse of both towns, you might say—at least, for folks on the margins or the down-and-out."

"Helps us a good deal." The magistrate sighed and leaned on his cane. "Just wish he'd let us do more than give him an occasional hot meal."

"I want to see him again," Ruthie said. "And his dog. Now I know they're not scary."

Absalom chuckled and squatted to her level. "And no doubt you will, Miss Ruth. But not till Hank wants to be seen."

"Well, that sets our minds at ease a bit. Thank you." Amalia sighed, ashamed she'd entertained Zelda's fears for even a short time. "I also have a few other questions for you, Magistrate."

"Of course, ask away. Would you like to come into my office?"

Amalia glanced at Ruthie, examining the workings of a mechanical pencil sharpener over at the counter with Absalom. "Takk, but we don't need to take that much of your time. I just wondered, does Forsberg House have any other resources? Zelda says there's no money, and she's sold nearly all the furniture. I know we need to start gathering boarders, but I'm not sure how to do that, and—"

"So you're low on funds." The magistrate's brows drew together.

"Well, ja. A bit."

"Absalom." He turned to his son. "You ever confirm what Miller told you? About the bank?"

The younger man straightened. "I did. I'm sorry, I meant to get out to Green Creek today, but Mrs. Nordberg came by about her troubles, and . . ."

"Well, then." The magistrate tipped his head toward Amalia.

"Of course." Absalom drew a breath and stepped closer. "I wanted to be sure before we told you, Miss Gunderson—Amalia. But that day I introduced you to Mr. Miller, he told me something before you and Ruthie came from the backyard. You know he's been farming the land for Mrs. Forsberg for some years for a share of the harvest, correct?"

"Ja." She nodded slowly. "But Zelda said the money was all gone."

"That's because he didn't give her the money from last year's harvest. He didn't trust her, because—well, he wanted it to go to the rightful heirs. But you and Ruth are. Amalia—you have over three hundred dollars in the bank."

Amalia clapped her hands to her mouth, then sank onto a nearby chair in a sudden onrush of tears.

Where had that come from? Avoiding the gentlemen's eyes, however kind, she dug for her handkerchief.

When she had wiped her tears, Absalom refilled her cup of water, then took Ruthie aside to show her a colorful copy of Audubon's *Birds of America* they kept for waiting clients to page through. His thoughtfulness while she regained her composure nearly made her start crying again. *What is the matter with you, Amalia?*

"I have an idea," the magistrate spoke softly. "Since you are here now, let's get the horse and buggy and go to the bank. I believe he put the money in an account for the boardinghouse since he didn't know your name. You can open an account yourself or put your name on that account. If Absalom and I are there to vouch for you, there shouldn't be a problem."

"But, but . . ." Amalia glanced down at her clothing.

"You look fine. Good idea to get this taken care of."

While she agreed with that, she felt like a rug was being pulled out from under her feet. Money . . . she'd be able to get the boardinghouse open more quickly. "All right, and takk for the information."

Within minutes, Absalom drove the horse and buggy up to the gate and helped them all into the shaded buggy.

"You ready to go for a ride?" he asked. Ruth was bouncing on the seat.

"Ja." Her grin was bright as the sun.

The four of them entered the coolness of the brick building and paused to look around.

"Magistrate, what brings you out today?" A man wearing a dark three-piece suit with a white shirt strode out of a glass-walled office, hand extended. He shook hands with both the magistrate and Absalom and tipped his head to Amalia.

"I brought you a new customer. These two lovely ladies, Amalia Gunderson and her ward, Ruth Forsberg, are the owners of the boardinghouse in Green Creek. They recently arrived from Norway."

"I'm sure there is a story here. Come sit down in my office." He asked one of the tellers to bring more chairs and motioned for them to follow him. With everyone seated, he took his chair and leaned forward with his arms on the desk. "Now, let the story begin."

Amalia tried to follow the tale Magistrate Karlsson told, wishing she had a better grasp of English.

"So, we need to either get the proper names on that account or open a new one." When the magistrate finished, the banker nodded.

"That we do." He pulled out a desk drawer and brought out some papers. Nodding at Amalia, he spoke in Norwegian.

Relief doused Amalia, feeling the smile crease both her face and her heart. "Takk." She answered all his questions, and he filled in the forms, then turned the paper around and, with the pen, pointed to a line for her to sign. He did the same with three other pages and tapped the edges on the desk.

"Now, would you like to take some cash with you today? Keep in mind that you can open accounts at the store in Green Creek and anywhere else you need. I don't recommend keeping much cash in the house."

Amalia nodded, laying a hand on Ruth's shoulder. "Tusen takk." She would just take enough now to help with some big purchases at the store.

"Stop at the teller's window on your way out to pick it up." He stood and walked them to the door. "Takk." He shook the men's hands. "Good to see you."

"Well, that was easy," Absalom said after he helped the others into the buggy and got in himself. "Now we'll get you home, unless you want to stop at ours."

The magistrate shrugged and nodded. "That might be best. Remember, I have a meeting at three."

Absalom nodded and stopped the buggy at the gate to their house. He helped his father mount the porch stairs and grinned at Ruth when he returned. "Next stop, the boardinghouse."

Amalia fingered the coins in her handbag. She needed to thank Mr. Miller—what foresight he'd had. Now all she had to do was get the boardinghouse ready for guests.

Twelve

Who can that be?

Amalia set her bucket of soapy water down to answer the knock at the front door. She opened the door to find a man with his hat in his hands standing on the porch. "Ja, how can I help you?"

"I heard you take in boarders."

"Ah, we will be, but we are not open yet." She began to close the door but hesitated.

"When?"

"Ah . . ." *Think, Amalia.* "Perhaps two weeks?" How were they going to do that? Even with the newfound money in the bank? In a burst of honesty, she added, "We need beds."

"Sleeping on the floor'd be fine. Used to that. A roof and four walls, with breakfast and supper'd be plenty." He studied his hat before looking back at her. "I work for the railroad, I'm a signalman. Be gone for a week. Don't have much but . . . be good to still have it when I get back."

"Are you always gone for a week?"

He nodded.

"What is your name?"

"Amos."

129

She waited then realized he wasn't going to say more. "Well, Mr. Amos, I will have a room for you when you return." She hoped she'd gotten all the English words in the right order. Mrs. Miller had been helping her and Ruthie practice, and Absalom said he would, too, though he hadn't come yet.

The man looked down at the bag at his feet. "Can I leave this here?"

She noticed a couple of fingers missing on his right hand. "Where will you sleep tonight?"

"Barn is good."

Oh, Lord above. What am I to do? Where was he last night? Questions pounded in her head. "Where have you been staying?"

"In Decorah."

"What brought you to Green Creek?"

"Mr. Karlsson said you opening a boardinghouse."

"So you know him?"

He nodded.

Was he hiding information or just a man of few words? Very few. Mr. Karlsson would not send someone to her if he were dangerous. Relief dropped her shoulders and let her breathe deep again. "Do you have somewhere else you need to be today?"

"No, ma'am."

"Would you be willing to help out here? We need to start cleaning the barn." Was that a flicker of a smile she caught in his dark-eyed gaze? He certainly looked like an honest man, but then who was she to judge? *Lord, if this isn't right, please stop me right now.*

Amos nodded.

Amalia smiled at him. Perhaps this quiet man came as another sign of God's provision. First the news about the money, then a boarder on their doorstep.

A scream came from the back yard. *Ruthie!*

Amalia spun around, tore through the house, and out the back door. "Ruthie!"

She was hiding behind a boy waving a big stick at the retreating rooster in the yard.

"What happened?"

"The r-rooster." Ruthie ran to Amalia and threw her arms around her waist. "H-he f-flew at m-me."

"He din't get her." The boy threw down his stick.

Amos plowed to a stop after running around the house. "She hurt?"

"Nei. Just frightened."

"Ya got ta carry a stick when that bird is around."

Amalia stared at the raggedy boy and big, black dog. "Who, how . . . ?"

"Was sleepin' in the barn when she screamed. Dog scared him off."

Amalia kissed the top of Ruth's head and mopped her tears with the corner of her apron.

"'Member the boy was sleeping on the straw last week?" Ruth sniffed as she looked up to Amalia. She turned back to the boy. "Then you were gone."

"Um . . ." He stared down at his dirty bare feet. "I shoulda asked. But that other lady told me to get outta here." The dog sat down, long pink tongue lolling out the side of his muzzle.

Zelda. "When was that?"

"Before the snow."

Before we came. How could she be so cruel? And why hadn't Zelda mentioned this when they talked about the boy before? Amalia blew out a breath. "So you are Hank?"

"Yep. Mr. Karlsson tole me to talk to you, but . . ." He shrugged.

Mr. Karlsson seemed to know all kinds of people. "Do you mean the magistrate or his son?"

"Both. They're together." He picked up the basket from the ground and handed it to Ruth. "Now watch out for that rooster."

Ruth looked around. "Don't see him."

"He's out scratching on the old manure pile. Chickens like bugs and worms an' such."

"What's his name?" She pointed at the dog.

"Dog."

"That's all?" Her face gave away what she was thinking.

"Ya want ta pet him?"

"He won't bite?"

"Nah, not 'less I tell him to."

Ruth looked up at Amalia, who shrugged and nodded. The little girl stood in front of the sitting dog whose feathery black tail brushed back and forth.

"Hold out your hand palm down so he can sniff you." Hank showed her how. "Then scratch behind his ears."

Ruth did as he said and giggled. "He tickles." Dog sniffed her hand and up her arm, then gave her a lick. "Good dog." He tipped his head forward to make the scratching easier for her.

"He likes you."

Amalia found herself blinking and sniffed. Ruthie glowed she was so happy. "All right, I have an idea." She paused to sort the words out in her mind. "This is Amos, and he will start cleaning the barn. Hank, would you please help him? Then you can stay here. Supper will be about six." She drew a breath. Giving directions in English made her brain ache. "Ruth, you gather the eggs and bring the basket into the house. Then you can help me finish scrubbing the top floor. Amos, you can stay on the second floor, if you don't mind not having a bed. After supper, we can all work in the garden till dark." Amalia glanced around. Everyone nodded and headed for their assigned tasks. She let out a breath and rubbed her temples. Well, her words must have worked. *Uff da.*

Amalia returned to the house and brought her pail back into the kitchen for hot water. Pail and broom in hand, she started up the stairs. Where was Zelda? She stepped back and rapped on the closed door. "Zelda?" She heard rustling inside and the door opened a crack.

"What?"

"Could you please come up to the third floor and help me scrub the rest of the floor? We have to get this place cleaned up. We already have one boarder."

"Can't have a boarder, there's no beds."

You made sure of that. Amalia bit back the words. "He said he was glad to sleep on the floor for now. He works for the railroad, so he will leave early in the morning and be gone for a week."

"Getting the garden in is more important than cleaning."

"We'll have more help with the garden after supper. Amos, our new boarder, and Hank are cleaning the barn now."

"Who's Hank?"

"The boy Ruth found in the barn the other day." *The one you chased off before winter.* "They will both be here for supper."

Zelda's head wagged side to side. "What you goin' to feed them?"

"Whatever we are having. I thought corn bread to go with the beans."

Zelda rolled her eyes. She heaved a sigh, stepped out, and closed the door behind her.

Suppertime was nearing when the three finished cleaning the third floor. They left the window at either end open to blow out the musty smell. Who knew when they would need the space, but Amalia felt much better about bringing in boarders to a clean house.

"When they were running this as a boardinghouse, what did they use the open third floor for?" Amalia asked Zelda.

"Mostly men passin' through, could bed folks down like a bunkhouse. A family with a passel of children rented the whole thing for a month or more."

"Why did Else stop taking in boarders?"

"Her health just kept declining after her husband passed away. She asked me to come help."

But Zelda hadn't been much help, by the look of things. "She died more than a year ago." Amalia was trying to figure out the family story of this place. At one time it must have been highly prosperous, both the farming and the boardinghouse.

"Else said I could stay here." Zelda clipped the words.

"You can, but legally this land now belongs to Ruth, and I am her guardian until she turns twenty-one." Amalia paused. Say more or leave it here? "As I said before, it is your choice. But should you decide to stay, you know what all needs to be done both to get ready and to provide a home for other people. I would be grateful for your advice and help. But most of all . . ." She felt her eyes narrow. "I appreciate you have been less harsh with Ruth lately and trust that will continue." She wanted to say more but swallowed the words.

Zelda met her gaze briefly. "She's a good girl."

Amalia felt her brows raise. "That she is."

On her way through the kitchen, Amalia stopped to put wood in the stove. She could hear Ruth laughing out on the back porch. Dog barked once.

"Ya have ta throw it harder." Hank.

How could she get him to clean up? She wondered if he had other clothes to change into while she washed his? He planned to sleep in the barn. Fine for now, but what about winter? Amalia heaved a sigh and settled the lids back in place. She checked the vents and stirred the pot of bean soup warming near the reservoir.

Outside, she watched Ruthie throw a stick for Dog. He brought it back and dropped it at her feet. What a delight to see her having a good time. *Thank you, Lord.*

A "hallo" came from the property fence, and Amalia shaded her eyes to see Mrs. Miller standing behind it, waving with one arm, the other holding something to her bosom. Amalia smiled and crossed the yard to their neighbor—so quickly becoming their friend. Ruthie dropped the stick and ran after Amalia, Dog running back to Hank's whistle.

"What good timing. I've been wanting to talk to you." Amalia laid her hands on the rough, sun-warmed wood of the fence.

"And I thought this little one might be big enough to come for a quick visit." Mrs. Miller lowered the squirming black-and-white kitten to Ruthie's eager arms.

"This is the one Mr. Eben said I could have when she's old enough." Ruthie snuggled the kitten against her chest. "I better keep her away from Dog, though."

"Dog?" Mrs. Miller looked across to where both Hank and Amos were digging and raking in the garden, Dog galumphing about. Zelda was nowhere to be seen. "Ah. I see you've met Hank."

"They must have finished in the barn."

"Who is the man?"

"Our new boarder."

Mrs. Miller raised her brows. "You have had a busy day."

Amalia sighed and chuckled, suddenly feeling tired. "Ja."

"But you had something to say. How can I help you?"

"First, I wanted to thank you, or rather, Mr. Miller. I found out about the money he put aside in the bank."

"You didn't know before?" The older woman's eyes widened. "Oh my dear! We should have said something to you. He told Mr. Karlsson . . ."

"Ja, I know. Anyway, we opened an account today. Please tell him mange takk—it takes such a load off my mind."

"Of course it does." Mrs. Miller shook her head. "Goodness."

"Also, now that we have funds, when might you be going to the store?"

"I can go day after tomorrow if need be. Your cupboards pretty bare?"

Amalia nodded.

"The men and teams are out planting, but we have an old mule and a trap, so we can go anytime."

"Ruth too?"

"Of course. To Nygards' in Green Creek or into Decorah?"

"Does Nygards' have oats for the chickens?"

Mrs. Miller nodded.

"Do they trade for eggs?" Despite their newfound security with the bank account, she still wanted to be careful.

"I believe they might. And if you need to start an account on credit, they will do that too."

"That's what the magistrate said."

"They know the family and the farm and Zelda. And now Hans and Tilda will get to know you and Ruth. They have owned that store for a long time." She brushed back a strand of graying hair. "I think his father started the store soon after they moved here, so Hans grew up in the store."

"That sounds good." Amalia drew a breath. "I'd better go check on Hank and Amos."

"Looks like you don't need to." Mrs. Miller nodded behind her, and Amalia turned to see.

Hank approached, stopping a ways back and keeping hold of Dog when he saw the kitten.

"You finished the barn?"

He nodded. "Spread straw in the stalls. Thought Dog and me could sleep in the horse stall?"

"If you want."

"You met JJ yet?"

She shook her head. "Not heard of him."

"Lives by the creek." Hank nodded to the north. "He builds things."

"You'll have to tell me more. Why don't you and Amos wash up for supper."

Hank nodded. "Evenin', Miz Miller. Come, Dog."

Amalia turned back to her friend as the boy and hound trotted toward the boardinghouse. "Everyone seems to know Hank around here."

"Only folks he allows to." Mrs. Miller shook her head. "He seems to have taken a liking to you. I'm glad. He needs—someone."

"Well, I'd best go get supper on the table and let you do the same. Ruthie, time to say good-bye to the kitten."

"She's ready to go back to her mama. Have you ever had a cat before?" Mrs. Miller leaned forward to take the mewling kitten from Ruthie.

Ruth shook her head. "Not mine. The one we had lived outside." She stroked the black-and-white fur once more. "So soft."

"I'll see you all Thursday for the mercantile, then."

After Mrs. Miller left, Ruth slipped her hand in Amalia's. "Takk for letting me get a kitten."

Amalia squeezed her hand. "Of course, den lille." Heading back toward the house, she looked out over the land lit with the golden glow of evening, marveling again how different the flat fields were from Norway. No mountains in sight, the slightly rolling hills more like swells, green leafing trees following Green Creek, aptly named.

Ruthie gave a little skip. "The kitten can live in our house when she comes, can't she?"

"Ja, she is yours and can be in the house." Amalia could only be prepared to go toe to toe with Zelda.

"And sleep with me?"

Uff da, what am I getting myself into?

Thirteen

"Tante Malia, my tooth fell out!"

Eyes and mouth wide, Ruthie felt the gap with her tongue at the end of supper that evening.

"So it did." Amalia leaned forward. "Where is it?"

"I don't know." Ruthie waggled her head and stuck her finger in her mouth. "I just took a bite of biscuit and I felt it pop out."

"Check in the biscuit." Amos, who'd hardly said a word through the meal, cleared his throat. "Mighta got stuck in there."

Ruthie grabbed up her half-eaten biscuit and examined it, then triumphantly pulled out the small white tooth and held it up. "I found it! Thank you, Mr. Amos."

He dipped his head and returned to cleaning his own plate.

"Your very first lost tooth." Amalia ran her hand over the little girl's head and bent close to examine the tiny incisor in Ruthie's palm. "I know it's been loose for a while—you've been very patient waiting for it to come out."

Zelda pushed back her chair and left the table.

Amalia fought to keep a smile on her face for Ruthie's sake. What, Zelda couldn't stand a little celebration over a child losing her first tooth? What was the matter with that woman, anyway, that she shunned any hint of joy or love?

"What do I do with it now?" Ruthie lifted her eyes to Amalia's.

"My brother used ta say, you put a lost tooth under your pillow. Then the tooth fairy comes an' takes it away, leaves money or somethin' instead." Hank shrugged his thin shoulders and reached for the last biscuit in the basket. "'Course, I didn't believe that."

Amalia hid a smile.

"Should I put it under my pillow?" Ruthie clutched her fingers around the tooth.

"Here." Zelda reappeared with a small glass of water and held it out to Ruthie. "Put it in here, safer than under your pillow. In Norway, you leave it on your nightstand, and they say that the Tannfe comes for your tooth."

"Tannfe?"

Zelda lifted her shoulders. "Tannfe, tooth fairy. Same idea."

Ruthie looked up at Zelda for a moment, then reached and took the glass of water, plopping her tooth inside with a plink. "Thank you, Miss Zelda."

Zelda grunted. "Might as well call me Cousin Zelda. That's what I am to you, after all—your great-onkel Amund was my first cousin."

Amalia rose to clear the plates, managing to keep from staring open-mouthed at Zelda. So the woman was capable of doing something kind. *Lord, am I seeing a miracle here?*

When she tucked Ruthie into bed that night, Ruthie craned her neck to see the glass of water on the floorboards nearby.

"Will the Tannfe see it, even though I don't have a nightstand?"

Amalia kissed her forehead. "I wouldn't worry."

Ruthie trailed her finger down Amalia's sleeve. "I wish I could show Mor my tooth."

Amalia's chest tightened. Of course she did. "I wish you could too, *den lille.*"

Ruthie lay quiet a moment, her eyes blinking pensively in the wavering light from the lamp Amalia had carried upstairs, then rolled over on her side, her breathing quickly turning slow and even with sleep.

Amalia smoothed the quilt over the little girl, the night still cool despite the warming days, then rose and carried the lamp over to their trunk. She set the lamp carefully on the floor, then lifted the lid. Inside she shifted aside the legal papers to dig out her pouch of coins from underneath. She selected one, then closed the trunk lid and crept to Ruthie's pallet. Slipping her fingers into the glass of water, she pulled out the tooth and slid the coin into its place.

But Ruthie woke sobbing in the night.

Roused from deep sleep by the mournful cries, Amalia dragged herself off her pallet, head groggy. Kneeling by the little girl's bed, she pulled Ruthie into her arms, the child's nightgown damp with sweat.

"Mor . . . Mor . . ." Ruthie's arms clung to Amalia's neck, the panicked whimpers tightening her own throat with tears.

"Ssh, den lille. Malia's here," she whispered into Ruthie's tangled hair, smoothing her hand over the small quivering back. Passing this first life milestone without her parents must have wakened the grieving afresh.

Slowly the gasping sobs subsided into hiccups, and Ruthie nestled down into Amalia's arms, never fully rousing. Amalia rocked her till the child's breathing evened and deepened, then laid her back on the pallet and drew the quilts over her, including the newer quilt Mrs. Miller had given them. Shivering in the chilly night air, Amalia slipped back under her own covers, tugging them up to her chin till her limbs warmed and relaxed. In the quiet darkness once more, tears slipped from her own eyes and slid toward her ears. She swiped them away.

Most of the time she was too busy to grieve for her parents. Always so much to do, so little time. But now, freshened by Ruthie's tears—the ache in her heart gaped as wide as the ocean that had received Mor and Far's precious bodies. She hadn't received a letter back from Norway yet, after writing home with the news. *Heavenly*

Father. She closed her eyes and shook with a muffled sob. *It hurts. I know you're taking care of us . . . you have, in so many ways. But still it hurts.*

The quiet tears fell for some time, wetting her pillow till comfort eased around her like invisible arms in the darkness. And then, as she fell back to sleep, a thought came, gentle like an offered hand.

I should ask Magistrate Karlsson how to find my brother.

The next morning, her tears seemingly forgotten, Ruthie proudly set their basket of gathered eggs on the table. "Cousin Zelda, the rooster didn't even try to bite me today. Hank showed me how to scare him off."

"Hmmph." Zelda, sipping her coffee on a chair near the stove, gave a scant nod.

"And I found a coin in that glass of water you gave me." Ruthie skipped around the table.

Thank the Lord for the resilience of children. Amalia washed her hands at the sink and tied on her kitchen apron. "Hank, would you fill the woodbox, please?"

"Sure. C'mon, Dog." Hank got up from tugging at a bone with his hound on the floor and slapped his thigh.

Zelda shifted her knees and held her skirt away as Hank and Dog passed her on their way out the back door. "Filthy animal."

Amalia bit back a sigh. Zelda missed no chance to parade her distaste for Hank and his dog. She insisted they should focus on gathering "paying boarders," though giving little idea how they were supposed to do that. Amalia slapped a bit of bacon grease in a pan and moved it to the hot part of the stove. "Ruthie, bring me the eggs, please."

Ruthie skipped off.

Hank tramped back in and dropped an armload of wood in the box by the stove. "Amos is out there choppin' enough wood for a snowstorm."

"Is he? Bless him." Amalia hadn't seen the older man when they'd been out feeding the chickens and thought he might have already left on the train. By the time they set the plates on the table, Amos came in the back door, carefully wiping his boots on the mat Amalia had added.

"Mange t—I mean, thank you for chopping wood." Amalia smiled at him and indicated a chair at the table. "We are ready to eat." She sat in her own chair and scanned the faces gathered round—Ruthie, Zelda, Hank, and now Amos. All new to her within these last few months, yet now among them she belonged—though only Ruthie felt like family. Yet.

Zelda reached for the biscuits, cutting off Amalia's thoughts.

"Shall we say grace?" Amalia kept her tone gentle but with a firm undercurrent.

Zelda pulled back her hand with only a slight eye roll. Ruthie reached for Amalia's hand and squeezed her eyes so tight her face scrunched. "I Jesu navn, går vi til bords, og spiser, drikker på ditt ord . . ."

Hank stared at them once the grace finished. "What's that mean?"

"It's a table grace we always say in Norway." Passing the biscuits to the children first, Amalia wracked her brain for the translation. "It's something like, 'In Jesus's name to the table we go, to eat and drink according to His Word. . . .'"

Amos nodded. "That's right nice."

Amalia's chest warmed. Good to have someone say something positive at the table, even if his words came few. Meanwhile, Hank and Ruthie enlivened the breakfast with their chatter. Seeing Ruthie's gap-toothed laugh at Hank's colorful stories made Amalia smile.

"Do you need any help in the garden today?" she asked Zelda. The garden so far remained the one place Zelda seemed to thrive, as the plants did under her hands. But the additional plot the

Millers had plowed up recently to expand the garden still lay bare, the turned earth unplanted. They'd need many more rows to feed their growing household this year—not to mention more coming boarders, Lord willing.

"Thought you were going to the store. We need more food."

"That's tomorrow."

"Well, the rows need weeding. And more planting." Zelda wiped her mouth. "But I've got an errand to run today."

"Oh?" Amalia stared, pausing her knife mid-buttered-biscuit. She'd barely seen Zelda leave the property since they arrived. "How? I mean, since we don't have the horses yet?"

"I've hired someone to drive me," the woman snapped. "Not that it's any of your business."

"Of course. I'm sorry." Amalia's ears stung as if slapped. But how did Zelda have funds to hire a driver? She made herself smile at the children. "We can look at the garden together later, then. We also need to order more seeds."

"Mind you don't go messing up my plants." Zelda rose from the table, leaving her plate dirty on the table.

With nary a by-your-leave. Amalia's tongue hurt from biting it. At least Zelda hadn't snapped at Ruthie. Deciding to let it go for today, since the woman would be out of the house anyway, she tackled the pile of dishes. Ruthie and Hank wiped them, then they all headed outside in time to see Zelda drive away in a rickety wagon driven by an older boy Amalia didn't recognize. Must be from one of the other neighboring farms.

"Now we can run and jump all we want." Ruthie took a flying leap off the porch steps and ran in a circle, giggling. Hank followed suit, then gamboled around the yard neighing like a pony, bringing shouts of laughter from Ruth.

Amalia chuckled, her own chest lighter to have Zelda off their property, if only for a few hours. "Let's go take a look at that garden."

---❖---

"I'm off to Green Creek shortly." Absalom gathered a stack of envelopes ready to mail on his way, various documents from cases currently under their care.

"To see Miss Gunderson and Ruth again, I take it?" His father paused on his way to the front door, headed to a city council meeting.

"Yes. You know I offered to help them with English." Absalom tried to speak naturally, though heat insisted on creeping up the back of his neck.

"Uh-hmm." His father eyed him. "No other reason, of course."

"Meaning what?"

His father chuckled and waved his hand. "Nothing, nothing. Forgive me, son. I'm just glad to see you taking some interest in a young woman, after . . ." He paused, sobered.

Now the heat sprinted to his ears. He pushed his spectacles up his nose. "Father, I've only honorable intentions toward Miss Gunderson. We are friends at most, nothing more."

"I know that. Do you think I don't know that?" He laid a hand on Absalom's shoulder, then backed toward the front door, hands lifted. "Holding my tongue now. I'm gone."

The door shut, and Absalom blew out a breath, then shook his head, trying to clear it. Here he'd been keeping focused on his goal, helping newly arrived immigrant clients as he did every day, keeping things professional—and his father had to go and get him all muddled in the head.

As if you aren't already whenever you think of her? He caught himself before tucking his ink blotter into his coat pocket instead of the letters. Giving himself a shake, he closed his eyes, trying to shut the image of Amalia and her golden crown of braids from his mind.

Blast it. His father was right.

The sunshine and spring wind cleared his head on the drive to

Green Creek, after stopping by the post office to mail his letters. He pulled up at the boardinghouse late in the morning, wondering if he should have waited till after the noon hour. He didn't want Miss Gunderson—Amalia—to feel the need to feed him. His stomach rumbled as if reading his mind.

He let Maybelle have a drink from the handy watering trough, then set the buggy brake and climbed down.

Just an hour or so. He'd see how they were, if they still wanted him to help them with English—he realized now he should have set a scheduled time. *Regardless, keep it pleasant, keep it professional.*

Keep his troublesome heart out of it.

He found Amalia and Ruth in the expanding garden patch behind the boardinghouse, kneeling in the dark rows of loosened loam behind the original garden, now a patch of sprouting green seedlings. They bent their golden heads over trowels and bags of seed, along with a brown-haired boy with familiar raggedy sleeves and too-small overalls.

"Hank!" The exclamation came out in a joyful burst.

All three gardeners jerked their heads up to stare.

"Mr. Absalom." Ruthie jumped to her feet and ran to give him a grubby-handed hug.

Hank sat back on his bare heels and nodded at him laconically. "Morning, Mr. Karlsson."

"I didn't know I'd find you here." Absalom patted Ruthie's head, then approached the garden.

"Hank is staying with us now." Amalia rose with a smile, wiping her hands on her apron. She pushed back a loose strand of hair from her braided crown with one wrist. "He's been such a help."

"That's wonderful." Absalom glanced between them, trying to assess the situation. He'd known about Hank sleeping in the barn, but actually staying here? "Since when do you condescend to staying in one place, young sir?"

145

Hank shrugged one shoulder, making his overall strap slip down. "They need help."

"Ja, indeed we do." Amalia fixed his overall strap. "What can we do for you, Mr. Karlsson?"

"I thought to offer you an English lesson." Absalom clasped his hands behind his back, feeling suddenly superfluous. "But judging from what I hear, Hank has that well in hand. And it doesn't look to be the best time."

"The more the merrier—isn't that what you say?" Amalia smiled, lighting her eyes as the bright sun lit her crown of braids, catching the loose strands with touches of gold. "You are most welcome to join us. It's a lovely day, ja?"

"And Cousin Zelda's gone." Ruthie shaded her eyes against the late morning sun to peer up at him. "So you don't gotta worry about her. Even if she's been a little nicer since I lost my tooth. See?"

"I see." Absalom smiled down at the little girl. "But Zelda's gone?"

"Just on some errand of her own." Amalia rubbed her gritty hands together. "I'm afraid we're a bit dirty for a proper lesson just now."

"Have it out in the garden." Hank dug his bare toes in the dirt. "Kill two birds with one stone."

"Kill birds?" Ruthie's eyes widened.

"That's just an English expression." Absalom shook his head. "It means to do two things at once—no killing involved."

"Uff da." Amalia shook her head. "We do have a lot to learn. But I suppose the best way to learn is by doing, ja?"

Absalom caught her eyes with his own, feeling like he could dance in their blue-gray depths. "Ja." His voice croaked, and he cleared his throat and made himself grin. "Or perhaps I should say, 'yes.'"

Soon he found himself kneeling in the dirt, on a rag Amalia had fetched to protect his city-pressed trousers from the worst of the soil. He dug with a trowel where Ruthie showed him, then helped push the seeds into the cool, moist earth—tiny carrot seeds, plump beans, wrinkled peas.

"I need to ask Mrs. Miller if she has any—how do you say it? Settepoteter."

"Seed potatoes, I believe. Though I'm no farmer." Still, the soil and sunshine soaked into his soul like water into parched ground. "If the Millers don't have any extra, she'd probably take you to the store for them."

"She's taking us tomorrow, actually. They've all been so kind." Amalia hesitated. "Sometimes, I think Eben Miller is a bit too kind."

"Oh?"

"Oh, nothing improper. I just sometimes think he hopes—never mind." Amalia's cheeks pinked, and she ducked her head to reach for another bag of seed.

Absalom returned to covering bean seeds and telling Ruthie the English names for all the vegetables, trying to calm the sudden thudding of his heart. Was Eben Miller interested in Amalia? Well, why shouldn't he be? She was a lovely, capable young woman in need of stability and protection. He hardly knew the man, but he seemed a kind, decent fellow, certainly an eligible young bachelor and from a successful farming family. Their farms even adjoined. A match made in heaven, many might say. Absalom's chest leadened. What a stupid fool he was to dare to think of . . .

"How do you say this in English?" Ruthie held up a wriggling worm between her fingers.

Absalom chuckled. "That's an earthworm."

"Earthworm." Ruthie placed it carefully back in the soil. "My far said they are good for the ground."

"So they are." Amalia drew a breath, seeming as grateful as he for the change in subject. "They turn the earth and loosen it and make it better for the plants to grow."

"My pa told me that too." Hank leaped over two rows to grab a shovel.

Absalom looked up. He'd never heard the boy mention his parents before, not naturally in conversation like this. "Was he a farmer too?" He kept his tone careful.

"Nope." The boy dug his spade into a section of earth that hadn't been fully loosened, the wall closing back over his face and past once more.

He shouldn't have pressed. Absalom shifted his jaw and handed Ruthie a fistful of beans.

"I'm hungry," Ruth announced half an hour later, sitting back on her haunches, her small face pink with sun and smudged with dirt from chin to forehead.

"You're right, it's the dinner hour." Amalia craned her head to look at the sun. "Will you eat with us, Mr. Karlsson?"

"Absalom, remember?" He stood and brushed dirt from his hands and thighs. "And I don't want to intrude on you."

"Nonsense. We'd love to have you, wouldn't we, children?"

Ruthie jumped up and down, while Hank gave a half grin. "They like feedin' people, Mr. Karlsson."

"Then I suppose I must oblige."

They filed into the boardinghouse to wash up, then Absalom prevailed upon Amalia to let him cut bread while she heated left-over soup.

"We'll dine simply, but there's plenty." She reached to lift a stack of bowls from the cupboard.

"Are you better off for food, then, now?"

"Much better, thanks to the chickens and the Millers—they share milk from their cows since ours hasn't calved yet. And Zelda is surprisingly adept in the garden, though of course we can't harvest much yet. But she planted rutabagas last fall, and they've been helping keep us fed. Did you know rutabagas can even be mashed and mixed in bread and cakes like applesauce, not to mention baked, fried, and stewed?"

He'd seldom heard her talk so much, though still a mingle of Norwegian and English. "I did not."

"Then of course there's the money in the bank now, thanks again to Mr. Miller. Though I don't want to use that more than we have to. What you helped us withdraw the other day should be enough to get us started on preparing the boardinghouse." She stirred the soup. "I want to speak to your father more sometime, get his advice on how to manage the money, and this property. Did you know we already have a boarder?"

"Really?" A lot sure had happened since he'd been here last.

"Well, almost. A man named Amos, he works on the railroad. He doesn't say much but seems to have a good heart. He stayed in the barn last night but will be back in a week." She winced. "I may have promised him a bed by then. Uff da, how am I going to do all this?"

"I see. Well, what needs to come first?" Absalom leaned on the counter, the bread now sliced.

She tapped her finger on her chin. "Well, more furniture for a start. We can't have boarders without beds to put them in."

"True."

"Hank told us a friend of his could make things. I still need to ask him how to find this friend. He was rather vague."

Could it be JJ? How was the old man? Absalom held his tongue, listening.

"Both porches need to be mended, not to mention the whole boardinghouse painted. We need a big dining table and chairs and parlor furniture, so people can be comfortable here. Plus a butter churn and more laundry kettles and . . ." She sucked in a breath. "It all makes me rather dizzy."

"One step at a time. Just tell us how we can help."

"Mange takk." She met his eyes. "You and your father have already helped us so much. Now that I have some money, I need to get quite a bit at the"—she stumbled over the word—"mercantile." She hesitated. "Thank you again for helping me at the bank the other day, you and your father. I wouldn't have known where to begin."

"Of course. I'm so glad you have that to fall back on now, though you've certainly managed well without it." He thought of her sudden tears when they'd given her the news—he'd never seen her cry before—and her flushed chagrin when she regained her composure. Had all the strain of the recent months just come suddenly flooding to the surface? His throat tightened. "By the way, I've been meaning to ask. Do you need more help at the boardinghouse, especially if you get more boarders? Mr. Jorstad, one of my immigrant clients, had asked if I knew anywhere his oldest daughter could work. She's young, but might be a good help with cleaning, maybe watching the children."

"Oh." Amalia nibbled her lower lip. "I—I don't think I should take on hiring someone right now. Not till we're more financially stable. But mange takk for asking."

"Of course."

She turned back to the soup, the bubbling mixture scenting the air with onion and thyme, and Absalom traced the contours of her profile with his gaze—her delicate nose, cheeks still rosy from the sun outside, a smudge of dirt on her forehead where she'd passed her wrist. Wisps of hair escaping her braids that he longed to smooth back, then brush his thumb over her cheekbone . . .

He shifted his gaze away, pulse thundering. *Hold it together, Absalom. She's not yours to claim.*

"There is another thing I want to ask your father, but maybe you would know something too." She set the wooden soup spoon aside and reached for a stack of bowls.

He drew a breath. "Ask away." At least his voice sounded fairly steady.

She turned to face him again. "It's about min bror—my brother."

"You have a brother? Why didn't—"

"He come with us?" The side of her mouth tipped as she ladled steaming soup into the bowls. "Because he's already here. At least, I think he is."

"In America?"

"Ja. He left Norway three years ago—to scout out the land, you might say, find a place for our family here. But once he arrived in New York, we never heard from him again. Mor, Far, and I finally came ourselves, hoping to find him." Her voice dropped at the end.

"And now they are gone too." His chest squeezed. How alone this young woman stood in the world. Yet not truly alone, he reminded himself. She had Ruthie and Zelda—small comfort though the latter might be. And now Hank. And Absalom . . . if she'd let him. *Don't get ahead of yourself.* "So you have no idea where he might be?"

She pursed her lips and sighed. "We had talked about Ohio, or Minnesota. But America is big . . . I don't know where to start."

"What is your brother's name?" He pulled out the small pad of paper and pencil he kept in his vest pocket.

"Erik Gunderson. Erik Hamre Gunderson, since I expect there are very many Erik Gundersons in America. If that helps at all."

"It does." He slipped the paper and pencil back. "I'll ask my father. He has connections with the Norwegian communities in Iowa, and some might have ties with those in other states. It's worth a try."

"Mange takk." She swiped below one of her eyes. "Sorry."

"You have nothing to be sorry for." He reached out, wanting to take her hand, but stopped himself, his fingers barely brushing her blouse sleeve before he lowered his arm. "You have borne so much, and so bravely."

She blinked, sniffed, and smiled. "At least I have not been alone."

Had she read his thoughts from earlier? "Amalia, I—"

151

With a stampede of running feet, the children burst into the kitchen. "Is dinner ready?"

"Ja, that it is." Amalia lifted the bowls. "Ruthie, set out the spoons please."

Absalom swallowed hard, breathing in through his nose till the thumping of his heart slowed. It was too soon, for—for anything. He would be her friend and advocate, nothing more. It's all he'd the right to.

Absalom smiled at the children, pulled out his chair, and sat down to his bowl of soup.

FOURTEEN

You want to add anything to my list?"

Zelda shook her head, then paused. "More seed potatoes. Planted all we have."

"Anything else?"

"Salt."

"On the list. Sugar too. Where do you usually get honey?"

"In Decorah." Zelda kneaded the mound of dough in front of her. Push, turn, fold, and push again. A universal rhythm.

"Perhaps we can have fried bread for dinner. We'll be back by then."

No answer.

Amalia hung her apron on the hook behind the stove. "Hank and Ruth are both going with me." She thought that might please the other woman, but stone-faced was the best description for her.

Stepping out on the porch, she paused to listen to the meadowlark calling from the fields. Other birds sang in the trees by the house. The apple, pear, and plum trees were finished blooming, not that she'd known which was which. Zelda was not forthcoming with information. Small green cherries already formed on the cherry tree, though.

"We're ready to go, Mrs. Miller is almost here."

Ruth looked down at a grass stain on her clean pinafore. "Sorry."

"You sure ya want me ta go?" Hank laid his hand on Dog's head. "He comes too."

"Ja."

"Good morning." Mrs. Miller twitched the reins and the mule stopped.

"How come your horse's ears are so big?" Ruth stared at the animal.

"That's 'cause he's a mule." Hank gave her a boost up to the seat and climbed in the back.

"What's a mule?" She looked up to their neighbor.

"His name is Leo, and his ma was a donkey and his pa a horse. He's getting old now, but we used to have a mule team. You can ride him sometime if you like."

"Really?" Ruth's eyes widened.

"Eben and the others used to ride him to school. He really likes cookies."

"Me too." She looked up to Amalia. "Gingerbread cookies."

Once they reached the center of town, Mrs. Miller stopped Leo on the shady side of the store building. Before she could get out of the trap, Hank had leaped down and tied the mule to the hitching rail.

"I better stay out here."

"Why?" Ruth jumped down.

"I—ah . . . just would be better." He drew circles in the dust with his big toe. "I'll water Leo."

Amalia took Ruth's hand. "We'll be back soon."

Something happened he doesn't want us to know.

They mounted the three steps to the porch where Mrs. Miller pulled open the door. "I'll introduce you to the Nygards." She waved to the woman behind the counter. "Good morning, I brought you a new customer, Amalia Gunderson. She has taken charge of Forsberg House."

"Ah, I've heard. What a pleasure to meet you."

"She is new from Norway, just learning English . . ."

Mrs. Nygard switched languages. "God dag. Welcome. How can I help you today?"

"God dag. We need most everything." Amalia laid the list on the well-aged counter and inhaled the store fragrance, from leather boots and saddles to pickles and coffee and who knew what else. "Do you sell eggs?"

"When I can get them. Might you have hens?"

Amalia nodded. "And they are laying more than we can use. I have some money to use today, but . . ."

"If you would like to start a tab, I will credit whatever eggs you can bring me. Butter too."

Mrs. Miller had mentioned a tab, but how did that work exactly? Amalia smiled her relief when the woman turned a ledger and flipped pages back to point to a page with the names and dates on the top and columns of numbers.

"We have earlier ledgers, too, from the time we opened the store." She traced down a column with her finger. "The Forsbergs were good people."

Ruth leaned on the counter and propped her chin on stacked fists. "Does Cousin Zelda buy things here?"

"She used to, but not so much anymore."

That's because she doesn't have any money. Amalia laid her list on the counter. "You have oats for the chickens?"

"We do. I'll have Kristoff load one bag—or two?—in your wagon."

"Two, and should I just bring the eggs in a basket?"

She nodded. "As you see we are out."

If the tab could help with groceries for now, perhaps she could save the money in the bank for bigger purchases, like furniture. "Do you carry heavy cloth for making pallets?"

"We have some already made. This for your boarders?"

"Ja." How did she know that?

"News travels quick around here." Mrs. Miller smiled at Amalia.

"We aren't open yet, we need furniture first. Like beds."

"You need to go into Decorah for that. They will deliver. You could order some smaller pieces here."

"Takk."

"You can go ahead and browse while I get the things on your list together for you. You have any questions, just holler."

Amalia smiled her thanks and started down an aisle. Ruth stayed close beside her.

"How many pallets would you like?" Mrs. Nygard asked when Amalia brought her selections up to the counter. She almost bought boots for Hank but knew he would not wear them until the weather turned cold in the fall. His overalls were ripped at the knee to the point that cutting them off wouldn't take much. But short for the summer would be cooler anyway.

So far Ruthie's dress hems could be let down if she sprouted up during the summer. But if it would be as hot and muggy in Iowa as she had heard, they would need lighter garments. Perhaps she should learn to use the sewing machine Ruthie said she'd seen in Zelda's room—though Amalia had had to scold her for snooping. Between needing to make clothing and pallets for the boarding-house, she should be grateful for a machine, and that Zelda hadn't sold it. As long as she'd allow Amalia to use it.

She turned to Mrs. Miller at her side, looking at buttons. "Do you know how to use a sewing machine?"

"Some, it's not hard to learn. In her later years, Else taught me so I could help her. Funny, the mister gave the machine to her for Christmas one year because he said he got tired of her begging and pleading. She said she only mentioned it once." Mrs. Miller rolled her eyes. "How I miss those folks."

Amalia studied the various fabrics on the shelves, rubbing the cloth between her fingers before she carried three pieces to the counter. "Do you know if Zelda ever uses the machine?"

"Ja, she used to make clothes for herself. Come to think of it, she upholstered furniture even. I wonder why she quit?"

One more thing to talk to Zelda about. Amalia wagged her head. Whatever turned her so bitter?

By the time all her purchases were loaded into the wagon, she tried to pay for peppermint sticks for Ruth and Hank, but Mrs. Nygard shook her head. "Not today, call that a welcome gift from me to you. And I heard you talking about sewing machines—if Zelda refuses to teach you how to use the sewing machine, I will gladly come out and show you. First you need to make sure you have needles for it. Oh." She slapped her hands on the counter. "We also run the post office here. Anyone who might have sent you a letter?"

Amalia sucked a breath. Probably too soon still to have heard back from her family in Norway, but . . . "Maybe. Would you mind checking?"

"Just a moment. Gunderson and Forsberg . . ." Mrs. Nygard disappeared into the back, then came out beaming, an envelope in hand. "Here you are."

"Mange takk." Amalia took the envelope as if it were made of glass. Not from Norway, but from Dakota Territory—Mrs. Haugen! Tears pricked the backs of her eyelids. Her insides danced with wanting to read it right there. Instead, she tucked the precious letter into her bag. "Takk. I'll bring you a basket of eggs on Monday."

"Any time you have extra eggs, I'll be happy to take them." Mrs. Nygard walked them to the door. "Butter and cheese too, if you have a cow." She waved them off and turned to greet another customer.

Amalia smiled at Mrs. Miller. "Thank you for bringing us here today."

"You are welcome. I asked Eben to come help us unload. Do you have a small wagon or a wheelbarrow?"

"Not that I know of." Amalia looked over her shoulder to see Hank back with Ruth, both of them sitting on the sacks of oats and licking their candy sticks. Hank raised his and grinned at her.

Zelda met them when the wagon stopped. "Did you bring me seed potatoes?"

Hank handed her a bumpy bag. "Here you go."

She thanked him with a glare and returned to the garden.

Amalia and Mrs. Miller looked at each other and, shaking their heads, climbed down from the wagon. Eben met them and lowered the tailgate. "Good day, Miss Amalia. Looks like you bought out the store."

"Ja, feels like it too." Grateful he spoke in Norwegian, learned from his mother, she answered with a smile.

Eben hefted the sack of flour and one of beans and carried them to the pantry. "If you show me where to put things . . ."

By the time everything was unloaded, the dinner hour was well past.

"Eben, did you bring the basket for our dinner?"

"Ja, I did. On the counter in the kitchen."

"Thank you." She looked to Amalia. "I thought we could eat on the back porch in the shade."

Amalia stared at their neighbor. "But you already took me to the mercantile and . . ."

"And now we are going to have dinner as friends can do. Nothing fancy, but good food, and then we can go back to work, and on Sunday we will go to Green Creek Lutheran Church and be grateful for all the blessings our Father spread out upon us. Our buggy will be here at ten thirty." She paused. "Unless you do not want to go to church."

Amalia stared, fighting back tears. "Of course we do. Tusen takk, for today, for everything."

Ruthie tugged on her skirt. "Can we eat? I'm hungry."

"Ja, you bring the chairs out and I'll set the coffee to heating."

Amalia added wood to the fire and pulled the coffeepot to the hot side, before going out to ask Zelda to come eat with them.

"She said no?" Mrs. Miller asked.

Amalia nodded and sat down with the others. After grace, everyone helped themselves to cheese sandwiches, along with pickles, hard-boiled eggs, and sour cream cookies. Hank and Ruth sat on the steps where Hank could slip a bite of his sandwich to Dog, which set Ruth to giggling, which set Hank to making faces.

Amalia's heart felt like it was about to burst with joy. She blinked away the incipient tears. *Takk, Lord God, for these gifts you pour out upon us.* Mrs. Miller reached over and patted her arm, smiling and nodding. And Amalia knew deep inside her heart they would be friends forever.

The thought of Zelda floated through her mind. What to do about her? Surely she couldn't be happy, keeping herself away from everyone like this.

They finished their meal, and after gathering up the things, Eben took the basket to the wagon. Mrs. Miller smiled at Amalia. "So we will see you at church on Sunday?"

Amalia nodded.

"Good, then we will be here to take you. Church is the best place to make new friends and having a friend along will make that far easier. Reverend Larsen and his wife started this congregation in Green Creek to make it easier for folks to get to church on Sundays. We used to drive the three miles to Decorah but never got there all winter. Now we can go year-round."

"Takk. We will be ready."

That afternoon, Amalia laid one of the ready-made pallets they'd bought on the table to study how it was made. She checked the seams inside and out, figuring she could rip the fabric to the sizes needed rather than cutting. *I can set the sewing machine up in the parlor in front of the window.* Before going any further, she folded the pallet from the mercantile along with the other fabric and laid it on a shelf. This would be best for winter work, but she hoped to need beds for boarders long before then. Good thing there were extra blankets in the trunks.

Glancing out the window, she was surprised how much time had passed. How long since she'd checked on Ruth? She paused on the back porch. Where was everybody?

She found Ruthie in the garden with Zelda, hoeing and raking the new addition to the garden to make it ready for planting. The seed potatoes were all cut into proper pieces, which meant two eyes for each piece. The eyes sprouted into new growth.

"Zelda?"

Ruthie dropped her hoe and ran to Amalia. "Zelda is teaching me more about the garden."

"That's wonderful." She smiled at Ruthie's greeting. "Ah, den lille, looks to me like you are getting sunburned, I need to make you a sunbonnet."

Ruthie shrugged and tugged on her hand. "Come see."

"Don't you go stepping on anything," Zelda warned.

"I won't." She pulled Amalia to the rows of small green leaves and squatted. "See, this is lettuce, and these tiny feathers are carrots. And oops, this is a weed." She jerked it out and shook off the clinging dirt.

"You be careful." The order carried clearly. "Don't you go pulling up our food."

"I won't. It's one of the weeds you showed me, see?" Ruthie held it out.

Zelda jutted her chin to examine it, then nodded. "Good."

Amalia blinked. An actual affirmation from Zelda. And she'd been investing in Ruthie a bit—after all, they were family. Maybe the woman wasn't beyond hope. She carefully walked in the space between the rows. "Back to what I came out here for." She stopped nearer to Zelda, who paid her no attention. "I purchased cloth to sew for pallets, and I'm thinking of setting the sewing machine up in the parlor. What do you think?"

"What sewing machine?" Zelda rocked back on her heels.

"Why, the one in your bedroom."

"How do you know I have a sewing machine in my bedroom?"

Amalia immediately recognized the trap. Ruthie had told her, but the little girl was not allowed in the woman's bedroom. "I— ah . . ." The pause thrummed with anger.

Ruthie, at her side, slipped her hand in Amalia's, all the while studying her dirty feet.

"I need the machine to get ready for boarders, and I understand it was Else's. So we must move the machine into the parlor, where I hope you will teach me how to use it. Otherwise, Mrs. Miller will come show me." Her heart felt like it was about to leap out of her chest. Was she being too bold?

"I will!" Daggers pelted the air.

"Takk." Amalia turned and walked out of the garden, collapsing on the steps of the back porch, not sure if she had won the war or not.

That night, after making Ruthie take a bath in the washtub, she tucked the little girl into her pallet and sat down beside her. Should she bring up the altercation or not? "Shall we say our prayers?" At Ruthie's nod, they joined their voices in the age-old prayer her mor had taught her and she taught the little one.

At the amen, Ruthie threw her arms around Amalia's neck and sniffled. "I'm sorry."

Amalia patted her back. "I know." The knowledge created a slow burn in Amalia's heart. "You go to sleep now, and I'll be back in a bit. I'm praying you sleep without nightmares tonight."

The little girl nodded and snuggled down on her pallet.

Amalia changed into her nightdress and hung her day clothes on one of the hooks on the wall. Might she have an extra sunbonnet in her trunk? If not, she could easily sew one for Ruthie, with or without the machine. She opened the trunk lid to search, but something was wrong. Someone else had been in her trunk. She searched again to be sure, but the guardianship papers, both originals and the copies Absalom had made, were missing.

FIFTEEN

W ill church be the same as back home in Norway?" Amalia's chest pinched as she buttoned the cuffs of Ruthie's Sunday blouse, then turned the little girl away from her to brush her fine blonde hair. "Not exactly the same, I don't think. But we'll find out."

"I had trouble sitting still in church back home sometimes. But then Mor would hold me on her lap and let me play with her fingers." Ruthie's voice wavered, but only a little. Were the memories of her mother growing fainter already? She was so young still.

Amalia used the comb to divide Ruthie's hair down the back of her head, then began weaving each half into a smooth braid. They'd had baths last night in the kitchen, lugging in a big washtub and dipping in enough water from the reservoir on the stove to warm the bath. She'd even insisted for Hank, though he made them all promise to "clear out," except for Dog.

Of course, when she'd gathered up courage and asked Zelda if she wanted to attend church with them, the woman had only sniffed and said it was "too far" to walk. Even when she'd mentioned the Millers' offer of a ride, Zelda looked at her like she'd made a crazy suggestion. Maybe if the woman would take a little time for the Lord, she wouldn't be such a crotchety burden to live with.

And not just crotchety—could Zelda possibly have taken the guardianship papers? Every time Amalia remembered that they were missing, the bottom seemed to drop out of her stomach.

"Ouch." Ruthie flinched and twisted away from Amalia's hands.

"Sorry, den lille." Amalia reached for the last braid, the end unraveling now. She must have pulled too tight. "I'll be more gentle, I promise." She finished the braid and tied both off with scraps of red fabric she'd found, then hooked the front of her own embroidered blue vest. Not what ladies of Iowa would probably be wearing at the Green Creek Lutheran Church, but the best she had. Glancing out the window at the sun fast rising in the sky, she hurried Ruthie down the stairs. Soon the church bells that had sounded every Sunday would peal, and this time they would be there.

Till now she hadn't felt it in her to tackle the Green Creek streets alone and brave an unfamiliar building full of strange people—especially since Zelda usually stayed in her room on Sundays. The past several weeks, she and Ruthie had passed their Sabbaths quietly, Amalia reading from her Norwegian family Bible to the little girl on the porch while Ruth played with her rag doll, then sometimes taking walks down by the creek.

But today—today they would go, especially with the Millers' kind invitation. It had been long enough without gathering with the people of God.

"Hank!" Amalia peered into the kitchen. "We're ready to go." But the kitchen stood empty, their porridge bowls from a hurried breakfast draining on the sideboard. Hank had downed three bowlfuls before she'd finished one—she'd have to make that boy some new clothes soon, though Mrs. Miller had shared some outgrown overalls of Eben's that Amalia had told Hank to wear today.

"Ruthie, see if Hank is on the front porch. I'll check the barn."

Amalia headed out the kitchen door, nearly tripping on the back steps in her haste. She hurried to the barn and pushed the door open. "Hank?" The barn stood silent and hay-scented, no boy or dog appearing from the stall where he still insisted on sleeping.

Amalia set her jaw and shut the door hard. Where was that boy? She'd told him to be ready when they came down. He'd shown little enthusiasm for the idea of churchgoing, but she felt responsibility for him under their roof—even their barn roof—for spiritual nourishment as well as physical. Zelda she'd no control over. But Hank . . .

Ruthie came running around the corner of the boardinghouse. "He isn't on the porch, or by the chickens."

"I'll check once more inside." She headed for the stairs, the heels of her good boots clicking out frustration. "Hank?"

Zelda's door thrust open. "Can't a woman get a Sunday's rest?"

Amalia paused two steps up and glanced down. "I can't find Hank."

"I saw him head off across the fields after breakfast." Zelda made to close her door.

And you didn't think to tell anyone? Amalia expelled a breath. "Well, we're leaving for church." She hesitated, then scolded herself for her cowardice and stepped back off the stairs. "Zelda, I can't find the legal papers I had in my trunk. Do you have any idea—"

"Certainly not. That boy probably took them." Zelda shut the door with a sound click.

Amalia pressed her fingers to her temples. No matter what, that woman always managed to get her heart rate up. She hadn't meant to accuse Zelda of taking the papers—or had she? Who else could have? Surely Ruthie wouldn't move them or even know what they were. Hank had no reason—and he hadn't even been upstairs, as far as she knew. Frustration simmered in her middle. Here she tried to do a good thing, get them all to community worship, and what thanks did she get? Runaway boy, the loss of the most important papers she owned, and a door slammed in her face.

She thrust open the front door, nearly bumping into Ruthie on the porch. The little girl jumped back with a squeal.

"Sorry, *den lille.*" How many times must she apologize this Sunday morning? Amalia drew a breath, willing her nerves to relax. *Forgive me, Lord.*

"Did you find Hank?" Ruthie's face upturned to hers, her brows pale question marks beneath the smooth part of her hair.

"Looks like it's just us this morning. Are you ready?"

Ruthie smiled up at her and reached for her hand. "Ja."

Amalia squeezed the small fingers in hers, the tension easing from her stomach. What had she done to deserve this precious child? Which was why those missing papers tore at her so. *Please, Lord, let me find them when we get home.* Maybe they were just shoved in some other corner of the trunk.

A halloo announced the arrival of the Miller buggy. Stepping off the front porch, she greeted their neighbors and let Eben assist them both up into the rear seat of the buggy. "Takk, such a perfect day."

"That it is." Mr. Miller smiled over his shoulder. "I hear you had quite a shopping adventure yesterday."

"Ja, we did."

They rode into the heart of Green Creek, birdsong mingling with the low peal of church bells guiding them forward. Clouds soared in a blue May sky, the morning sun warm on their faces. Where had Hank gone off to? Not that she was really surprised, but Amalia's middle pinched that he'd left without a word to her. Had she pressed him too much about going to church? Would he come back at all?

"Is that it?" Ruthie pointed to a brick building with a square bell tower ahead, lines of people streaming inside.

"Ja, I think so." Amalia swallowed. So many people, and so different from the wooden peaks of their stave church in Norway. She smiled down at Ruthie. "Here we go." Eben lifted Ruth down and gave Amalia a hand. Did he hold her hand slightly longer than necessary, or was she imagining things?

Along with the Millers they entered the dark coolness of the sanctuary and found seats in a pew near the back. Amalia scanned the whitewashed walls, her eyes slowly adjusting after the brightness outside, and breathed in the scent of old hymnals and a faint hint of communion wine. At least those smells were familiar, and when the white-surpliced minister stood and gave the invocation first in Norwegian, then in English, her throat swelled with tears.

"In the name of the Father and of the Son and of the Holy Spirit . . ."

She knelt beside Ruthie for the Confession and Absolution and closed her eyes, leaning her forehead on hands folded upon the wooden back of the pew before her, letting the balm of the words wash over her. *Mange takk, Father. Forgive me my frustration this morning . . . thank you for bringing us here.*

"Look." Ruthie tugged at her wrist and whispered. "It's Mr. Absalom."

Amalia glanced across the aisle, her heart skittering a bit with surprise. She'd thought he would attend church in Decorah. But sure enough, his familiar dark curly head bent over in his pew, passing his handkerchief to a sniffly small boy in the family sharing his pew. How like him. A moment later Absalom straightened and glanced over, his dark eyes lighting when he saw them. "I'll talk with you after," he mouthed.

Amalia nodded and sat back with Ruthie. Communion, sermon, and prayers passed in soothing rhythm, though she had to blink back tears again when she went forward to kneel and receive the bread and cup. It had been so long.

They stood for the closing hymn, then the pastor raised his full-sleeved arms for the benediction.

"The Lord bless you and keep you. The Lord make His face shine on you and be gracious to you. The Lord lift up His countenance upon you and give you peace."

Amalia lifted her face and joined in the "Amen."

They chatted with the Nygards for a bit, even greeted Mr. Gruber, the stationmaster who'd given them a ride that first day. At last Amalia had a chance to glance about for Absalom. He stood off to the side, waiting for them, and caught her eye with a smile.

Amalia led Ruthie sidling along the pew till they reached him. "I'm surprised you come here."

"I've attended First Lutheran in Decorah with my father as long as I can remember, but . . ." He shrugged the shoulders of his brown Sunday suit. "Lately I feel the need for a change, for—well, several reasons. For one, our church sadly went through a split this January after a theological argument that carried on for several years. Nothing essential for salvation and fellowship, as far as I see it, but others disagree."

"I'm sorry."

"At any rate, I thought I'd visit here." He gave a playful tweak to Ruthie's nose, making her squeak.

"Well, I'm glad you did. This is our first time coming, thanks to our neighbors, the Millers. It feels so good to be in church again." The crowd about them thinned, and at Absalom's gesture for them to precede him, Amalia led Ruthie toward the door. "Would you care to join us for Sunday dinner?" She mentally scanned their larder to be sure they'd have enough. Amos shouldn't be back till tomorrow or Tuesday, so she could probably stretch the rest of the ham she'd bought at the mercantile.

"You're very kind, but I can't let you be feeding me all the time." Absalom hesitated outside the church door, twirling his hat in his hands. "What if you joined my father and me for dinner instead?"

"Truly?" Amalia met his brown eyes and knew he meant it. Well, why not? Hank was off on his own, and Zelda could get herself dinner. Surely the Millers wouldn't mind. A smile tugged at her cheeks. "If you're sure we won't be imposing."

"My father will be delighted. Wait and see."

She thanked the Millers for the buggy ride and told them about the invitation.

Mrs. Miller nodded. "That's fine. I'm glad we could be the ones to bring you today. We'll talk soon."

"You're sure?"

"Of course."

Indeed, Magistrate Karlsson met them on the porch of their gracious, shaded home with a broad smile when they drove up in Absalom's buggy.

"I hope you don't mind us showing up uninvited like this, Magistrate." Amalia accepted Absalom's hand to help her down before he swung Ruthie to the ground. "Your son insisted."

"And rightfully so. He knows our housekeeper, Mrs. Skivens, always cooks such a big roast for Sunday that we're hard-pressed to eat through it by the end of the week. Why, it seems like half the time Absalom manages to rope someone or other into Sunday dinner."

That sounded like him. Did that ever include other young women? Amalia squelched the thought. It certainly didn't matter whom his good heart sought to bless.

"I like your trees." Ruthie climbed the porch steps, gazing up at the gabled roof under the shade of spreading branches.

"Planted most of them when my Absalom and I moved out here after the war, when he was no bigger than you. Maple, white oak, elm. They've grown tall and sturdy now."

"Why didn't your mor come too?" She cocked her head at Absalom.

He crouched to her eye level. "She died, Ruthie. When I was younger than you."

"I'm sorry." She touched the cuff of his coat sleeve. "My mor died too."

"I know. But we'll see them again in heaven someday, ja?"

"Ja." The gap in her teeth peeked out again.

"I'm surprised Hank isn't with you." The magistrate opened the door and led the way through the familiar law office rooms through a doorway they'd never passed before. They stepped into a hallway of polished wood.

"True, I didn't think to ask." They entered a cozy sitting room, and Absalom hung his felt derby hat on a nearby brass hatstand. "Though I've never seen him in church, so I suppose that's why I didn't question it earlier. He'll be sorry to miss dinner, though."

"He disappeared this morning before we left." The prickle of worry crept up Amalia's spine again. "I don't know where he ran off to."

"That's Hank for you." Magistrate Karlsson sighed and limped toward a paneled door leading to a formal dining room. "Here one day, off again the next. Truth be told, with you at the boarding-house is the longest I've ever seen him settle anyplace."

"I agree." Absalom pulled out chairs for Amalia and Ruthie at the dark walnut table, already laid with linen and white china, simple yet elegant.

"Can't we help with the meal first?" Amalia hesitated, one hand on the curved back of the chair.

"Mrs. Skivens left it ready last night, and I put it all to heat in the oven when I got back from church. Absalom will bring it in." The magistrate sat in his chair at the head of the table with a wince from his bad leg. "You'll find him no mean hand in the kitchen, growing up without a woman in the house."

Sure enough, Absalom carried in the tray of steaming roast, surrounded with potatoes, carrots, onions, and parsnips, as capably as any waiter in a fine restaurant—not that Amalia had ever been to one. He did let Amalia fill the water glasses, then they all sat and bowed their heads for the magistrate to give the blessing.

"Lord, we give thee thanks for these friends, this food, and all thy bounty. Bless the hands that prepared this, and lead us in thy service. In Christ's name we pray, Amen."

"Amen," Amalia murmured with the others. Worship in church and fellowship at table, all in one day—what richness.

She waited till the plates had been passed, steaming with slices of juice-dripping beef and redolent with the scent of onions and carrots, before asking the questions pressing her mind.

"You said you came 'out' to Iowa, Magistrate, when Absalom was little. Where did you come from?"

"Pennsylvania." He spread his napkin. "My wife died of a fever when Absalom was only a year old, when I was still off fighting in the war. My parents cared for him till I got wounded and returned. Afterwards, we were both ready for a new start."

She knew about that—though her new start had been rather thrust upon her.

"What about you?" he asked. "From what part of Norway do you hail?"

"The Bjerkreim region."

"Ah, in the southwest. You'll find many immigrants in this area from there as well."

"I loved hearing Norwegian in the service today. It felt like a taste of home."

"Do you still have family back in Norway?"

"My grandparents, and an uncle, aunt, and cousins." Sudden longing for her family squeezed her chest. When might she receive a letter back? It had been lovely reading the one from Mrs. Haugen, but . . .

"As I mentioned the other day, Father . . ." Absalom leaned forward over his plate. "Amalia has a brother in America, but she doesn't know where."

"That's right." The magistrate quirked a heavy gray brow. "You've no idea?"

Amalia swallowed a savory bite of beef. "We haven't heard from him since he left three years ago. Absalom said you have contacts in the Norwegian communities and that you might be able to ask around?"

"I can certainly try. Being magistrate does put one's fingers in a good many pies. I believe Absalom already gave me his name, but write down as much information about your brother's information as you can for me, after dinner. I'll see what I can do."

"Mange takk. I will."

They ate till they could hold no more, Ruthie polishing off a second helping, then sat on the shady front porch and visited till the sun began to lower through the trees.

"This has been so lovely, Magistrate, Absalom." Amalia at last pushed herself to her feet. "But we must get home to feed the chickens and get supper."

"Let me get you a pen and paper, about your brother." The older man stood and limped into the house.

"I certainly hope Hank will be back when we get there." Amalia smiled to watch Ruthie running in the grass of the front yard, then stooping to smell the opening rosebuds. "You say he's stayed with us longer than you've seen before?"

Absalom nodded, stepping to the edge of the porch beside her and pushing his spectacles up his nose. "He has. I think perhaps he feels needed with you—that he isn't just a charity case, if you know what I mean. He wants, like everyone, a place to contribute—to belong. He'll turn up, try not to worry."

"I am."

"Here we are." Magistrate Karlsson emerged from the house with a small pad of paper and a pen.

Amalia propped the pad on the porch railing and wrote *Erik Hamre Gunderson* once more, along with his birthdate, a physical description, the approximate date he would have arrived in New York, and the last date they'd heard from him. She added *Minnesota or Ohio?* then passed paper and pen back to the magistrate. "Mange takk for whatever you can do."

He gave a firm nod. "I'll let you know."

She hesitated, but she should tell them, shouldn't she? "Also—maybe I've just misplaced them, but I—I can't find my guardianship papers."

Absalom's brows disappeared under the curls falling over his forehead. "Your legal papers from the ship?"

She nodded, her stomach sinking again. "I was looking in my trunk last night, and they were gone."

The magistrate frowned. "Could they have fallen out? Or gotten pushed under something else?"

"I need to check again."

"You still have the extra copy I made for you, right?" Absalom leaned his hand on the porch railing, watching her.

Amalia's middle tightened further. "I—I kept them together." A foolish idea, she could see that now. How could she be so stupid? Her eyes stung.

Absalom laid his hand on her arm. "Try not to worry. Most misplaced things turn up, don't they? And we still have our copies, so legally speaking, you needn't fret too much."

Amalia drew in an easier breath, whether from the truth of his words or the warm comfort of his touch, she wasn't sure. "I will look again."

Absalom drove them back to Green Creek and out to the boardinghouse, late afternoon sunlight slanting across the greening fields.

"We'll be able to bring our cows over to the pasture soon, Ruthie. Maybe the horses too." She glanced at Absalom. "Thank you for helping make our Sunday special."

"You are welcome." He shot her a smile.

Zelda was standing on the front porch of the boardinghouse, arms crossed, when they pulled up.

"Where have you been?" Her words carried sharply across the yard before Amalia even alighted from the buggy.

"We went to church with the Millers, as you know." Amalia kept her tone even as she reached up for Ruthie, though her heart rate increased. Why did she let the woman get to her so? "Then Mr. Karlsson was kind enough to invite us back for Sunday dinner with the magistrate."

"And never a thought for me, I suppose."

"You didn't want to come with us." Amalia turned to face her, holding Ruthie's hand. "I trust you found plenty for your dinner in the larder."

"Hmmph." Zelda shifted her hands to her hips. "Never going to make a working boardinghouse if everyone keeps running off."

Had Zelda been—lonely? Or just finding fault everywhere as usual? Amalia sighed, not up to ferreting out the woman's motives tonight. She turned back toward Absalom. "Thank you again. We truly enjoyed it."

"Of course." His eyes met hers. "You'll be all right?"

She nodded, though her throat tightened at his concern. "We will."

The buggy clopped away, and Amalia led Ruthie toward the steps, feeling a bit like they were returning to the lions' den. "So Hank isn't back yet?"

"No." Zelda turned and headed back into the boardinghouse.

"The Karlssons say it's not unusual for him to run off like this. They think he'll be back soon—I hope they're right." Heading into the kitchen, Amalia kept glancing out the window, hoping to see Hank returning soon.

"It's what comes of inviting orphans in like this. Don't say I didn't warn you."

Amalia's lips tightened. Was the woman determined to chase

174

out every vestige of their pleasant Sunday? "Come, Ruthie, let's change and feed the chickens."

They had just shut the chicken-house door when Hank and Dog, along with a slow-moving older man, appeared with a string of fish. The man coughed into his sleeve and nodded to Amalia.

"Brought my friend James Johann, goes by JJ." Hank motioned to the old man. "Amalia is a guardian for Ruth, like I told you. Figured you could build some furniture for her and the boarding-house." Hank looked to Amalia. "You can trust JJ."

JJ held out the string of gutted trout. "Thought maybe these might taste good for supper."

"Takk, er thank you." Amalia looked into fading blue eyes that never wavered. Another coughing attack left the older man fighting to breathe.

"JJ's been bad sick." Hank watched his friend with concern.

"But Hank brought me a bottle of cough syrup, so gettin' better."

Amalia looked to Hank, who shrugged. "Mr. Karlson helped."

She looked down to see Dog snuffling Ruth's hair, making her giggle.

Hank was safe. *Thank you, Lord.* "Please join us for supper and we will talk about furniture."

With the fish cornmeal-breaded and fried, along with cooked rice, canned green beans, and leftover biscuits, they sat down to a hearty meal.

"Zelda, this is Mr. JJ. He will be building bed frames for us."

Her glare could have withered a willow tree.

Amalia started the grace, to be finished by her and Ruth. They passed the platter and bowls around and Dog lay down with a thump between Hank and Ruthie.

"So Mr. JJ . . ."

"Please call me JJ."

Amalia nodded. "Where do you come from?" The English words were starting to come easier, thanks be to God.

"Headed west after the Civil War, no family left, guess you could call me a drifter."

"He can turn a piece of wood into whatever is needed." Hank dropped his hand down to Dog and slipped a bite of biscuit to him.

"No feeding that dog at the table!" Zelda snapped.

"Yes, ma'am."

Amalia took another bite of fried trout. "Delicious. You caught these in Green Creek?"

JJ nodded.

"His shack is fallin' down."

"But the cough is going away."

"He could build bed frames and whatever you need if you can buy the supplies. In exchange for livin' here." Hank finished with a nod. "Even the barn would be better than the shack."

Zelda snorted. "One paying boarder won't cover all this."

And I am not going to tell you about the money in the bank. Amalia made the decision at that moment. After all, Zelda was the one who sold all the furniture.

Zelda pushed her chair back. "I'm going out to the garden." She picked up her dishes and set them into the pan of soapy steaming water on the stove.

Amalia watched her go out the door, amazed that it didn't slam behind her. Shaking her head, she turned back to Hank and JJ. "You tell me what you need. There must be a lumberyard nearby where we can order wood?"

JJ nodded. "Yup, right in Decorah."

"Good. Also, our porches both have missing boards. Could you fix them?"

He nodded. "Whatever you need."

"Wonderful." Her heart lifted. *Thank you, Lord.* "You can sleep on a pallet in one of the rooms. . . ."

"Or out in the barn with Hank." A cough ripped through him, leaving him wheezing.

"There will be less dust in the house because Ruth and I have been scrubbing all the rooms." Amalia smiled to take any sting out of her words. "We even have a couple more pallets ready to stuff." She thought a moment. "Perhaps you should go with us to the lumberyard in the morning. Make sure we get all we need. Would that be all right?" She struggled with some of the words, mixing her English and Norwegian.

He nodded. "You want to start with six beds?" He coughed again. "Perhaps we could stop and get me more of that cough syrup."

They finished eating, and Amalia stacked the dirty dishes in the sink. She glanced at the pile, then out the window at Zelda out in the garden. Did she dare?

Amalia took her courage in hand and marched outside before she could talk herself out of it. "Zelda, I need to run over to the Millers', so could you please do the dishes tonight?"

Zelda rolled her eyes. "I'm working in the garden, if you can't tell."

"I know, but the light is fading anyway. I need to ask if they can take us to the lumberyard tomorrow. We can't get more paying boarders without furniture." Perhaps that double reminder, of the paying boarders she kept harping on and the furniture she'd sold off . . . ? Amalia held her breath.

Zelda stared at her a moment, as if waiting for Amalia to change her mind, then sighed and set her hoe aside. "All right."

Amalia let out the breath. "Mange takk. I appreciate it."

"Go on with you, then." Zelda made a shooing motion and followed Amalia toward the house.

Amalia stepped back into the kitchen and hung her apron on the hook behind the stove. "I'm going to ask the Millers about tomorrow, be right back." So strange to leave the pile of dishes behind. The feeling of freedom made her want to dance.

Ruthie clasped her hands together. "Can I go see the kittens?"

Amalia started to shake her head, then changed her mind at the droop of Ruthie's face. "All right, but we won't be staying but a minute."

Hand in hand, she and Ruthie hurried out the front door into the dusk. What a day it had been, and not over yet.

Sixteen

"Going to see the kittens," Ruth sang, swinging her and Amalia's locked hands as they left the house in the falling twilight.

Amalia inhaled. Surely there was nothing better than the fragrances of growing grass, freshly turned earth, and trees coming alive again after winter slumber. A meadowlark sang an evening song, and two crows carried on a conversation in one of the budding trees. *Thank you, Lord for this world you created. And for Mr. JJ and his help getting the boardinghouse ready for guests.* The train echoed across the prairie.

She pushed open the gate and crossed the Millers' porch to knock on the screen door.

"Coming."

Ruth grinned up at her and squeezed her hand.

"Why, look who is here. Come in, come in." Mrs. Miller pushed open the door, her smile lighting the shadowed porch. "Abram, we have company."

"I just came to ask a favor."

"Surely you have time for a cup of coffee. Abram and I were just talking about you."

Amalia and Ruth followed her to the kitchen where indeed the coffeepot was steaming.

"Can I please go see the kittens?"

"Of course, Eben is out at the barn."

"Thank you." Ruth slipped out the door.

Mr. Miller pulled out a chair. "Have a seat, have a seat."

"I need to get back." She smiled at Mrs. Miller. "I don't want you to go to any trouble."

"Can I tempt you with a piece of custard pie? I tried a new recipe and I'd like to hear what you think."

Amalia settled back in her chair and picked up her coffee cup. "What a treat that would be." After a sip, she set her cup back. "I have a favor to ask." At the other woman's nod, she continued. "I wondered if you would take me to the lumberyard tomorrow so I can order boards for Mr. JJ to make beds for guests at the boardinghouse."

"Oh, good, how did you meet him?" She set the plates in front of both her and the mister. "He's been living in that shack out by the creek, hasn't he?"

"I can guess who introduced you." Abram nodded around the smile the bite of pie brought forth.

"If you are thinking Hank, you would be right." Amalia laid her fork back down.

"What time would you like to go?" Mrs. Miller sat down with her own plate.

"Whatever is convenient for you."

"I'll be over right after breakfast. Will JJ be going too?"

"And Ruthie."

"Fine. We may stop at Nygards' on the way home, if you don't mind. I could use a few things."

"Not at all."

The next morning, Amalia felt like she was getting a tour of Decorah, as the lumberyard was on the other side of the town. They drove past First Lutheran Church, Main Street, and saw the train station. When they drove under the Wilbur Lumber Company sign, she inhaled the scent of freshly sawed wood.

A man with a straw hat and pencils in his shirt pocket greeted them before Mrs. Miller stopped her mule. "How can I help you today? Long time since I saw you, Mrs. Miller."

"Lucas, I'd like you to meet the new owner of the boardinghouse in Green Creek. Miss Amalia Gunderson, guardian for Ruth Forsberg. Newly arrived from Norway. They plan on reopening the Forsberg House. Mr. JJ is going to build them some new furniture."

"Starting with beds. Good to see you, Lucas." JJ leaned forward, extending his hand to shake.

"Well, I'll be. I wondered whatever happened to you."

Amalia watched the exchange. For living in a cabin by the creek, JJ sure seemed to know a lot of people.

"Come on in the office, and let's see what we can do." He helped Amalia down. "Glad to meet you. I'm Lucas Engbertson, and I'm pleased that house is going to be useful again. My far helped build it right out in the middle of nowhere; Green Creek town wasn't even a dream yet. Prime piece of property that."

By the time they got home again, Mr. Engbertson having promised to deliver the order that afternoon, a bank of clouds was building in the west. Mrs. Miller dropped them off. "Thanks for needing me today. Been a pleasure. JJ, you take care of that cough. Glad to hear you'll be helping get that house up and being useful again."

"Thank you for taking us." Amalia stroked the mule's muzzle. "Soon the pasture will be high enough our team can come home, but I am grateful Mr. Miller and Eben will keep on with the field work. Be a shame to let them lie fallow." She switched to Norwegian, since while improving, her English still lacked many words.

Ruth stopped beside the old mule. "Can I come ride you?" she asked, stroking his cheek with gentle fingers. He snuffled her arm and leaned into her petting.

"Leo likes being fussed over like that. I think he gets lonesome when the teams are all out in the field."

"Wish I had a carrot for you." Ruth stepped back. "May I come ride him soon?"

Mrs. Miller nodded. "And you know he likes cookies." She flicked the reins and turned him toward the barn to back up again.

"I wonder where Hank is." Amalia scanned the barnyard.

JJ took a couple of packages from Amalia to carry to the house. He looked to Mrs. Miller's retreating back and called out, "Do you have any sawhorses?"

"We do, you are welcome to use them."

"Thank you."

Ruthie came running around the corner of the house. "Malia, Hank and Dog aren't anywhere."

"Probably went fishing." JJ gave a knowing nod.

Amalia mounted the steps to the back porch, her feet tired. Good thing they had leftovers for dinner.

Zelda was standing at the sink, draining her coffee and setting the cup down. "I'm going out to the garden."

"They'll be delivering the wood for the beds later this afternoon." Amalia reached for an apron. "Have you seen Hank?"

"No." Zelda let the door slam behind her.

Amalia closed her eyes and heaved a sigh. *Think about the pleasant morning,* she reminded herself, making sure she dropped her shoulders at the same time. Shame she didn't include a pleasant demeanor in the list of required behavior for Zelda to stay. At least the bean soup was warm; they could eat pretty soon.

Spreading butter on the cornmeal biscuits, she slid the plate into the hot oven. "Please set the table."

Ruth did as asked. "Where do you think Hank went?"

"Well, Mr. JJ said maybe he went fishing."

"But he went yesterday. Why would he be gone so long?"

"Depends on how well the fish are biting, I s'pose." How easy it was to slip into Norwegian when it was just she and Ruth. "Go call Mr. JJ."

JJ pulled off his battered hat as he stepped inside. "Sure smells good in here."

"You sit down, and I'll dish up."

JJ nodded, caught by a sneeze that turned into a coughing spell. He pushed back from the table and staggered outside.

"Where's his cough syrup?" Eyes wide, Ruth looked to Amalia.

Amalia left the ladle in the pot and followed after the man who was still coughing out on the porch. "Can I get your medicine?"

"On—the window—sill . . . above the s-sink." He held tight to the post at the steps, fighting to catch his breath.

Feeling about to panic, Amalia found the brown bottle and took it back out to him. "Drink this, and I'll get some honey for you."

Back in the kitchen, Amalia fetched the honey from the pantry. Filling a cup with hot water from the reservoir, she spooned the golden honey into it and stirred as she returned to the porch where JJ was now sitting on the top step, breathing hard but no longer coughing.

"Drink this."

"Sorry, not sure what happened there."

"Better?"

"Yep."

"Has that ever happened before?"

He slowly wagged his head. "And I hope never again."

Takk, Lord, please let it be so.

The afternoon seemed to crawl by. Amalia found herself looking up the road as often as Ruthie did. Surely Hank would not leave them without at least saying good-bye. She even missed Dog. She reminded herself Hank had disappeared yesterday too, but that was because he was with JJ. She knew he'd been on his own for years, but . . .

JJ walked over to the Millers' for the sawhorses so that when the lumber did arrive, he could get started on the beds.

Clouds piled higher and darker in the west, the wind driving them eastward, lightning forking the darkness. Amalia went all around the house, closing all the windows, Ruth shadowing her.

"Tante Malia, you think he is coming back?"

"I'm sure he is. You fill the woodbox, and I'll make biscuits for supper." She looked out the window to see the chickens heading for their house, their feathers puffed out as if the wind was going to blow them away.

The wagon driver from the lumberyard backed up to the barn and the men stacked the supplies inside.

"Thank you," Amalia called to them as they headed back to the road, hupping the team into a trot.

The storm hit with a vengeance, not a sprinkle, darkness falling like a curtain. They ate supper by the light of the kerosene lamp and still no Hank. At least the storm blew on as fast as it blew in.

Unable to endure Zelda's "I told you so" looks anymore, Amalia took Ruthie upstairs and put her to bed, then stood by the window, looking out over the barnyard now lit by a slender crescent moon. *Father, protect him, wherever he is. He's only a boy. Please bring him back to us.* At length she lay down on her pallet, still on the floor though JJ had promised to make bed frames for them as soon as he finished the one for Amos, and fell asleep in her chore clothes.

A thumping on the door woke her sometime later with a start. Her heart pounding, Amalia shoved to her feet and hurried out into the hall, closing the door behind her to try and keep Ruthie asleep. She flew down the stairs.

Zelda met her at the door, candle in hand and nightcap framing her face. "Mind you take a rolling pin from the kitchen. He coulda brought back a gang to rob us."

Then why would he—if it was Hank—knock on the door?

JJ came from the kitchen, where Amalia had convinced him

to sleep on the floor rather than in the barn. "Let me get it, young miss."

Amalia swallowed and nodded, then followed him to the front door. Was it Hank? Or someone more sinister?

Grasping some sort of tool in his left hand, JJ unlatched and swung open the front door with his right.

No threatening shapes met them, only a small figure leaning against the doorframe.

Zelda held up her candle behind them.

The circle of wavering light fell on Hank, breathless and nearly collapsing, with a small, whimpering child clinging on his back.

SEVENTEEN

"What in land sakes?"

Zelda's sharp exclamation behind her jolted Amalia into action. She reached toward Hank, lifting the smaller child from his back. The new little boy clung to her, sniffling, clad only in an oversized nightshirt.

"His foot's hurt," Hank gasped. He leaned on Dog, whining beside him.

JJ grasped the boy's shoulder and guided him inside, Dog padding after them. "Let's get both of you young'uns into the kitchen."

Right—he was right. Holding the child tight—he couldn't be more than three or four—Amalia headed for the kitchen, feeling her way by the moonlight from the front windows, since Zelda stood as if frozen by the door with the only candle in her hand.

Once in the kitchen, JJ lighted a kerosene lamp, bringing a soft glow to the room. He bent to start up the fire in the stove while Hank collapsed into a chair, Dog at his feet.

"What happened? Who is this child?" Amalia set the little one on the table so she could see him better. Dark, close curls covered his head, and his small shoulders quivered. She wrapped her shawl around him, and he rubbed a fist across his nose and sniffled, clutching a stuffed toy in his other arm. "You said he's hurt?" She lifted the nightshirt's worn hem to reveal scuffed knees and an oozing scrape from big toe to ankle, one toenail partially torn off. "Poor little one."

"He tripped on the road, fell on a rock or something." Hank sat hunched in his chair. "So I carried 'im the rest of the way."

"Where from?" JJ straightened from the stove, coals and tinder now glowing bright inside. He added wood, shut the iron door with a muffled thud, and adjusted the damper.

"Decorah."

Amalia turned from wetting a rag at the sink pump to stare at him. "You and this child walked all the way from Decorah?"

"Noah. His name's Noah." Hank shrugged his shoulders. "Din't have no choice."

And he had carried the younger boy who knew how much of the way. Mind whirling, Amalia squeezed the excess water into the sink and turned back to the little one. "Noah, that's your name?" He looked up at her, big dark-lashed eyes blinking. "I'm going to clean your foot, all right, Noah? I'll be as gentle as I can."

"You got a passel of explainin' to do, boy." JJ thumped down into a chair across from Hank. "Where did you pick up this young'un?"

"His ma's dead." Hank swiped a dirty sleeve across his nose. "I went to check on her today, while y'all was at the lumberyard."

So why hadn't he gotten a ride with them? "Who's his ma?"

"I knew Lottie, that was her name, knew she'd been ailin', so went to see. They were in a state when I got there, almost no food in the house, Noah cryin', and his ma like to breathin' her last in the bed. I tried to get some water and bread down her, but it weren't no use." Hank's voice quivered, then flattened. "She was a goner by 'round suppertime. So I laid her out best I could and made to bring Noah out here."

Noah made a small sound in his throat, a tiny whimper that cut to Amalia's heart. She dabbed at the dirty, raw skin about his torn nail as gently as she could, trying to clean the worst of the dirt, but it stuck, embedded. He flinched and tugged his foot back, clutching his toy close. "We need a basin. JJ, is there hot water in the reservoir?"

He checked. "No, but warm."

"Warm is better." Amalia poked a finger in to check the temperature, then dipped some out into a basin from beneath the sink. She set the bowl on a chair and drew it near the table where Noah sat. "Here, den lille. Put your feet in the water."

The little boy hesitated, then obeyed. A small sigh slipped out as his feet slid into the warm water.

"Why didn't you go to the magistrate for help, Hank?" Amalia set aside some clean cheesecloth to use for a bandage, then dipped her rag in the water and gently wiped the child's scraped knees. "He's right there in Decorah."

"Too late, I figured. And I know he'll help most anybody, but . . ."

"But what?"

"I wasn't sure if he'd help somebody like . . . Noah."

Startled, Amalia looked up, first at Hank, then at the child's face before her. His dark eyes and close curls, beautifully full lips and flared nose. The dusky tone of his skin hardly differed from hers in the dim lamplight.

JJ heaved a sigh and leaned his hands on his thighs. "I thought so. He's a mixed-race young'un, ain't he?"

Amalia closed her hands gently around the child's feet in the warm water, wishing she could protect him from whatever this meant. "You mean—he's part Negro?" She'd heard of America's tensions between races, but this was the first hint she'd seen.

"Yep." Hank looked up. "His ma, Lottie, met his pa when he stayed in town awhile from workin' on the railroad. He hired on to work for her family for a time."

"I heard about this." JJ nodded slowly, rubbing his hand over his scruffy beard. "Her family threatened to disown her when they found out she'd taken up with a black man, but she defied them, said love didn't know no color. And here in Iowa, marriage between races been legal for, oh, over thirty years now, so they had no legal leg to stand on."

Amalia stared at him. Since when did this elderly man have so much legal knowledge? "So they married?"

"Yep, and I guess had little Noah here. I have not heard much tell of them in some time."

"Her family kicked her out, so she's been takin' in sewin' and laundry and such tryin' to make ends meet while her husband, Curtis his name is, travels with the railroad. He's been tryin' to save up enough to take Lottie and Noah further west where they can make their own way. But now . . ." Hank slammed his fist on the table suddenly, making Noah jump. "It ain't fair."

"No, it ain't." JJ nibbled his mustache and shook his head, gazing at the stove.

"But surely Magistrate Karlsson would have helped." The color of a person's skin wouldn't matter to such a good man—would it? Amalia finished bathing Noah's feet and set the basin aside to dump later, patting his feet in a dry towel in her lap. She fetched some salve from the pantry and smoothed it over the scrape, then wrapped the cheesecloth to bind his injured toe.

Hank lifted one shoulder. "Just weren't sure. But I knew you wouldn't turn him out."

Had he? Amalia caught the hope in the glance he sent her and met it with a smile, the words nestling in her heart. How she'd earned this boy's trust, she wasn't sure. But she sensed it was a treasure not to take lightly.

"Of course we won't." She ran her hand over Noah's curls. "You'll stay right here with us tonight, Noah. I'll make a bed for you right next to mine, would you like that?"

He stared up at her, wordless, the lamplight flickering in his wide eyes. Could the child speak? Or was he too stunned from shock and grief just now? She could see now the worn toy in his arms was a stuffed elephant, with black button eyes and a stitched flannel trunk.

"You know you'll never run a respectable boardinghouse like this."

At the flat words, they all looked up toward the door. Zelda stood there, candle sputtering in her hand, her face set in hard lines.

"You're collecting nothing but a passel of orphans and vagrants—and now a mulatto child?" She huffed. "Never did think you'd much of a head on your shoulders, Amalia, but that's downright crazy."

Amalia picked Noah up and hugged him close, wishing she could shield him from Zelda's words. "I will never turn away any of God's children who need help, Zelda, if that's what you're wondering."

The older woman snorted and turned away. A moment later her slippers padded back to her room.

Amalia let out a breath. The hate that woman spewed at every turn—where did it come from? Should she even keep letting her stay?

The child in her arms stirred, twisting to get down. "Need to go. In pot."

Amalia caught her breath in a laugh. "So you can talk, den lille." She set him on the floor and took his hand. "Let's go."

The next morning, Amalia woke from heavy slumber to a steady knocking from below. She pushed up on her elbow on her pallet, squinting against bright sunlight streaming through the window, head foggy. Had she only dreamed the incident the night before? A glance at the floor beside her pallet showed a small curly head peeking from a mound of quilts and settled her doubts there. She pushed back her own covers and bent over Noah. He lay breathing deep, rosebud mouth parted in sleep, thick lashes fanned on perfect cheeks. She glanced over at Ruthie's pallet, her steady breathing showing she still slept too.

The knocking came again, and Amalia hurried to slip off her nightgown and into her simple chemise, petticoat, work blouse and skirt. Who could it be now? A fleeting wish that the magistrate or Absalom would appear on their doorstep shot through her mind, but how could they know about Noah?

She flew down the stairs toward the patient tapping on the door. Goodness, by the sun streaming through the front windows, it must be near eight o'clock. Where was everyone?

She flung open the door to see Amos standing there, satchel in one hand.

"Oh, Amos, welcome." She laid her hand on her chest. She'd gone and forgotten he might show up today. And JJ hadn't even started on his bed, though at least they had the lumber now. "Forgive me for making you wait, we had quite a night. Please, come in."

He dipped his head and stepped in, pulling off his hat.

"Have you had breakfast?" Had anyone?

He shook his head. "But don't go to no trouble."

"We all need to eat anyway." Where were Hank and JJ? Zelda's door stood shut, but that was nothing new.

Amalia strode into the kitchen and stirred up the stove, still finding embers from their episode in the night. She put the coffee on, then pulled sourdough starter from the warmer over the stove and set about mixing biscuits. Eggs and slices from the rasher of bacon, that would be quick and easy.

"How was your trip?" She glanced at the silent man now sitting at the table.

He lifted one shoulder. "Well enough."

What did a signalman even do on the railroad? She'd no idea but should find out.

Footsteps scuffed at the back door and Hank came plowing in, basket in hand. "I picked the eggs and fed the chickens."

"Oh, bless you." Amalia blew out a breath. "Sorry I slept so late."

"Noah all right?"

"Still sleeping. Ruth too. Wash up, I'll have breakfast on soon." She slid the tray of biscuits into the now-hot oven. "Where's JJ?"

"Out back making Amos's bed."

Thank heaven. She smiled at Amos. "We promised you a bed, and a bed you shall have."

"Malia!"

At the holler, Amalia scurried into the hall to see Ruthie standing at the stairs, hair mussed, eyes wide.

"I found another boy!"

A chortle snorted through Amalia's nose. Goodness, their life certainly had become full of the unexpected. "I'm sure you did, Ruthie. His name is Noah."

"Is he staying with us?"

"For now, at least. Try not to wake him."

A wail came from the bedroom. Ruthie flinched. "I think I already did."

Amalia sighed. "Hank, would you make sure the biscuits don't burn, please? And pour Amos a cup of coffee." Poor man, she hadn't even done that yet.

Amalia hurried upstairs, beginning to feel a bit like the rhyme Absalom had read Ruthie last week, the woman who lived in a shoe and had so many children she didn't know what to do. She knew three wasn't that many, but . . .

She found Noah sitting up in a tangle of quilts, tears running down his cheeks. Her irritation melted away. "Good morning, Noah." She knelt beside him, not wanting to startle him. "Did you have a good sleep?"

He wiped the back of his hand across his eyes and sniffled, but at least he wasn't wailing anymore. "Eh-phant?"

Of course. Amalia dug under the covers till she found the flannel elephant and handed it to him. He hugged the stuffed animal tight.

Ruthie came to stand behind her shoulder, still in nightgown and bare feet.

"We're glad you are here, Noah. I'm Amalia, and this is Ruthie."

He glanced between them, wide-eyed.

"We'll have some breakfast ready soon, downstairs. But first, would you like to use the pot?" Hopefully he hadn't had an accident—he couldn't be long out of diapers.

Noah nodded and held out his arms.

"I'll get it!" Ruthie dashed for the chamber pot in the corner and brought it near.

"Thank you, Ruthie." Amalia pulled down the little boy's drawers and set him on the pot, hearing an immediate tinkle. His mor had trained him well. And now—she was gone. Amalia's chest constricted. What must be going through his little mind and heart?

She helped Ruthie dress and braid her hair, then led both children downstairs.

In the kitchen, Hank sat at the table talking with—or rather, at—Amos. The tray of nicely browned biscuits sat on the sideboard. Dog lay at Hank's feet, as usual.

"Mange takk, Hank." Amalia set Noah on a chair and gave him a crust of bread from yesterday's loaf as something to nibble on. "Amos, this is Noah. Hank brought him to join us last night."

"His ma passed, so I brought him here." Hank shrugged and reached down to ruffle Dog's ears as if no further explanation were needed.

Noah stared at the hound, then laid his bread crust on the table untouched and slid off his chair. He toddled toward Dog, limping with his bandaged foot, then reached to stroke the silky black ears, elephant still clutched in the other arm. Dog leaned his head against Noah's nightshirt, tongue lolling in a grin. An answering smile peeked out on the child's face.

Amalia smiled, her throat tightening. What a gift animals were. But of course, Noah knew Hank and probably Dog from before.

"We must get word to the sheriff today about his mother. Some-one will have to go out to their home and take care of her body." She turned sizzling slices of bacon in the skillet. "Noah's father works on the railroad, so we don't know where he is or when he might be back." An idea sparked. "Amos, have you known a man named Curtis on the railroad?"

Amos cleared his throat, always seeming to need time to get words out. "Not sure."

"Hank, do you know his last name?"

Hank squinted and reached for Noah's untouched bread. "Williams, I think. He's a black man."

Amos shook his head slowly. "Can't say as I heard of him. Can keep an ear out, though."

Well, at least that was something. Amalia slid bacon and eggs onto plates and popped the biscuits into a basket. She stepped to the door and called JJ for breakfast, the older man straightening from sanding the clean yellow frame of the new bedstead.

Zelda didn't come till they were halfway through breakfast, appearing in the kitchen and serving up her own plate without a word, though she glanced at Noah, sharing his biscuit with Dog, with a snort and shake of her head.

Amalia drew a breath when everyone had nearly cleaned their plates. "I could use your help today, Zelda. We need to do laundry and make up beds for our new guests." She smiled around the table, heart suddenly growing so full. Hank and Noah, JJ and Amos, Ruthie and Zelda and her. After the bedsteads, she'd have JJ start on a big dining table—they wouldn't all fit in the kitchen much longer.

"I've got my own business to handle." Zelda wiped her biscuit around her plate, sopping up the last of the egg yolk.

What business? Another of her mysterious errands? The missing papers snaked through Amalia's mind once more, but when she'd gathered the courage to ask Zelda about them again the other day, she had only accused Amalia of losing them herself, implying she wasn't a fit guardian if she couldn't even keep track of Ruthie's papers. Her stomach tensed at the memory. Still . . .

"If we're going to run a boardinghouse, I'm going to need your help more." Amalia straightened her shoulders and tightened her fingers in her lap below the table. "Especially if you want a portion of the proceeds."

"What proceeds?" Zelda snapped. "From taking in foundlings and vagrants? You'll turn this place into a charity house before we see any hint of any proceeds." She shoved her chair back and snatched up her plate, banging it into the sink before stalking out of the kitchen.

Amalia swallowed and glanced at the staring faces around the table, her scalp burning. "I'm sorry. I shouldn't have brought that up just now."

"Not your fault she's such a crab apple." JJ tipped back his chair and poked a wood sliver between his teeth. "You just keep on, young lady. You've got a good heart, and you're doin' just fine. And all of us here sure do appreciate you putting a roof over our heads."

Amalia smiled at him, then lunged to catch Noah's plate before he dumped the entire remains of his bacon and eggs on the floor for Dog. She set the plate safely aside and blew out a breath.

Zelda did have a point. With Amos their only paying boarder, how on earth was she to keep putting food on the table for all these bellies? That money in the bank would only last so long. They simply had to find more paying boarders. But how?

EIGHTEEN

EARLY JUNE, 1889

W e're bringing our cows and horses home!"
Whooping, Ruthie ran ahead of Amalia toward
the Millers' barn, Noah trotting at her heels. Amalia
and Mrs. Miller followed more slowly.

"She's so excited. I hope we're not taking on too much yet."
Amalia glanced at the pastures spreading beyond both their
farms, now growing green and lush and dotted with wildflowers.
She really had no reason to impose on their neighbors' hospitality
any longer. "It will be nice to milk our own cow and have a way
to go to town. We can never say mange takk enough for all you
have done."

"Nonsense, what are neighbors for?" Mrs. Miller, wisps of graying hair blowing from her bun in the late spring breeze, pushed
the barn door open, the children ducking in ahead. "I daresay my
Abram will miss having an extra team."

"He's always welcome to use the horses. He'll still be farming
our fields with them, after all."

"Here she be." Eben led the cow forward. Her sides bulging
with calf, Honey followed the rope with a docile plod, regarding
the children with large dark eyes. "I'll bring the heifer next."

"Look, Noah. You can pet her neck." Ruthie showed him how, having already assumed the role of older sister to the little boy. "Gentle, like that."

Noah reached up to pat the cow's smooth, golden-brown neck. He beamed, eyes seeking Amalia.

"Yes, very good, den lille." She smiled back at him.

"Such a precious child." Mrs. Miller's forehead pinched. "Did you know his mother? Her family?"

"Only a little. Her father is a banker, and they held themselves a bit above us farmers, you know. But we'd see them at community functions. I suppose that's partly why they took it so hard when their daughter . . ."

Amalia sighed. "I find it hard to understand people sometimes."

"I know the feeling. Have you any idea where his father is?" Mrs. Miller stepped out of the way for Eben to lead the cow past them. Outside, Mr. Miller was hitching up the team to the wagon—their wagon.

"On the railroad, somewhere. Amos, our new boarder, is going to see what he can find out. Speaking of that, do you have any ideas how we might advertise for more boarders? We've got to get more income somehow."

"Well, you've already spoken to Mrs. Nygard at the mercantile." Mrs. Miller tapped her finger on her chin. "Oh, I nearly forgot— land sakes, where is my mind today? I saw Helen Stenerson, the schoolteacher, in town yesterday. She said she's looking for a permanent place to board, rather than always boarding round with different families. I told her to speak with you."

"Really?" Amalia's heart lifted. "That would be wonderful."

"I suggested she stop by the boardinghouse, so hopefully she'll do that."

"I hope so. Our house is certainly getting fuller—just mostly not with paying boarders."

"You certainly have been becoming a shelter, haven't you?" Mrs.

Miller's clear blue eyes met her own. "Something of an ark of refuge for orphans and those left out by others, it seems."

Amalia blinked back a sudden stinging. "It certainly wasn't something I set out for."

"I know that. But you have an open heart and open hands, such as the Lord loves to use."

Was He truly using her in this new land? She'd never thought of it that way. She'd been so busy just trying to survive, to care for Ruthie and now the other children, to manage with Zelda, to put food on the table and furniture in the place . . .

Eben finished tying the yearling heifer to the back of the wagon beside Honey, then approached. "We've got 'em all set, Miss Gunderson. I can drive you over if'n you like." He pulled off his hat. "Also, I was wonderin' if you might like to ride along with me to Decorah next Saturday night. They're havin' a sort of a—" He glanced at his mother. "Shindig?"

"A dance." Mrs. Miller beamed. "A Springtime Community Dance, they're calling it. It may become somewhat of an annual thing, to celebrate once planting is done."

"Oh—I see." Amalia's cheeks warmed. She hadn't seen this coming. "That's very kind of you, Mr. Miller—"

"Eben."

"Eben." She glanced at Ruthie and Noah, absorbed in the kittens' antics as they gamboled in a patch of sunshine by the barn door. "It's just, I don't think I could leave the children."

"Oh, you could bring them here for the evening." Mrs. Miller gave a firm nod. "No problem at all."

"I see." Amalia tried to think, brain scrambling. "Well, I—I suppose I'll have to think about it."

"Of course." Mrs. Miller squeezed her arm. "But I do hope you'll go. You deserve a nice evening out, and I know Eben will take good care of you."

Ruthie ran up, black-and-white kitten squirming in her arms.

"Mr. Miller says the kittens are old enough to leave their mor now. Can I bring mine home now? Please, please, please?"

"I—I suppose so. Into the wagon now, we mustn't keep Mr. Eben waiting." Amalia scooped up Noah and plopped him into the wagon bed, then lifted Ruthie and kitten in, being sure to secure the wagon gate behind. She hugged Mrs. Miller good-bye, fighting a prickle of awkwardness, and climbed up onto the seat next to Eben, avoiding the young man's gaze.

An invitation to a dance—just a complication she hadn't needed right now. Uff da.

"Ruthie, not on the table!" That afternoon, Amalia spun around from trying to chop rutabagas at the kitchen counter for the fifth time. Would she never be able to get supper started tonight?

Ruthie snatched up the kitten, now christened Magpie, just before she stepped into the waiting butter dish. "Sorry?"

"I told you, if you want to have her in the kitchen, you have to keep her from underfoot. And Noah, no." The little boy looked up from picking at his bandaged foot where he sat on the floor near the woodbox. Amalia scooped him up and set him in a chair. "Ruthie, get a string or something for the kitten to play with; that will entertain Noah too."

She turned back to her chopping, blowing a breath upward to try and shift the sweaty strings of hair sticking to her forehead. The kitchen steamed with heat from the stove and the still-beaming sun outside. Only June, and it already felt like summer. Her blouse's high collar stuck to the back of her neck, and she fought the urge to rip off her woolen bodice. A smirk tugged despite her frustration. Now that would get a comment from Zelda.

Ruthie and Noah shrieked with glee behind her, the kitten's claws scampering on the floor. At least they seemed entertained for the moment. As soon as she had the stew set and simmering, she'd have to see about getting the horses and Honey and the heifer—they really needed to give the young cow a name—their evening feed and making sure they were settled in the barn for the night.

Amalia finished chopping the rutabagas and scraped them into the bubbling pot of beans. Everyone might be tired of bean stew with rutabagas and bits of ham, but she didn't know what else to cook tonight. None of the chickens could be spared for butchering yet, and she didn't want to spend too much money on meat. If only they had mutton so she could make sodd. Her mouth watered at the thought of the rich Norwegian soup with lamb meatballs, potatoes, and carrots. It would be a while before they could dig new potatoes from the garden.

At least she had found a few wild leeks by the creek to add some flavor this time. Amalia pulled the slender green stalks from her gathering basket and set to chopping them fine.

"That cow is bellering." Hank banged the kitchen door open, his hound with him. Dog halted, stiff-legged, then barked and dashed past Amalia's skirt.

Ruthie shrieked. "He's chasing Magpie!"

Amalia slammed down her knife, nicking the tip of her finger, and spun around. "Ruthie, grab her!"

The kitten dashed under the table, Dog crashing after her, then clawed up the tablecloth, scampering across the table and right through the butter dish. Dog lunged at her, barking, and Magpie took a flying leap to the counter, crashing into the small pitcher of wildflowers the children had picked earlier. It tipped, spilling water onto the tray of rising biscuits. Amalia grabbed at the kitten and held her to her chest, wrapping her apron over the ball of spitting, scratching fur.

"Hank, get Dog out of here. Ruthie, take your kitten. All of you, outside, now!"

Hank grabbed Dog and dragged him, still barking, out the door. Amalia thrust the quivering kitten into Ruthie's arms. "Take her

200

to the barn, and Noah too. Go." The children scurried out past Zelda, entering the kitchen from the hall.

"What on earth is going on now?"

Amalia flung up her palm, finger still bleeding. "I can't talk to you right now." She stomped right past Zelda's scowling face, through the front hall, and out the door.

Ten minutes later, trailing her throbbing finger in the cool water of the creek, Amalia's breathing finally eased, her thudding pulse calming. She drew her knees up close to her on the creek bank and leaned her head on the wool of her skirt, her bare feet pressing into the pebbly mud. Her skirt would get muddied too, but she didn't care just now.

"Father in heaven, I don't know how to do this." A sob jerked out. "I can't do all this. Not by myself. It's too much."

Did I ever ask you to?

Had that been a response or simply her own imaginings? Amalia rested her damp cheek on her knees. *Not by might, nor by power, but by my Spirit.* The words trickled through her memory with the murmur of the creek, like a gentle hand caressing her bent head. She released a long, shuddering breath. So much . . . children to care for, a farm to tend, a boardinghouse to run. She hadn't signed up for any of this—it had all just been thrust upon her, though she supposed she'd accepted it. A burden? . . . Or a gift?

Absalom's suggestion to hire more help nudged from a corner of her mind. She hadn't thought she could afford that yet—had thought she could keep handling it all herself. But . . .

Help me. Too weary to think any more just now, she closed her eyes and let the burble of the creek lull her nearly to dozing, till a muffled moo jerked her head upright.

The cows—the children. She'd sent them to the barn alone, hound and cat and three- and five-year-olds, with only Hank to watch them all. What had she been thinking? She shoved to her feet and hurried along the creek bank toward the barn, digging out her handkerchief to wrap her finger as she went. *Please, Lord, let there be no catastrophe.*

Silence hung over the barn as she approached. She creaked open the aged door and peeked inside.

Nearby at the foot of the strawstack, Ruthie petted the kitten curled in her lap. Noah lay on his tummy beside her, playing with fistfuls of straw. Hank stood forking hay into the stalls for the horses, while Honey and the heifer already munched contentedly.

Amalia expelled a long breath and stepped inside. "Where is Dog?"

"I tied 'im up to the clothesline." Hank glanced over his shoulder, from under his shock of untrimmed brown hair. "Sorry 'bout . . . everything."

"It's all right, Hank. And I don't want you to keep him tied up." Goodness, this was the first she'd seen Hank without Dog by his side. "We'll just have to figure out how to keep him and Magpie separate, at least for a while."

She knelt beside Ruthie and reached a finger to brush the silky head of the sleeping kitten.

"She just got scared." Ruthie looked up at Amalia, blue eyes solemn.

"I know. I'm sorry I yelled at you all."

Ruthie leaned into her side. Noah sat up and reached for her injured hand. "Owie?"

"Ja. But it will heal." As would they all, Lord willing.

Coming out of the barn after feeding the stock the next evening before supper, Amalia braced herself to see Zelda heading her direction.

"Some woman is here. Wants to talk to you." For a change, a glint shone in Zelda's eye instead of a glare.

"All right." Could it be the schoolteacher Mrs. Miller had mentioned? Amalia hurried up the back steps into the kitchen, washed her hands, and pulled off her barn apron, then headed into the front parlor—if one could call it that. In addition to Amos's bed, JJ had cobbled together a couple more chairs over the last few days. The man was a wonder with wood, but they could dearly use a couch or settee. The sewing machine sat in front of the window.

"I'm so sorry to keep you waiting." Careful with her English, Amalia held out her hand, finger still bandaged, to the tall young woman who rose from one of the chairs. "I'm Amalia Gunderson."

"Helen Stenerson." She gave Amalia's hand a squeeze. "And I speak Norwegian, if that helps. I'm the schoolteacher here in Green Creek."

"Mrs. Miller mentioned that." Amalia gestured for the teacher to sit again, then took the other chair, slipping gratefully into Norwegian, still so much easier. "I apologize for our lack of furnishings. We still have much to do to make this boardinghouse what it should be."

"I understand. Though it seems you have done a great deal already." Helen clasped her hands on her lap over her dark gray skirt. She held her head erect above the high collar of her white blouse, her blonde hair pulled back softly from her face and wound into a simple bun. "Perhaps Mrs. Miller told you I'm looking for a place to board?"

"She did, ja." Amalia examined the teacher's clear features. She liked Helen's directness and wanted to be equally so. "We would love to have you, though I cannot promise more than the simple necessities yet."

"That's all I need." Helen drew a breath. "I've grown . . . weary, of constantly boarding 'round, moving from one family to another each term. To have one place to set my hat, as it were, would be a gift, however simple. And a room to call my own."

"We can give you that." Amalia thought hard. JJ was working on simple bedsteads for her and Ruthie just now, but he could start on one for Helen next. They had eight bedrooms on the second floor—that one at the end of the hall, with a pretty view, would do well for the teacher. Mrs. Nygard said they could order smaller pieces of furniture for fairly low cost at the mercantile, so perhaps they could add a washstand and dresser without too much trouble. She needed to make more pallets. "How soon would you want to move in?"

"Next week is our last of the term, so we'll end at noon that Friday, the fourteenth of June. Would it be possible for me to come over that afternoon? Or is a week too soon?"

"I think we can do that." *Lord, please let me not be stretching too far.* "We're charging three dollars and seventy-five cents a week. Will that be acceptable for you?" Mrs. Miller said the going rate for room and board was four dollars a week in Decorah, but with such bare furnishings she daren't charge that much yet.

"Yes, I think that's quite reasonable."

She smiled at the young woman. "We will look forward to your coming, Helen."

"Thank you." The schoolteacher drew a breath, the pleating on the front of her blouse rising and falling. "You don't know what a relief this will be to me."

Amalia examined the faint color flushing the young woman's face. Was there more to Helen's eagerness to move into the board-inghouse than she'd said?

NINETEEN

W hy was he so nervous?

Absalom pressed his feet against the floor of the courthouse hallway to still them from tapping. He leaned his head back against the wall where he sat on a wooden bench, waiting for his meeting.

Only a couple more months before he'd be a full-fledged lawyer, walking these halls. Which was why he sat here today, waiting to meet with his mentor to go over the last requirements he needed to complete before taking his legal exams.

He pulled out his watch and glanced at it, the hands ticking agonizingly slow. He pulled a book on criminal law out of his satchel and thumped the weight of it on his lap. Not his favorite area of law, but he had to know it—and he'd been spending too little time studying of late.

He cracked the heavy tome and ran his finger down a page of statutes, reviewing them aloud under his breath. Last year had been his principal year of academics, with this year constituting more practical "legal study" under a practitioner of law—handily, his father. Still, he had a written dissertation to complete before he took his final exam in August.

"Karlsson, there you are. Apologies for the delay."

Absalom closed the book and looked up to meet the piercing gray gaze of Judge Alfelt. "Not a problem, Your Honor."

"Come now, 'sir' does well enough outside the courtroom." Alfelt gave a wink that belied his austere silver hair and black robes. "Into my office now, and we'll have a chat."

"So." A few moments later, the judge leaned back in his leather chair behind his massive mahogany desk and regarded Absalom. "Feeling ready to walk these halls as A. Karlsson, Esquire?"

"Not sure about ready, sir." Absalom leaned forward and steepled his fingers on his knees. "But eager to be."

"That's what I like to hear." Alfelt shook a finger in the air. "You have a passion for law, son, that I've rarely seen in a student your age—I've told this to your father. Oh, plenty of young men come 'eager,' as you put it, to practice law, but often more for the money than the rights and wrongs of it, if you take my meaning. You seem to want to do justly and love mercy and walk humbly with thy God, to quote words more eloquent than my own."

Absalom swallowed, not sure how to take such praise. Should he be wary of a catch? "I just see plenty of wrongs to be righted in this world, sir."

"And so there are, son. So there are." Judge Alfelt put on a pair of silver-rimmed spectacles and peered at a collection of papers on his desk. "So, you're to come for your oral examination the nineteenth of August, is that correct?"

"I believe so."

"And your written dissertation will be due the week prior." The judge looked over his glasses at him. "What topic have you chosen?"

Absalom cleared his throat. "I am thinking something on immigrant law."

Alfelt nodded. "No surprise there, given what I know of your interests. But what, exactly?"

Absalom fought the urge to squirm like a schoolboy. "I, uh, haven't exactly decided." He'd been bouncing ideas around with his father, hashing them out in his brain night after night, tossing on his pillow, but pinning the subject down eluded him. And during the day, he had so much to think about—helping his father, other immigrant cases, how to help Hank and Amalia . . .

"I see." Judge Alfelt plucked off his spectacles and stared at Absalom. "Well, you only have a few weeks, young man. You need to decide."

His ears burned. "Yes, sir."

A few moments later, Absalom emerged from the judge's office, feeling like a chastened schoolboy. Why couldn't he nail his topic down? He should have started writing the dissertation weeks ago, as Judge Alfelt's raised brows and crisp tone had made abundantly clear.

He sighed, clapped his hat back on his head, and headed back down the hallway toward the atrium of the courthouse, his footfalls echoing below the vaulted ceiling.

A lawyer stepped out from a side room, talking with an older woman in a bonnet, doubtless a client. Absalom stepped aside to avoid getting in their way as the woman headed away from him toward the exit, but the attorney glanced back, meeting Absalom's gaze with a spark of recognition.

A knot twisted in Absalom's stomach. Uffe Bernhard, who took any case, the more crooked, the better.

"Karlsson. Greetings." The lawyer's voice came smooth as snake oil. "Still haunting these halls as a legal clerk, or have you actually made it to attorney?"

"I take my examinations in August." Absalom kept his tone even.

"Ah, excellent. Perhaps then we can face each other on equal ground, rather than you hiding behind your father."

Absalom tightened his jaw. "I had no need to hide. Your client hadn't a leg to stand on, cheating immigrants right and left. The Jorstads were only one of many families he defrauded."

"Well, we all have to make a living." Bernhard's eyes narrowed. "Even you. You'll never be able to keep a fiancée if you don't." He clucked his tongue. "Ought to think about providing for a family, Karlsson. Dirt-poor immigrants and vagrants won't go far to paying the bills."

Absalom stepped around the man and headed for the front doors. The lawyer, who'd represented the unscrupulous landlord in the Jorstad case, of course knew of his broken engagement two years ago, like everyone else.

"When I heard you'd taken up law, I thought you'd be a fine provider. I didn't know you meant to do law like that." Rebecca's remembered words, flung at him the night she jilted him, stung again—but not, this time, because of Rebecca herself. That hole in his heart had finally healed, thanks be to God. But could Uffe Bernhard have a point? He'd been a bully since their school days. However, did Absalom have the right, with his fledgling career, to the other dreams daring to sprout unspoken in his heart of late . . . of another possibility for a family of his own someday?

Surely God would provide, and lead, when the time came. But still, Bernhard's words rankled.

Blinking in the bright sun outside, Absalom paused on the courthouse steps a moment. Below at the bottom of the steps, the older woman Bernhard had met with climbed into a wagon driven by a farm boy—a bit of an odd conveyance. He frowned and peered more closely. Was that Zelda Berg? What on earth would she be doing at the Decorah courthouse?

He hurried down the steps, but the wagon drove away before he could hail her. Or even be sure he'd seen right.

Back home, Absalom pushed open the door to the familiar office bell's jangle. He'd eat the sandwich Mrs. Skivens had left, then dive into his studies for the afternoon. Perhaps he could finally pinpoint his dissertation topic—the run-in with Bernhard had given him an idea.

But a feminine murmur from within the open door of his father's private office pricked up his ears and quickened his steps. He peeked inside to see Amalia Gunderson sitting in the chair opposite his father's desk. Absalom fought the grin that sprang to his face. He shouldn't be so obvious.

"Absalom, come in." His father glanced over at him. "How did it go with the judge?"

He tipped his head. He'd fill his father in later. "I'm set for the examinations."

"Excellent. As you can see, I have company."

"God dag." Amalia smiled up at him. "Your father has very kindly been giving me some advice."

"Is everything all right?" Absalom sat down on the green upholstered chair opposite hers. What a gift to see her again—her steady blue-gray eyes and crown of golden braids. Sudden gratitude to be free of Rebecca made him breathe deep.

She nodded. "Ja—at least, I think so. But so much is happening. I feel the need for some guidance."

"Have you found those missing papers?"

Her face dimmed. "Not yet."

"We've been discussing the money." His father tapped his fountain pen on his desk. "Miss Gunderson wisely wants to save as much as she can, yet draw on some of the funds to finish furnishing the boardinghouse."

"Have you new boarders?"

"One. Miss Helen Stenerson, the schoolteacher of Green Creek."

"Splendid." Absalom leaned forward, clasping his hands. "So with the man from the railroad, that makes two?"

"Two paying boarders, ja. But as I was about to tell your father, Hank also has brought us another child."

Absalom sat up straight. "What? Who?"

"A little boy, Noah. I think he's only about three." Amalia drew a breath. "He's mixed-race and seems to be alone in the world now. His mother just died, and Hank knew her. So did JJ—or at least, of her. Have you heard of Lottie Williams?"

His father let out a low sigh. "Of course I have. Dear God, she is gone?"

Amalia pressed her palms together in her lap. "I'm afraid so."

"Who is this, Father?"

"A few years ago, when you were in college"—his father stared at his desktop, turning his pen between his hands—"a couple came to me to be married, a young Negro man who worked on the railroad and Lottie Larsen."

"The banking Larsens?" Absalom felt his eyes widen.

"Yes. Her parents were adamantly opposed, of course, but she insisted she didn't care, that they'd run away together regardless. And I knew the young man a bit—Curtis, I believe his name was."

Amalia nodded. "Ja, Curtis Williams."

"That was it. He'd been of assistance in a train robbery case that the Pinkertons pursued; I'd helped him come forward as a witness. Got two men put away for the crime. He was a good, honorable young man, and Lottie was head over heels for him, I could see that. So I married them." He sighed. "Knew they'd have a rough time of it, but through no fault of their own—and who was I to stand in the way of lawful marriage? I haven't heard much of them for a couple of years, thought perhaps they'd moved out of town."

"They wanted to, according to Hank. Curtis has been working on the railroad, trying to save enough to take his family west where they'd encounter less prejudice, could have their own land. Lottie had been taking in washing and sewing, but she got sick."

"Why didn't Hank come to me?" His father rubbed his hand

over his face. "Didn't he know I would have helped? Since her parents certainly wouldn't."

"I don't know." Amalia bit her lip. "But we have Noah now."

"Is the boy all right?" Absalom asked.

"He injured his foot when Hank was bringing him—they walked all the way from Decorah in the middle of the night. But it's healing now. I hope that is also true of his heart. I feel an urgency to find his father. Amos, that's our boarder who works on the railroad, is going to try and find someone who knows him, but if you have any other advice?"

"Of course." A spark of energy came back into his father's voice. "I have contacts with some of the railway executives in this area. I'll write to them and see what I can learn."

"Mange takk."

"Hank, Ruthie, now this little fellow." Absalom shook his head. "You are practically running an orphanage."

She lifted her shoulders. "So it seems at times. And I love them all, but I hope we can keep putting food on the table."

"And so you need boarders." Absalom glanced at his father. "How else can we help?"

"I wondered if there's a way to advertise on the railroad. How might I print a—what do you call it, pamphlet?"

"There's a print shop in town." Absalom nodded. "I can take you over now, if you like."

"Takk." She smiled at him, sending his pulse thrumming in that way she had. "That would be wonderful." She stood. "Mrs. Miller came over to watch the children for me today, but I shouldn't stay long. Which reminds me . . ." She drew a breath. "You mentioned a client of yours, with a daughter—do you think she might still be looking for work?"

Absalom raised a brow. "Of course, Carl Jorstad and his daughter. I can ask. Could you use the help?" Silly question. He'd no idea how she'd managed this long on her own as it was, as little help as he guessed Zelda gave.

"I—I think so." She twisted her fingers together. "I'm a bit nervous about paying for everything still, but especially with trying for more boarders, I'm realizing—I can't do everything."

"A wise realization some of us take decades to reach." His father nodded, his gray eyes warm as they rested on her.

"Takk for all your help, Magistrate. I do hope I haven't troubled you too much."

His father stood, grunting slightly with the weight on his bad leg. "No trouble at all, Miss Gunderson. It's just this news about Lottie's child. I can't help feeling a mite responsible."

"You're not responsible for people's hate." Her voice came soft and firm. "You only sought to side with love."

One corner of his mouth tipped up. "Thank you, my dear. I'll let you know if I can learn anything about Curtis Williams's whereabouts."

Absalom grabbed his hat, so recently on his head, and headed back out into the sunlit street, this time with Amalia by his side.

"I hope I'm not making you miss your lunch. You only just returned from the courthouse." She glanced up at him with a furrow in her brow.

"Not a worry. My sandwich will keep perfectly well." *And I'd skip lunch every day if it meant time with you.* He clamped the words inside his head and smiled down at her. "The print shop is just around the corner."

She fell into step beside him, her braided head bobbing only a few inches below his own. "Mange takk. It sounds so simple, to have something printed up, but I didn't know where to start."

"Mr. Brynild Anundsen publishes the *Decorah-Posten* newspaper here." As they turned the corner, Absalom gestured to the sign above the shop ahead. "But they also print whatever else a customer might need on paper. Calling cards, handbills, custom stationery, advertisements. Even wedding invitations." Now why had he mentioned that last item? Perhaps because he and Rebecca had come here early in their engagement to look at possibilities— only to have their very different ideas on how much they should spend widen the rift already opening between them. Absalom bit the inside of his cheek. "Here we are."

The scent of fresh ink and new paper greeted them along with the clatter of the printing presses. Absalom lifted his hand to hail a black-aproned young clerk, who hurried over to the counter.

"What can I do for you, mister and missus?"

"I, ah." Absalom's neck heated. He thought they were married? "This is Miss Gunderson. She runs the old Forsberg boardinghouse now."

"Right, I heard they were back in business." The young man grabbed a pen from behind his ear, not seeming to notice or care about his mistaken assumption. "You needin' some pamphlets printed up, miss?"

"Ja." Amalia laid her fingertips on the edge of the counter. "How much are they?"

He named the price. "'Course, if you buy in bulk, that'll be less."

"I suppose I'll take fifty, then." She swallowed. "Do you think that's too many, Absalom?"

"Not if you really want to get the word out." He itched to reach into his wallet and pay for them himself, but he knew she'd refuse. "What do you want them to say?"

"Rooms for let, three-seventy-five a week." She sounded the English words carefully. "And that we're in Green Creek, of course, since I hope we can pass the pamphlets through the trains to other places, as well as in Decorah."

"What's the name of your boardinghouse?" The clerk looked up from writing.

She hesitated. "I believe it was known as Forsberg House, and it should still be, since it will belong to Ruthie." She glanced at Absalom. "I just hope Zelda doesn't protest."

A fair concern. The memory from the courthouse prickled in the back of Absalom's brain like a nettle. Had that woman been Zelda? If so, what on earth had she been doing there? Her and Bernhard together . . . well, he didn't like the feeling in his gut.

"What else should I say?"

Absalom focused back on Amalia and the clerk, their heads bent over the paper on the counter.

"Well, lady, you've got three more lines you can use before the price goes up again."

Absalom leaned on the counter. "What else is special that you offer at the boardinghouse? What would appeal to what folks need?"

"Well, we have hot, home-cooked meals. And laundry is included. Clean rooms—at least, they are now."

The clerk scribbled fast. "Home-cooked meals, clean rooms, laundry. How 'bout 'Less than three miles from Decorah station'? Since folks might not know where Green Creek is."

"Good idea." She nodded. "Takk—I mean, thank you."

"Not to worry." He cracked a grin. "I'm Irish, but I hear as much Norwegian as English around here. Matter of fact—" He reached over and whipped a newspaper off a stack, landing it in front of her. "Like a copy of the newest issue of the *Decorah-Posten*?"

Amalia ran her fingers down the freshly printed page, eyes wide. "It's in Norwegian?"

"Sure is. Reports on local news and stuff back in Norway. Circulation approaching twenty thousand throughout this region, last report I heard. We've even got serial stories and Norwegian folk songs."

Absalom fought a grin at the wonder on Amalia's face. The boy could make a living as a salesman.

"How much?" Amalia turned the first page as if it were made of precious parchment.

"On the house today, miss, bein' as you're new in town. Anything else on your pamphlet?"

"Mange takk. And no, I think that should be fine." Her eyes sought Absalom's. "Do you agree?"

He nodded. "Straightforward and clear. I think weary travelers would take an interest."

"All right, then." She paused at the sight of another flyer hanging from the counter. "Is this for the spring dance I've heard about?"

"That's right. Going to be at the town hall next Saturday. A real shindig, by the sound of it." He winked. "I'm takin' my girl."

"I see." Her cheeks pinking, Amalia dug the coins out of her purse to pay for the leaflets.

Absalom clenched his hands at the thought suddenly beating hard in his chest. He'd barely heard his father mention the town festivities, but with all his heart he suddenly yearned to ask Amalia to it. Did he dare? Would she be affronted, and their friendship altered? Or . . . might she possibly say yes?

Mind tumbling, he followed her out the door of the print shop, where she paused on the wooden sidewalk.

"Eben Miller asked me to that dance. I still don't know if I should go."

Absalom's pulse halted a moment, then resumed a dull, steady throb.

"How nice," he heard himself say. For what else could he?

TWENTY

How had she agreed to this?

Amalia flung her best dark red woolen skirt on her bed, plopped herself next to it, and covered her face with her hands. She could sit here comfortably now and rest her feet on the ground, thanks to the bed frame from JJ's capable hands. But that proved small comfort at the moment.

With a groan, she peered through the tangle of her fingers at the open trunk against the wall, where she still kept most of her clothing and belongings brought from Norway. Little Noah bent over it, pulling out scarves and stockings to strew on the floor, and she didn't have the energy to hinder him at the moment. None of that clothing seemed right for an American dance. She should never have agreed to go with Eben. And now the dance was tomorrow. What on earth had she been thinking?

Something white Noah flung aside caught her eye. She stared a moment, then scrambled to her knees and snatched the roll of papers on the floor into her hands, scarcely daring to breathe lest they disappear again. The guardianship papers. Had they been here all along, somewhere in the trunk and now found by Noah's little hands? Had she missed them, in all the times she'd looked? Or . . . the back of her neck prickled. Had Zelda indeed taken them and now brought them back . . . and her with enough gall to have seethed at them about noticing the sewing machine in her room. Amalia rubbed her forehead and tucked the papers into the farthest corner of the trunk, covering them with her mor's shawl-wrapped Bible and saving aside the original to keep elsewhere. She wouldn't chance them all going missing at once again.

And Zelda had finally agreed to teach her to use the sewing machine next week. Should she just act as if nothing had happened?

"Malia!" Ruthie's holler drifted up the stairs.

Amalia sighed and pushed herself off the floor. As usual, any moments marginally to herself came swiftly to a close. She crossed to the door and leaned out. "What is it?"

"The teacher lady is here."

Uff da, that's right—it was Friday afternoon already.

"Come, Noah." Amalia tugged him away from the trunk and hurried down the stairs as fast as his three-year-old legs could keep up, mentally examining the room at the end of the hall they'd prepared for Miss Stenerson. Room freshly swept and scrubbed, newly built bed in place, the washstand set with a porcelain pitcher and basin she'd splurged on from the mercantile with part of her withdrawal from the bank. "Strategic use of your resources," the magistrate called it—spending enough to create a welcoming space for boarders, thus eventually bringing in more funds. But had she remembered to put out towels?

"Miss Stenerson, welcome." Amalia pasted on a smile as she reached the foot of the stairs, hoping her braids weren't too mussed from trying on both her good blouses. Ruthie stood still holding the door open, with the schoolteacher in the doorway, a satchel in her hands. "Please, come in."

"Thank you." Miss Stenerson stepped inside.

Amalia glanced past her to the porch. "Have you nothing else?" Surely a schoolteacher had more belongings than would fit in one small carpetbag.

"I do have a trunk, but it's still at my student's family's home. I wondered if someone might be able to take a wagon and bring it for me tomorrow?"

"Of course. We have a team and wagon now; Mr. JJ should be able to fetch it for you. I wish I had realized—we could have offered to come and get you and your belongings all together. Then you wouldn't have had to walk all this way."

"I enjoy walking. And I—well, I wanted to come here as soon as possible." Though she smiled, something in Helen's eyes told a different story.

Amalia pushed her questions back for now. "Well, let us get you settled. May I?" She took the satchel Helen relinquished. "Ruthie, you may close the door, and bring Noah." Amalia led the way to the stairs, the teacher following.

"Do you teach English at your school?" Ruthie tagged at Miss Stenerson's heels, Noah trotting at her side.

"Yes, we teach English and many other things."

"Like what?"

"Mathematics, and history, and geography. Penmanship and music."

"I love music. Tante Malia, can I go to school?"

"Ja, I've been thinking about that." Amalia reached the top of the stairs and turned down the hallway. "When does the fall term start?"

"Usually late August or early September, depending how haying and harvest go." Miss Stenerson paused as Amalia opened the door to her room. "So at the end of the summer, Ruthie, perhaps you can start school in my primer class. Would you like that?"

"Ja." Ruthie gave a little skip.

They stepped into the room. Afternoon sunshine beamed through the window in golden stripes across the bare planked floor, adding to the stuffy heat upstairs. Amalia set the satchel beside the bed and crossed to open the window, letting in a cooling breeze.

"This is lovely." Miss Stenerson drew a breath and unpinned her light gray hat. She crossed to the window and gazed out over the waving green of the pasture below. The breeze teased tendrils of hair from her bun. Noah ran to peer out the window too, chubby hands gripping the sill that his chin barely reached.

"I'm sorry I don't have curtains yet—or a rug. Hopefully soon."

"I don't need that. This is just perfect." The teacher turned and smiled down at the little boy. "Thank you—or should I say, mange takk?"

"Velbekommen. We are trying to work on our English."

"And you are doing very well."

"Ruth—ie! No—ah!" Hank's holler echoed up the stairs. Both children ran to the hallway.

"What?" Ruthie shouted back.

Amalia winced. She hurried to the doorway. "Hank, Ruthie, what have we said about yelling inside?" If Zelda were here, she'd have snapped off heads by now.

"Sorry." Hank paused halfway up the stairs. "But that broody hen, her chicks are hatching. JJ found them, told me to get the young'uns."

"Oh, my." Amalia drew a breath. Baby chicks—she yearned to see them too. "All right, then. You can take them, but watch Noah, all right? Mama hens can peck."

"I will." Hank reached up for the little boy's hand, already climbing down the stairs toward him, clinging to the banister. Ruthie hurtled past them, braids flying.

Amalia sighed and turned back to Miss Stenerson, waiting just inside her room with a smile teasing the corners of her mouth.

"You must think you've entered a madhouse. I'm sorry."

The schoolteacher laughed. "I teach eight grades in one room, remember? This will be calm by comparison."

"Are you sure we can't send someone for your trunk today? I could ask JJ—he's our handyman."

She shook her head. "Tomorrow morning will be fine."

"I'll leave you to settle in, then. Supper will be at six." Amalia turned to go, then hesitated. "Miss Stenerson—is everything all right? With your previous boarding place, I mean."

The young woman's smile dimmed. "You are quite perceptive, Miss Gunderson."

"Forgive me." Amalia shook her head. "I shouldn't pry."

"No, I've doubtless given enough hints." She sighed. "Let's just say, a member of that family showed a—well, an interest in me that went beyond what was welcome. Or proper."

Amalia's middle twisted. "I'm sorry."

"It's fine. That is, I'm fine. Now." Miss Stenerson put on a smile that almost reached her eyes. "Thanks to you and this lovely place. Life can just be complicated, can't it?"

"Ja." Amalia gave a half chuckle, half sigh. "Even the littlest things. I'm ashamed to say that before you arrived, I nearly lost my temper over what to wear to the spring dance tomorrow."

"Oh, are you attending?"

"Ja—I suppose so. That is, I've been invited." Her ears warmed. Why had she brought this up?

"How lovely. By whom?"

"Eben Miller." Amalia drew a breath and twisted her fingers together. "His family's farm is next door."

"Did you find a dress to wear?"

"I don't really have any American dresses. I suppose I'll just wear my Sunday bunad."

"Well, goodness, I think I have a dress you could borrow. We're about the same size."

Amalia stared at her. "I couldn't ask that."

"You're not asking, I'm offering. Please, it would give me such joy."

Her eyes suddenly pricked. "You are so kind. Mange takk, Miss Stenerson."

"It's settled, then, once my trunk arrives. On one condition."

Amalia blinked. "Ja?"

The teacher smiled. "That you call me Helen."

She reached to squeeze the teacher's offered hand. "Only if you call me Amalia."

———

The next afternoon, standing in her room in petticoat and corset with Helen laying out the fashionable blue dress on her bed, Amalia gripped the bedpost and fought a wave of nausea.

"I don't think I can do this."

"Nonsense. You can't back out now."

"I can if I'm going to be ill."

"And spoil the most fun I've had since I can remember?" Helen put her hands on her hips and gave a mock frown.

"Why don't you just go? You'll wear that lovely dress much better than I." Amalia scanned the garment, a soft French-blue trimmed with darker blue shirring on the overskirt, bodice, and sleeves, not to mention tiny cloth buttons all down the front.

"I don't have anyone to go with. You do. Now, no more nonsense, let's get you into this."

Amalia stepped into the skirt and let Helen help her button it securely around her waist, then lifted her arms for the top of the dress to slip heavy over her head. She worked on the buttons while Helen arranged the bustle in the back—a complete mystery to Amalia. How strange these American clothes were. Give her a simple Norwegian blouse and skirt.

"Oh, it fits you like a dream." Helen stepped back and clasped her hands. "Now we have only to do your hair. Where's your hairbrush?"

"My hair?" She reached to touch her crown of braids, no doubt mussed by the dress. But she could just redo them. "I don't want anything fancy."

"Trust me. Sit." Helen guided her toward a chair.

Amalia sat. Helen certainly must make a good schoolmarm.

But oh, how had she gotten herself into this? She should be making more pallets or interviewing Inga Jorstad, the girl Absalom had found to help her. And how could she run off and leave the children for a whole evening? Despite Mrs. Miller's kind offer, Zelda had announced at lunch that she would watch the children. Amalia's face must have showed her shock, as Zelda's thin cheeks actually reddened.

"What, you think I'm not capable to keep eyes on three young rascals?" she'd snapped.

Amalia held serious misgivings on that. But JJ promised he'd stay close, and him she did trust. Helen would also keep a watchful eye. Amalia would simply tell Eben she couldn't stay late.

"There." Helen stepped back, a note of satisfaction in her voice. "Do you have a mirror?"

"Nei, I'm afraid not." Amalia lifted a hand to feel her hair. What had Helen done?

"Come into my room, then." Helen tugged her out the doorway and across the hall. In the teacher's room, she plucked a pewter-backed hand mirror from her dresser and held it out. "Look."

Amalia gripped the mirror's cool handle and peeked at herself. She caught her breath. Her head rose elegantly from the high collar of the dress, braids rewoven and pinned up in coils behind her head rather than over it. Helen had somehow fluffed out her front hair to softly frame her face, even teasing out a curl or two. A breath of a laugh escaped her.

"I hardly recognize me." Amalia handed the mirror back.

"You look lovely." Helen gave her arm a quick squeeze and took the mirror back. "But you should get downstairs. Your escort will be here soon."

Her escort. Middle tightening, Amalia lifted her heavy skirts to descend the stairs.

Ruthie met her at the bottom, eyes wide. "You look like a princess, Tante Malia."

"Takk, den lille." Amalia hugged the little girl to her side, careful not to muss Helen's dress. "You be good for Cousin Zelda, all right?"

Ruthie scrunched up her face. "I'll try. She said she'd teach me to knit socks for Noah."

Well, that sounded encouraging. "Good girl. Where are Noah and Hank?"

"Helping JJ in the barn."

Would JJ make sure Noah stayed away from the horses' hooves? Oh, perhaps she shouldn't go after all.

The rumble of a buggy outside the front door set her heart to pattering.

"Go." Helen gave her a gentle push from behind. "Ruthie and I will go check on the boys."

"Mange takk. For everything." Amalia sent her a glance she hoped conveyed the gratitude she felt. How had this young woman become such a friend already? She drew a steadying breath, then headed straight toward the knock on their door. She opened it and smiled at Eben Miller, standing there in collar and jacket, hat in hand and a grin on his face. "Good evening, Mr. Miller."

She accepted the arm he held out and followed him to the buggy without a backward glance. She would make the best of this evening.

At least, she would try.

They had little conversation on the way—Eben didn't attempt much, and neither did she, focusing on breathing despite the unfamiliar corset and company. He helped her down from the wagon when they arrived at the town hall where the dance was to be held.

"You sure look pretty." Eben beamed down at her.

"Takk—thank you." Amalia swallowed and took the arm he held out.

Within the hall laughter and lamplight swirled, chatter rising like a cloud of insects above the hum of fiddles being tuned in the corner. The scent of punch and cake mingled with that of so many people crowded together on a warm evening. Amalia held tighter to Eben's sturdy arm despite herself. He led her to some empty chairs set on the side, where she sank and scanned the crowd for anyone she knew. She spied a few people she'd seen at church, and the clerk from the print shop where Absalom had taken her. Was Absalom here? She didn't see him.

She'd hardly caught her breath before the band struck up the first tune. Eben set his hat on his chair, then held out his hand to her.

"Want to dance?"

Well, that was what they were here for, wasn't it? Amalia made herself smile and stand. "Ja, thank you."

He led her onto the floor where couples already gathered in circles. At least she recognized the music and form as the Seksmannsril—a six-man reel she'd often done in gatherings in Norway as a girl. If only her far or bror were here to partner with her now. She pushed back the tightness in her throat and gripped Eben's offered hand on one side, that of fatherly Mr. Gruber, the stationmaster, on her other. The music launched into the dance, and she circled with the others, first to the left, then to the right. She spun to face Eben, gripping both his hands as she skipped backward around the circle. When it came Eben's turn to skip backward with his corner partner, though, he stumbled and fell, crashing into Amalia from behind. She helped him up—red in the face, poor fellow—and guided him back into the right-hand chain now winding through the circle, hoping she sent him in the right direction. They connected back into circling left without major mishap, and she drew a breath of relief. But when they had to skip backward again, clapping this time, the strain on Eben's face made her middle pinch for him. The poor man, was he going through all this for her? It seemed torment to him.

They both drew long breaths of relief when the music ended—or as long a breath as Amalia could draw in her tight bodice—and joined in the applause.

"Sorry 'bout that." Eben's neck bloomed red above his collar. "Never can get the hang of these Norwegian dances."

"That's all right. Would you like a drink of water?" By the shine on his forehead, he could use it.

The music struck up again, and Eben's face brightened. "Is this a polka?"

Amalia listened to the lilting strains. "Ja, I think it's a pols."

"I know this one—my mor taught me." Before she could reply, he caught her by the waist and pulled her out onto the dance floor again.

Amalia clung to his broad shoulder and hand, desperately trying to make her feet fly in step with his. Eben might know the polka steps, but he hadn't the faintest notion about timing. He whirled her about till her feet left the floor and the room spun about her like the roundabout Far had taken her on once as a little girl.

The music finally stopped, Amalia still gripping Eben's hand for balance till the room stopped turning. Her head pounded.

"That was fun." He grinned. "Want a drink now?"

Amalia nodded mutely and let him lead her through the crowd to a table with bowls of punch and platters of cookies and cakes. She took the punch in a shaky hand and sipped, the liquid cool but so sweet it puckered her mouth.

"How 'bout a plate of food?" Eben scanned the platters.

"I'm really not hungry." Amalia laid a hand on her middle, queasy from spinning. "You go ahead."

"You sure?"

"Ja."

"Be right back."

She stepped to the side of the room and breathed a sigh to have a moment alone. Sipping her punch, she scanned the crowd, wishing she knew more people. But how could she, having been here barely a month and a half, and always so busy at the boardinghouse? She should be thankful for the dear friends they had already made . . . the Millers, the Karlssons. Warmth circled her heart at the thought, despite the pang of missing home. She needed to write her remaining family again, and the Haugens. Mrs. Haugen had written that Lars had already found a sweetheart in Dakota Territory—they sounded happy, building a new life though not forgetting the old.

Another dance struck up, and the clerk from the newspaper office claimed her for it before she could look for Eben. Next she danced with a stout young man she'd never seen before, and wove her way through a reel on Mr. Gruber's arm.

At last she made her way to their chairs and sat down, trying not to crush Helen's bustle. What had made her agree to wear this dress? She'd have been much more comfortable in her own skirt and vest, if less fashionable. She scanned the crowd for Eben and saw him visiting animatedly with the Nygards by the refreshment tables. Her lips quirked. Talking definitely seemed more his suit than dancing.

"Amalia?"

She looked up to see Absalom approaching, brown eyes wide behind his spectacles.

"Mr. Karlsson—Absalom." She rose, a smile coming unbidden at the sight of his familiar face. "I didn't see you—I mean, how good to see you here."

"To tell the truth, I almost didn't come." He passed a hand through his tousled dark curls. He wore a light brown herringbone suit that seemed better suited for the law office than at a dance— which somehow made her feel more at ease in her stuffy ensemble.

"Why not?"

He lifted a shoulder with a half smile. "I didn't have anyone to go with. But my father urged me, and finally I thought—why not? Anyway—" He cleared his throat. "You look beautiful."

She sighed. "You're kind to say so. Our new boarder, Helen Stenerson, loaned me this lovely dress. But I feel like a fashion doll."

The gentle strains of a vals began. Absalom glanced around. "Where is your escort?"

"Eben went to get food." She scanned the tables and saw him now forking food into his mouth from a plate and chatting with a plump young blonde woman. She smiled. "I think he's quite occupied."

"Well, then." Absalom's throat worked slightly, and he held out his hand. "Might I have this dance?"

She smiled, some of the tension in her chest easing. "You certainly may."

He led her out onto the dance floor and took her hand in his, his other resting lightly on the small of her back. Their steps fell into rhythm together—a simple waltz, but like a drink of cool water after the flurry of the last few dances. Amalia floated on the lilt of the music, Absalom steering her gentle but sure, their feet moving in time. When the music finished, he gave her a little spin under his arm. She dipped into a curtsey and rose, laughing.

"That was lovely." She joined in the clapping with everyone else. "Mange takk, Absalom."

"Velbekommen." He swallowed and clasped his hands behind his back.

Was he flushed? Perhaps the heat of the room was getting to him too. Just then she spied Eben crossing the floor to her once more.

"Evenin', Karlsson." He gave Absalom a genial nod. "Thanks for takin' care of my partner for me. Didn't mean to leave her for so long."

"Of course. Till later then, Miller, Miss Gunderson." Absalom dipped a quick bow, then slipped away through the crowd.

Amalia watched him go, fighting a sense of loss. She forced a smile back up at Eben's towering figure. She hadn't had to look up so high for Absalom. "Did you want to dance again?"

"Actually." The young man hesitated. "I'm not much good at dancin'. Not sure if you could tell."

Amalia bit her lips to hide a smile. "It was very kind of you to invite me here, then. Would you rather just go home?"

His eyes widened. "Would you mind?"

"Of course not. You've given me a lovely time, but I'm rather tired." And stifled, and alone in a sea of strangers—at least now that Absalom had disappeared. She scanned the milling group of dancers for him again but could spy no young legal clerk in a herringbone suit.

Eben fetched his hat and her shawl, and they headed out into the moonlit evening. Amalia drew a breath of cool night air, wishing she could loosen her corset. Eben helped her up onto the buggy seat, then climbed up beside her.

Holding the reins in his hands, he sat still a moment, leaving the brake set.

Amalia shifted on the seat. "Are you all right?"

"My pa wants me to marry you." He spoke the words low, gazing at the reins in his hands.

Amalia's tongue froze. Her pulse pounded in her head. "He does?" she finally managed. Not that she hadn't guessed, but she hadn't expected to hear this tonight.

"Do you want to?" He glanced up at her at last. She couldn't read his face beneath the shadow of his hat.

"Eben." She swallowed past the dryness in her throat. "You're a good man. You've shown me much kindness, and I respect you. But . . ."

"But you don't see your way clear to marryin' me."

She sat silent a moment. Was she being a fool, to throw away this chance? A secure future, not just for her but for Ruthie, Noah, Hank. The boardinghouse itself. Marriage, a husband, more children to come. A good man willing to walk by her side. And yet . . . somehow, she couldn't. "I'm afraid not."

He let out a long sigh, then released the wagon brake and softly hupped the horses. "That's all right. I figured maybe we weren't rightly cut out for each other."

"Really?" She dared to glance at him.

"Just a feelin'." A grin peeked through his voice. "'Sides, I was talkin' to Holman's daughter at the dance. They have the farm on t'other side of our'n. Might be she'd be amenable to goin' courtin', if you ain't."

A laugh burbled from Amalia's chest. "Well, I'm glad to hear it."

Eben drove her up to the boardinghouse porch, then walked her to the door. Amalia bid him thank you and good-night, then stepped inside and fastened the door as quietly as she could, the house still and darkened. She crept up the stairs, hearing Zelda's snoring from below. In her room, she slipped Helen's dress over her head and unlaced her corset, exhaling a long breath, then pulled her own cotton nightdress over her head.

"Malia." Ruthie's whisper could have been heard by the chickens outside.

"Ssh." Amalia buttoned her nightgown and padded over to sit on the side of the little girl's bed. Noah slumbered in a silent heap on his cot nearby. "Why aren't you asleep?"

"I was waiting for you to come home."

"I'm here now, den lille." Amalia laid her hand on Ruthie's cheek. "Sleep now." Magpie curled near Ruthie's back, a small dark purring mound.

"Did you have fun at the party?"

"I did—and I didn't. But I'm glad I went." It had clarified some things, at least. "How was your evening?"

"All right." Ruthie yawned. "Cousin Zelda taught me to turn a heel."

Amalia smiled in the darkness. "Well done."

"Are you going to marry Mr. Eben? Cousin Zelda says you are."

Amalia caught her breath, then pushed down the hot prick of

anger. She shouldn't be surprised, though, that Zelda would speak of such things to the children . . . "No, Ruthie. I am not."

"All right." Ruthie turned onto her side and put her arm over the kitten, pillowing her cheek on her other hand. "I'd rather you marry Mr. Absalom anyway."

Amalia paused her hand in stroking Ruthie's hair. Now where had that come from?

TWENTY-ONE

R uthie loved going barefoot in the garden.

She wiggled her bare toes in the dark brown earth between the rows of beans, then bent to pull out another weed. "Like this, Cousin Zelda?"

Cousin Zelda, her face shielded from the beaming sun with a giant brown gingham sunbonnet, nodded. "Just remember to pull gentle."

"Because we don't want to pull up the bean plants with the weeds."

"That's a good girl." Cousin Zelda straightened from where she knelt between the rows and moved to another plant, peeking under the leaves.

She was checking for bean beetles, Ruthie knew that. Cousin Zelda had taught her to do that too. She'd been teaching her a lot of things lately, and seemed nicer, at least sometimes. Ruthie peeked under a broad green leaf, but no orangey-tan spotted bugs.

"Root-ee!"

Ruthie popped up and shaded her eyes to see Noah running toward her through the garden, Tante Amalia following behind.

231

Noah's little brown feet scampered bare too, and he beamed that special grin he had just for her.

"Noah!" Ruthie held out her arms for his hug, and he tackled her, knocking them both to the soft earth. Giggling, she sat up and brushed her hair out of her eyes. "Silly boy. Come on, I'll show you how to check for bean beetles."

"Bean beetles." Noah nodded.

"How goes the gardening?" Tante Amalia wore a sunbonnet too, made from the same yellow calico as Ruthie's, though Ruthie's hung down her back just now. She didn't like the way the brim made it hard to see.

"Well enough," Cousin Zelda grunted as she stood and moved farther away from Ruthie and Noah. She never seemed as nice when Noah was around, or Tante Amalia. When Tante Amalia had been away at the party, Cousin Zelda had even called Noah a funny name, and she'd looked mean when she said it. It made Ruthie feel like her stomach had a knot tied in it. Mr. JJ had heard and snapped at her never to use such language again, or he'd see to it she got kicked into the streets.

Ruthie didn't want Cousin Zelda kicked into the streets. She just wanted her to be nice, like when she helped Ruthie with her knitting every night after Noah went to bed. Why couldn't everybody just be nice?

Noah turned over a leaf. "Look, Root-ie. Bean beetle."

Ruthie peered close at the spotted insect. "You're right, Noah. You're a good bean beetle–finder."

Noah stuck his finger up to the leaf and let the beetle crawl onto it. He held it out to Ruthie with a question on his face.

"Cousin Zelda says to squish them."

Noah frowned.

"I know." It made her feel squirmy inside. "But they'll eat the beans otherwise."

The beetle flew away from Noah's finger. At least they didn't have to worry about whether to squish that one now.

"Mr. JJ says to sprinkle wood ashes on the bean plants. That will get rid of the beetles." Tante Amalia looked out over the rows of bush bean plants to the staked tomatoes and waving cornfield beyond. "The garden is doing well. You are becoming a good little gardener, Ruthie."

"Can we pick beans for dinner?"

Tante Amalia smiled and held out her gathering basket. "What do you think I brought this for?"

Noah did a dance on his bare toes. Ruthie grabbed his hands and spun in a little circle with him between the rows, both of them giggling. Her heart did its own happy dance, happier than she'd felt in a long time.

That afternoon, Ruthie was heading upstairs to get her rag doll and Noah's toy elephant so they could play when Cousin Zelda called her from the parlor doorway.

"Ruthie. Come in here." Cousin Zelda hesitated. "Please."

Ruthie paused a moment, dangling one foot off the bottom step, then let go of the banister and followed.

Cousin Zelda sat on the worn velvet settee and patted the empty space beside her. "I want to show you something."

Ruthie sat on the springy cushion and gazed around the room. It looked more like a parlor now. Not just because of the settee, which was an old one the storekeeper's family had been getting rid of, but JJ had carved a side table and two more chairs, nicer than the ones in the kitchen, and Tante Amalia had made cushions for them. They even had two lamps ordered from a big catalog—Sears Roebuck, Hank called it. Ruthie liked to slip in here sometimes and look at the pretty designs etched on their glass globes.

"Now look at this here." Cousin Zelda thumped a fat book in her lap.

"What is it?" Ruthie ran her finger over the raised flowers and leaves trailing over the velvet cover and tried to sound out the letters Miss Stenerson had been teaching her in the evenings. "A-L-B-U-M."

"That's right. You're a smart little girl. This is our family photo album."

"Ours?" Ruthie looked up into Cousin Zelda's face, so close to hers.

"Ja. Our family—yours and mine. We're the only ones who are really family here, aren't we?"

Ruthie looked down. "Tante Amalia is my family."

"Well, I mean by blood. I'm one of your father's cous—"

"And Noah, and Hank, and Mr. JJ. They're all my family too, now."

Cousin Zelda huffed a sigh and opened the album. "Look. I wanted to show you something." She tapped her finger on a page of faded brown and white photographs. "These are your grandparents, did you know that?"

"Ja." Ruthie put her finger near their sober faces. "Far had a picture like this in our Bible. They died before I was born."

"True. Your grandfather, Olaf—he stayed back in Norway to marry your grandmother, but his parents and brother, Amund, came to America and started this boardinghouse many years ago. When Amund grew up, he married Else."

"I know who she is. That's why we came to live here." Ruthie bounced on the springy cushion a little bit, stopping before Zelda could scold her. "Far told me about his Tante Else; he came to visit her in America once, and he liked it here. Because she and Onkel Amund didn't have any children, she decided to give the boardinghouse to us."

"Yes—to us. To you and me, Ruthie. Remember, your Great-Onkel Amund was my cousin, so I'm your first cousin twice removed."

"All right." Ruthie wondered why Zelda was telling her all this. Noah would be wondering where she was. But at least Zelda was being nice and talking to her. Ruthie leaned over and turned the page. "Who are these people?"

"Those are Else's family on her mother's side." The front door clicked. Zelda stiffened and pulled the book away a little bit.

Ruthie looked up to see Tante Amalia standing in the open doorway. She stared at Ruthie and Cousin Zelda with a funny look on her face.

"Yes?" Cousin Zelda's voice had that hard sound back in it again.

"I—I thought you were going to show me how to use the sewing machine."

Zelda snapped the album shut and set it on the side table. "I was just waiting for you."

What had Zelda been showing Ruthie? Amalia shook off the questions and tried to focus on Zelda's taciturn instructions about the sewing machine now set by the parlor window. *Wheel, belt, treadle, needle.* At least the older woman seemed to take more interest in the little girl lately. Any increase in kindness was something to be grateful for.

"Now first you've got to wind your shuttle bobbin. Been a while since I used this thing, the thread is about out."

Amalia tried to follow the quick movements of Zelda's fingers, passing the thread through various points and parts of the machine, slipping the bullet-shaped bobbin onto the bobbin-winder, then pressing a lever and spinning the wheel. The thread wound upon the bobbin as if by magic.

"It's so fast. Did Else teach you to use this machine?"

"My mother had one. She taught me before I was married."

Amalia swiveled her head to stare. "You were married? But— but I thought . . ."

235

"You can shut your mouth now. We're getting flies about."

Was that a tug of humor at the corner of Zelda's lips? Amalia clamped her mouth shut. But—why had she gone by "Miss Berg"? She tried to focus on Zelda's fingers, remarkably deft as she re-inserted the bobbin into the machine, then drew the top thread across the machine, around various small knobs and hooks.

"Now you thread the needle." Zelda held out the thread. "Just like threading any other, but outside to inside."

Amalia drew a breath and took the thread between her fingers. Just like any other—except she'd never known a needle to be stuck upside down in some contraption of a machine. Ducking her head low, Amalia managed to thread it after three tries.

Zelda nodded. "Now we begin." She spun the wheel to start the machine, then used her foot to rock the treadle, a lever plate of woven iron suspended below the machine, back and forth. "You're not so much giving it power as just keepin' it going." The machine hummed throatily, stitching a straight seam across the scrap of muslin Amalia had brought to practice with.

After a moment, Zelda stopped, but didn't get up for Amalia to take her place yet. "I was only married two years. Just seemed easier to go back to bein' 'Miss.' That way not everybody needed to know."

Amalia frowned. Why wouldn't she want others to know? "What happened to your husband? If—if I may ask." She'd never had so close to a real conversation with Zelda.

"Thrown off a horse. Cracked his neck." Her tone lay flat.

"I'm so sorry."

Zelda sniffed. "Good riddance to bad rubbish." She stood. "Here. You try."

Amalia slipped onto the sewing machine stool, her ears tingling to think what hatred could make Zelda speak so about her late husband. Had the man been cruel? Unfaithful? Was that part of what left her so bitter?

"Now give the wheel a spin. That's it. Then keep it going with the treadle—no, I said keep it going, don't push it."

The machine made a clunking sound and went backward. Amalia snatched her finger out of the needle's way and flinched. "Sorry."

"You have to get the rhythm of it."

"I see." Only she didn't. Sweat pricked at Amalia's hairline and under her collar. How would she ever get the hang of this? Yet she'd begged Zelda to teach her this machine. And while she could sew sunbonnets and even dresses for her and Ruthie by hand, outfitting a whole boardinghouse would require faster sewing. Amalia set her teeth and tried again.

"Spin the wheel again and rock with it. Listen to the machine, don't try to make it listen to you."

A novel way to put it. Who would have thought Zelda had a poetic line in her? Amalia gave the wheel another spin, this time managing to rock with the pedal for a few seconds before it clunked and seized up again.

"Almost."

Was that nearly encouragement from Zelda? Amalia drew a breath and fresh courage. She spun the wheel again, this time letting the machine's rhythm guide the rocking of her foot on the treadle. A line of even stiches marched away from her across the muslin strip. A giggle burst from her lips. "I did it." She kept rocking, treadling, stitching till she reached the end of the piece of cloth.

"That's it." Zelda nodded, arms crossed as she stood to the side. "You'll need a lot of practice, but getting the rhythm is the hardest."

"Thank you so much for teaching me." Amalia cut the thread and examined the line of stitches, so neat and even—so fast. "I need to make summer clothes for Ruthie and me, and then more pallets for boarders. I thought curtains for the boardinghouse windows too—don't you think that would brighten things up? Then we'll need more tablecloths, and other linens too." She drew a breath. "Some of it will have to be done over the winter, but if we both can sew, it will go much faster."

"You never run out of ideas, do you?" Zelda pursed her lips.

"It's just things are finally starting to come together. I have a young girl, Inga Jorstad, coming over tomorrow to see about working here, and the flyers for the boardinghouse should be spreading the word now. We may have more boarders by next week."

Zelda's face hardened. "Well, aren't you a wonder." She turned and left the room, her heels stomping on the floor.

Amalia dropped her hands to her lap, still holding the strip of cloth. Here she'd thought she and Zelda had finally been beginning to understand each other a bit more. What had she said wrong?

TWENTY-TWO

*T*wo new boarders! *Mange takk, Lord.*

Amalia hurried the team home from her trip to the mercantile, thankful to have the means to drive herself now, though part of her missed having reason to see the Millers so often. She needed to call on Mrs. Miller for a chat soon. There was just always so much to do—and now Mrs. Nygard had introduced her to two burly brothers at the mercantile, both needing a place to stay. Asgar and Eivor Rykavyk had worked on the construction of the new train station and stayed for other building jobs in Decorah, but they were looking for a quieter, more reasonable spot to board. Their bearded faces had lit up when Amalia mentioned their prices, not to mention hot meals and clean beds. They'd paid her a deposit on the spot.

Even better, Mrs. Nygard had handed her not one but two letters from home in Norway—she could hardly wait to get home and open them. Now if only she hadn't missed Inga Jorstad, who was to come this afternoon.

Amalia drove into the barnyard and braked the wagon, thanking JJ when he came to unhitch the team for her.

"Got a young lady waitin' for you in the kitchen. Nice little thing, but mighty quiet."

That would be Inga. Scolding herself for being late, Amalia

239

gathered her purchases into her arms and hastened up the back porch steps, nearly tripping in her hurry. At least JJ had mended the holes in the back porch and the missing railing out front.

"Inga." She dumped her parcels on the table and smiled at the young girl who stood from a kitchen chair when Amalia came in. "I'm so sorry to keep you waiting." At the faint wrinkle in Inga's brow, Amalia switched to Norwegian. "Takk for coming today."

Inga's face cleared, and she nodded.

JJ was right—what a shy, quiet girl. Seeing Inga Jorstad standing before her in the boardinghouse kitchen, Amalia felt she was looking at herself five years ago. The fifteen-year-old girl stood shoulders straight, hands folded before her clean white apron, hair neatly twisted into one long blonde braid down her back.

"So, Inga, do you like working in the kitchen? You know how to bake bread and biscuits?"

Inga nodded. "Ja. Yeast and sourdough."

Of course she would—Amalia had been baking for years at that age. "What is your favorite thing to bake?" She wanted to draw the girl out a bit more.

Inga tipped her head ever so slightly. "Maybe julekake."

"Oh, my mor used to make that every Christmas." Amalia's mouth watered at the thought of the Norwegian Christmas bread studded with candied fruit. What would Christmas be like for them this year? Her chest squeezed at the thought. "Will this be your first Christmas in America, you and your family?" She thought Absalom had said Inga was the eldest daughter of a large family.

A nod and nibble of her lower lip.

"Well, I can use some help in the kitchen, especially when we have more boarders, but Zelda and I already both do a great deal in here. I may especially need you with extra laundry and cleaning, and sometimes watching the little ones."

Inga nodded. "Whatever you need."

She certainly was willing, if less than conversational. "Mange takk. Let's try two afternoons a week to start. I may be able to in-crease your hours once we have more boarders." If they did—no, surely it would be *when*, as today had already shown. Such a strange mode she'd been in the last few months, planning for people who might or might not materialize. "Would fifty cents a week be acceptable?"

Inga dipped her head. "Ja. Takk."

"Wonderful." Amalia tapped a finger on her chin. Inga had come all the way out here, and her family's farm lay a mile away—she should put her to work on something while she was here. "Might you help me with freshening up the third floor? I just got news that we'll have two more boarders coming in a few days, but they're brothers, so they can bunk down in the open space up there. I'll have Mr. JJ, he's our handyman, put together a couple more bedsteads. I hope one day we can finish off separate rooms up there, but for now I can offer it to bachelors at a reduced rate." Thankfully they'd done all the heavy cleaning weeks ago, but the top floor still needed to be swept again, dusted, and aired and the windows wiped down.

The boardinghouse no longer felt so empty. Zelda's room of course was near the front door, while JJ, Amalia and Ruthie, and Miss Stenerson had rooms on the second floor—and they'd only recently persuaded Hank to move into one there too, rooming with Noah. Amos had expressed willingness to move up to the third floor, which would free up another private room. The Rykavyk brothers, like Amos, would be gone periodically for work.

Inga followed Amalia upstairs, where they opened all the third-floor windows to let summer breezes ease the stuffy heat. "Uff da. The ground floor certainly is cooler. You're sure you'll be all right up here?"

Inga was already tying a handkerchief over her head and at-tacking a corner with the broom Amalia brought. She nodded.

Amalia smiled. "Mange takk. Come down for a drink of water whenever you need it." She strolled downstairs, marveling at the feeling of someone else to share her labor. Guilt tried to pinch, but she squeezed it away. *Mange takk again, Lord. I'm trying not to do everything on my own so much. Thank you for providing—and may this job be a blessing to Inga and her family too.*

Back in the kitchen, she spread out her packages on the table to organize and put away. Beans, flour, salt, sugar. Salt pork and even some canned peaches for a treat. With more boarders coming, it was a good thing she'd just stocked up, else they'd run short on supplies. Amalia smiled to herself. Those Rykavyk brothers looked like they certainly could eat. So much to be thankful for.

Two envelopes fell out from between her packages, and Amalia snatched them up. Her letters from home, and she'd nearly forgotten them. She let the packages sit on the table a bit longer and slit the first envelope with a kitchen knife, this one from her tante, her mor's sister. Reading the carefully penned lines, she sniffed back tears at her aunt's grief-stricken yet comforting words. Blinking hard, Amalia folded the letter and tucked it away to read over again later, then opened the second, this one from her cousin Maya, one of her dearest friends back in Norway.

Min kjære Amalia . . .

Tears filled her eyes again. How the familiar Norwegian endearment balmed her heart. She read on.

> *How your letter grieved us! To think of you losing not just one but both of your parents in that terrible cholera epidemic. We all wept when we read the news, and I know my mor has written to you also. How I wish I could be there to comfort you, cousin. I am glad, however, to hear that you have at least found a place for yourself, for now, though it aches my heart to think of you so far from any family. How good of you to take on care for little Ruthie. How does she fare? So much*

grief for a young one. And to think that you will be in charge of a boardinghouse! Truly we do not know what each day will bring forth, do we?

My sisters send their love and prayers, as does Ødger. My brother is still the handsomest bachelor in Norway, even if he pretends to be so serious with his seminary studies. He has such a heart to serve our Lord—though sometimes the books overwhelm him—and he jokes of coming to Amerika to track down Erik and make him take care of his sister. Have you learned any news of your brother at all?

Einar and I are settling in to married life. How I wish you could have been bridesmaid at my wedding, but I am grateful to have found a good husband. He works so hard for us and is often gone on his fishing boat, as farming here, you know, is nothing but a battle. This is the first I've said of this to anyone, but Einar and I are thinking about coming to Amerika also. Do you think there would be room for us at the boardinghouse, at least for a while? We could help you until we get our own land or Einar finds work. Of course, the voyage is daunting, especially knowing the tragedy you have suffered, but life is full of dangers wherever one is. At least there we would have a chance at building a new life, and we would still be with family.

Let me know what you think, dear Amalia. We wouldn't set sail before March, but we have much to plan and ponder over.

We pray for you daily. Please write soon and tell me how you are keeping.

> *With all my love,*
> *Your cousin,*
> *Maya Bredesen*

Amalia folded the letter and hugged it to her chest a moment. Maya and her husband, coming here? To actually have beloved family at this boardinghouse, willing and ready to help shoulder the load? The weight on her chest lifted even further at the thought, but she drew a steadying breath—she mustn't get her hopes up too much yet, and anyway they wouldn't be here before spring. But oh, how that hope could help carry her through the long winter to come.

"Amalia!" The kitchen door banged open, and Hank burst in.

"What's wrong?" Amalia dropped the envelope back onto the table.

"Noah got kicked by a horse."

"What?" Amalia dashed out the back door after Hank, her heart thudding with the pounding of her feet, Dog barking at their heels. *Dear God, please God, please*—visions of Noah dashed, bloodied to the ground flashed through her mind.

They found JJ bent over Noah, crumpled and sobbing on the barn floor.

Crying, so alive and conscious. Air rushed into Amalia's lungs as she fell to her knees beside the child. "Where is he hurt?"

"Think the horse got his leg. Happened so fast—"

Amalia gently worked off the little boy's trousers, streaked with manure and mud, as he wailed. A darkening bruise seeped a trickle of blood from his thigh. She sucked a breath. "At least it's his leg and not his stomach." Dog snuffled Noah's hair and licked his wet cheek.

JJ shook his head. "You kin say that again. I had a cousin who died from gettin' kicked in the belly as a child."

Amalia shuddered. "We should go for a doctor. Hank, can you?"

Hank scrunched up his face. "The doctor in Decorah don't like me too much."

"And why is that?"

JJ laid a hand on her shoulder. "The boy's right, and it's my fault. But no time for that now. I'll go, take the team and wagon with Noah in it. Be faster anyway."

Amalia shook her head. She'd have to tug more of this story out of them later. But for now, JJ was right. "I'll come too."

Ruthie ran into the barn, Magpie in her arms. "Why is Noah crying?"

Hank whirled on her. "Because you were supposed to keep him away from the horses while JJ and I cleaned out their stalls. And you ran off, so he got kicked! Where were you?"

Ruthie froze, tears filling her eyes. She stared from Hank to Noah, who now lay sniffling in Amalia's arms. "I—I went to look for Magpie—"

"He'll be all right, Ruthie." Amalia forced her voice steady. "But we need to take him to the doctor. You stay with Cousin Zelda, understand?"

Her face red and quivering, Ruthie gave a faint nod, still clutching the kitten.

"Hank, Inga Jorstad is up on the third floor, cleaning. Please tell her she's free to leave when she's finished, and I'll pay her next week." Amalia gathered up Noah in her arms as JJ led out the team and hitched them to the wagon. She'd have to deal with Hank and Ruthie more later. Right now she had to focus on this injured little one.

The drive to Decorah seemed long with Noah whimpering every time the wagon hit a rut in the road. Amalia had wrapped a towel around his leg and tried to keep it cushioned on her lap. At last they pulled up in front of the doctor's office. JJ set the brake and jumped down, spryer than she'd ever have thought a man of his age could move. He reached up to lift Noah gently from Amalia's arms so she could climb down.

Lord, please let the doctor be in. Amalia took Noah back, and he clung to her, little arms tight around her neck.

A handsome, dark-haired young man looked up from a desk when they stepped inside. "I'm Dr. Armitage. How can I help you?"

"This child got kicked by a horse." JJ nodded at Noah in Amalia's arms. "His leg needs lookin' at."

"I see." The doctor raised dark brows and stood. "Please, step into my examining room."

"I'll wait out here." JJ gave her arm a squeeze.

Amalia held Noah tight and followed the doctor.

"I assume this is your child, ma'am?" The doctor spoke while washing his hands at a basin in the corner of the room. It was small but clean, holding an examining table covered with a sheet, and a cabinet of medicines.

"No." Amalia swallowed. "But I'm his guardian." Perhaps not officially, as with Ruthie, but she was all Noah had, for now.

"Put him on the examining table, please."

Amalia tried setting Noah down, but he clung to her and screamed. "It's all right, den lille." Tears stung her own eyes. So much pain this little boy had gone through already in his short life. "You need to sit here so the doctor can help your leg, all right?" She pried his arms from her neck and sat him on the table, holding his hands still.

The doctor paused in his approach and glanced at her. "How did you come by a Negro child?"

Half Negro, but that didn't matter either way. Or shouldn't. "His mother died, and we are searching for his father. I am caring for him at the boardinghouse in the meantime." Her words came clipped, her English stronger than it had ever been. "I hope the color God chose for him does not affect your treatment?"

"Certainly not." The doctor hesitated an instant, then pushed up his sleeves and removed the towel from Noah's leg. "Kicked by a horse, you say?"

"Ja." Amalia drew a shaky breath. "I don't think it's broken, but we want to be sure."

Dr. Armitage examined Noah's leg, his hands gentle and skilled despite his demeanor. Noah sat still, hiccupping a bit and looking from the doctor to Amalia with big eyes.

"You're right, it's not broken." The doctor straightened. "Bad bruise, though. He'll be in pain for a few days. I'll clean the cut and give you some St. Jacob's Oil to aid the bruise's healing."

"Thank you." Amalia held Noah still for the wound cleaning, which brought more tears, then watched as the doctor anointed the bruise and bandaged the little leg. Noah at last safely back on her hip, sobs reduced to sniffles, she thanked the doctor once more and followed him out to the office. JJ stood from a chair where he'd been waiting.

"What do we owe you?" Amalia asked, shifting Noah's weight on her hip. He was growing heavy.

"It's two dollars for a first visit. Twenty-five cents for the St. Jacob's Oil." He wrapped the bottle of ointment.

Amalia swallowed. She hadn't that much in her handbag. "Is there a way to put it on credit and pay the next time I come to town? We left in such a hurry—"

"I'll take care of this." JJ dug a handful of coins out of his pocket and laid them on the doctor's desk.

"JJ, you don't need to do that."

He held up his hand. "You've been payin' me, even though you don't have to, not to mention puttin' food on my plate. 'Sides, I owe the doc for fixin' up my little friend here." He gently wiggled Noah's foot, bringing the first smile since the accident.

"Very well, then. Summon me if his leg swells overmuch, or if you see redness or pus. Otherwise, it should heal within a few weeks." The doctor glanced up as another patient came in, a middle-aged woman in a silk dress and feathered hat. "Now if you'll excuse me." He made a shooing motion, and Amalia and JJ hurried out with Noah. The woman turned and raised her shapely brows as they passed.

"Feller ain't got much of a bedside manner, does he?" After helping Amalia and Noah up to the wagon seat, JJ slapped the reins and clucked the horses toward home.

247

"At least he treated him." Amalia sighed and snuggled Noah closer on her lap. "JJ, I'll pay you back."

"No, you won't. I owe the doc anyway." The older man sucked his teeth. "Fact is, Hank stole some medicine from him, month or so ago. For me."

"He did what?" Amalia blew out a breath. "So that's why he didn't want to come."

"Your Absalom Karlsson smoothed it over and paid for the medicine. And 'course won't take anythin' from me. Didn't even tell me what happened, till Hank spilled it a few days ago, guess he felt guilty-like. Which shows your influence on him, ma'am, and no mistake. He never had no scruples 'bout swiping what he felt he'd a right to now and again, not before. But 'tany rate, payin' for this little feller's visit today makes me set a mite easier."

"Well, mange takk." Amalia sighed. "And what do you mean, 'my Absalom Karlsson'?"

JJ slanted a glance at her, then chuckled. "If you don't know yet, young lady, it ain't for me to tell you."

Noah fell asleep against Amalia by the time they got home, so she carried him upstairs to his cot, then came down to find Zelda frying potato lefse in the kitchen. Something savory bubbled on the stove.

Amalia stared. "You started supper?"

"Just because you always take over, doesn't mean I don't know my way around a kitchen," Zelda snapped.

Amalia swallowed back a retort, willing her ears not to burn. *Don't let her bother you.* "Thank you. It smells good." She peeked under the lid of the stewpot. Meatballs simmered in a rich broth.

"Thought those children could use a bit of a treat tonight." Zelda flipped the rolled piecrust-thin potato pancake. "How's the little boy?"

Did she actually detect a note of concern in the woman's voice?

Amalia darted a look at her. "Nothing broken, thanks be to God. He's going to be all right."

Zelda nodded and stirred the meatballs. Perhaps she had a heart after all—if kept carefully hidden.

Amalia left the kitchen in search of Ruthie. She found her under the back steps, curled in a ball with tearstained cheeks, Magpie twining about her shoulders. The kitten looked up at Amalia's approach and meowed.

"Oh, den lille." Amalia pulled Ruthie out and into her arms. "He's going to be all right."

"I didn't—mean to—let him get hurt." The words sniffled out between sobs. "He wanted—to see Magpie—so I went to look for her—and I couldn't find her at first—and—and—"

"I know. I know." Amalia kissed the damp hair above the little girl's forehead and drew the mewling kitten close to cuddle too. "You would never hurt Noah on purpose. And I'm sure Hank didn't mean to yell at you. He was just worried about Noah too."

"That's right." Hank approached and stopped a few feet away, rubbing one dirty bare foot atop the other. "I'm sorry, Ruthie." Dog left his side and, tail wagging, licked away Ruthie's tears. Magpie, snug in her arms, hissed at the dog, shrinking closer to the little girl.

Amalia chuckled and held out her arm to Hank, and after a moment, he came and knelt beside them there on the dirt by the back steps, awkwardly patting Ruthie's shoulder.

"Perhaps we all learned something today." Amalia laid her cheek on Ruthie's head and let out a long sigh. "Thank God the lesson didn't come at an even higher cost."

TWENTY-THREE

Why did English have to be so complicated?

Amalia rubbed her forehead at the kitchen table, trying to concentrate on the verb conjugations Helen chalked out. The schoolteacher had propped a small blackboard against the bread box for the daily lessons. Amalia thought she'd been making strong progress in English, but why did this language have so many verbs that did not follow the rules?

"So, Ruthie." Helen sketched a rising sun on the slate surface, then the word *awake*. "If you want to tell me that you woke up yesterday, what do you say?"

"I awoke."

"And if your Tante Amalia woke you earlier than usual, and it's now in the past?" She glanced at Amalia and pointed to the column on the board labeled *past participle*.

Amalia nibbled her lip. "I—had awaked her?"

"Actually, it's had awoken." Helen wrote the words, her script elegant and looping, even in chalk.

Uff da. How many different verb endings were there? She thought she'd conquered past tense a while ago.

"Now, Ruthie, what will you do tomorrow morning when the sun comes up?"

"I—will awake!" Beaming, Ruthie hopped off her chair and threw her arms wide to match the sun's rays.

Noah giggled and clapped his hands from his perch on Amalia's lap, never mind that one chubby hand held a cookie.

"Very good." Helen smiled and held out the cookie plate to Ruthie. "You have earned another."

The little girl clambered back up on her chair and palmed another from the pile of havrekjeks, the Norwegian oatcakes Amalia had stirred up this morning. Simple and nourishing, they made an easy treat for the children. And for adults, especially those struggling with their English lesson. She reached for one herself. Why did grasping the language seem so much easier for Ruthie?

"Hank, would you like to join us?" Helen glanced beyond the group to where Hank knelt on the floor next to a chair by the stove. Bare feet akimbo behind him, he scribbled something on a scrap of paper flattened against the chair seat.

He snorted, not looking up. "I already know English."

"So perhaps you could help me teach."

He looked up at that. "I ain't no teacher."

"Nonsense. I saw you teaching Noah to gather eggs yesterday." Something flickered in his eyes. "That's different."

"Not so much. Here, I'll show you." Helen wiped the board with a rag. "Let's take the verb 'to bring.'" She wrote it on the board. "How would you conjugate that for the past?"

"Huh?"

She smiled. "Forgive me. We teachers fall too easily into grammatical jargon. If you want to tell Ruthie to bring you a cookie, what would you say?"

Hank's mouth tipped. "Bring me one o' them cookies."

"And if she already did?"

"I'd say—she brought me one."

"Excellent." Helen wrote the words on the board. "You just conjugated that irregular verb."

"Don't see as it makes much difference." Hank twisted the pencil between his fingers. "Can't read them words anyway."

Helen paused her bit of chalk. "Would you like to?"

"Don't need me no school larnin'." Hank turned back to his scribbling. "Get along just fine without it."

Helen met Amalia's eyes, one brow lifted. Amalia gave a slight shrug back. So hard to know, with Hank.

Ruthie slipped off her chair and crossed to Hank, holding out an oatcake. "Here."

"What's this for?" Hank looked up.

She tipped her head. "Well, you did say to bring you one of them cookies."

Hank's grin slipped out, and he took the cookie. "Guess I did."

"What'cha drawing?" Ruthie craned her head to look over Hank's shoulder.

"Nothin'." Hank shifted away and stuffed the cookie in his mouth.

"That looks like Miss Helen. And Tante Amalia holding Noah. Oh, is that me?"

"What do you think?" His mouth still full, Hank snatched the paper back from her eager fingers.

"Hank, are you an artist?" Helen rose and approached, holding out her hand. "May I see?"

"No! Ain't nothin' but a bunch of junk." Hank stuffed the paper under his arm, crumpling it, and sprang to his feet, dashing out the door. It slammed behind him.

Helen halted in the center of the floor. "Oh, dear." She turned to look back at Amalia, her forehead creased. "Sometimes I'm afraid I push too far."

"Hank is still a bit of—what do you say? A mystery, to all of us." Amalia sighed and lapsed back into Norwegian. "Magistrate Karlsson and Absalom say this is the longest they've known him to even stay anywhere, since he ran off from the orphan train."

"And why did he? Run off from the train." Helen sat back down and took Noah into her lap.

"I'm not sure." Amalia's middle clenched that she hadn't pressed Hank for more of his story herself—but he always clammed up so quickly when she asked anything at all. "He had an older brother, and they ran off together so they wouldn't get separated. Something happened to his older brother soon after, he got sick and died, but I haven't been able to learn more than that."

Helen shook her head. "There must be a better way of caring for orphans in this land."

"I know!" Ruthie flung out her arms. "They can all come here. We already have lots of orphans—Hank, and Noah, and me, and Tante Malia—"

"I suppose even I'm an orphan, come to think of it." The schoolteacher chuckled, then sighed. "If even half our country had as open arms as you and your Tante Amalia, Ruthie, it would be a much warmer, more welcoming place."

Noah slid down to play on the floor with Ruthie and Magpie, and Amalia leaned forward to concentrate on the verbs written out on the blackboard.

Awake—awoke—awoken.

Forbid—forbade—forbidden.

Go—went—gone. She shook her head. Who came up with these?

The back door slammed open again, making her jump. She pressed her hand to her pounding heart and twisted to peer at Hank panting in the doorway. "Uff da. Now what?"

"Sorry—but it's Honey. She's having her calf!"

Ruthie and Noah jumped up and dashed for the door.

"Oh my." Helen raised her brows. "Will you follow?"

A grin tickled Amalia's cheeks. "I think I'd better."

She hurried after the children. In the barn they found JJ leaning over the half door of Honey's stall. He turned to hold a finger to his lips.

"Come real quiet, now. She's doin' mighty important work."

They crept forward. Hank helped Ruthie climb up on the grain bin so she could see. Amalia scooped up Noah.

Honey shifted where she stood against the other side of the stall, her hooves rustling the straw. Her sides heaved, and she lifted her tail and strained. Two tiny hooves poked from beneath her tail, a string of fluid hanging down. Slowly her front knees buckled, and she rolled on her side.

"Where's the baby calf's head?" Ruthie's voice sounded small. "I don't see a head."

"It's comin'." Hank put his arm around her shoulders and pointed. "Look."

Honey pushed again, and a small, dark nose poked out above the hooves, then receded.

"She's doin' fine." JJ nodded slowly. "Just fine. Not her first time, she knows what she's about."

They all waited, breathless, as more and more of the calf's head slid into view with each push. Then the shoulders emerged, and in one long, slippery motion, the entire calf slid, dark and wet, to the straw. Honey staggered to her feet and started licking her baby hard, nose first.

"Baby calf." Noah pointed from Amalia's arms.

"Ja, baby calf." Amalia wiped her eyes and sniffled.

Hank leaned over the stall. "Is it all right?"

"Looks to be." JJ nodded. "I can see its sides movin', so it's breathin'."

Amalia let out a breath. *Tusen takk, Lord.*

The calf lifted its head on a wobbly neck and looked around, nearly knocked over again by the force of Honey's tongue.

"Is it a boy or a girl?" Ruthie whispered loud.

"Can't tell yet. Wait till she gets up and suckles from her mama."

Before long the calf struggled to her knees, sprawling flat in the straw several times before she made it to her feet, spread wobbly beneath her like one of the long-legged water bugs down at the creek.

"Looks to be a heifer." JJ nodded. "Good, give you another milker in a couple years."

So with Fawn, as they'd christened Honey's other heifer, they'd have three cows to supply the boardinghouse. What a gift.

The calf took short, stiff-legged steps, making Ruthie and Noah giggle. Her hair started to dry, turning from nearly black to dark golden-brown. Honey nosed her gently from behind till the calf nuzzled at her full udder, then mouthed a teat and started to suck. After a moment, foamy droplets of colostrum dripped from the corners of her mouth. The little tail swished, brushing Honey's nose as she continued to clean her baby.

"Good." Hank let out a breath. "Now she's nursin', she'll be okay, right, JJ?"

"That's right, boy." JJ lightly tapped the top of the stall door. "Why'nt you go get Honey a bucket o' warm water with a swig o' molasses in it. She deserves a treat."

"Sure thing. I tied Dog up outside so he wouldn't interfere." Hank hopped down from the grain bin and headed for the house.

Amalia took his place next to Ruthie and gave the little girl a squeeze. "What do you think we should name the little one?"

Ruthie nibbled her lip. "What about Kaprifol, since she is Honey's daughter?"

"Honeysuckle in Norwegian." Amalia smiled and tugged Ruthie's braid. "I like it. We can call her Kapri for short."

A new life for the farm, just as they'd been given a new life here in this land. Amalia laid her cheek on Ruthie's head and wrapped her arms around her as they watched the calf nurse. Even Hank wore a smile back on his face as he brought a bucket of water and one of mash for Honey.

New life for all of them, please God.

Now, how to get Hank to open up about his drawing.

How was it already July 4th?

Absalom bit into a cherry from the boardinghouse's expansive picnic basket, the sweet juice exploding in his mouth. He sat on a quilt spread on the grass of the church grounds, sharing the space with Helen Stenerson, JJ, Amos, and his father. They'd been invited to join the Independence Day celebration here in Green Creek, and he'd gladly accepted. The Millers' quilt bordered theirs, surrounding them with friends. He felt more and more connected with the Lutheran church here—not to mention not having to see Rebecca every Sunday. Though he realized that he hadn't even thought about her in quite some time. The notion made him smile.

"Mr. Absalom, look!" Ruthie ran up, beaming in her new red-and-white gingham dress Amalia had sewn her for the summer, now she'd learned to use the boardinghouse sewing machine. "Hank won the watermelon eating contest, and he got another watermelon for a prize! He gave me a piece." She held out the dripping slice, juice already coating her chin.

"How about that." He grinned at her. "Having fun?"

She nodded hard, blonde braids bouncing, and bit into her slice again.

"Where's your Tante Amalia?" Absalom propped one knee up on the blanket and scanned the church grounds.

"She was watching Hank in the contest, and now she's keeping Noah away from the firecrackers."

Absalom chuckled. That sounded like a job. The distant pop of the firecrackers from the street hailed where the boys would be.

Perhaps he should join them. He'd hardly seen Amalia the last few weeks, between writing his dissertation and her busyness at the filling boardinghouse. Absalom nodded to Zelda Berg as she approached and thumped into a chair set back from the quilt a bit.

"Uff da, this heat." The older woman fanned herself. "Crazy to be out in it like this."

So why had she come? Absalom pressed down the thought and stood. "I believe I saw a lemonade stand earlier. May I fetch you some?"

She nodded and dabbed at her neck with her handkerchief. "Ja, please."

An errand of mercy and a chance to look for Amalia. Absalom grinned as he wended his way through the picnic blankets patchworking the grassy expanse on one side of the church—the graveyard anchored the other. He neared the street to the strains of bugle, tin whistle, and drum, an impromptu band of town musicians striking up "Yankee Doodle" under a canopy while small boys circled in the street, their firecracker bangs and puffs of smoke startling nearby horses.

Absalom spied Amalia holding tight to Noah's hand near the lemonade stand on the other side. He glanced both ways to see the street was clear and crossed to her.

"I can't get him away from watching." She smiled at him in greeting, then was tugged sideways by Noah, lunging toward the firecrackers again. "Nei, den lille. Those can hurt you."

"How is his leg healing?"

"Only a faint bruise now, thanks be to God." She wore a new dress too, a light blue calico that looked far cooler than her woolen vests and skirts. And brought out the blueness in her eyes. With her ribboned straw hat, she looked more American than he'd ever seen her, though her Norwegian lilt still gave a musical softness to her words.

"Any word on his father?"

"Oh, I forgot to tell you. I asked at the post office, and they had a letter Curtis Williams had sent his wife—of course, she had never picked it up. So I wrote to him at the town where the letter was mailed, telling him about Lottie's death and that we were caring for his son—though I grieve for him to hear such news from a stranger." She sighed. "Who knows if it will actually reach him, but I had to try."

"Good idea." Absalom crouched to the little boy's level. "Noah, would you like a cup of lemonade?"

The child regarded him a moment with big eyes, then nodded hard.

Absalom stood and winked at Amalia. "Let's see if this works." He took Noah's free hand and led them both over to the lemonade stand, where he paid a young girl for four cups of lemonade. He juggled three while Amalia carried one, also leading Noah back to their quilt in the shade.

"Mange takk." Amalia sank down on the quilt and handed Noah his cup. "I thought I'd be stuck by the fireworks all afternoon." She relieved Absalom of her cup, and he passed one over to Zelda.

"Wondered what took you so long" came her comment.

"Where's Ruthie?" Amalia asked.

"Mrs. Miller took her to see the music."

"There'll be real fireworks later after it gets dark." Absalom sipped his own lemonade. Lightly sweet and tart, just as he liked it. "Did you ever see fireworks in Norway?"

"My far took me to see some once at New Year's." Amalia took off her hat and laid it aside. "But that was far away, and I was little. Will they be very loud?"

He smiled at the wrinkle in her forehead. "You may want to cover your ears."

She tipped back her braid-crowned head, gazing at the pattern of leaves dancing on the branches overhead. "It's so lovely here."

Absalom noted the delicate sprinkle of freckles across her nose, brought out by her hours in the Iowa sun, gardening, doing laundry, caring for the children and animals. He so rarely saw her actually sit down and rest. Her hand, reddened from work, lay near his on the quilt, and he had to clench his fist to keep from reaching for it.

When would he gather the courage to tell her of his feelings? Should he, even, with all she carried on her shoulders? If only Zelda and his father weren't around just now . . .

"Have you started writing your dissertation?" She reached for the bowl of cherries to set between them. The boardinghouse cherry trees had started to bear in abundance.

"I have." He pushed his glasses up his nose, a bit slippery from the heat. "I've decided to write on the importance of proper legal assistance for new immigrants to this country. Far too many get taken advantage of almost as soon as they set foot in America."

"Well, there's a topic that suits you."

"I suppose so. I've a ways to go, but the ideas are coming together. Finally."

He glanced behind them. Zelda seemed occupied in watching a baseball game shaping up in a nearby field, and his father and Mr. Miller dozed off in their chairs. Eben Miller proved nowhere to be seen. *Now or never.* He drew a breath, heart thumping. "Amalia, I—"

"Hey, Mr. Absalom." Hank ran up, Ruthie at his heels. "We need you to help judge a three-legged race."

Popping a cherry into her mouth, Amalia smiled at him. "Have fun."

He smiled back, hating himself for resenting Hank at that moment. But as he fell into step beside the boy toward the field where races were being set up, the knot in his middle eased. He rested his hand on Hank's shoulder, not so skinny as it used to be, and squeezed it. A few months ago, he'd never have thought to be sharing a community picnic with this boy. What a difference Amalia had brought to this town already. Had she any idea?

Hank ran to strap his leg to that of a stocky redheaded boy, and Absalom joined Eben Miller and Mr. Nygard to make a tie-breaking panel. Hank and his partner placed second, and the boy grinned as Absalom pinned the red ribbons on their shirts.

"Never thought I'd win anythin', least of all twice in one day."

Dusk fell at last as they finished eating the piles of fried chicken, ham, lefse, buns, baked beans, pickles, and cherries and raspberries that came from the trees and bushes behind the boardinghouse. Hank, Ruthie, and Noah played rounds of tag and ring-around-the-rosy with other children between the picnic blankets. As darkness fell, they tumbled onto the boardinghouse quilt, out of breath and laughing. Noah crawled into Amalia's lap and stuck his thumb in his mouth.

"The fireworks will start soon." Absalom scooted closer to Amalia, hoping he wasn't too brazen.

At the first explosion of color in the night sky, Ruthie shrieked and clapped her hands over her ears. Amalia reached to draw her close, one arm still around Noah, who stared open-mouthed at the pyrotechnics. Hank, holding his knees to his chest, gazed silently up at the blossoming sky.

Amalia hugged the children to her, her uplifted face as bright as the fireworks themselves. As were her dreams for this new land, crushed at first, but now slowly bursting into bloom.

Absalom swallowed, unable to tear his gaze away from her—or his heart either. If only she could hear him right now to tell her so.

TWENTY-FOUR

MID-JULY, 1889

H
ave you seen Hank?"

Amalia looked up from kneading a batch of sourdough rye bread to see Helen poke her head into the kitchen. "I think he's out by the pasture. What did you need?"

"Nothing." Helen stepped into the kitchen, absently brushing at her dark blue skirt. That with her high-collared white blouse made her seem she should already be back in the schoolroom. "I just wanted to speak to him, see if I could apologize for sticking my nose into his business before. About the drawing. He's been so scarce lately, I haven't had the chance."

Smiling at the American expression, Amalia dug the heels of her hands into the soft dough, then pulled it toward her and flipped the floury lump over. "You meant well."

"Well, you know what they say about the road paved with good intentions." Helen chuckled. "Then again, maybe you don't."

"Do I want to?"

"Probably not. Can I help you?"

"You can grease those bread pans for me."

Helen tied on an apron and smeared lard inside the loaf pans. Amalia divided the dough and set the loaves to rise.

"Where are the other children?" Helen asked.

"Ruthie and Noah are helping Zelda in the garden—once I finally got them to leave the calf alone for a while. Honey does not like them coming near her calf. We need to build a pen for Kapri."

"Isn't Mr. JJ busy building the big dining table just now?"

Amalia sighed. "He is. And with our rooms filling, we sure need it. Asgar and Eivor said some of their fellow workmen might want to board here too. It all rather makes my head spin." She wiped her floury hands and grabbed a basket from the pantry. "I'm going to go pick some peas and dig new potatoes for supper if you'd like to come help."

"Please. I love the space for solitude with my own room, but I'm starting to not know what to do with myself till school starts."

"Well, work for willing hands we can always provide."

"You have a gift for alliteration."

Amalia laughed and opened the back door. "Allite-what?"

Out on the back porch, Amalia meant to head for the garden, but she spied Hank perched on the pasture fence on the other side of the barn. She glanced at Helen and tipped her head toward the boy, raising a brow.

Helen nodded and stepped off the porch. "Would you come too, please?"

They strolled together along the pasture fence, bright-faced sunflowers waving over it in the summer breeze, to where Hank perched on a lower rung, his ragged sketch pad propped atop one flat fence post.

Amalia hung back a bit while Helen stepped closer. "Hello, Hank."

He looked up and shifted, closing the pad of paper Amalia had bought him at the store. "'Lo."

She lifted her hand. "I'm not asking to look at your drawings. I wanted to apologize, actually. I should never have pressed you the way I did."

262

Hank shrugged and glanced away. "That's all right. You din't mean no harm."

"That's true, I didn't. But I don't like it when people invade my privacy, and I shouldn't invade yours either. Will you forgive me?"

He stared at her a moment, then nodded with a slight shrug.

"If you ever would like to share your drawings, I—and I'm sure Amalia"—Helen glanced toward her—"would love to see them. But only if and when you want to."

Hank ducked his head. "I don't mind. I just don't think they're much of any good. Figured folks would just laugh at 'em." He shoved the paper toward Helen.

She raised her brows. "Are you sure? You don't have to show me."

He shrugged. "I know."

Helen took the notepad and gently opened the cover. At Hank's nod, Amalia came near and peered over the teacher's shoulder.

"Hank." Amalia caught her breath. "These are beautiful."

He snorted. "You're just sayin' that."

"But I'm not." She ran her finger down one page, the paper yellowed and water-spotted, one edge tattered. But on the page, so real she might have bawled, Honey's calf struggled to her feet, each limb wobbly and wet. Honey nosed near, her eyes dark and loving. Some rough strokes, true, but each penciled line breathed with life.

"Where did you learn to draw like this?" Helen turned the page to one of Ruthie and Noah watching the baby chicks, Ruthie cradling one tiny cheeping puffball in her hands.

He shrugged, digging with his thumbnail into the wood of the fence post. "Just try to draw what I see, that's all. What sticks in my mind."

"I would love to have you come and give drawing lessons at school." Helen paged through the rest of the book. "Show the other children what you can do."

Hank narrowed his eyes at her. "You just tryin' a sneaky way of gettin' me to school?"

She breathed a laugh. "Hank, you are too smart for your own good. But truly, you could teach the children things about art I never could. I can barely draw a straight line. And you needn't stay if you don't like it."

He nibbled his lip. "I'll think on it."

"Thank you for sharing with us, Hank."

He took the sketchbook back and tucked it under his arm. "'Course." He stepped down from the fence, then frowned across the yard. "What's Zelda hollerin' at the young'uns about?"

Amalia spun around and shielded her eyes with her hand against the slanting afternoon sun. Sure enough, Zelda towered over Ruthie and Noah in the garden, gesturing sharply. Her strident tones carried across the yard to them, though she couldn't make out the words.

Uff da, what now? Amalia lifted her skirts and hurried for the garden, her basket bumping against her knees.

She'd only made it halfway when Ruthie and Noah came scurrying toward her, Noah tumbling to the ground along the way. Ruthie tugged him to his feet, and they kept running, both throwing themselves at Amalia's skirts.

"What happened?" She crouched to their level, trying not to let them bowl her over.

Noah rubbed his eyes with garden-smudged fists, hiccupping sobs. Ruthie swiped a hand at her cheeks too, the tears running.

"Noah, he thought he was helping, pulling up weeds, but then by accident he pulled up some carrots—a lot of carrots. And Zelda got really mad and yelled at him. I told her he didn't mean to"—she sniffed back a sob—"and then she yelled at me."

No surprise there. Amalia suppressed a groan and hugged the children to her. She could understand Zelda being frustrated, but didn't she have any understanding of children? And here she'd thought things were going better in that department.

"Come, we will talk to her." She took both their hands and tugged them along, small feet dragging.

She found Zelda bending between the rows of feathery carrot tops, muttering to herself and digging with sharp jerks.

Lord, give me grace and wisdom. "I understand you had a bit of a mishap out here."

Zelda snapped her head up and glared at them. "Of course they would go crying to you."

"If you treat them harshly, then *ja*." Amalia breathed slowly, trying to cool the fire heating in her chest. "What happened?"

"I told that young nuisance"—she jerked her thumb at Noah— "to pull up weeds and what does he do? Ruin near half a row of carrots. Too small to pick yet and can't be replanted. Ruined."

"I fought they weeds," Noah spoke up, pressing against Amalia's skirt.

Good for you, little one. Stand up for yourself. "It is a shame about the carrots. But he was trying to help. We all make mistakes. Did you even show the children how to tell which are weeds and which not?"

"Do you take me for a fool?" Zelda's glare seemed to singe Amalia's ears.

"No, but if you cannot forgive an innocent mistake, you are behaving like one." Her own tone sharpened. "I must ask you to apologize to the children."

Zelda set down her tools, snatched up a handful of the spindly, too-young carrots. She stood. "I? Apologize to them?" She shook the carrots at Noah.

Amalia tightened her grip on the children's hands, her stomach tensing. "That's what I said."

Zelda stepped closer till she breathed nearly right into Amalia's face. "You, young lady, have gone just about too far. First you take

265

over my home, then you have the gall to—" She reared her arm back, and Amalia cried out, reaching to shelter the children.

But Zelda just flung her handful of carrots across the garden. They dropped between the rows of cabbages like dirty bullets.

Zelda stomped off toward the cornfield, muttering under her breath.

Ruthie wailed, turning her face into Amalia's dress. Noah stared after Zelda, stunned into silence.

Amalia wrapped her arms around the children, her own eyes stinging now and pulse still thudding from the altercation. *Lord, was I wrong to let Zelda stay here? How can I keep these little ones from such hostility? Please, show me what to do.*

Absalom missed Amalia.

Summer's weeks had passed in a blur of heat, humidity, and writing his dissertation. He'd little excuse to go offer English lessons at the boardinghouse, not with teacher Helen Stenerson living there now. Hank, though, still visited him and his father often and served as a veritable newsboy. The boardinghouse had three new boarders, a couple of workers on the railway and an elderly lady. Ruthie had lost another tooth. Helen wanted Hank to go to school.

And how was Amalia? he yearned to ask. But how could he, without giving away something of the state of his heart? Once he figured out exactly what that was himself.

He turned in his dissertation the ninth of August, twenty-some pages of his sweat, head, and heart written in type, then had ten more days to cram for his oral examination. And then—August 19 dawned.

He arrived at the courthouse early, the clouds still gilded with gold and apricot in the east. Too early, in fact, so he sat down on the courthouse steps to wait and pray, pressing his palms together between his knees.

*Father, thank you for getting me this far. Help me do my best—
and be ready to use what I've learned to serve you and others.*

"Early bird, eh, Karlsson?" Judge Alfelt arrived nearly an hour later, his polished boots stopping beside Absalom on the steps.

"I suppose so, sir."

"Well, get on your feet, son. You've an exam to take."

Within a few minutes, Absalom stood before Judge Alfelt in his office. The judge leaned back in his expansive chair and regarded him.

"So, young Karlsson. Do you feel yourself ready to take up the practice of the law?"

Absalom swallowed. "God helping me, I believe so."

"A good answer." The judge folded his hands over his robed middle. "I've observed you for two years now, Karlsson, as has your father. While many in recent decades have slid into allowing so-called 'diploma privilege,' letting any graduate from a law school to automatically practice law, I despise that method. I think anyone aspiring to handle such delicate matters as the laws that govern our human lives should at least have to give an account for himself. Do you agree?"

Absalom clasped his hands behind his back. "I do, sir."

"Good. I hear measures are forming in many states to require written bar exams, but till then, there's nothing like a good old-fashioned oral examination to my mind. So." The judge slid on his spectacles, leaned forward to a sheaf of papers on his desk, and turned over the first page. "What is the definition of a contract?"

Two hours later, Absalom stepped out into bright sunlight, voice hoarse, and blinking like a groundhog emerging from hibernation. He had finished. His head ached from trying to keep up with Alfelt's rapid-fire questions, and his knees wobbled slightly. But he'd passed, as the judge had informed him with a slight smile and a firm handshake.

He had passed.

He took the long way round walking back home. It might be some weeks before his official license to practice law would come in the mail. But for all intents and purposes, he'd completed all the steps to becoming Absalom Karlsson, attorney-at-law.

A grin tugged at his cheeks. He tipped his head back, listening to the summer serenade of cicadas and katydids in the trees. He felt like singing too.

He pushed through the gate, jogged up the porch steps, then swung open the door, jangling their bell. His father poked his head out of his private office before Absalom could reach him, eyes bright beneath his bushy gray brows. "Well?"

"The judge said I passed."

His father breathed a long sigh, then limped his way to Absalom. "I knew you would." He gripped his shoulders. "Congratulations, son. I couldn't be prouder to share this office with any other attorney-at-law."

Absalom's eyes stung, and he gripped back. "Thank you. I owe so much to you for this."

"You owe the gifts God gave you and your own hard work." His father clapped him on the back and scanned the waiting room. "Now. We've got to find space in here to give you your own office."

He hadn't thought of that. "I thought I'd just keep using the front desk."

"Nonsense. You must have a private space for meeting with your own clients." His father rubbed one sideburn. "Perhaps that back parlor we rarely use. We could cut another door, add an entrance to it from the front waiting area. What do you think?"

Absalom nodded slowly. "That could work."

"Now." His father pointed a finger in the air. "We've got casework piling up from your focus on your studies this summer. Since you're a bona fide lawyer, grease your heels and get to work."

Absalom lifted his shoulders. "I don't actually have my license yet."

"Didn't ask you to argue in court yet, did I?" His father winked. "Now get to it. Then we're invited to the boardinghouse for supper tonight."

Absalom spun back from heading to the front desk. "We are?"

His father chuckled. "Hold your horses, son. You've got plenty to keep you busy till then."

Never had the day stretched so long. Still, finally they pulled up outside the boardinghouse in Green Creek. The summer sun still slanted bright over the gingerbread-trimmed building and barn, gilding the green fields with gold. An evening breeze brought hints of coolness.

Ruthie met them on the porch. "Mr. Absalom! We have a surprise for dessert."

He bent to her level. "What is it?"

She giggled, showing a tooth starting to come in. "Silly. If I tell you, it's not a surprise." She grabbed his hand and pulled him toward the door. "Come on."

Amalia came out of the kitchen to greet them, wearing a red-trimmed white apron, cheeks pink with heat from cooking. "Thank you for coming, Magistrate and Absalom."

"Thank you for having us. Can we help?"

She smiled but shook her head. "Please, have a seat in the dining room. Supper is almost ready."

Absalom stepped through the doorway she indicated, realizing he'd never eaten in there, only in the kitchen a time or two. A long, broad table nearly filled the room now, JJ's handiwork, and was spread with a woven yellow tablecloth, the color brightening the room like sunshine. Ruthie darted in with a basket of rolls, then out again like a flitting bird, small Noah tagging at her heels with a tattered stuffed elephant under his arm.

At last they gathered round the table—a larger group than he'd realized. The Millers all came, plus Amalia, Zelda, and JJ, of course.

Hank, Ruthie, and Noah. Miss Stenerson, Amos the railroad signalman, the Rykavyk brothers, and the three new boarders. His father and him.

Amalia extended her hands to Ruthie and Noah, who flanked her. "Magistrate, would you say the blessing?"

"I'd be honored." His father gripped Absalom's hand on one side and Hank's on the other and bowed his head. "Our Father, we thank thee for this bountiful table and still more the dear friends who have provided it. Thank you for how you provide family even for those of us who have lost it." His voice grew husky, and he cleared it. "Thank you for Absalom and his hard work that he might better work for justice and mercy in our community. Bless him as he steps into this new season, and this food to our bodies. In Christ's name, Amen."

"Amen" came a chorus from around the table. Only Zelda stayed silent, glaring at her plate. Did she seem even ornerier than usual? Absalom noticed Amalia avoided her eyes, but otherwise she seemed calm.

Absalom gazed at the food spread before them. Ham and meatballs, lefse and biscuits. Fresh corn and green beans from the garden, and Norwegian cucumber salad. His mouth watered. "I hope you didn't go to all this trouble just for me."

Amalia laughed. "Don't worry, we all still need to eat. And we also all need cause for celebration now and then—and what better reason than celebrating our dear friend?" She looked at him, eyes bright. He found it difficult to swallow.

"To Attorney Karlsson." JJ raised his glass of water.

"I'm not quite an attorney yet." Absalom managed a grin. "But I'll drink to it anyway. And thank you—all." He sought Amalia's gaze, hoping she could see how much he meant it, but she'd turned to tie a napkin round Noah's neck. The tender bend of her head over the little boy caught him in the chest. *Lord, I love this woman—I really do. How can I find a way to tell her?*

Once everyone had eaten all they could hold, the meal crowned with a delectable Norwegian cream cake, they headed out onto the porch to breathe in the evening's coolness. The children chased fireflies in the yard below, darting after the glowing mites like gamboling moths. Absalom leaned on the porch railing, watching them, while Mrs. Miller engaged Zelda in conversation on the other side of the porch.

Amalia came to stand beside him. She ran a hand down the porch post and drew a long breath. "I love the evenings here in summer. Though I miss the midnight sun of Norway."

He leaned his elbow on the railing and twisted to face her. "Does it really still shine at midnight?"

"Well, not quite, not where we lived in the south. Though the sky stayed light all through the night in June. But once my parents took me to the north to visit family around midsummer, and the sun didn't set at all."

"I can't imagine." He glanced at her profile in the darkening twilight. "You must miss your parents horribly."

"I do." She leaned against the post. "Though for much of these recent months, I've hardly had time. Sometimes I feel guilty for that. And for not doing more to find my brother."

"I'm sure they wouldn't want you to. They would be so proud of you, Amalia. Look at what you've done—bringing all these people together. We were gathered round this table tonight because of you. And you've done all you can about your brother right now. My father is still waiting to hear back from his contacts."

She lifted one shoulder. "I feel like I've just been trying to keep up with whoever the Lord drops on my doorstep." She glanced at him. "In spite of everything we've accomplished, I still sometimes don't feel at all sure I'm going to make this work."

The faint tremor in her voice made him frown. "Has something happened?"

"Ja—and no. Just still some tension with Zelda. She's been

kinder to the children lately, so I should be grateful, but she seems to hate me more than ever." She sighed. "Sorry. I shouldn't burden you with this."

"Friends are for sharing burdens. And I hope we are that." And how he wished they could be more—but when would it be time to speak?

"You and your father surely have been friends to us in this new land. We might not have been able to stay at all, if you hadn't helped us—along with the Millers, and so many others. It's one reason I wanted to say 'thank you' tonight." She leaned on the railing, her slim, hardworking hands so close to his.

Had she any notion how his life had changed—opened, brightened—when she and Ruthie showed up in their law office that day? He swallowed, inching his hand nearer hers on the railing. "Amalia." Something urged forward to be told, before he could share his heart. "I—I was engaged to be married, a couple of years ago."

Her head snapped toward him in the darkness. "You were?" He heard the shift in her tone.

"Ja." The Norwegian word slipped out, softer here in the darkness, somehow. "Her name was—is—Rebecca. She still lives in Decorah, or rather she recently moved back. With her husband, Dr. Armitage."

"Armitage." Amalia shifted back from him, wrapped her arms around herself. "That's the doctor JJ and I took Noah to."

"I expect you did." He drew a breath, searching for more words.

"So what happened?" Her voice softened.

"She broke it off." The words still cut a little, though not near as sharply.

"Why?"

How to put this succinctly? Kindly? "Rebecca and I grew up together, went through school together, though I didn't know her well till I came back from college. Then we started to be thrown together at various social functions, church events and so on. She seemed to take a liking to me—at least once she heard I was pursuing law. She was lovely, charming. Girls had never paid me much attention, the awkward scholar, you know. I was smitten." He paused, realizing the usual surge of shame no longer stalked him.

"And then?" Her voice came gentle through the darkness, as if she could sense his pain then, though not so much now.

"We got engaged almost before I knew how. It wasn't till I started focusing on immigrant cases that I realized why Rebecca had pursued me. She thought that a lawyer would be—well, how did she put it? A 'fine provider.'"

"So money."

"Yes. To her, my 'charity cases' made me unfit to provide for a family." He drew a breath, grateful to find it all more a remembered wound now than a present one. "So that—was that."

"I'm sorry, Absalom." Amalia laid her hand beside his on the railing, the side of her finger brushing his and sending a thrill clear to his shoulder. "You didn't deserve that."

He shrugged and smiled. "We all have our trials. Mine lighter than most."

She hesitated. "May I ask why you told me? Now?"

He shifted his jaw. "I suppose I want you to . . . know me. All of me—and my story."

He felt her quick intake of breath in the darkness. Did she sense what he meant by that?

"Malia!" Ruthie ran up the steps, holding up a jar flitting with glowing bugs. "Hank showed us how to trap fireflies. Look!"

"They're lovely, den lille." Amalia traced a finger down the side of the jar, her voice trembling only a touch. "But now it's time for bed. Let the fireflies go and bring Noah, please."

A flurry of good-nights rose, and Absalom didn't manage more than another brief exchanged glance with Amalia. He couldn't read her face in the dim light from the boardinghouse door. Soon he sat on the buggy seat, driving himself and his father toward home.

What she thought of him now, he couldn't say. But he was glad he'd gotten this far, glad she knew this part of him. Even if he hadn't managed to tell her the most important piece.

TWENTY-FIVE

LATE AUGUST, 1889

W hat happened to your fingers, Mr. Amos?"

Amalia looked up at the supper table to see Ruthie staring at Amos's hand, gripping his coffee cup across the table from her. As Amalia had noticed before, the ring finger on his right hand showed only a stub, the little finger missing completely.

"Ruthie," Hank hissed. "You don't ask people about such things."

"I just wanted to know." Ruthie subsided into her milk cup.

Amos cleared his throat and spread his hand on the table. His work-roughened knuckles trembled slightly. "That's all right, little lady. I lost 'em."

"How?" Her eyes rounded.

"Used to be a brakeman. Had to stand between the railcars, coupling and uncoupling them old link-and-pin couplers. If your attention slipped for just a second, well." He flexed his maimed hand.

"Your fingers got smashed off?" Ruthie's voice squeaked.

"Happened to many a lad," Declan Murphy put in. The red-headed young man and his friend, Finley O'Dowd, also railway workers, formed the newest additions to the boardinghouse, along

275

with Mrs. Askeland, an elderly widow seated on the other side of the table. "Had a friend once who lost a hand."

"Now I hear they're switchin' to them Miller hook couplers," Eivor Rykavyk said.

His brother, Asgar, nodded. "Sounds to be a lot safer."

"So your fingers won't get smashed anymore?" Ruthie's forehead puckered.

"Well, I'm a signalman now." Amos picked up his fork. "Don't have to worry about that so much."

"What does a signalman do?" Hank reached a lanky arm across the table toward the biscuit basket, then caught Amalia's eye and rolled his. "Please pass the biscuits?"

She handed the basket over. Helen hid a smile.

"So, are signalmen the ones who tell the trains when to go?" Hank crammed a biscuit in his mouth, then passed the basket along to Finley, who grinned and took two.

"That's the idea." Amos nodded. "Got to keep the lamps clean, maintain the semaphores. Check each train that passes and tell when the section is clear."

"What's a sempafore?"

"Semaphore." Amos punctuated the word with his fork in the air. "That's the signals that light up to tell the engineers what's happenin' on the track ahead."

Declan shook his head. "You young ones sure ask a heap o' questions."

Eivor chuckled and reached for another drumstick. The children had been begging for chicken again since the Fourth of July, so they'd finally butchered another of the older hens who'd stopped laying.

Amalia laid a hand on Ruthie's arm. "Children, let's allow Mr. Amos to finish his supper, all right? He's been very gracious."

"Now she'll step in," muttered Zelda. She swiped her biscuit around her plate, sopping up gravy from the roast chicken.

Amalia set her jaw. She'd promised herself she'd just ignore Zelda's under-the-breath remarks. Easier said than done, as Helen had said the other day. English did have a lot of apropos phrases. She pushed back her chair and stood. "Is everyone ready for dessert?"

Inga Jorstad helped Amalia clear the plates. She now helped out Monday and Friday afternoons and evenings, plus some Saturdays, getting her supper at the boardinghouse those days besides. Together they carried in bowls of rømmegrøt, Norwegian pudding made of cream, flour, milk, a little sugar, and topped with melted butter and cinnamon. Warm, simple, and easy to mix up for a crowd, as Amalia was learning.

"Thank you, dear." Mrs. Askeland glanced up with a smile as Amalia set her bowl in front of her. "This smells just like my mother used to make."

Amalia smiled back. Already the elderly woman reminded her of her bestemor back home.

Having served all the boarders, she set bowls in front of Hank, Ruthie, and Noah, then slipped back into her own place. But Noah ignored his pudding, instead studying Amos's hand beside him on the table. The little boy reached to gently touch the finger stubs with his dimpled hand. He looked up at Amos, dark eyes solemn.

"Owie?" he asked.

"Not anymore, little fella." Amos opened his hand and patted Noah's. "Don't you fret." He looked down at the little boy, and a smile cracked amid his black beard. Noah stared at him a moment, then grinned back, pearly teeth peeking through.

Amalia looked down and dipped her spoon into her rømmegrøt, blinking back the stinging in her eyes. Many wounded souls at this table. But moments like this made her hope for at least some of them to be made whole.

After supper, Amos stepped into the kitchen when Amalia was washing the dishes, Helen wiping. She'd already sent Inga home.

"'Scuse me, ma'am. Might I have a word?"

Amalia turned, wiping her hands on her apron. "Of course."

"The talk at supper reminded me." Amos cleared his throat. "I did hear somethin' about the little fella's father."

"Curtis Williams?" Amalia stepped closer. "What did you hear?"

"Well, it was through another feller I worked with when I was a brakeman. Sounds like Williams was a brakeman too—no surprise, they used to like black fellers for that job, 'count of the danger. I hear white workers are startin' to push 'em out now that it's safer. Anyway—my friend said he heard Williams had hired on to the Cheyenne and Northern Railway, to help build a new line out there in Wyoming."

Wyoming. Amalia tried to recall what she'd studied of United States geography. "I sent that letter to somewhere in Dakota Territory. Wyoming is further west, isn't it?"

"It's a fur piece. Might be they'd forward the letter, might not."

"Well, at least we know something. Thank you. Do you think your friend would know how to get a message to Mr. Williams?"

"If'n you can write another one, I can give it to him."

"I will. Mange takk." Amalia watched Amos dip his head and slip out of the kitchen. The creak of the stairs told he'd headed up to his room.

"Well, that's good news."

"It is. I love having Noah here, but it aches my heart to think of his father so far away, and not even knowing his wife has died."

"Whenever he does get your message, I know he'll be grateful his son has been loved and cared for." Helen resumed drying the dishes. "And I suppose we know a bit more about our strong and silent friend after tonight."

"You're right. More than we did, anyway." Amalia dipped more hot water into the sink from the pot on the stove. "I wonder if Amos has always been so quiet, or if something else in his life caused that?"

"He wasn't particularly quiet tonight." Helen arched a brow.

"True." She smiled and set back to scrubbing the roasting pan. "Thanks to the children. So, do you feel ready for school to start again week after next?"

"Yes and no. The summer break always seems to stretch unending when the summer begins, then once August comes, it's gone in a flash." She sighed. "Still, the itch for my classroom is beginning. Lesson plans have started dancing in my head, so that's always a good sign."

"Ruthie can hardly wait to start school. Hank, on the other hand . . ."

Helen chuckled. "One step at a time."

"Can I really have my own slate, Tante Malia?"

A few days later, Amalia smiled down at Ruthie's upturned face and ran her finger over the smooth surface of one of the slates on the mercantile shelf. "Ja. And you may pick one of those slate pencils in that bin too. We want you well prepared for your first day of school on Monday." What a luxury to have a bit of money to spend, even if she still had to count coins carefully. But with five boarders giving steady income, she'd paid off some of her tab at the mercantile with a bit leftover. And once the harvest was finished, Mr. Miller assured her she could pay off the rest and more.

"I like this one." Ruthie fingered a slender gray pencil.

"Then put it into my basket." Amalia scanned the shelves for any other items she needed. "Ruthie, we should make you a new dress for fall."

"Truly?" The little girl's blue eyes went round.

"Ja." Pushing away the fear of being extravagant, Amalia crossed to the counter and scanned the bolts of fabric behind it. After all, Ruthie would need a warmer, sturdy dress for school. She'd outgrown at least one set of blouses and skirts from Norway already. "Do you like the dark red calico or the blue flannel?"

"The red." Ruthie balanced on her tiptoes, gripping the edge of the counter.

Amalia asked Mr. Nygard to cut the yardage, ignoring the inner nudge at the price. She had enough now, she reminded herself. She could do this, and they could still fill their bellies without worry. "And let's add a pair of new boots too." She chuckled at the look on Ruthie's face. "You can't go to school all winter barefoot, den lille." She'd get some denim and boots for Hank too.

She and Ruthie drove toward home in the wagon, the back loaded with pantry provisions as well as the yard goods and school supplies, including plenty for Hank. Such bounty. *Thank you, Lord.*

"When can we see Mr. Absalom again?" Ruthie asked.

"I don't know. Why?"

"I miss him. And he said he'd teach us English."

"Well, he did teach us some. And Miss Stenerson has been doing a fine job."

"I know. But he makes me laugh more."

He made her laugh too—or at least smile. Amalia tightened her hands on the reins. What had Absalom meant the other night, that he wanted her to know him—all of him? So help her, that sounded like—well, almost like . . .

If only she could see him again, and they could have time to talk. Really talk, without the constant distractions of children and boarders.

Amalia turned the team off into the lane leading to the boardinghouse. An unfamiliar black buggy sat out front. She frowned and pulled the wagon up by the barn. A new boarder?

Hank emerged from the barn and hefted a crate of supplies from the back of the wagon.

"Mange takk, Hank. Do you know who is here?"

"Some man talkin' to Zelda." Hank's tone said he didn't approve, but he headed up the back porch steps with his load without further comment.

280

"I'd better go see what that's about. Ruthie, you help Hank unload, then you can go see Mr. JJ and Noah in the garden." She spied the little boy tagging at JJ's heels as the older man hoed the rows of root vegetables. He'd become a surrogate grandfather to all the children, and certainly a godsend to her.

Amalia hefted a sack of flour in one arm and the yard goods in the other and climbed the steps, depositing her purchases on the kitchen table. She smoothed the front of her dress and removed her hat, ready to meet potential boarders, then headed into the parlor.

A slender young man in a black suit and tie rose when she entered. Zelda did not.

"Good afternoon." Amalia smiled and held out her hand. "I am Miss Gunderson. Welcome to our boardinghouse."

"He's not here as a boarder." Zelda stood now, lifting her sharp chin.

Amalia stilled, lowering her hand. "Then?"

"Uffe Bernhard, attorney-at-law." The young man swept his hat from his head with a smooth motion.

Attorney? Amalia stared from him to Zelda.

"This is my lawyer." Zelda returned her gaze with a glint in her eyes. "I'm suing for custody of Ruthie and trusteeship of this boardinghouse."

The room tipped. A buzzing filled her ears. *What?*

Bernhard cleared his throat and stepped forward. "It's all quite aboveboard, I assure you." He handed her a sheaf of papers.

Amalia took them in shaking hands, her vision too blurry to try and make out the English words. "Nei, nei. You cannot do this. I have papers, papers that show Ruthie's mother entrusted her care to me. I am her legal guardian, and trustee of this house until she comes of age."

"Well, we all have papers, don't we?" The attorney cocked his head with a slight smile beneath his brown mustache. "And of course nothing will be settled till the court hearing."

Court hearing? Amalia tried to swallow, but her throat was too dry.

"But I assure you, Miss Berg has a strong legal case. She is, after all, young Ruth's only living relative in this country. And she claims you have been filling this place with—" He cocked a brow. "Vagrants and orphans? Surely you can see how that jeopardizes the child's inheritance, raising definite questions as to your fitness for guardianship."

Zelda cracked a small smile. Amalia met her gaze for an instant, then blinked away, seared by the hatred there. What—how—she'd thought Zelda was softening. She gripped the horrid papers, her hands shaking. "I have my own lawyer." And a lawyer he truly was, now. "You will not get away with this."

"Ah, Absalom Karlsson, isn't it?" He gave a small sigh and shook his head. "Yes, Miss Berg has told me about your intimate relationship. Unfortunately, romantic entanglements with your defense only add weight to the case against you. And Karlsson—well, I've known him most of my life. He has high ideals, but as a lawyer?" He chuckled. "He's barely past his exams. I doubt he could argue a chicken into laying an egg."

Heat seared Amalia's cheeks. "There is no 'romantic entanglement' between us, Mr. Bernhard. And now, I must ask you to leave this place. I still have authority here." *For now.* She couldn't contemplate beyond that.

"As you wish." The lawyer bowed and put on his hat. Heading for the door, he turned back with lifted hand. "Oh, you'll find the date and time of the hearing at Decorah courthouse on those papers. I would highly suggest you not be late. A pleasant day to you both."

The door banged shut behind him.

Amalia turned to Zelda. "You—how could you? What have I ever done to you?" She still shook, her vision swimming red. So this was all Zelda's recent kindness had meant—her currying favor with Ruthie. All a facade, for her own twisted endeavors.

"Done to me?" The woman huffed a laugh. "You've taken over my home and filled it with ruffians. You've taken the one family member I have left and made her love you more than anyone. You think you can just waltz in here and change everything, take all I've—" Shaking with anger herself, her voice broke off. "You ask what you've done to me?"

Amalia flung up her hands like a shield, still clutching the papers. "I would ask you to leave these premises right now, but I will not react in the heat of anger. I am going to see Absalom."

Her head throbbing in rhythm with her pulse, she hurried back through the kitchen to find Ruthie, then paused at the back door. Ruthie would be with JJ and Noah by now, happy and looked after. Telling her anything of this would only upset her—not before she talked to Absalom. She would just go.

She caught up her handbag from the table and hurried out the front door, not even glancing at Zelda, who still stood in the parlor. The door slamming behind her, she half ran to the barn where the horses and wagon still stood, Hank just starting to un-hitch the team.

"Wait, Hank. Don't." Amalia stepped up the side of the wagon and onto the seat.

"Jiminy." Hank sprang back. "What's goin' on?"

"I have to go back to town—to see Absalom." She stuffed the papers under the seat and tried to smile at the boy, gathering the reins with shaking hands.

"Why? What happened? Who was that man?" He glanced behind her to the west. "There's a storm comin'."

Even as he spoke, a gust of wind whipped her hair into her face, fluttering the papers at her feet. She snatched them up and tucked them beneath her on the seat for safekeeping. "Don't worry, I'll be back soon."

Thunder grumbled low in a bank of dark clouds on the horizon as Amalia drove toward Decorah, urging the horses as fast as she dared. Lightning spiked in the distance. They'd had these summer storms once or twice a week, typically blowing in and out late in the day like this. But she couldn't wait—she had to talk to Absalom.

The road passed in a blur, tumbled with her thoughts. She couldn't lose Ruthie—couldn't let Zelda take her. Ruthie was finally blossoming, emerging from her grief and finding a place to belong. This would destroy her. A sob caught in her throat. *Please, God.*

She reached the law office and clambered out of the wagon just as the first drops of rain splatted her hair. She'd forgotten to bring her hat, but no matter. She snatched the papers from the seat and hurried through the gate, bending her face against the wind.

Absalom opened the door at her pounding knock. "Amalia?" Frowning, he drew her inside. "What are you doing out in this weather?"

"Zelda, she—" She gasped a breath, threatening tears suddenly sucking away her words as the wind tossed her hair. "She's trying to take Ruthie away."

"What?" Absalom's brows shot up to hide under his thick curls. Taking her arm, he led her through the waiting area to the magistrate's private office and shut the door behind them. "Father's at the courthouse right now. We won't be disturbed in here if someone else stops by. Here, sit and tell me." He led her to one of the chairs, then drew another close for himself and leaned forward, his eyes on hers.

"She—I—" Amalia struggled to breathe. She covered her mouth with her hands, the papers falling to her lap. "I can't lose her—I can't." Tears brimmed and overflowed.

"There." Absalom drew one of her hands down and rubbed it between his own, the pressure warm, gentle. "Take a few deep breaths. In—out. That's it."

Closing her eyes, Amalia managed to slow her breathing. "I'm sorry."

"Don't be. Take your time."

She blew out a long shuddering breath and opened her eyes again. It was a mercy he spoke Norwegian; she couldn't think in English just now. "Zelda was waiting with an attorney when I got home from town today. She says she is suing for custody of Ruthie—and guardianship of the estate. The boardinghouse."

"What?" Absalom sat back, still holding Amalia's hand between his. "Who's her lawyer?"

"Someone I'd never heard of. Something Bernhard."

His face tightened. "Uffe Bernhard?"

"That's it." She swallowed. "You know him?"

"Unfortunately." He pushed his glasses up his nose and rubbed the bridge beneath with his fingers, keeping his other hand over Amalia's. "Makes sense, though. If you want to do something underhanded, Bernhard's your man."

The vise in Amalia's chest tightened still more. "Do you think he could win?"

"Did he give you papers?"

"Ja." She held them out.

Absalom released her hand to thumb through the stack. Amalia clasped her hands in her lap, feeling the loss of his touch.

At last he blew out a sigh, then grimaced.

"It is bad?" She twisted her fingers together.

"He's done his homework. They're doing their best to paint you as an unfit guardian, Zelda as the faithful, abused family member."

Amalia squeezed her hands till they hurt.

"But honestly, contesting the last will and testament of a dying parent is a hard case to win. Especially when Ruthie is so clearly attached to you. I don't think they've got near as strong a leg to stand on as Bernhard might try to paint it."

Air rushed into Amalia's lungs again. "Really?"

"That's my take right now. But I'll need to talk this over with my father. He's helped me beat Bernhard before—a few months ago, in fact. May I keep these?"

She nodded. "Ja, please. And takk. I'm sorry for flying in on you like this. Perhaps I should have waited till tomorrow. . . ."

"Amalia." He set the papers aside and took both her hands in his, this time leaning forward to meet her eyes. "Don't you apologize for anything, you hear me? I just can't believe that woman would try to do this to you." His jaw hardened, his brown eyes flashing.

She wanted to say so much but couldn't. Instead, she gave his hands a little squeeze. "Mange takk."

"Now, let's try and get you home before this storm unleashes its full wrath upon us." He stood and pulled her to her feet, then hesitated. "Does Ruthie know?"

Amalia shook her head. "I left without telling her."

He expelled a breath. "Good."

They drove back to Green Creek through fitful rain that turned to sheets. Absalom drove the wagon, and Amalia huddled beside him, holding the umbrella. Despite the downpour, she felt somehow warm beside him—safe. As she had ever since they'd met him, she realized. He'd become her anchor in this new and tumultuous land. How could she tell him that? Or did he already know?

They pulled up in front of the barn to the welcome of a booming clap of thunder. Hank tore out of the barn to meet them, drenched and wild-eyed.

"Ruthie," he gasped out, his words barely heard above the storm. "She's gone."

TWENTY-SIX

Where was God?

Huddled under the bushes by the creek, Ruthie hugged her knees, rocking back and forth on the muddy ground. She'd thought the overhanging branches would protect her from the storm, but the rain streamed through anyway. She pressed her face into the sodden fabric of her skirt.

Mor had said God was with them in the storms. So was He here now? She didn't feel Him.

Ruthie wiped her eyes and nose on her sleeve, but it was too wet to work.

She missed Mor. She wanted Tante Amalia. Tante Amalia had gotten to be almost as good as Mor—nearly. But now, Cousin Zelda was going to take her away from Tante Amalia. Ruthie hadn't understood everything she heard when she went looking for Malia and stopped in the hallway, frozen by the angry words coming from the parlor.

But she had understood that.

And then Tante Amalia had driven away. Did she not want Ruthie anymore? Was she just going to let Cousin Zelda take her? Was she never coming back?

She'd walked so far along the creek, her legs got tired, and then the rain came. She couldn't try to find her way back home right now. She wasn't even sure she could, though Tante Amalia always said if she followed the creek, she'd never get lost.

But Tante Amalia also said she'd never leave her. And she had.

Ruthie buried her face in her damp dress and let her tears mix with the rain.

Where was she? Amalia wanted to scream. They'd already searched the boardinghouse, but she flung open the door of each room upstairs again, including Mrs. Askeland's, who was away visiting a friend this weekend. She then searched the third floor, dropping on her knees to peer under each railroad worker's bed. Amalia could apologize for invading their privacy later.

But no Ruthie.

She hurried down the stairs again, boots clopping on the steps, and into the kitchen. Noah sat on the floor, whimpering. Zelda stood by the stove, looking stone-faced out the window.

Fire blazed in Amalia's chest again, and she had to look away from the woman lest she grab her by the shoulders and shake her. JJ burst through the door, panting, his balding head dripping with rain.

"She ain't in the barn. Hank an' me searched it stalls to loft."

"We'll have to spread out farther. Is Absalom still here?"

"Yep, searchin' the henhouse and outbuildings with Amos."

"Malia." Noah tugged on her skirt, sniffling. "Hold?"

"You have to stay here, den lille." She ran a trembling hand over his curls. "Zelda." She heard the steel in her own voice. "I need you to watch him. And if any harm comes to him—"

"All right, all right." Zelda turned from the window and came to pick up the child, who squirmed and twisted against her. "I'll see he's looked after. Just find her." Her voice trembled slightly.

As if this weren't all her fault. Amalia grabbed for her coat, no matter she was already soaked, then headed out into the lashing wind and rain after JJ.

Absalom came from the chicken coop, shielding his face with his arm. "She's not in there." He nearly had to shout over the storm.

"How 'bout the Millers?" JJ asked.

The pressure in Amalia's lungs eased a fraction. She should have gone for their neighbors' help at the beginning. "Ja, she might go there. Hank, can you?"

The boy tore off without a word, Dog scampering soaked at his heels.

The frenzy in Hank's face tugged at Amalia's heart, but she couldn't think about that right now. Only of Ruthie—they had to find Ruthie.

Please, God. Please.

"Where else does she like to go?" Absalom pulled his hat lower over his face.

Amalia pressed her fingers to her temples, trying to think. "The barn—the henhouse. Upstairs in her room." Could she have missed something up there? But no, she'd searched every cranny.

"The creek," Amos spoke up.

Cold gripped her.

Absalom's face mirrored hers. "Let's go."

They crashed through the sodden brush and branches along the edge of the creek, the sight of the rising, rushing water clutching Amalia's heart with steel. *Please, God, no.* Could Ruthie have been swept away?

"Ruthie!" She screamed till her throat hurt. "*Ruthie!*"

Amos and JJ caught up with them after a bit. "Nothin'?"

Amalia shook her head. "I don't know which direction to even look."

"Hank's back. She's not at the Millers', but Abram and Eben came to help."

That hope snuffed like a last candle flame, Amalia stumbled in the mud.

Lightning knifed almost over their heads, followed by a deafening crash. Absalom snatched Amalia out of the way as a big willow tree she'd loved came crashing to the ground. She landed in the mud, Absalom half-shielding on top of her.

"We gotta get inside." JJ helped Absalom pull her to her feet. "It's right dangerous out here. Can't do Ruthie no good if you get hit by a tree. Storm should pass pretty soon, then we'll send out a search party."

Through tear-blurred eyes, Amalia stumbled after the men toward the boardinghouse through the lashing rain, clinging to Absalom's wet hand, hardly seeing where she stepped.

Please, Lord. Please don't take Ruthie. Please—shelter her like a little bird under your wings.

Ruthie couldn't stop shivering.

The rain was stopping, splatting slower onto her hair through the branches, but she was cold—so cold. It made her so tired she didn't want to move. She huddled farther under the bushes and laid her cheek on her knees, trying to remember the verses Mor had taught her.

"God is our refuge and strength, a very present help in trouble. Therefore will not we fear, though the earth be removed, and though the mountains be carried into the midst of the sea. . . ."

They didn't have mountains or sea, in this strange new land of Iowa. She missed Norway. But Iowa had started to feel like home . . . until today.

"Our help is in the name of the Lord, who made heaven and earth. . . ."

"What time I am afraid, I will trust in thee. . . ."

The rain stopped after a while. A late sunbeam peeked through the branches above her. Ruthie lifted her head, and a sparrow hopped out onto a wet twig, cocking its little head at her.

"Even the very hairs of your head are all numbered. Fear not therefore: ye are of more value than many sparrows."

Mor had said that meant God took care of every sparrow, and so she could know He would always take care of her too, because she was even more important than the birdies. She could trust Him and not be afraid.

Even if Cousin Zelda took her away.

Ruthie took a deep breath and pushed to her feet. Her bare feet and ankles squished in the mud. It felt good on her scratches. She shivered again—she was still cold.

A snuffling noise came through the bushes, then padding foot-steps. Ruthie froze. A bear? Or a wolf? Did they have those in Iowa, like back in Norway?

More snuffling, then a bark.

Dog's wet, black face came crashing through the bushes, tongue lolling out at her in a grin.

"Dog!" Ruthie flung her arms around his neck, burying her face in the wet ruff of his fur, not caring about the stink. "You found me." She poked up her head. "Is Hank here?"

But no one else appeared alongside the rushing creek. Ruthie saw now how close she'd come to the edge of its rushing waters, and she shuddered.

"Will you take me home, Dog?" She gripped her fingers into his fur. "It's starting to get dark."

He turned and headed up the creek bank, pausing to give her time to get her footing. Still, she stumbled a lot while trying to climb back up, bruising her toes. She was so tired—so cold. If only she could find someplace warm to lie down. Twilight was turning to darkness around them awfully fast. She couldn't tell if Dog was leading her the right way. It almost seemed like they were heading away from the boardinghouse.

But at least Dog was here. She wasn't alone. Maybe that was God taking care of her, just as Mor had said.

"Let's go, please." Amalia pressed her chilled hands together. The men seemed to take forever to put on their boots.

The storm had broken just before sundown, the sun slanting triumphant gold through the gray clouds. They'd all changed into dry clothes while they waited, Absalom wearing a shirt and trousers lent by Amos—a bit long on him, but better than his sodden suit.

"Better take lanterns." Amos carefully struck a match. "Be gettin' dark soon."

Dark—and a little girl out there somewhere, alone.

She threw on a shawl, the evening cool after the rain and hinting of fall, though it was still late August, and hurried outside.

Hank stood in the yard, calling for Dog.

"Can't you find him?" Amalia hugged herself.

"He took off when that ol' tree got hit by lightning." Hank swiped his sleeve across his nose. "He never did that afore."

He was crying, Amalia could tell, though he hunched his shoulders away from her. She gave him a quick squeeze. "We're going to find them, Hank. Ruthie and Dog both." If only she could feel as sure as she sounded.

The men spread out in the yard, Mr. Miller and Eben, JJ and Amos, Absalom, all wearing hats and holding lanterns. Mrs. Miller had come too, to help Zelda cook supper and watch Noah—and be a friendly face should Ruthie find her way home.

JJ took charge, thankfully. Amalia couldn't.

"Mr. Miller and Eben, you search the pasture and wheat fields, you know them well. Amos and Absalom, try the cornfield, orchard, and outbuildings ag'in. Miss Amalia, you and Hank come foller the creek with me." He stumped on ahead, a wiry, stooped little leader.

"Sure wish Dog hadn't took off." Hank's feet slipped in the mud. "Might be he coulda sniffed her out."

Amalia tried to keep up, her skirts catching on the wet rushes, calling for Ruthie.

Oh, Ruthie. Why did you run off? Didn't you know I'll do whatever it takes to keep you? To protect you? She never should have left in the wagon like that. She should have made sure Ruthie didn't overhear Zelda. She should have taken her with her. She should have—

Lord, I already lost Mor and Far. You can't take Ruthie too. Rebellion tasted sharp in her mouth.

They searched the creek bank in the falling shadows. Hank and JJ went one way toward town, Amalia the other toward the barn and beyond to the open fields. Which way would Ruthie have gone, if she came here? How could they possibly know?

Please, please show us, God.

She'd gotten too far to hear Hank and JJ anymore, so she turned back in the other direction. A chill shook her, and she stumbled, falling to her hands and knees in the mud.

A sob burst from her chest, guttural and raw. *I can't—I can't lose her. Please.* Her fingers clenched, squishing in the mud. *How can I bear this?*

I am with you. And I am with Ruthie.

Slowly, her breathing evened. God never promised to shield them from heartache, or even death—she knew that wrenching truth from these last months. But He did promise to never leave them, no matter what. And He hadn't, all through their heartbreaking losses so far. Whatever happened, the trials of this world would not be the end.

"Forgive me, Lord. I trust you. I do trust you." The words choked, but she whispered them out. "Help us, please. And help Ruthie . . . to know you're with her, wherever she is."

She pushed to her feet and stumbled onward, farther and farther from the boardinghouse, till she could hear Hank and JJ's voices ahead. Could Ruthie have walked this far? But JJ held up his lantern and beckoned through the deepening twilight.

"What is it?" She rushed forward.

He held out a sodden blue ribbon. "This look familiar?"

"Ja." Amalia snatched at it. "It's one of Ruthie's hair ribbons. She had it on today. Where did you find it?"

"Right over here." JJ forged ahead, his steps quicker.

Amalia's heartbeat picked up, and she hurried after him. So Ruthie had come this way. *Thank you, God.* But how close had the ribbon been to the creek? Could Ruthie have fallen in?

Hank crouched and held his lantern closer to the ground. "Footprints."

"From Ruthie?"

"From an animal. Maybe Dog." He traced the faint outlines in the mud. "Had to be after the storm, or they'd have been washed away."

"An' up here." JJ bent ahead, peering at the ground. "More paw prints, but look—think this might be a bare foot?"

Amalia shook her head, clenching the ribbon between her muddy fingers. "Maybe. I can't tell."

"Looks like they're headin' thisaway. I wonder." JJ straightened and stood still a moment, then took off crashing through the bushes away from the creek. "Worth a chance to look."

Amalia stared after him. "What is he doing?"

"I don't—oh." Hank lifted his head. "Could be!" And he took off after JJ.

Amalia plunged after them in the falling darkness.

They emerged into a small clearing, the air lighter gray here than amid the trees. A shadowy shack rose before them at the end of the clearing.

"JJ useta live here." Hank's voice came breathless at her shoulder. "Dog an' me came here lotsa times. I think he's wonderin' if Dog—"

JJ already mounted the steps ahead of them. "Watch your step." He shone his lantern for their feet as Amalia and Hank followed, picking their way over the rotten boards. JJ pushed on the door, which hung open, and it gave way with a creak.

Amalia followed JJ's lantern beam, her breath catching in her chest. JJ, ahead of them, gave an incoherent exclamation.

"Thank God A'mighty."

Amalia rushed forward and fell to her knees beside the rough pallet on the floor, throwing her arms across Ruthie, who lay sound asleep under a faded quilt. Dog flung himself at Hank, sending the boy tumbling, laughing and crying, into a heap on the floor.

Amalia rocked Ruthie long by the kitchen stove that night, after giving her a warm bath and a bowl of hot soup. Noah and Hank lay asleep upstairs, Amos and JJ too. Mrs. Miller, who had stayed to help feed everyone, at last laid her hand on Amalia's shoulder.

"You'll be all right now?"

"Ja." Amalia reached up to squeeze her hand. "Mange takk—for everything."

"Of course. Thanks be to God for this happy ending."

Amalia's throat tightened. Ja. Only the ending hadn't come yet—she hadn't been able to bear saying anything about the lawsuit to Mrs. Miller tonight. Not that she'd had a chance.

"Good night, Amalia. Mr. Karlsson."

The front door closed behind her friend. Now only Absalom still sat with her, by the winking red light of the stove.

Amalia ran her hand over Ruthie's still damp hair, the sleeping little girl's head pillowed on her arm. She pressed a kiss to her soft cheek.

"I was so frightened," she whispered.

Absalom leaned forward, pressing his palms together between his knees. "We all were."

"After losing Mor and Far, I felt—like it was happening again." Amalia's throat squeezed tight. "I'm afraid I had some harsh words with God."

"It's easy to fear. Especially when you've suffered loss. You know it could happen again." He sat up straighter, rubbing his hands on his thighs. "Surely the Lord knows that. He remembers we are dust, as the psalm says."

"And He gave her back to me." Amalia traced the perfect, rosy ear pillowed on her arm.

"To all of us." Absalom reached to lay his hand gently over Ruthie's bare foot, sticking out from beneath her nightgown. "Thanks be to God indeed."

"I suppose I should lay her down." She sighed, shifting Ruthie's head to her shoulder. Her arm ached, but she still hated to put her to bed.

Absalom helped her stand and followed her up the stairs, staying outside in the hall while she laid Ruthie on her pallet. She peeked at Noah and Hank, slumbering in the next room, then shut both doors.

At a noise below, she looked to see Zelda standing in her bedroom doorway near the foot of the stairs.

"She all right?" Her usual abrupt tone came a bit hoarse tonight.

"I think so." Amalia gripped her elbows. Absalom stepped slightly nearer to her. "She got awfully chilled, but she's warm and sleeping now. Hopefully she won't catch cold."

"Always did think these children were too much for you to keep track of." Zelda turned to go back into her room.

Amalia's scalp burned. After what she'd done today, did this woman really think she could . . . ?

Absalom took a step forward, but Amalia held out a hand to him and shook her head. She needed to do this. She hurried down the stairs to Zelda's door before she could close it.

"Zelda?"

Zelda frowned, holding the door half-shut. "Ja?"

Amalia straightened her shoulders. "I will give you a few days to find another place. But I'm afraid I cannot allow you to continue living here. Not after today."

Something flickered across Zelda's face. "So you're throwing me out. Always knew you wanted to."

"I didn't want to." Amalia swallowed. "But I must protect these children."

Zelda's face twisted. "Fine, then." She slammed the door hard enough to shake the whole house.

Amalia groaned and gripped her head in her hands. "Now I feel like a bully."

"She is the bully." Absalom descended the stairs, then took her elbow and guided her toward the kitchen. "You are doing the right thing."

Amalia drew a breath, his words unwinding something in her chest. "Mange takk."

She pushed the coffeepot to the hotter part of the stove. "Cup of coffee before you go?" Her voice almost sounded normal now.

He nodded. "Thanks." He sat down and ran a hand through his hair, drying curlier than ever after the storm.

She added more water to the pot, then sat down in her chair by him, their knees nearly touching. "It's you I should thank. You've been here with us so long. Won't your father worry?"

"The Millers' hired boy took a message to him hours ago." He met her gaze. "And there's nowhere else I wanted to be."

Her stomach did a little flip-flop. She glanced away from him to the flames in the stove, face heating from more than the warmth there. Why did he say things like that? What was it supposed to mean?

"Amalia."

"Ja?" She didn't look at him.

He leaned forward, bridging the gap between their chairs. "I'm sorry. Saying such things . . . it isn't fair to you. Not unless I explain myself."

She snuck a glance at him. Had he read her mind?

"I mean that—I have come to care very much for you." He reached out and took her hands in his, his grip warm and firm, though his fingers trembled a little. "In fact . . . I love you, Amalia."

She caught her breath. Her heart thumped hard.

"I know this may not be the best time to say it." He tightened his grip on her hands. "But there never seems to be the right time. You have brought so much light and love and joy into my life, Amalia. You've opened up—hope in me again. For a future . . . for love. Though I don't know what you think about that idea, or about me. I'm barely a lawyer, and I'll certainly never be a rich one. I—"

"Stop." She breathed the word, trying to withdraw her hands.

He released her immediately, his forehead creasing beneath his curls. "I'm sorry. I shouldn't have spoken—"

"No—it's not that. I just—" The storm, Zelda's news, losing and then finding Ruthie—and now this—a warm rush filled her eyes, and she clasped her hands to her face. "I need a moment."

"Of course." He pressed his fingers together between his knees and waited.

The fire crackled in the stove. A night breeze wafted through the half-open window, carrying the sweet scent after the rain.

She drew a long breath through her nose, lowered her hands. She didn't need to fear, to rush. This was Absalom. She knew him. "You have been so good to us, Absalom. You are—such a good man." Her throat tightened. "And I care for you too. But—there's so much right now. Ruthie running off, Zelda leaving, the court hearing. Can I have a little time—to think? And pray?"

"Of course. I've stayed long enough." He rose, hesitated, then touched her shoulder briefly, his hand warm, gentle. "You'll be all right?"

She nodded, reaching up to touch his fingers with hers. The faintest brush, yet her fingertips tingled with it. "Mange takk. For everything. We'll talk soon."

"Of course. We should meet soon about the hearing; I'll speak to my father. Good-night."

After the faint click of the front door from the entryway behind her, she buried her face in her arms and let the tears come.

TWENTY-SEVEN

I will have to give my statements in English, ja?"

"That will be best." Absalom nodded, sitting at his father's desk across from Amalia. "Judge Alfelt is Swedish, but he conducts everything in English."

"What sort of a judge is he?"

Absalom hesitated. "He can seem severe, but I've always known him to be fair. I'm grateful he'll be the one hearing your case. The following week he goes on vacation, and an interim judge will take over."

She nodded. Her fingers twisted together in her lap, her thumb rubbing her knuckle over and over.

"We should go over what you want to say, practice now ahead of time, so you'll feel more confident at the hearing."

She flinched. "I can't imagine feeling confident there."

He itched to go to her, to take her hands in his and reassure her, but held himself back. He'd shared his feelings, now he needed to give her the space, the time she'd asked for. And right now, they needed to focus on preparing for court next week. This was about her and Ruthie, not him.

He set his notes aside and leaned forward, clasping his hands on the desk. "Have you thought about what you'll say?"

"Only every few minutes during the days and quite a bit of the nights." Her mouth tipped wryly. "But I still don't know what would be best to focus on and to leave out. Should I describe how awful Zelda has been? Or just focus on Ruth and me?"

Absalom shifted his jaw. "A good question. But I'd focus on your story, how you came to be Ruthie's guardian. Answer any questions about Zelda truthfully, but you don't want to seem vindictive—not that you are, but let me handle telling the uglier side of things." He cracked a grin. "Lawyers are known for doing the dirty work, after all."

She gave him a tremulous smile. "I'm so glad you'll be there with us."

"So am I." His throat suddenly dry, he tried to swallow and jerked his gaze away from her blue-gray eyes, pulling out his notepad. "So, what are the key points you'll want to tell of your story? Let's make a list, and I can help you practice them in English."

She drew a breath. "Well, the cholera epidemic, I suppose, how Ruthie and I both lost our parents. And how Mrs. Forsberg asked me to become her guardian."

"You'll want to share that in detail, emphasizing the legal papers, the captain being there and all. Don't forget to mention being trustee of the boardinghouse also."

"So much to remember." She swiped her palms against her skirt as if damp. "What if I make a mistake?"

"Your English has gotten stronger than you think. And as I said, we'll write the basic points out in English for you to practice. I can always step in with a clarification if needed. Amalia . . ." He waited till she met his eyes, his chest twisting with the mingle of emotions in her gaze. "You're going to do fine."

Together they compiled a list of the most important points she needed to cover, then Amalia dictated the wording she wanted while Absalom typed the sentences up for her, correcting grammar as needed along the way. At last he tugged the paper from the typewriter with a flourish and handed it to her.

"There you are, my lady."

"Mange takk for going to all that trouble. I can't believe how fast that machine goes."

"My favorite wonder of the modern era." Absalom gave his trusty typewriter a pat. "My father spoiled me with this when I started law school. A mercy for all my future clients, as anyone who has ever seen my handwriting knows well."

She laughed, a joy to his ears, then stood. "Well, takk for everything. Now I must stop by the lumberyard to see about setting up coal delivery for the boardinghouse for the fall."

"Already?" He stood also and opened the office door for her.

"Ja, well, Zelda didn't use the coal furnace in the basement the last few years. Since she only lived on the ground floor, the heat from the cooking range was enough, I guess—and she didn't have the money. But we'll need to heat the whole boardinghouse this winter. I want to be ready."

"And Zelda has moved out?"

"She took the remainder of her things last week." Amalia sighed. "I don't know where she's staying, but we're all breathing easier already."

He shook his head. "You put up with her much longer than many would have. Are all your rooms full?"

"Not yet. We have three rooms open out of eight on the second floor since Mrs. Askeland moved down to Zelda's old room, and several beds open on the third floor still. But I've had a note from a writer who is moving to this area in the spring and looking for lodging."

"A writer. Interesting." He followed her out the front door.

"I thought so. We are developing a rather fascinating collection of people. Did you know Mrs. Askeland used to teach music? And she insists on helping out where she can, despite her arthritis." She sighed. "Well, I'd better go if I'm to get back in time to welcome Ruthie home from school. I'd rather stay and keep talking to you." Her cheeks pinked as if she hadn't meant to say that.

Absalom's heart suddenly thudded hard. She wanted to stay with him? To be with him? He shouldn't take it to mean too much—and yet, the way she flushed and glanced down, then back up at him, as if afraid yet wanting to meet his eyes . . . "May I walk with you?" he blurted.

"Don't you have work to do?"

"It can wait." He shoved his hands into his pockets, tongue suddenly thick. "I—I'd rather be with you too." Bold, doubtless far too bold. But she'd started it this time, hadn't she?

She nibbled her lip, then nodded and smiled a bit. "I'd like that."

They strolled down Main Street side by side under the September sunshine. A few early-yellowing leaves drifted down to skitter on the wooden sidewalk before them.

"How is Ruthie?"

"She's loving school so far." Amalia sighed. "I think it's been a merciful distraction from—all this. Helen is so good with her, and she feels safe there. Her nightmares have started again, though."

Absalom's gut clenched. "I'm so sorry." A flash of anger burned again, that someone would cause these two such blatant and inexcusable turmoil. They'd been through more than enough without having their lives upended again.

"Ja, well." Amalia drew a breath. "Just trying to keep taking one day at a time."

They turned the corner to head toward the lumberyard. A young woman pushing a baby carriage came toward them along the sidewalk, her hat hiding her face as she bent toward the infant. But Absalom knew her before she looked up, her face changing as she recognized him. She stopped the carriage.

"Rebecca." He smiled and tipped his hat. "Good to see you." And it was, he realized. The old pang had completely gone.

"And you." She glanced at Amalia, a question in her eyes.

"This is Miss Gunderson, a friend and client." Gently, he touched Amalia's elbow. "She has reopened the old Forsberg House in Green Creek."

"How lovely." Rebecca's shapely brows raised.

"A pleasure to meet you." Amalia smiled, her English clear and precise. She slipped her hand into the crook of Absalom's elbow, startling him, then glanced at the carriage. "And who is your little one here?"

"This is little David." Rebecca turned the carriage for him to see a chubby, dark-haired infant arrayed in a laced and beribboned gown. He blinked sleepily at them. "Named for my husband, the doctor here in town." Pride colored her voice.

"What a beautiful child. And oh, ja, Dr. Armitage has helped some of our boardinghouse family."

"Really?" Rebecca looked up. "He didn't mention it."

Absalom fought a sudden urge to laugh, so hard he had to clamp his jaw to keep from snorting.

The baby started to fuss, and Rebecca moved the carriage. "Well, I'd best be on my way."

"As had we." Amalia tightened her hand slightly on Absalom's arm. "It was nice to meet you."

"And you."

The carriage rolled away behind them, and Absalom and Amalia crossed the street to the lumberyard without saying anything. She slipped her hand off his arm once they reached the lumberyard fence.

"Sorry if I shouldn't have done that." She flushed and glanced away. "I'm not sure what came over me."

"I didn't mind." More like having her so close, and at her initiative, made him want to kick his heels in the air, but he wouldn't say that.

"So that was her."

He nodded and blew out a breath. "That was Rebecca."

"I'm glad you told me about her—before."

"I don't want to have any secrets from you." He met her gaze.

She examined his face a moment, blue-gray eyes thoughtful. "Do you still have regrets?"

He leaned on the fence under a sheltering elm, not wanting to answer too fast. Just as he wanted no secrets from her, he wanted to give no pat assurances either. But as he searched his heart, the answer came clear. "No. The memories might still hurt a bit at times, maybe. But regrets? Never. Rebecca is happy with a husband who can give her the fine things she wants, the things I couldn't—at least not and pursue the path I believe God wants for me. And I am happy with where I am. Far happier than I'd have been with her—I see that now." *"Happy with you,"* he wanted to say. But it wasn't the time, not today while she was still dealing with so much.

Suddenly, the laugh he'd squelched crept up his throat and exploded into a guffaw.

"What?" She stared at him.

"Sorry. Just what you said—about her husband helping folks from the boardinghouse." He shook his head, trying to stop the chuckles. "So Dr. Armitage didn't mention his encounters with Hank and Noah, what a shock."

She stared a moment longer, then burst out laughing too. "Probably would have made some interesting supper conversation if he had."

They chortled till a nearby mule turned and stared at them and Amalia had to wipe her eyes.

"Oh my." She sniffed and sighed. "Well, I'd best get back to business. Mange takk for walking me here."

"Velbekommen. I will see you soon—before the hearing, if I can."

She nodded, the shadow falling over her eyes again. "Do you—do you think we will win?"

His chest tightened. "I pray so."

The following week, he stopped by the post office after a preliminary meeting with Judge Alfelt and Bernhard—a meeting that left him with even more dislike for his former schoolmate than before, if that were possible.

"Letter for your father, Mr. Karlsson."

"Thank you." Absalom took the envelope from the postal clerk and headed out of the post office back down the street. A brisk breeze flapped his coat, the leaves on the trees turning from green to gold over his head and reminding him fall was coming.

Just like the hearing for Amalia and Ruthie. Tomorrow already. Had he sufficiently prepared? Never had a day in court weighed on him like this.

He pushed through the gate toward home and pressed the worn brass handle on their front door. Stepping inside, the familiar dark wooden interior and scent of ink and paper only faintly soothed the tension in his chest.

"Mail for you." He poked his head inside his father's open office door and tossed the letter onto his desk.

"Thank you." His father didn't look up from the scratching of his fountain pen.

Absalom started to step away, then hesitated. "Later, could I go over my arguments for tomorrow with you?"

His father did look up then, the lines of his face softening. "Of course, son."

Absalom sat down behind the front desk. Though they'd spoken to JJ about their plans to cut a door to the small parlor and turn it into a private office for him, far more important items had been taking everyone's attention of late. He opened a locked drawer and pulled out all his files on the Forsberg/Gunderson/Berg case.

Methodically he laid out the papers before him. His copies of the original papers from Ruthie's mother, signed on board ship. The English translation of those papers. Zelda's filing for custody and trusteeship. His notes on everything he'd found regarding law and precedent.

He knew from his studies that even grandparents didn't always have the right to file for custody once another guardian was established. Amalia's case should be solid. Still, Zelda and Bernhard made a twisted combination. He couldn't rest easy, not till this whole ugly business was over and done with.

He leaned forward and rested his head in his hands, thinking of Amalia, as it seemed he did so much of the time. Had he been right to tell her he cared? More, that he loved her? He'd sensed so at the time . . . and the memory of her whispered *"I care for you too,"* the brush of her fingers against his, sent a warm tingle through his whole body. Not to mention the sweetness of their walk the other day, the pressure of her hand on his elbow—so dear, so right-feeling. But what if he had only added an unnecessary burden on her mind at such a time?

Lord . . . we surely need you right now. Please hold your hand over us all, in these coming days. Cover Amalia and Ruthie with your peace. Rescue and vindicate them, Lord. Let justice be done, and truth win out. Help me do my job well. And for whatever you want for me and Amalia . . . he drew a long, slow breath, then let it out. *Guide us. Cover her with your love. And thy will be done.*

At last, a measure of the peace he'd sought released in his heart. Opening his eyes, he sat up and made a few more notes on his arguments for tomorrow.

"Absalom?" His father's cane tapped through the doorway.

"Yes?" He looked up.

His father held out the unfolded letter in his hand. "You should see this. It's about Erik Gunderson."

Amalia's brother? Absalom shoved to his feet and took the single page.

"It's from an old acquaintance of mine who used to work at Castle Garden. He was able to make inquiries into the immigrant records of the last few years."

Absalom scanned the written lines. "Oh no."

His father leaned on his cane and nodded, his mouth grave beneath his mustache. "Sounds like yet another testimony to what you wrote in your dissertation."

The letter stated that Erik Hamre Gunderson had indeed arrived in New York three years ago, but soon after seemed to have been taken advantage of by a dishonest interpreter, preying on newly arrived Norwegians. He'd lost all his money and was stranded on the streets of New York, had fallen in with the wrong crowd, and finally been arrested for a group robbery.

"In prison for the last two years?" Absalom looked up at his father. "How am I going to tell Amalia?"

He shook his head. "At least she will know he is alive. But perhaps wait till after the hearing."

"I think you are right." Absalom blew out a breath and pushed his spectacles up his nose. "One thing after another, isn't it?"

"At least it says he will soon be released on good behavior. Perhaps she can make contact, bring him here."

"If he is willing to come." Would the young man be too hardened by now to care about seeing his innocent younger sister? Or, if the upright raising he and Amalia had clearly known still held effect, too ashamed?

"Best put it aside for now." His father held out his hand for the letter. "We've more immediate concerns to deal with. Tell me your arguments for tomorrow."

TWENTY-EIGHT

She'd never been to court before.

Amalia held tight to Ruthie's hand as they mounted the steps leading to the pillared front of the Decorah courthouse. Her heart hammered so hard she could barely breathe. *Far i himmelen, be with us. Protect us, help us. And please—please don't let Zelda take Ruthie.* Her prayers jumbled in a panicked mush in her mind, but surely the Lord understood.

They entered the building, and she paused and scanned the atrium. People hurried back and forth, speaking to each other in hushed voices. Ruthie hung behind her, her little fingers digging into Amalia's hand. She'd had to keep Ruthie out of school today for this. Where were they supposed to go?

"Amalia." Absalom hurried toward them, his footsteps echoing in the vaulted chamber.

His familiar tousled curls, spectacles, and reassuring smile felt like a welcoming home in a wilderness.

"Where do we go?"

"Right this way. Come with me." He touched her elbow, gently guiding her, and sent a smile over to Ruthie.

They entered a vast courtroom, filled with benches dotted with various people, with a raised podium at the far end. No one sat there yet.

"You can sit here in the back till your turn," Absalom whispered.

"Is Cousin Zelda here?" Ruthie asked.

Absalom scanned the room. "Not yet."

They sat on the hard wooden bench for what seemed like hours. A tall judge with silver hair and wearing a long black robe came in shortly, and all rose in his presence, then sat when he took his seat at the raised podium. He said a few words to open the court session, then began to call different cases, small groups of people at a time going forward to tables at the front. In whispers, Absalom explained which were the plaintiffs and which the defendants.

Amalia had no idea so many cases would be heard before theirs. She wished she'd brought something to entertain Ruthie, but Absalom pulled a small pad of paper and pencil from his pocket for her to draw on and tied his handkerchief into various animals, making her softly giggle. His warm, suit-coated shoulder next to Amalia's kept her able to breathe from one moment to the next.

"Where is Noah today?" he asked her, voice low.

"Mrs. Miller came over to watch him, bless her. Along with helping Inga get dinner on for the boarders."

He nodded, then straightened in his seat. "There she is."

A knot tightened Amalia's chest and throat. Zelda walked into the courtroom and down the aisle right past them, trailing Uffe Bernhard. She didn't look at Amalia or Ruthie.

Amalia swallowed, her palms dampening. On the bench beside her, Absalom slipped his hand over hers and gave her fingers a squeeze. Not caring whether it was proper or not, she squeezed back. Thank God for Absalom. How would she make it through this day without him?

After another half hour, she slipped out to take Ruthie to the necessary. They were just coming back into the courtroom when she heard the judge say, "I will now hear the case of Zelda Berg versus Amalia Gunderson."

Absalom stood and nodded to her. The knot jumping into her

throat, Amalia squeezed Ruthie's hand and followed him down the aisle to the defendant's table on the left. Zelda and her lawyer sat themselves at the table to the right.

Amalia darted a glance at Zelda. The older woman's face was impassive beneath her bonnet. She still didn't look at Amalia or Ruthie.

Judge Alfelt, a tall man with a long face, glanced between them over silver-rimmed spectacles. "Will the plaintiff please state their case?"

"Certainly, Your Honor." Uffe Bernhard stood, clad in an expensive dark suit. He withdrew a stack of notes. "Miss Zelda Berg has been an upstanding member of our community for some years now. She ran the formerly well-known Forsberg boardinghouse along with her cousin-in-law, Else Forsberg, as a jewel of Green Creek until that lady's passing. In the last few months, she has been joined by one of her few living relatives, Miss Ruth Forsberg, who, with her parents, was to come from Norway and assist in reopening the boardinghouse." The lawyer looked over his nose at Ruthie. "To Miss Berg's shock, young Ruth's parents died on the voyage across, and Ruth was thrust into the care of a stranger, Miss Amalia Gunderson. This woman invaded Miss Berg's home, claiming not only guardianship of the child but ownership of the boardinghouse. She has since proceeded to fill it with unpaying boarders of the most questionable type, from runaways to vagrants to half-breeds."

Amalia's breath came quickly, her scalp hot. How many hateful half-truths could one person spew in a row? She held tightly to Ruthie's hand, only the gentle pressure of Absalom's arm against hers keeping her focused and upright.

Bernhard licked a finger and turned a page, seeming to read verbatim. "At last, seeing her cousin's legacy dragged through the mud and her young relative endangered, Miss Berg saw no other choice than to file for custody of Ruth and trusteeship of the boardinghouse, along with all funds. She will then fulfill her long-held plans to reopen the boardinghouse under her own name." Bernhard folded his notes and clasped them in his hands. "I would urge the Court to grant her request lest this formerly fine establishment become a blemish on our entire community."

Judge Alfelt raised silver brows. "Very well, Bernhard. Karlsson, the defendant's response?"

"Yes, Your Honor." Absalom rose. He, too, held notes in his hand, though he only glanced at them. "Your Honor, the plaintiff's argument displays not only woeful misrepresentation of the case, but outright falsehoods. To begin with, Miss Berg herself had run Forsberg House nearly into ruin before Miss Gunderson and Ruth Forsberg arrived. She had stopped taking boarders, sold most of the furniture, farmed out the animals, and let all buildings fall into extreme disrepair. Only by Miss Gunderson's hard work and diligence has the boardinghouse been able to open again, and even begin to turn a profit. Moreover, Miss Gunderson never claimed ownership of the place. She is well aware she runs it only as a trustee and by Ruth Forsberg's mother's dying wishes, when she gave her child into Miss Gunderson's guardianship, as laid out clearly in these papers, signed and witnessed aboard ship in April of this year, 1889." He held up the papers—the originals this time, provided by Amalia at his request, along with the translation, though Judge Alfelt could read some Norwegian.

"May I?" Judge Alfelt extended his hand.

"Of course, Your Honor." Absalom stepped quickly up to the bench and passed the papers over.

A hush fell over the courtroom as the judge perused the papers. After a moment, he looked over his spectacles directly at Amalia. "You are Miss Amalia Gunderson."

She swallowed. "Ja, Your Honor." She flinched at accidentally using the Norwegian word, but he didn't blink.

"And Hilda Forsberg gave her child into your custody on board ship before she died?"

Amalia glanced at Absalom. He nodded. "She did. She was dying of cholera, just after my own parents succumbed to the same disease. We had an epidemic." Her throat tightened, remembering. "A few hours before she passed, the captain called me to Mrs. Forsberg's cabin. She asked me to become guardian of her little girl, as her husband had already died. She said Ruth was to inherit a boardinghouse, and I would bear charge for it, and her child, until Ruth turned twenty-one, if I were willing. The captain was there to witness it, to make it legal."

"And why did you undertake such a task? It's a heavy burden— you can't be more than twenty-one yourself."

She swallowed. "I'll be twenty-one next month."

"So did you see a chance for profit here? To make your fortune in America by taking advantage of this child's inheritance? With no parents of your own, perhaps you thought it best to grab what you could." His gray eyes pierced.

"Nei, Your Honor." Shock accentuated her words. "That never entered my head. I didn't ask for this. It's been—" Her throat nearly closed. "Not easy."

"No doubt." His eyes softened. "So, why you, Miss Gunderson? You're no relation to the family. Why did Hilda Forsberg pick you in her dying moments?"

"I . . ." The courtroom swam around her. "I don't know, Your Honor."

"Because Tante Amalia loves people." A little voice piped up beside her. Ruthie stood and squeezed Amalia's hand, hard. "She loves me. Mor knew she'd take good care of me. And she did."

"I see." The judge leaned forward, meeting Ruthie's eyes. "And perhaps we should ask you, young lady, since you form the central spoke of this case. With whom do you wish to stay? Your Cousin Zelda? Or Miss Gunderson?"

"Tante Amalia, always." Turning, Ruthie threw her arms about Amalia's waist, burying her face in her skirt and hugging hard.

Amalia's eyes blurred. She wrapped her arms about the little girl's shoulders.

Absalom cleared his throat. "Your Honor, if I may. Miss Berg's suit against Miss Gunderson stems from, though I hate to say so, nothing more than jealousy and pure spite. Miss Gunderson was chosen as guardian for Ruth while she was not. Miss Gunderson has begun to make the boardinghouse a success again where Miss Berg did not. True, some of Miss Gunderson's early guests may seem unconventional, but none of them pose any danger to the community. Instead, they have begun to form a true working kinship—one might say, a family. As you can see, Ruth is safe, cared for, and loved with Miss Gunderson. She is an excellent guardian, to Ruth and to the other children who have come into her care. Just as Hilda Forsberg knew she would be."

"Thank you, Counselor." Judge Alfelt looked down and made a notation. "Does the counsel for the plaintiff wish to respond? Question Miss Gunderson?"

Uffe Bernhard rose. A faint sheen of sweat glistened on the edges of his dark hair. "No further questions, Your Honor."

A rustle came from Zelda as he sat back down. She leaned forward, whispering harshly. Her lawyer muttered sharply back.

At a nod from Absalom, Amalia sat, her legs trembling. Ruthie still clung to her, and Amalia put her arm around the child, cuddling her close to her side. She hardly dared breathe.

Judge Alfelt cleared his throat, glaring down at Zelda and her lawyer till they both quieted. "I've no need to call a recess. I have my decision."

Silence fell. All eyes turned to the judge.

"I grant continued custody of Ruth Forsberg to Amalia Gunderson, along with trusteeship of Forsberg House till Ruth comes of age, as detailed by her mother's will. Zelda Berg shall pay any outstanding legal fees incurred by Miss Gunderson." Judge Alfelt brought his gavel down with a firm rap. "Case dismissed."

TWENTY-NINE

They had won.

Amalia sagged against the wooden back of the court bench, all the strength fled from her spine. *Thank you, God. Tusen takk, mange takk.*

"Did we win, Tante Malia?" Ruthie got up on her knees on the bench beside her. "Do I get to stay with you?"

"Ja, den lille." Amalia gave one of the little girl's braids a gentle tug, then hugged her. "You do."

"Hurra!" Ruthie twisted on the seat. "I want to say mange takk to Mr. Absalom."

"Ja, and we should probably get out of the way." No doubt the judge had more cases to hear. Amalia stood. Where was Absalom? She hadn't even noticed him leaving her side, but now he stood on the other side of the aisle with Zelda and her lawyer.

"You told me this would work, Bernhard." Zelda wasn't exactly trying to keep her voice low anymore. "You lied to me."

"What do you want from me, lady? You should've known better than to contest a dying mother's final wishes." Her attorney turned his back on her and gathered his papers, muttering under his breath.

"I've paid you most of my savings. You promised I'd get it all back and much more." She grabbed Bernhard's arm.

He shook her off with a jerk. "No guarantees in court, Miss Berg. You should know that." He snatched up his briefcase to leave.

"What am I supposed to do?" Her voice rose.

"Miss Berg does have a point, Bernhard." Absalom's voice cut in. "If you promised something you couldn't deliver, she could file a complaint, even sue you for malpractice."

Zelda glared at Bernhard and Absalom alike. "Well then, I will."

The judge cleared his throat. "If you've quite finished, Counselors? I have other cases to hear."

"Of course, Your Honor. Apologies." Absalom dipped his head and stepped back across the aisle to Amalia and Ruthie, holding out his arm. "Let's go." Though he kept his demeanor professional, he met Amalia's eyes with a brief smile that melted her middle and strengthened her legs down the aisle and out the courthouse door.

At the bottom of the steps, Absalom finally blew out a sigh. "Whew. What a day."

"Mange takk, Absalom." She turned to him, holding Ruthie's hand. "That seems far too little to say."

"You have little need to thank me. Your own words helped win the day—and yours, Miss Ruthie." He tweaked her nose, earning a giggle. "Most of all, thank the Lord. I thought we'd win, but . . . you never know. God is gracious. And as I told you, Alfelt is a good judge." He shook his head. "I sure wouldn't want to be in Bernhard's shoes just now."

"Nor I in Zelda's." Amalia glanced back to see Zelda standing just outside the courthouse door, alone. She gazed after them, silent, her hands clenched on her elbows.

Amalia turned back, a pang in her middle. But no, she wouldn't give into guilt. She had given Zelda many chances, and she'd thrown them back into her face—and worse, at the children who'd been entrusted into Amalia's care. Even Christ told His followers that sometimes they'd have to shake the dust off their feet and move on. But she would still pray for her. What an unhappy woman.

"Ready to go?" Absalom extended his hand toward his buggy, his black mare waiting patiently.

"You really don't have to give us a ride back."

He gave her a look. "On today of all days, don't deprive me of the pleasure."

A smile tickled her cheeks. "Then thank you, kind sir."

The September sun warmed their shoulders as they drove back to Green Creek, their stomachs rumbling for dinner. Cornfields waved on either side of the road, tassels browning, nearly ready for harvest. Along the creek, the green of the trees had started to turn russet and gold.

"Look, Ruthie." An arrow of geese flew overhead, honking toward the south.

"Miss Stenerson said that means fall is coming." Ruthie leaned her head against Amalia's shoulder. "Tante Malia, what will happen to Cousin Zelda now?"

"I don't know, Ruthie, I really don't."

Absalom glanced at her. "Don't let yourself feel guilty."

Had he read her mind? Amalia sighed and tipped her head back to follow the geese. She couldn't deny a cloud had lifted from over the boardinghouse without Zelda there. Ruthie and Noah seemed happier, more content. She'd caught Hank whistling while milking and felt her own heart settling, her body no longer having to tense at the sound of Zelda's footsteps.

Absalom pulled up in front of the boardinghouse, its freshly painted walls and dark blue gingerbread trim warm in the golden sunlight. More of JJ's handiwork. Hank came running out of the front door.

"What happened? Did we win?"

Amalia smiled at him and let Absalom help her down. "Ja. By God's grace, we won."

He whooped and spun Ruthie in a circle. Mrs. Miller came out onto the porch smiling, Noah on her hip, Inga behind her. "Dinner's ready. Come on in and tell us all about it."

Amalia turned to Absalom, still holding her hand from helping her down. Had he forgotten to let go? "Won't you join us for dinner?" She gave his hand a gentle tug.

"Just a moment." He glanced at the children, filing inside after Mrs. Miller and Inga, then drew her closer to him. "I have something else to tell you. I didn't want to mention it before the hearing—you had enough on your mind. But you've a right to know."

He released her hand to draw a letter from his inner jacket pocket.

Amalia took it, cold creeping over the warmth around her heart. What was this? Absalom's smile had faded, replaced by creases around his eyes. She unfolded the letter.

"It came to my father yesterday. We agreed you should know."

Amalia tried to focus on the penned lines, her English reading still shaky.

". . . in response to your inquiry regarding Erik Hamre Gunderson . . ."

She choked and looked up at him. "Min bror—is he alive?" She thrust the letter at him, hand shaking. "I can't read it fast enough—please, just tell me."

"Ja, he's alive." He caught the letter from her, then pressed her hand between his. "As best we can tell, that is."

"Where is he? How can I reach him? Why hasn't he—"

"Amalia." He waited till she met his eyes. "He's in prison. Has been for the last two years."

She stilled. A faint breeze stirred her hair, the only movement save the pounding of her heart. "Why?"

"He got cheated by a dishonest interpreter, shortly after he arrived in New York. He lost everything. After that, it seems he fell in with the wrong sort of people—trying the wrong way to set their lives right, if you know what I mean."

"Nei." She covered her mouth with her hand. "Oh, Erik. How could you?" Her brother had always had a good heart. He knew what was right. But sometimes . . . oh, sometimes his rashness got the better of him. But to steal? To break the law? She shook her head, tears spilling over. She'd never have thought.

"I know it's a great deal to take in." Absalom touched her arm. "But at least you know."

"Ja." She sucked a breath through the tears. "Ja, knowing is better than not knowing. But can I write to him?"

"We are looking into that. It seems he will soon be released. My father has already responded to this contact, to see what else he can learn. But it may take time."

"Time is all right. But oh, just to know this—mange takk, Absalom." She looked up at him then, at his concerned brown eyes behind his spectacles, at his dear shock of unruly curls. Warmth flooded through her, and she lifted her hand to brush a yellow leaf from the shoulder of his brown jacket. What a good man he was—a dear, thoughtful, wonderful man. Could he be—her man?

He cocked his head. "What are you thinking?"

"Of all that's happened since we came to Green Creek." She drew a breath through her nose, remembering the nightmarish voyage, that awful first night at the boardinghouse. But then the brightening days that followed—building a home here, seeing Ruthie grow and heal. Meeting Hank and JJ and Amos, Noah and Helen. Getting to know the Millers, and seeing this place burst into life with a growing garden and animals. Baby chicks in the henhouse—a newborn calf in the barn. Getting boarders . . . going to the dance. And Absalom—always Absalom. Advocating for them, thinking of them. Tending to their legal needs and waltzing with her at the dance. Making Ruthie laugh and defending them in the courtroom. Loving them, in every way he could.

She wrapped her hands over his. "I was wondering . . . why it's taken me so long to realize that I love you too."

He caught his breath, shifted his feet. "Amalia, I didn't mean to rush you into anything."

"I know that. And you haven't." She met his eyes. "I'm not saying I won't still need to take things . . . slowly. So much has happened, and I have so much to still figure out. But I hope to have you beside me, as I do. As you already have been, in so many ways."

A slow smile spread across his face. "I think you'll find it hard to get rid of me."

She smiled back. "Good."

He lifted his hand and ever so gently trailed his finger along her check to her chin, asking permission with his eyes.

A warm flush tingled from her chest to her cheeks. She tipped her face up to his, and he bent his head and met her lips with his own as they shared their gentle first kiss, with the patient chaperoning of the black mare.

"Malia!" Ruthie's shout from the porch made them startle apart, both flushing a bit.

The little girl leapt down the steps and darted toward them, squeezing in between and putting an arm around each. Ruthie looked up between Amalia and Absalom, beaming. "Isn't this the best day since we came to America, Tante Malia? Doesn't it just feel like finally coming home?"

Amalia exchanged a smile with Absalom and hugged her. "Ja, den lille. It does."

EPILOGUE

MID-DECEMBER, 1889

How could December be here already?

Amalia lay perfectly still, wishing she could go back to sleep, until she heard the clanking of a stove lid being set back in place. JJ was already up. She got out of bed as quietly as possible so Ruthie could sleep a few more minutes and dressed in the darkness. Bundling her hair into a snood, she carefully made her way down the stairs, not bothering with a lamp or candle. The light from the kitchen was plenty to keep her from bumping into the dining table and chairs, already set up for the morning.

"Good morning." She trapped a yawn. "Thanks for starting the stove." Her Norwegian accent was always more pronounced in the early morning.

"You always bank it well." JJ had assumed the job of assistant through the months since Zelda had left, not that she had ever really been that.

"Is the water still warm in the reservoir?" Helen Stenerson asked, pitcher in hand. "I need to leave for school a bit early this morning so the room can be warm for the children."

"I thought Nygard's grandson was going to start doing that?" JJ pulled the large pot with rolled oats over the hotter part of the stove next to the coffeepot. The diminishing heat had been enough to cook it through the night.

"He has been, but he said he would not be there today." She filled her pitcher from the reservoir and returned to her room to complete her toilet.

Hank and Dog appeared next on their way out to milk the cow and take care of the chickens. JJ shrugged into his coat and clamped his hat on to go with him. Between them they took care of all the livestock.

"God dag." Mrs. Askeland, now moved into Zelda's old room since stairs were difficult for her, her cane tapping, always greeted Amalia with a smile that lit up the entire kitchen. "What would you like me to do first?" She rubbed her hands together, then lifted an apron from the hooks on the wall and tied it on, her arthritic fingers making that difficult. "I see the table is all set."

"Ja, we need both the milk and cream pitchers from the pantry, and bacon. Oh, and the basket of eggs. We have oatmeal, and we'll scramble eggs and heat the bread. Since Amos and the Rykavyk brothers won't be back until day after tomorrow, we have fewer to feed." She paused. "You know you do not have to do this."

"I know, but I can't sleep late anyway, so at least I can be useful. And if I don't use my hands, they will only get worse." She used her cane to push back the rolled-up rug keeping the pantry cold out of the kitchen.

Breakfast flew by in the usual flurry, and JJ handed Miss Stenerson up to the front seat of the wagon and tucked a robe around her. He tossed a quilt over Ruthie in the back. They would stop at two farms on the way to pick up three other children on the way to school. Perhaps next term, they'd get Hank to go consistently too. So far, he'd consented to go once with Helen for a drawing lesson, but hadn't been back, spending his days helping JJ instead. At least today was the last day of school before Christmas break.

When JJ returned from driving and taking care of the horses, he stamped the snow off his boots on the porch.

"Coffee's hot," Amalia said when he dumped an armload of wood into the woodbox. He rubbed his hands together in the heat of the stove.

"Going to let the cows and horses out for a while, so I can clean the barn."

Dropping her voice, she motioned to the parlor where Noah was playing with blocks at Mrs. Askeland's feet as she kept the sewing machine busy. "How is the surprise coming for . . . ?"

"Nearly finished." JJ accepted the steaming cup of coffee and sipped carefully. "Think it's about time I feed the furnace too. They delivered that new load of coal just in time."

"What would I ever do without you?"

"Just grateful for a roof over my head and walls to keep out the wind and the cold." He gave her a grandfatherly wink.

A few days later, new snow barely disguised the old but glittered like scattered jewels. Amalia grabbed a shawl off the coat-tree by the front door and stepped out onto the porch, all to see more of nature's miracle. Fence posts wore top hats and tree branches drooped with the weight of the icicles. *"Christmas,"* this world whispered the news.

She heard Noah call her name. With Ruthie in school, the little one tagged after her, as if afraid she might leave him too. Although, at least now he understood Ruthie was coming back. Stepping back inside, she hung her shawl on the hat tree. "In here, Noah."

He ran to her as if she had been gone for hours and flung his arms around her. "I couldn't find you."

"I stepped outside to see how beautiful the snow is." She scooped him up in her arms and moved to the window that, thanks to Mrs. Askeland, now had curtains. The woman's fingers could no longer hold a needle, but she could sew on the machine. And she did. All the rooms on the first floor now were curtained.

"He was playing here by me until he looked around and you weren't there." The elderly woman leaned back in her chair. "So hard to believe Christmas is almost here, and now I live near enough to church that I can go to the service."

"Ja. You'll come with us."

"Are you sure you have room?"

"We have to go early for the children's choir to practice, so the Millers will give you a ride."

"I haven't been to a Christmas service for years. And to think the children will be singing."

The two women smiled, Amalia holding Noah on her hip. She could feel him relaxing with his head on her shoulder. The letter she'd received two days earlier nearly burned a hole in her apron pocket. Noah's pa was coming for his son to take him west. But he was not sure when.

For some reason, Absalom tiptoed into her thoughts. That happened often. For Christmas, she had embroidered his three initials on the corner of a white handkerchief to wear in the chest pocket of the suit he wore in court. He and the magistrate would be joining them for dinner tomorrow on Christmas Day. As usual, thoughts of him sent tingling in to warm her middle. She knew the exact moment she'd realized she not only loved him but was in love with him. With all her heart and soul.

But how to let him know that? Or when. Or if?

The house lay dark and silent as Amalia made her way down the stairs on Christmas morning. Hearing a clanking sound, she stopped. It came from under her feet, so she knew it was JJ down in the cellar, feeding the furnace. He had set up a cot down there and moved his tools from the barn so that he now had a workshop in the cellar; so as long as he had a lantern, he could work whenever he felt like it. She knew he'd been making presents.

She fumbled for the lid lifter, delighted to see winking coals after setting the lids aside. Taking a straw from the full jar, she held it to the coals till it flared so she could light the candle in the holder she kept on the stove shelf. *Tusen takk, Lord, for light and heat and this blessed morning*. Gratitude filled her for the people who shared this house with her, so many friends, all the blessings He heaped upon her. Never could she have even dreamed all this. And Absalom. He and his father would join them for dinner and the rest of the day. All the while her mind found more to be grateful for. Her hands started the fire, pulled the coffeepot she'd set the night before to the heating stove, and fetched food from the pantry.

"Let me do that." Amos spoke softly to keep from startling her. "Merry Christmas."

"Merry Christmas. Takk." She handed him the pan of cornmeal mush and nodded to the basket of eggs. The chill of the room was seeping in despite her woolen clothing. She took the ham from the counter under the window, where the world outside was lighting with the coming dawn. The magistrate had sent out the ham as his contribution to the dinner. That and a jar of pickled herring.

Amalia slid the ham into the oven and shut the door, figuring the ham could heat up along with the oven.

"I'm goin' out to do chores. Tell Hank to start with the chickens when he comes down; he was sleeping so sound I let him be."

He'd no sooner shut the door when Hank and Dog yawned their way in. "Where's JJ?"

"Merry Christmas to you too." She smiled at him and patted Dog's head. "Amos is milking, he said start with the chickens. JJ is in the cellar." She turned from setting cookies on a plate and held it out to him. "Thought you might need something to get you started." She handed a cookie to Dog. "God Jule." The draft from his feathery tail made her smile and nod. "Breakfast will be ready in about half an hour."

"Takk."

She grinned and wagged her head.

Ruth and Noah padded in with Mrs. Askeland, who pulled out a chair for Noah. Ruthie set his box before helping him up.

"Cookie?"

At Amalia's nod, Ruthie handed him a cookie and her hairbrush to Amalia. "God Jule, Tante Malia."

Amalia hugged her. "God Jule, den lille." Certainly not how either of them would have imagined their first Christmas in America a year ago . . . yet surrounded by blessings, certainly a god Jule all the same.

With the Rykavyk brothers and railway workers gone home, as was Miss Stenerson, the gathering at the breakfast table felt cozy, candlelight dancing above the greenery Ruthie had helped decorate the table with. Afterward, JJ, Amos, and Hank dragged the two bulky items from the barn, still draped with canvas, into the parlor.

Ruthie stared, holding Noah's hand. "What are those?"

Amalia kissed the part between her braids. "Why don't you see. That long one is for you, the larger one for Noah."

Noah pulled off his canvas first, with help from Hank. A wooden barn emerged, fashioned by JJ's loving hands, filled with carved farm animals of every type—horses, chickens, pigs.

Noah gazed round-eyed a moment, then looked back at Amalia, mouth agape.

"Ja, for you, little one. Go on."

He looked back at the barn, then clapped his hands and danced on his toes, a delighted giggle bursting forth and bringing chuckles from them all.

"Lookie here." Hank dove onto his knees by the barn and reached in. "I carved these 'uns. JJ showed me how." He held forth a miniature wooden cow and calf.

Noah took them in his chubby hands, turned them over, then waved them in the air. "Honey an' Kapri." He beamed.

"That's right." Hank grinned back. "Just like them."

JJ had crafted the barn before they heard from Noah's father, but surely the little boy could at least take some of the animals with him out west.

"Now you, Ruthie." Amalia drew her down by the lower, longer bundle.

Ruthie knelt and slowly lifted the canvas, peeking under, then with a little gasp, she flung the covering off and clapped both hands over her mouth.

Amalia laughed, tears blurring her eyes. "You like it?"

The wooden doll cradle rocked before them, hearts carved in the headboard and footboard. Amalia had sewn a wee pallet, pillow, and quilt of rose-and-yellow calico squares to add to JJ's handiwork.

"Mange takk, tusen takk." Ruthie flung herself into Amalia's arms, then at JJ. "I have to get Anna." She dashed up the stairs for her beloved rag doll, sewn by Amalia for Ruthie's sixth birthday in November.

"There's one more thing." Amalia drew out a small, soft package from behind her back when Ruthie returned, her well-loved doll with yellow yarn braids hugged close in her arms. "I thought maybe Anna could use a Christmas dress."

"Oh," Ruthie breathed, unwrapping the small frock made of scraps of blue velvet and lace. "She will love it." She leaned against Amalia's side. "Takk."

"You are most welcome." Amalia hugged her again, then fetched another package from behind the sewing machine. She crossed to the boys, investigating the hayloft ladder of the barn, and knelt beside them. "Hank, this is for you."

He looked up, face startled. "For me?"

"Of course. Don't you know you're part of our family too?"

"Yeah, but—well." He fumbled with the string around the brown paper package, then opened it to reveal a fine drawing tablet and several charcoal pencils. He ran his hand over them and blinked hard. "Thanks."

"We look forward to seeing what you create with them." She squeezed his shoulder. "You deserve real art supplies."

Sometime later, the smoky sweet scent of the ham roused Amalia from watching the children play to check on their dinner. She'd just removed the sizzling ham, redolent of honey and cloves, from the oven when a knock sounded at the door.

Absalom. Amalia couldn't hold back her smile. She flung her apron aside and hurried to the door, reaching it just before JJ did. The older man chuckled and stepped back. "After you, young lady."

Her cheeks warming, Amalia opened the door. "God Jule—merry Christmas, Magistrate, Absalom." But it was the second man who held her gaze, as he stood there, cheeks ruddy and eyes twinkling in his dark brown overcoat, smiling in that way that seemed just for her.

"Merry Christmas." He followed his father inside and squeezed her hands, and suddenly her world felt complete.

Dinner stretched long and merry, full of good food and fellowship and children's laughter. At last they all gathered back in the parlor, decked with red-ribboned garlands of greenery and warmed by lamplight as snow softly began to fall again outside the windows.

Noah fell asleep on the braided rug, curled beside his beloved barn, the wooden calf held tightly in his hand. Ruthie rocked her doll in the cradle, murmuring to her some story of her own creation. Hank lay on his stomach near them on the rug, sketching on his new tablet, lips pursed in concentration.

Absalom sat beside Amalia on the settee. She felt like a queen each time she ran her hand over the red velvet cushions, even if they were a bit faded, being secondhand.

"They look so happy." He gazed at the children, then nudged her arm. "That's thanks to you, you know."

Amalia shook her head. "Not just me. So many people have come together to love them. And God is the one who brought us all together in the first place."

"True." He placed his hand over hers. "But you were willing to let Him use you."

328

She surveyed the room, the three children, contented and loved. Mrs. Askeland nodding in her chair, JJ, Amos, and the magistrate deep in conversation—three unlikely friends. Then she glanced at the man beside her, who was studying her face with those thoughtful brown eyes behind his spectacles.

"What is it?"

"I was just thinking"—he squeezed her hand—"that I love you."

Warmth curled through her as it always did at those words. She squeezed back. "And I you."

"And also that . . ." He cleared his throat and pushed his spectacles up his nose. His fingers tightened on hers. "That . . . I want to marry you."

"Absalom Karlsson." She sat up straighter and glanced about, but no one else sat near or seemed to note their conversation. "Are you—proposing? Right now?"

"I suppose I am." He took both her hands in his. "Yes. I definitely am."

A soft laugh snuck from her throat, then she blinked back tears. "Then yes. Ja. Of course I will marry you. But where will we live?"

He grinned, though moisture shone in his own eyes. "After all that's happened these last months, that's what you're worried about? We'll figure that out when we come to it." And he kissed her, there by the windowpane showing softly falling snow.

AUTHOR'S LETTER

My dear readers,

I know I don't always write letters to you, but the story behind this series is part of my family history on my father's side. I moved the time back a few years because what I wanted to do had to happen before the turn of the century. And I moved the setting from northern Minnesota to northern Iowa—an author's privilege.

My grandpa worked in a bank, and Grandma raised their large family in a house big enough to take in a few boarders too. Her main job was keeping everyone fed, so that included a huge garden, keeping chickens, and caring for a cow or two. One year, spring brought a late frost, and much of the garden had to be replanted—except for the rutabagas and other root crops. Despite covering tender plants with sheets, an early fall frost did even more damage.

That year, my ever-creative grandma used rutabagas in every recipe: soups, stews, baked, fried, even like applesauce in cake. When an early snowmelt happened, they raked back the dirt and dug out frozen rutabagas. While they might have missed a few meals, they all made it through the winter, and stories passed down through the family (and probably the boarders' too).

I know that my younger self asked a million questions—nearly drove people nuts—but now I'm wishing I had asked more. Grandma Clauson made the best lutefisk and lefse at Christmas, and other times too, and how I loved that big house in Bemidji. And you never went to her house without finding two or three kinds of cookies in the cookie jars and for dinner, a choice of three pies.

It's thanks to my delightful writing partner, Kiersti Giron, that this series is continuing, since I had a slight altercation with the floor and am now recuperating from a broken femur. Never a dull moment at my house.

My thanks, too, to agent and friend Wendy Lawton for being coach, guide, and all the myriad things agents do of which authors are not aware. We are all part of the Books & Such Literary Agency, who keep raising the bar in our Christian writing industry. Through all my writing career, I have had the honor of working with Bethany House Publishers, beginning with two series of horse books for girls (boys have enjoyed them too)—first the GOLDEN FILLY series and then THE HIGH HURDLES. Then I wanted to know more about my Norwegian heritage, so I proposed two novels with a character named Ingeborg, a combination of my mother, Thelma, and her sister Inga. Thus the rest of my writing career grew into being.

I am grateful for my husband Wayne, who has now gone on to his heavenly home, for all our years as he supported his wife's career and his growing children. When he was forced to retire from his carpentry career due to asthma, he discovered the part he came to enjoy most. We traveled for research and promotion for the books I kept dreaming up. I can still see him sitting with a group of old-time farmers, swapping tales and enjoying life.

And most of all, thanks be to our loving and gracious Lord, who loves us all beyond our understanding and never lets us go.

Thank you, my reader family, as we flow and grow through the years, for reading and enjoying our books, sharing them with others and sometimes sending me great ideas for more books and characters. May the Lord bless and keep us all. You can contact me at my website, LauraineSnelling.com. Blessings and happy reading.

Lauraine Snelling

DISCUSSION QUESTIONS

1. Amalia and Ruth come as immigrants to America. Do you have immigrant stories in your family history? Share!

2. Zelda brings a great deal of strife and stress to Amalia's and Ruth's lives. How do they handle it? Do you think there's anything Amalia could or should have done differently? How did the conflict with Zelda make you feel?

3. How have you handled situations with difficult people in your life? How did you feel about how the conflict with Zelda was resolved?

4. Absalom carries hurt from his broken engagement with Rebecca. How does meeting Amalia and Ruthie help bring healing to his heart?

5. Many people show welcome and assistance to Amalia and Ruth when they arrive, from Magistrate and Absalom Karlsson to the Miller family. How can we show welcome and give help to new immigrants in our own communities?

6. The boardinghouse becomes a sort of shelter for a wide variety of people in this story—Hank, JJ, Noah, Helen, etc. Which characters did you especially enjoy "meeting"? How does each contribute in their own way to the story and the boardinghouse "family"?

7. Amalia and Ruthie both experience deep grief over the loss of their parents. How does the process of grief affect them similarly and differently? How do they help each other step toward healing in this book?

8. Hank struggles to let anyone help him. How does he become part of the boardinghouse family? Why do you think he lets Amalia and Ruth take him in?

9. Magistrate Karlsson does much to help those in his community, from Hank to JJ to Noah's parents to Amalia and Ruth, but he doesn't want to be noticed for it. Do you think he is a reflection of Jesus's words to not let our right hand know what our left is doing? How is the magistrate an inspiration to you?

10. Later in the book, Amalia reaches a point of realizing she can't do it all on her own—that she needs to both lean on the Lord's strength and also accept the help of those He has put around her. Do you ever have trouble asking for help? How can Christian community help shoulder the burdens we find too heavy on our own?

For more from

LAURAINE SNELLING,

read on for an excerpt from

The
Seeds
of
Change

After turning the tables on a crooked gambler, Larkspur Nielsen flees her home with her sisters on a wagon train bound for Oregon. Knowing four women will draw unwanted attention, she dons a disguise as a man. But maintaining the ruse is harder than she imagined, as is protecting her sisters from difficult circumstances and eligible young men.

Available now wherever books are sold.

ONE

I truly hate that man."

"Lark, you know Ma said we should never hate anybody."

Larkspur's sister Forsythia, third of the Nielsen daughters, spoke out of the side of her mouth, the way they had learned so as not to be heard by anybody else. Especially in church. Forsythia had spent a good part of her young life trying to keep her older sister out of trouble.

Larkspur refocused her attention forward, clenching her fingers in her lap to keep from leaping out of the pew.

Deacon Wiesel raised his Bible, the pages rippling from the force of his shaking. His voice nearly tore the hinges from the doors. "Women, if you are indeed following God's Word . . ."

Larkspur watched the red of his face deepen. Perhaps a heart attack? A stroke?

"You are ordered to submit to your husband's every utterance. God says so, right here." The words thundered, and spittle spattered the pulpit. "If you are not married, your father is in charge. For too many of you, your mouth is your biggest sin." Little pig eyes slit nearly shut, he stared right at Larkspur as if daring her to speak.

337

Lark returned stare for stare, knowing she was aggravating the deacon but no longer caring. According to him, women should never raise their eyes—only a downcast posture was proper.

Forsythia laid a gentle hand on Larkspur's shaking knee, and Lark felt an elbow digging into her left side. Her sister Delphinium was only reminding her that were their mother here, she would be mortified by the actions of her eldest daughter. Surely she had taught her daughters better than to let their emotions show like this in church. But then, Ma had never met Deacon Wiesel or watched him drive their dear Pastor Earling to his deathbed. At least, Lark sure found it suspicious that the two men had gone for a buggy ride and only the deacon returned alive, lamenting that their pastor had died in an accident. But how had Wiesel survived a runaway horse and Pastor Earling hadn't? And if their mother could see how the weasel took out his furies on his wife . . .

Lark glanced at Climie Wiesel, cowering in a forward pew. Bruised, bones broken, terrified he would one day abuse their dreamed-of children, Climie made excuses for her husband whenever she and Larkspur talked. But they all knew that Climie had lost that last baby and those before because the deacon beat her so badly. When Wiesel got liquored up, there was no stopping him. They all knew that, but their mother had gone on to heaven before Climie started taking refuge with the Nielsens when her husband went deep in his cups. Sadly, often not soon enough.

Something had to be done. After the accident, Deacon Wiesel had taken over, ignoring all efforts of the other church leaders to find a new pastor. Larkspur tried to shut down her mind by running through multiplication tables. It didn't help. She tried adding columns of three numbers. Nothing helped. She raised her head when she no longer heard the weasel haranguing them with the Bible verses.

But he was staring right at her. "Women, obey your husbands, for that is the word of the Lord."

For Forsythia's sake, Larkspur stared down at her clenched hands. She was shaking so hard the entire pew shuddered. *Thank heaven I am not married, and if all men are like you, I never will be.*

At a faint thud from the front of the church, Larkspur looked up.

Climie had slumped over in the pew where she sat. Fainted from the sheer force of her husband's hypocrisy?

Lark half rose to go to her.

"Young woman," Deacon Wiesel fairly roared, "sit down!"

"Your wife, sir." Lark shook off Forsythia's restraining hand and stood to her full stature, taller than the deacon himself if he hadn't been in the pulpit. "She's fainted."

"She has merely fallen asleep. You should concern yourself with hearing the word of the Lord and leave my family to me."

Mrs. Smutly, the woman on the piano bench who thought Deacon Wiesel ordered the sun to rise in the morning, gave a firm nod and cast a disapproving glance at the slender woman collapsed in the front pew.

Lark once again matched Wiesel glare for glare, then pushed past her two sisters and strode up the outside aisle toward the exit as if she were stomping ants. She ignored the scowls she could feel stabbing her and let the outside door click shut behind her. Shaking her head, Larkspur sucked in a deep breath, pausing at the top step to inhale the clean, quiet air.

"'Onward, Christian soldiers . . .'" The closing hymn floated out through the walls and windows, giving no hint of what had gone on inside.

Or what was going on inside of her.

She had to get away before the congregation was released from the evening service. Deacon Wiesel would make his way up the aisle to stand at the door and greet everyone, and she didn't want to be here when that happened.

Starting down the walk to the street, she heard her siblings exiting behind her.

"You've done it now." Her brother Anders, the eldest of the Nielsen clan, joined her. "I'm going back to the store. You're welcome to join me. Dealing with numbers always calms you down."

Larkspur shook her head. "If someone came in, I might bite their head off."

"Why can't you just ignore him? Or stop going to church?"

"That would really do it. Both Pa and Ma would be shuddering in their graves."

"Wait, Lark," Delphinium, next in age below Larkspur, called from behind them. "Let's walk together."

"I don't think you want to hear or even feel what I am thinking, Del."

"We know what you're thinking, but it doesn't do any good."

"Look, several of us from the board have written to the head church office requesting that they send us a new pastor," Anders said. "Till then, we'll have to ignore him."

"Ignore when his poor abused wife keels over in the front pew?" Lark demanded.

Anders stopped at the wooden porch of Nielsen Mercantile, which had been started by their father. "So what are you going to do, then?"

"I'm going home, that's what I'm doing." Larkspur turned to her sisters. "You can go back there and make nice with everybody, but I'm finished." She stomped ahead of them, the other three trailing behind.

"What are we going to do?" Delphinium whispered. "When she gets like this, she won't back down."

On the corner of the next block, rowdy piano music poured out of the swinging door of a saloon, inviting passersby to come on in. The sisters automatically stepped off the boardwalk to move to the other side of the street.

"Deacon Wiesel already blames Lark for all his problems. He thinks she influenced Climie and turned her against him. Now he's going to come after us, and if he doesn't do that, he'll at least tell everybody else how horrible we are, and there go our reputations right down the drain." That was Lilac, the youngest of the sisters at nineteen.

"Reputation isn't the most important thing here," Forsythia's gentle voice cut in. She caught up to Larkspur and put her hand through her sister's arm. Forsythia said nothing more, just walked quietly with her for a few moments.

A measure of peace seeped into Lark's bones bit by bit, radiating from her sister's spirit. She lowered her stiff shoulders with a sigh. "I just couldn't sit there anymore."

"I know."

"When I saw Climie crumple . . . Isn't there anything else we can do?"

Before Forsythia could respond, someone burst through the saloon doors and charged across the street in the waning light, nearly running into them.

"You gotta help me! I'm in bad trouble." Their baby brother, seventeen-year-old Jonah, grabbed Larkspur's hand and tried to drag her across the street.

"Jonah George Nielsen!" Larkspur jerked her hand free. "What in the world do you think you're doing?"

He fell to his knees, clutching her skirt. "He's a new man in town, and he's got all our money, and Bernie gave him a deed, and he's got that too and . . ." His words tripped over each other, tumbling into a cacophony of sound.

Shaking her head, Lark pulled him back to his feet. "How many times have you promised me you would stay out of that place?"

"Just this once! All I ask is that you come help me. You know cards. We were just playing for a good time, but I think he's cheating." He sucked in a deep breath. "You could stop him."

Lark sighed. "The stupidest thing I ever did was teach you to play cards."

"He would have learned from someone else." Delphinium had caught up and rolled her eyes. "Come on, Jonah, just come home with us, and—"

"I can't. Jasper lost his horse and saddle, and Bernie bet his land."

"And lost it. Won't you fellows ever learn?" Del asked.

"He's cheating, I know he is."

"Makes no never mind. Had you stayed out of the saloon, you wouldn't be in this mess." Larkspur stared at her youngest brother. Were those tears in his eyes? Was he that afraid? She noticed details no one else did, and that tended to help her win at cards, but she'd promised herself not to help him again.

But since, according to Deacon Wiesel, she was a fallen woman anyway—and worthless, at that—she straightened her spine and sucked in a deep breath. Maybe giving someone their comeuppance would be a relief to her feelings right now.

Turning to her sisters, she said gently, "You go on home, and I'll bring Jonah in a little while."

"Larkspur, surely you're not going to—"

"Just go on home and put on the coffeepot. This won't take long."

"Oh, dear Lord, protect us." Lilac glared at the youngest of the family. "You, Jonah George Nielsen, are nothing but trouble. Have been since the day you were born."

Jonah swallowed and nodded, penitence dripping from his eyes. "I know, but this is the end. Just get me out of this, Larkspur, and I promise I'll never gamble again."

"We've heard that before," Del said.

Larkspur tucked her arm in Jonah's and gave a tug. "Let's get this over with."

Sign Up for Lauraine's Newsletter

Keep up to date with Lauraine's latest news on book releases and events by signing up for her email list at the website below.

LauraineSnelling.com

FOLLOW LAURAINE ON SOCIAL MEDIA

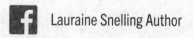 Lauraine Snelling Author

More from Lauraine Snelling

  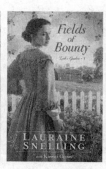 

This series shares a journey of sisterhood, romance, and faith in the midst of adversity. When the Nielsen family faces unforeseen trials during their wagon-train trek, the four sisters must learn to flourish under difficult circumstances. Join a frontier adventure of wagon rides and westward futures on the Oregon trail in this series that will harvest abundant faith and resilience, keeping you turning pages.

LEAH'S GARDEN:
The Seeds of Change, A Time to Bloom, Fields of Bounty, A Season of Harvest

 BETHANYHOUSE

 Bethany House Fiction

 @BethanyHouseFiction

 @Bethany_House

 @BethanyHouseFiction

 Free exclusive resources for your book group at BethanyHouseOpenBook.com

 Sign up for our fiction newsletter today at BethanyHouse.com